The Lights of London

Gilda O'Neill

D0332525

ARROW

Published in the United Kingdom in 1999 by
Arrow Books

3 5 7 9 10 8 6 4 2

Copyright © Gilda O'Neill 1998

The right of Gilda O'Neill to be identified as the author of this
work has been asserted by her in accordance with the
Copyright, Designs and Patents Act, 1988

First published in the United Kingdom in 1998 by William Heinemann

Arrow Books Limited
Random House UK Ltd
20 Vauxhall Bridge Road, London SW1V 2SA

Random House Australia (Pty) Limited
20 Alfred Street, Milsons Point, Sydney
New South Wales 2061, Australia

Random House New Zealand Limited
18 Poland Road, Glenfield, Auckland 10, New Zealand

Random House South Africa (Pty) Limited
Endulini, 5a Jubilee Road, Parktown 2193, South Africa

Random House UK Limited Reg. No. 954009

A CIP catalogue record for this book
is available from the British Library

Papers used by Random House UK Limited
are natural, recyclable products made from wood grown in
sustainable forests. The manufacturing processes conform to
the environmental regulations of the country of origin

Printed and bound in the Great Britain by
Mackays of Chatham PLC, Chatham, Kent

ISBN 0 7493 2177 6

The Lights of London

Kitty caught her breath in a fearful gasp at the sudden, unmistakable sound of laughter and music. Skidding to a halt on the filth-strewn cobbles, she steadied herself against a wall. The raucous male voices had her shaking uncontrollably. She must be close to a pub. She couldn't risk being near the light, where she might be seen. Might even be found by the boatmen.

Kitty's eyes brimmed with tears of helpless terror. It was all she could do to turn herself round and stagger off in another direction. She had to find the river, her salvation.

She started to move quickly again, picking up speed, running on blindly, ever more lost in the unfamiliar streets of London's East End, swerving and veering like a hound's quarry at every little noise; her chest hurting, the blood pounding in her ears and her heart thumping faster and faster.

Gilda O'Neill was born in the East End of London and now lives in Essex with her husband and two grown-up children. Her grandmother owned a pie and mash shop, her grandfather was a tug skipper on the Thames and her great uncle was a minder in a Chinese gambling den in Limehouse. She has written six other novels and two non-fiction books.

Also by Gilda O'Neill

FICTION
The Cockney Girl
Whitechapel Girl
The Bells of Bow
Just Around the Corner
Cissie Flowers
Dream On

NON-FICTION
Pull No More Bines: An Oral History
of East London Women Hop Pickers
A Night Out with the Girls:
Women Having Fun

In memory of Dolly, my much-loved and
much-missed mum

And I said to the man who stood at the gate of the year: 'Give me a light that I may tread safely into the unknown.'

M. Louise Haskins
The Desert (1908)

Prologue

Editorial: *Daily Messenger*, 4 March 1899

With no more than months left until the beginning of the new century, the focus of our concerns must be the signs we see around us of a deterioration in the national character. There is the degeneration of a once moral people, careering down in a giddy, headlong descent to barbarism. This not only alarms decent men and women, but emphasises the ever greater divide between the haves and have-nots, with the feckless poor being encouraged by anarchists and the continual threat of violence in our once safe land.

Everywhere we see evidence of an underclass, creatures whose lives are dominated by crime, loutishness and sexual licence. Brutes made more brutish by their daily diet of cheap, popular entertainment, alcohol and drugs. Lives lived in gaudy imitation of the less edifying aspects of the USA.

These individuals – many of them homeless, some openly unmarried but still with children, others begging on the streets – complain of lack of opportunity and unemployment, but we all know there are jobs to be had, and places to stay, for any who choose, or can be bothered, to look for them.

It isn't only the unsightly presence of these low-lifes which makes our streets unsafe for decent people; there is now the increasingly unavoidable menace of motor cars congesting our roads and choking our children.

What, we ask, are the police doing to protect us from all of this? Most of us know the answer to that question. They are more concerned with harassing honest citizens over petty rule-keeping than with the real criminals; leaving them to carry on with their nefarious activities, as they laugh at the stupidity of the do-gooders who call for ever softer punishments, while the hapless victims are left without thought or sympathy. This is without even mentioning the troubles in Africa.

Men who once ruled the home are now in second place to the so-called New Women. There is nothing new in behaving like Jezebel.

This is Great Britain, our country, the centre of an Empire of which we could once be proud. Let us act before it is too late. Let us make our country worthy of the new century.

Chapter 1

The dank night air resonated with the bass moaning of fog-horns, as craft – from the grand to the all but derelict – made their way cautiously up- and downriver through the dense, rolling mist blanketing the Thames.

But, unlike most other people in the crime-ridden, poverty-stricken neighbourhoods east of the great City, Kitty Wallis was oblivious of their mournful warnings. She felt too sick, too weary, too dazed, to register their existence. In fact, she had long since ceased to notice anything of the wintry London nightscape which surrounded her, even though she was standing so high up and the cruel west wind was stinging her face, whipping around her legs, and pulling and flapping at her patched, filthy skirts. After the terrifying, icy climb to the top of the bridge, just remaining upright took every scrap of strength she had left in her.

But exhaustion, cold and fear weren't her only problems; nor was it the hunger gnawing away at her guts that was making her so despondent; nor even the stomach-churningly rancid stench that rose up from the bitterly cold waters swirling far below.

Kitty was beyond all that. Beyond even the reach of the nuns who had preached of the wickedness of the sin she was about to commit.

As she had stood there, clinging to the low parapet that ran the span of the bridge, her fingers growing numb with the cold, she had worried, over and over again, about what choices she had, what she could possibly do next. What she could come up with, this one last time.

Finally, she had come to the tragic conclusion that she had no choice. It was either this or going through the further agonies of starving to death.

For a few glorious weeks she had been fool enough to believe that getting the skivvy's job in the big house was going to be her salvation, that things were, at last, improving in her short, hard life. But then, like a slap in the face when she had been expecting a kiss, it had all gone wrong.

She should have known. Things turning out badly was obviously Kitty's lot. Even when she had been starving in the gutter and, in wild desperation, had tried to follow the example of others in her situation by stealing an unwanted morsel of food, Kitty had been unable to bring herself to take what wasn't hers. She had staggered away, her empty belly screaming and burning in protest, rather than slip a stale, moulding loaf into the folds of her shabby skirts.

She almost smiled. *Things turning out badly*. That was hardly a description to suit her situation. Things were worse than that. Almost unbelievably worse.

To have come to this . . .

With a deep, sobbing breath, Kitty loosened the grip of her aching fingers from the rough, unyielding stone and leaned forward.

All at once she was tumbling; down and over she went in the bitterly cold air, a plunging, accelerating arc of flailing limbs, ragged clothes and shattered dreams.

She was unconscious before her frail body had even touched the filthy, unforgiving waters.

Her fall went unnoticed, or maybe unheeded, by the wild-looking creatures on the river bank. They were too busy trying to warm their chilled bones by the

4

crackling, spitting bonfires to bother themselves with yet another soul lost to the river.

'I'm telling you, Buggy,' Teezer slurred, 'I've had enough. I'm getting out of this game.'

'Oh yeah,' sneered Buggy, his voice only slightly less the worse for drink than his governor's, 'how's that then, Teeze?'

Buggy was as bored as Teezer with rowing up and down the Thames for the best part of every day and night, selling glasses of purl to a bunch of big-mouthed, mean-minded ingrates, who were as likely to cosh you over the head as pay you, but he'd heard his boss – who was also his supposed best mate – complain too many times before to take him seriously.

'I'm gonna find myself a few pretty girls, ain't I?' Teezer continued. 'Have someone graft for me for a change, while I take it easy. Get some proper money in me pocket for once. It's gonna be the new century soon, the twentieth century, Bugs. Just think about it.' He paused, a far-away look in his drunken, unfocused eyes. 'Things have gotta change. Gotta be different.' He let go of the oars, flexed his aching shoulder muscles and scratched thoughtfully at his unshaven chin. 'I've been doing a lot of thinking about the future, see, and I reckon . . .'

'Oi, watch it, Teeze!' yelled Buggy, as the bridge suddenly loomed up at them out of the thick, yellow-grey fog. 'If you ain't bleedin' careful we won't *have* no future to worry about. And what d'you mean, you wanna get people working for you? What am I here for, bloody decoration?'

Teezer, despite the half-dozen measures of purl – the potent mixture of beer and gin, flavoured with ginger and sugar – he'd already swallowed that night, was immediately alert. He ignored Buggy's whining and concentrated on leaning hard on his left oar, setting the little skiff spinning away from the bridge's massive stone and iron columns. But as the boat pitched there was a sudden unexpected impact and a shower of sparks flared from the brazier set on the floor between them.

With Teezer now pulling wildly at both oars and the boat bucking like an oat-fed pony, Buggy burrowed his head under the skirt of his leather apron to protect himself from the now decidedly unsteady container full of flaming coals. Having a fire on board was a hazard even on calm, sunlit waters, but they couldn't do without it; it was an essential part of their trade, as their customers – the sailors, stevedores and lightermen – only considered purl to be palatable if taken piping hot. But when the bloke steering the boat was as pissed as Teezer, having a blazing, unsteady cauldron so alarmingly close to your private parts was rather more of a hazard than usual. A bloke who'd been drinking all night could go up like a firework.

Buggy breathed a weary, muffled sigh from under his leather canopy. He was that fed up. It wasn't as though having your bits singed was the only drawback to being a purl-man. There was the almost continual state of drunkenness that most of the trade found themselves in. You couldn't escape it. And not only did it mean you felt fit for nothing most mornings, it also meant you earned very little for your efforts, as you were always too woozy to realise that you were being conned rotten by the customers, who must have been laughing up their sleeves, as they beckoned from their barges and ships and along the wharves, for the little boat to come closer and ply its alcoholic wares.

'We've hit something,' mused Teezer, staring squiffily into the water.

'I know that, you great lummocking piece of driftwood,' Buggy snarled, as he slapped his apron back into his lap. 'What's got into you tonight, Teeze? That's twice you've nearly had us over. Do you wanna get us drowned like puppies, *and* roasted to death like a pair of mutton chops? 'Cos if you do . . .'

'I'll ignore your rudeness. Now just shut up, Buggy,' Teezer sternly instructed his verbose assistant, 'and give your eyes a chance for once.' He reached over the side. 'Now, will you look at that?' he said, obviously impressed.

Buggy couldn't make out a thing in the dark. 'Hold it nearer the fire.'

As Teezer heaved his catch closer to the glowing coals, Buggy found himself staring at a pale, bony hand, smeared with river mud and what looked like the stringy remains of an overboiled cabbage.

'Here, there might be a ring,' Buggy said, leaning perilously close to the brazier, all thoughts of being reduced to a pile of ashes apparently forgotten. 'Or a bracelet, even.'

'That's what I thought,' Teezer said, his excitement rising. 'Hang on, it ain't just an arm. And it's still warm!' He took a firmer grip and twisted round so that he could get a better purchase on his find. 'It's caught up by the bridge here.' He wedged his feet against the side and yanked, making the boat rock wildly. 'With a bit of luck it won't be too bashed up. Just right for them saw-bones over at St Thomas's.' He peered over his shoulder at Buggy and winked happily. 'Looks like we'll be earning ourselves a nice few bob tonight, me laddo.'

Tibs screwed her eyes tight and pushed her even, pearly little teeth hard into the compressed rosebud of her tiny mouth.

Why couldn't he hurry up and get on with it? She hated it when they went on and on, grunting and groaning into her neck, breathing boozy fumes all over her until she almost suffocated.

This one might have looked and talked like a gentleman, but Tibs hadn't been fooled by any of that and hadn't been in the least surprised when, for all his finery, he turned out to be as disgusting as any mark straight out of the rookeries. It made Tibs laugh when people called the likes of him the 'Quality'. *Quality*? This bloke wouldn't know the meaning of the word. And as for the noises he was making . . . They were repulsive. Just like the animals made when they were being herded through the dung-slicked back streets of Whitechapel to the underground slaughterhouses.

Tibs squirmed as he thrust into her. No, she was wrong, he sounded even worse than those poor beasts. She gulped and swallowed hard, as her mouth and nostrils filled with the odour she knew so well: that of a man who was beyond control.

What he was *really* like was the boys who'd lived in the tenement where she'd once managed to get a proper place to stay. They made noises like him when they dragged her up the stairs and shoved her on to her back on the landing. And then, when they'd finished with her, they'd call for all the other boys in the surrounding buildings to come and take their turn and, as they watched, they'd pant, and they'd . . .

She shook her head to rid herself of the hateful images.

At least she was getting paid for this.

'Keep still.' The man grabbed at her hair, snapping her head back and slamming it – whack! – against the slimy alley wall. 'Now, do as you're told, or you'll feel the back of my hand across that pretty face of yours.'

*

8

Teezer cocked his head to one side and regarded the soaking-wet bundle that he and Buggy had eventually managed to haul into the skiff.

'Well, Bug,' he puffed, 'what d'you reckon to her?'

Buggy considered their trophy. 'Well, Teeze,' he began, 'from the look of her I don't reckon she's no lady. Not one of them what's been out on a boat trip to a riverside inn, like. You know, one of them what goes out to enjoy the sunset, while she gorges herself on a fine whitebait supper and a glass or two of best Madeira, but has one too many, forgets she's a lady and falls arse over tit into the drink. I don't reckon she's one of them.'

Teezer plucked at their prize's filthy rags and tutted contemptuously. 'Buggy, with a brain like your'n, mate, I do not understand how you're still only working for a purl-seller. It's a wonder you ain't standing for sodding parliament, or . . .'

'Christ, Teeze!' Buggy squealed like a frightened child and threw himself as far away from the body as the little boat would allow. 'It only pissing moved!'

Thank Gawd for that was Tibs's first thought as she finally pulled her drab, threadbare skirts down over her saggy, darned stockings. She pulled out her hatpin and refastened her battered straw bonnet, fingering its greasy feather into momentary pertness, all the while smiling up at the man who – thank the Lord – was about to give her money.

With a bit of luck she might not only have the price of a bed for the night but, if he felt inclined to give her a little bit extra – as they occasionally did – she'd have enough to pay Mrs Bowdall and some over to give her pimp, Albert Symes. All of which added up to peace of mind, a decent kip in a common lodging house and being safely off the streets for a couple of hours. What bliss that would be, and all without having to go searching for other punters.

The thought of it had Tibs smiling again, this time with genuine pleasure.

Please Gawd, she prayed silently, let this gent treat me to a few extra shillings. Please.

She held out her hand, her dirt-ingrained nails poking through the torn ends of her tatty lace gloves. 'Glad you enjoyed yourself, mister,' she cooed as softly as she could manage with her gruff cockney growl. 'Now if you'll just settle up, like, I'll be on me way.'

The man's lip twisted into an ugly sneer. 'You want payment? From me? For that?' He shoved his clean white shirt down into his trousers and shook his head in contempt. 'Get out of my sight, you whore.'

Such language coming from an elegant-looking gentleman might not have shocked Tibs, but the idea that he might try to get away without paying her had her boiling. He could have been the Prince of Wales himself, but he still wasn't going to have one over on her. She grabbed at his sleeve. 'You don't reckon you're getting away with this do you, you thieving, dirty-eyed . . .'

'Get your hands off me.' The words hissed through the man's teeth as he shoved Tibs hard in the chest.

Unusually, for Tibs, she hadn't seen the blow coming and her head hit the wall again, making her eyes roll and her ears ring. It took her only a moment to recover, but it was time enough for the man to disappear out of the alley.

Even as Tibs recovered, he was swaggering along the Highway in search of a pint of thick, creamy porter and a steaming-hot beef and oyster pie – another slummer's treat he enjoyed – before returning to the more salubrious surroundings of his home in Belgravia.

Tibs was incensed both at him and at her own stupidity. 'You bastard,' she hollered pointlessly into the night.

Ordinarily, she would have hitched up her skirts and given chase, but what with her aching head and the fog which was now so bad that the whole of Tower Bridge had disappeared into its folds, she knew there was little point. He could be anywhere in the maze of rat-infested streets, courts and alleys surrounding the Ratcliffe Highway.

She spat noisily and expertly, imagining the man to be her target, then dug her hand deep into the secret pocket she'd stitched into one of her layers of flannel petticoats.

Having pulled out her total wealth, she counted it with mounting disbelief. 'A tosheroon?' she wailed. 'Half a sodding bloody crown?'

Squatting down on her haunches, Tibs ran her hand over the mucky cobbles of the alley floor, frantically searching in the dark for the rest of her money, but knowing in her heart that she'd been robbed and that her efforts to find it were in vain.

What made it worse was that she knew it couldn't have been that posh old bleeder who'd done it. He might have been a heartless, sneery bastard, but he wouldn't have had the skills to flimp her without her noticing. No, it would have been one of the other tarts and, as clear as a summer's morning in the Essex countryside, she knew exactly when it would have happened.

The brides had all been standing outside the Hope and Anchor, up by the Minories, before they started their night's work. All of them eager to hear the latest rumours as to the identity of the madman who'd slit the throat, carved up and murdered the girl who'd been found dumped near the Royal Mint opposite the dock

11

gates. They didn't show it, but most of them were really scared and were making all sorts of excuses to work close to one another. It was the third similar murder in the past year, but nothing was being done. The police weren't interested in a few dead whores. Just as they wouldn't have given a damn about one of them being robbed.

But while Tibs knew there wasn't one of those tarts she'd been talking to who wouldn't take the opportunity to earn a bit extra by dipping the marks they'd picked up, flimping one of your own kind was definitely not acceptable. That was only done by someone low. Someone as low as they came. And that, as far as Tibs was concerned, could mean only one person.

'Blast your eyes and damn you to hell, you stinking, rotten tea-leaf, Lily Perkins,' growled Tibs. 'You know I have to pay Mrs Bowdall, you swindling, low-life whore. I'll kill you stone dead if I get hold of you. I bloody swear I will.'

She was going to have to go back to work after all.

As weary and wretched as she felt, Tibs hauled herself out of the alley and back towards the alehouses that lined the notorious dockside streets.

She rubbed her hands over her face with a groan of self-pity. 'Ne'mind no bed in no common lodging house for the night, Tibs girl, or being scared of some murdering maniac on the loose. If you don't earn some money a bit lively, Mrs Bowdall's gonna say she can't help you out no more, and worse than that, Albert'll get hold of you and knock your block clean off your shoulders, and you won't be needing no bed not ever again. And poor little Polly won't have a flaming mother. Not even a useless, stupid, careless whore like me.'

*

Slowly, Kitty opened her eyes and blinked uneasily. Was she going mad? It looked and felt, from the swaying and rocking, just as though she was on the floor of some sort of boat.

A boat?

Warily, she ran her fingers about her and probed the rough but unmistakably soggy texture of overlapping wooden planks.

It was a boat.

If she hadn't actually lost her mind, then how on earth had she got here?

She blinked again, more wildly this time as she realised she wasn't alone.

Gradually, bit by awful bit, it dawned on her that not only had she failed to end her miserable disaster of a life, but she was in a tiny bucketing craft, squeezed between two strange men – both drunk by the stink coming off them – with her soaking-wet clothes steaming in the heat of what looked like a brazier full of red-hot coals.

She didn't have time to consider whether she was actually relieved to find herself alive; her bodily reflexes took over and she was far too involved with physical reactions even to consider such philosophical matters. Just in time to avoid vomiting all over herself, Kitty stuck her head over the side and choked up what looked like several gallons of Thames water, back into the river from where it had come.

Buggy watched, fascinated, actually leaning over her to get a better look. Teezer, on the other hand, was interested in more than the projected contents of Kitty's stomach.

He gripped Buggy's shoulder. 'What d'you reckon, Bug? Not a bad-looking sort, is she? Too skinny and a bit on the lanky side maybe, but some fellers like 'em tall, don't they? Makes a change, like, from the little 'uns.'

'Eh?' Buggy said absently, his attention now fixed on Kitty's struggle to stop retching.

'You see,' Teezer went on, grimacing with the effort of keeping his purl-addled thinking on track, 'I saved her life, didn't I? So I reckon in return, like, she owes me some sort of a favour.'

'How d'you mean?' Buggy asked vaguely.

'She could be the first of my girls, couldn't she? The start of my . . .' Teezer paused for effect, then added grandly, 'my *harem*. Come on, let's get her back on dry land and see how she cleans up.' He nodded at Buggy. 'Play your cards right, mate, and you can be in on this with me. I might even make you a proper partner.'

Buggy, suddenly interested, flashed him a lop-sided grin. 'You know, Teeze, maybe you ain't as stupid as you look.'

Teezer winked and raised his chin triumphantly. 'Me mother didn't just keep the pretty ones, now did she, Bug.'

Tibs stood in the shadow of one of the huge bonded warehouses – a storehouse packed full of riches that the likes of her couldn't even begin to imagine, let alone dream of ever owning. She sighed loudly, leaned back against the soot-covered wall and massaged her aching calves. Despite the cold her stiff, leather-cramped toes felt as hot and as damp as a plateful of steaming saveloys. At least in the summer she could pull off her boots, stuff her stockings down into the toes and dangle them round her neck by the laces.

She loved that feeling, having her feet free. Especially when she took ten minutes to get herself down to the river at low tide and walked along the edge, letting the mud ooze and squidge up between her bare toes.

She'd get herself a decent pair of boots one day, ones that really fitted her, and a pot of Elliman's Embrocation to rub into her legs, and a nice basin of water with Epsom Salts to soak her dogs in. Yeah, and she'd get herself a new tiara and all, while she was about it. You could hardly keep turning up at Windsor Castle in the same old gear every time. . . .

When she saw people, like the bloke who'd just diddled her, being able to spend so much on fine clothes, just because they liked the look of them, just for the sake of it, it really amazed her how much money there was in the world. Especially when all she needed was probably no more than a fraction of what they'd throw away on a new bonnet for their fat, lazy wives, that would be worn no more than a few times and discarded for the next fashionable style or colour.

That money could change her life.

And Polly's.

Still, it was no good dreaming. Life wasn't fair now, and it probably never had been and never would be.

She puffed out her cheeks and blew noisily. Where was the nearest likely gaff to find a mark at this time of night? By now, most of them would have picked up a girl already, or else they'd be too pissed to give a damn about having a bit of the other. And because the crossing sweepers didn't exactly queue up to ply their trade in this part of London, the streets were that mucky by this hour it was like wading through a swamp made up of dung. Especially when the air was so damp.

Maybe there was a boat just in.

The thought of trailing down to the dock gates and fighting for customers with all the other brides was even more depressing than admitting she'd been stupid enough to let herself be robbed.

'Bloody, rotten bastard, thieving off me like that,' she

15

muttered angrily. 'If there was any thieving to be done it should have been *me* doing it. Off of that posh geezer. Not Lily pissing Perkins, and definitely not off of me. Sodding cheeky . . .'

'Hello, Tibs, me old love.'

The sound of the gruff, tobacco-thickened voice coming out of the fog had Tibs straining to see who it was who had spotted her without her even realising she was being watched.

She must be getting soft. First Lily, then the bloke, now this. She'd have to get her wits about her or she'd really be in trouble.

The voice spoke again. 'That is you, ain't it, sweetheart?'

The figure of a heavily built woman in her late thirties stepped towards Tibs out of the mist.

A smile of recognition lit up Tibs's pretty, if dirt-ingrained, face. She stretched out and took the far less attractive, smallpox-scarred face of the woman in her little hands and kissed her, smack, on her cracked, dry lips.

'One-eyed Sal, you old bugger,' Tibs greeted her, as she leaned back to get a better look at her friend. 'How are you, me darling? I ain't seen you for weeks.'

'This is how I am. Cop a load of this.' Sal whipped off her shawl and affected an ungainly pirouette, showing off the full, heavy swirl of her black-trimmed scarlet dress. 'Not been this well off in years, have I, ducks? Proper swanky, ain't I? Not even this bloody fog's getting me down. Well, not much, but it's still good to see a familiar face. Bit of company never comes amiss in this weather, eh, girl? You never know who you might run into. And what with that poor girl getting done in . . . '

As interested in avoiding the dangers of working

alone in the London fog as any other bride in the area Tibs, for the moment anyway, was more concerned with how Sal had managed to earn enough to pay for such luxury. 'What the hell you been up to? That ain't no fourth-hand rubbish off a barrow.'

'It certainly ain't. Look, leg-o'mutton sleeves, neat little bustle *and* it's hardly been worn,' Sal informed her proudly. 'No darns or nothing. Well, not many. In fact, if it hadn't been so foggy I'd have been twirling me little parasol what matches the hat. But I don't wanna go ruining it.'

Tibs fingered the thick woollen cloth and the stiff black frogging trim. She was flabbergasted. It wasn't only beautiful, it was as good as clean. And so warm. Wearing it must be like being all wrapped up in a big, soft blanket. 'Blimey, Sal, you got yourself a fancy man or something?'

Sal threw back her head and roared with laughter. 'One-eyed Sal with a fancy man?' she spluttered, her hand instinctively going to the black patch that covered the empty socket of her left eye. 'He'd have to have one more of his minces missing than I have to bother with an old haybag like me.'

'Don't be so hard on yourself, Sal,' said Tibs, flinching as she remembered how Albert, who 'looked after' Sal, as well as her and half a dozen other tarts, had taken the boat hook to her face for daring to answer him back that night. 'You're still a good-looking woman.'

'Yeah and I was such a success at her Diamond Jubilee the other year that Queen Victoria's asked me round to tea again, to show off me drawers to all her fine friends. Her parties'd be nothing without me.'

'Sal . . .'

'I don't kid meself, Tibs. I know I'm almost fit for the knackers.' She chortled wheezily to herself as she reached under her skirt and pulled out a short, squat flask. 'Here, have a drop of this nerve tonic to warm your cockles, me little love.'

Tibs took a pull of the liquor, screwing up her eyes as she waited for it to hit the back of her throat. But then she realised that her mouth wasn't burning and her eyes weren't watering either.

She examined the gin bottle in disbelief. It was proper stuff, not the sort of rot-gut that was brewed up in a bucket in someone's backyard. 'It's good gear, this,' she said after a long pause. 'Right nice stuff.'

'It's that all right. And how about this.' She scratched purposefully at her tightly corseted waist. 'I might still be cootie, but look.'

Sal affected a mad grimace, showing a wide gap where her front teeth had once stood like rotting tree stumps. 'I even got myself enough to go and see the dentist. Mind you, I ain't never been before. That cocaine lark he gave me was a bit frightening. Made *that* seem like water,' she said, pointing to the gin that Tibs was still holding. 'I don't think I'll be going back to get the rest done.'

'So where'd it all come from then? The bottle of jacky' – Tibs held up the flask – 'all the new clobber.' She frowned with concern; they both knew Albert's views on girls who made private arrangements with their punters. 'Here, you sure you ain't got no one on the quiet? I wouldn't say nothing, Sal, you know me, but you'd better watch yourself if you have.'

One-eyed Sal had a swallow of gin, put the bottle back under her skirt, leaned forward and pinched Tibs's cheek. 'I've got better than that, my little pet, I've got a new hall I'm working. And you know how the halls attract the posh sorts out slumming. They're always on the look-out for business. And this one, well, even old

18

crows like me are getting plenty of custom.' She slapped Tibs playfully on the shoulder. 'Specially from the ones what've been to fancy West End parties and have spent all night staring at their friends' wives' titties bulging out of them fancy frocks, and all without getting even a little squeeze of 'em. By the time they get down here they're bloody screaming for it. Us brides are well away.'

'Where's this hall then, Sal?'

'You know, down the Old Black Dog.' Sal took a pipe from her pocket, tried and failed to light it. 'Bugger this weather. It's colder and damper than a witch's tit. If this fog don't . . .'

'They're putting on turns at the Dog? The one in Rosemary Lane?' Tibs broke in impatiently.

'Yeah, Jack Fisher, the new landlord there, he's opened up that big room upstairs. The one old Mary Fishguts used to . . .'

'Mary who?'

Sal chuckled deep in her throat. 'I forget, Tibs, you're just a youngster, ain't you. Wish I was. You know, when I was your age . . .'

'So how long's it been open then?' Tibs interrupted again. She didn't want to be rude to her old friend but she had to find out more. This could be the answer to her prayers.

'Been going for almost a fortnight, it has.' Sal sniffed loudly and wiped her nose along the back of her hand, leaving a trail of silvery snot that traced its way up and along her scarlet sleeve. 'They can try all they like with their licensing nonsense, but I'm telling you, they'll never close down the halls. Never. They can . . .'

'Look, Sal, I know I've been working more over towards Aldgate,' Tibs said a bit more sulkily than she'd intended. 'Trying to keep out of Albert's way to tell you the truth. That old cow Mrs Bowdall stung me for more money over the last fortnight and I sort of owe him a bit. But someone could've mentioned it to me.'

'Don't be like that, love. No one who knew about it reckoned it was gonna last more than a week. See, it ain't exactly Drury Lane. I mean, brides like me don't usually get a look-in at the better sort of halls. You have to be done up like a sodding duchess even to get your foot through the door at the Empire or the Alhambra. But down the Dog . . .'

'What? What about the Dog?'

Sal chuckled. 'The turns really stink, but 'cos it's new it's still a bit of a novelty. That's how it's managing to pull in the punters. But they don't hang around for long. They start looking for other distractions, if you know what I mean.'

Suddenly there was a distant look in her eye. 'You know, Tibs, I really thought I was ready to start walking the parks of a night. Doing Gawd knows what for all them strange ones with their funny ideas and that. But now the Dog's come along.' She grinned broadly, showing her few remaining back teeth to be as brown and broken as a set of ill-kept railings. 'It's not only brought a lot of that mob back who'd moved on to the boozers down Shadwell, it's brought in all these toffs and all. For now, anyway. But wait till it gets around what a load of old shit Fisher's putting on every night and the novelty of having a laugh at all the old tripe wears off.' She winked gleefully. 'You wanna get yourself down there with me, young 'un. And make it a bit sharpish and all. Make hay while the sun shines, as they say. But don't let on about it to too many others, eh, 'cos it's got what I think you might call a very limited potential for any sort of a run.'

Tibs pinched Sal's crêpey cheek gently between her

fingers. 'You are an angel from above, sweet Sal, a genuine angel of mercy.'

Sal laughed coarsely. 'I've been called some things in me time, darling, but it's the first time I've ever been called that.'

Despite being a tall, country-bred young woman, with shoulders almost as broad as a boy's, Kitty was no match for Buggy and Teezer. What with having been half drowned, and with her sopping-wet clothes and soaking boots weighing her battered body down like lead, they were able to push and shove her up the flight of waterman's stairs with no more effort than it would have taken to shift an uncooperative five-year-old.

She tripped up the final step, coughing and panting, and stumbled along the shoreway – one of the shadowy narrow walkways that ran between the massive warehouses – that led from the river to the Ratcliffe Highway.

Her stomach heaved and she vomited again, fetching up what she could only pray was the very last scrap of anything left inside her.

Wretchedly she slumped against a rough brick wall, not even noticing how it scraped her bony back. But the very next moment Kitty was standing as rigid as a barber's pole, her senses sharp as freshly stropped razors, as she listened in open-mouthed astonishment to Teezer outlining his plans to Buggy.

Kitty had honestly believed, as she had tried to end it all by throwing herself into the Thames, that things could get no worse. Then she had been saved and had, just for a moment as she'd been dragged out of the boat and along the alley, wondered if it was meant to be. But now, here she was, with two apparently raving madmen, who seemed to be under the impression that, out of gratitude, she'd be more than happy to go on the game for them. Maybe when she explained she'd rather go pure-finding for the South London tanning factories – collecting dog dung at a few pennies a bucketful for them to use for their leather dressing – than ever have a man touch her again, they'd throw her back in the river where they'd found her and she would sink into the oblivion she had obviously been right to prefer to this terrible life.

But her disgust at their idea clearly did not convey itself to either of the purl-men.

'Gotta be realistic, Teeze,' Buggy offered with a drunkard's reason. 'No point wasting time scrubbing her down if she ain't gonna be any good. If you know what I mean.' His tongue flicked over his lips and the suggestiveness of his meaning grew more evident. 'She's gotta be, you know, fit for the purpose, now ain't she? Take me, for instance, I always go for a nice sort of a bosom. Big and firm. So if we have a butcher's at hers we can see how she matches up. And her legs, we'll have to have a look at them. I must admit I do like a nice pair of pins. And a nice sort of arse to grab hold of while I'm doing the business and all.'

'And we might as well give her a seeing to while we're at it,' added Teezer, his voice thick with lust. 'Try her out, like. Make sure there's nothing wrong with her or nothing.'

The very thought of having these men's hands – any man's hands – anywhere near her ever again had Kitty wide-eyed and as taut as a fully wound clock-spring.

Summoning every bit of courage she had left, she spat at Teezer's face.

She missed. Spitting wasn't something she was used to, but the men's slack-jawed shock at Kitty's sudden and unexpected display of anger gave her the few precious moments she needed to make a run for it.

She'd almost reached the end of the shoreway when Teezer recovered from his stunned silence. He roared into the darkness after her, 'I'll kill you, you no-good, ungrateful trollop!' and began swinging his arms about him, as if he were a punch-drunk prize-fighter in a penny booth.

Unfortunately, his wild flailings threw him off his already unsteady balance and he staggered backwards, knocking Buggy over into the bargain.

Kitty could hear them curse as they fell to the ground in a drunken heap of arms and legs and rapidly spreading bruises, but she couldn't risk slowing down. She ran as though the devil himself – the one she'd been threatened with at the convent – were at her heels, not stopping even though she was being sucked deeper and deeper into the maze of fetid streets and byways of the dockside rookeries.

Past locked doors and secretive alleyways she ran, with the sound of fog-horns echoing in her ears, and the memories of once welcome hands touching her, then pawing her and crawling over her skin. Memories which drove her on.

She had to get away. And somehow she would find the river.

This time there would be no mistakes, she would finish it all for ever.

But what was that?

Kitty caught her breath in a fearful gasp at the sudden, unmistakable sound of laughter and music. Skidding to a halt on the filth-strewn cobbles, she steadied herself against a wall. The raucous male voices had her shaking uncontrollably. She must be close to a pub. She couldn't risk being near the light, where she might be seen. Might even be found by the boatmen.

Kitty's eyes brimmed with tears of helpless terror. It

was all she could do to turn herself round and stagger off in another direction. She had to find the river, her salvation.

She started to move quickly again, picking up speed, running on blindly, ever more lost in the unfamiliar streets of London's East End, swerving and veering like a hound's quarry at every little noise; her chest hurting, the blood pounding in her ears and her heart thumping faster and faster.

Then it was all over.

Someone grabbed her, spun her round, and crashed her already bruised and aching body hard against the wall. This was finally it. Forget about finding the river. Her heart was about to burst. She would simply die there and then.

Chapter 2

'For Christ's sake belt up!' One-eyed Sal, with her fists stuck in her waist, was bellowing furiously at Kitty who, to Sal's increasing annoyance, continued to scream like a stuck pig.

Sal flapped her arms in impotent exasperation. 'Just shut up and listen will you? Just *shut up*. Tell her, Tibs, tell the noisy mare how lucky she is that I never gave her a right-hander when she come running into me like that.'

But Tibs didn't have a chance to tell anyone anything, not with Sal in full flow.

'I'm telling you,' Sal went on, 'if you don't shut that bleed'n' gob of your'n I'm gonna forget I'm a lady and bloody well shut it for you. *Do you hear me*?'

This time Tibs actually managed to slip in a few words. 'All right, Sal, that's enough. Leave her alone, eh?' She eased her friend out of the way and reached out to touch Kitty on the sleeve to reassure her, but Kitty, wild-eyed with fear, snatched her arm away as though Tibs was about to grab her. She had no intention of letting anyone lay a single finger on her ever again.

Tibs dropped her hands to her sides and looked up into Kitty's face. 'It's all right, darling, no one's gonna hurt you.' She moved a tentative step closer. 'Here, you're soaking. What you been up to? Someone chucked you in the drink, did they?'

Kitty shook her head frantically and backed away from the garishly made-up women.

'Bloody hell, what a performance.' Sal rolled her single eye in undisguised annoyance. 'I hate simpering twerps like her. It's all toffee, you know. She should be on the boards. Mind you, at least she's shut her cake-hole at last. That's something to be thankful for. Come on, Tibs, let's get going or we'll miss our chance down the Dog. The third show'll be starting any . . .'

'Hang on, Sal.' Tibs hadn't taken her eyes off Kitty's terrified face. 'That's better, sweetheart,' she soothed her. 'Now, why don't you tell us what's happened? You hurt, are you? Someone bash you up or something?'

Kitty's mouth turned down, her face crumpled and she began snivelling pitifully.

Sal started groaning. 'Leave her alone, Tibs. Can't you see she's barmy?'

'No, she ain't. Look at her. She's scared.' Tibs held up her hands as though she were surrendering. 'Don't worry, love, I ain't coming near you and I ain't gonna touch you. I just wanna help. All right?' All the while she was talking, Tibs was sighing inwardly; she wouldn't be able to go to work with this one tagging along. But she couldn't just leave her. She was too soft to be left alone in an area as tough as this.

'Look, Tibs,' One-eyed Sal hissed into her ear, 'you said if you didn't earn another few bob you was gonna be in trouble with Albert. And that old cow Mrs Bowdall won't take kindly to you missing giving her her wages neither. So why you have to go and give a flying fart about this soppy mare, whoever she is, I do not know. She ain't nothing to you. Come on, she'll be all right. Let's be on our way.'

'How can I leave her? Especially here of all places.'

Sal grabbed Tibs's arm. 'Easy.'

She shook herself free. 'No, Sal. I can't.' As she spoke, Tibs smiled gently at Kitty. It seemed to be calming her down a bit. Either that, or the shock of whatever had happened to her had sent her into some sort of a trance. Tibs had seen people in trances before, in the mesmerist's act at the Pavilion – and this was pretty much how they looked: pole-axed.

'You can leave her,' Sal insisted.

'No, Sal, I can't. Look, thanks for the tip about the Dog and everything, but you go on. If I can, I'll catch up with you later.'

'You're too good, Tibs, that's your trouble.'

'If I was good I'd never have wound up in this dump in the first place, now would I?' she said with a weak attempt at a smile.

'I'm being a fool to myself,' Sal bristled, 'but I'll do you a favour and hang on for a bit. But only till you see sense, mind.' With that she folded her arms tightly across her bosom and stared hard at Kitty, daring her to cause any more trouble.

One-eyed Sal liked Tibs, genuinely so. Not only because she was the sort who'd help anyone – even this dopey great rasher of streaky bacon – but she was a good laugh, who could always be depended on to cheer everyone up. But Sal also had other reasons to wait for her. Tibs was a nice-looking girl, the type who attracted the kind of punters who had lovely fat wallets. And apart from that, it was always useful to have a bit of company on a filthy night like this. You never knew who might be lurking in the foggy alleyways, ready to jump out and slit your throat for the few coppers you had tucked in the leg of your drawers. Sal shuddered involuntarily. She would definitely feel more secure with a companion, especially so close to the river . . .

'What's your name then, darling?' Tibs asked softly.

'Kitty,' the girl rasped in a voice made almost as harsh as Tibs's own by the overwhelming combination of swallowed Thames water, vomiting and weeping.

'Here, what a coincidence. We're a right pair of pussycats, we are.'

'They call her Tibs,' Sal explained flatly, jerking her thumb towards Tibs's face. 'Got them slanty eyes, see.'

'Yeah, me best feature they reckon. Well, me best till I get me corsets off!' Tibs, realising immediately from Kitty's expression that she wasn't used to such ripe talk, tried another tack. 'You can't stand here and catch your death, now can you, love? You come with me. Come on, sweetheart, and we'll have you all warmed up and dried out in a trice. All right? Come on, let's get going, shall we?'

Kitty stiffened, her eyes widening in apprehension.

'Darling, believe me, you ain't got no choice. You don't know this place. Anyone could tell from a mile off that you're a stranger round here, and if . . .'

'Not in this fog, they couldn't tell,' snapped Sal sarcastically.

Tibs ignored her. 'Look at you. You're as nervous as a rabbit and with them soaking-wet things hanging off you, slowing you down, you won't last five minutes with some of the tripe hounds you get roaming around these parts. I wouldn't trust 'em with me old granny, let alone a fine-looking girl like you.' She smiled winningly. 'You might not realise it, you know, but it's lucky you bashed into me mate Sal here. If you'd have kept on running in the direction you was heading you'd have wound up in Chinatown.'

'Yeah, I can just see her in an opium den.' Sal puffed out her cheeks and slapped her arms about her shoulders to keep warm. If *she* was cold in her thick woollen dress, this dopey cow must be perishing in all that wet gear. Why wouldn't she just get walking? That'd be a start.

'I won't take no for an answer, Kit.'

'She won't,' emphasised Sal, eager for something, anything, to happen, so she could get off with Tibs and on with the business of earning a few bob.

'Let's at least go somewhere where you can find a bit of shelter and have a little rest,' Tibs coaxed her. 'You look like you've done a three-day shift in a sweat-shop.' As she spoke, she stretched out her hand as cautiously as if she were trying to trap a butterfly. 'I'm just gonna slip me arm through your'n, so as we don't lose one another in this fog. Then we can walk part of the way with Sal.'

'That'll be nice,' said Sal, narrowing her eye at Kitty, 'you can let me go off alone and earn a few bob, while you look after your new friend here and earn bugger all. Still, I'll enjoy your company while you can spare it, I suppose.'

'Enjoy me company? Enjoy me protection more like,' retorted Tibs.

One-eyed Sal smiled in resigned agreement. 'Don't look so surprised, Kitty, or whatever you reckon your name is. She's a right street scrapper this one. Might look like a pretty little pussycat but she acts more like a terrier.' Without so much as a pause, Sal added, 'You in the family way, are you? That why you chucked yourself in the drink? I suppose you reckoned that *that'd* make 'em all feel sorry for you. Guilty, like.'

Kitty didn't answer, but some progress had been made: she was so bewildered by Sal's barrage of words and questions that she was allowing Tibs to steer her gently forward.

'He pissed off and left you, I'll bet. That's the usual story, eh Tibs?'

'No.' Kitty dropped her chin. 'It weren't like that.'

'Here, Tibs. Listen to that voice. She's only a sodding

carrot cruncher. Up from the sticks, are you, dear?' Still walking along, she turned to Tibs. 'No wonder she's so flaming dopey. They're all like that down there.' She gestured vaguely over her shoulder towards where she imagined the countryside might be. 'It's all that fresh air, see. Can't be no good for you, can it?'

Tibs flashed a warning glare at Sal, then returned her attention to Kitty. 'Here, I'm a country girl and all,' she enthused in her broad cockney croak. 'I come from . . .'

'Here, hang on a minute.' Agitated by her friend's siding with this feeble-minded bumpkin of an interloper, Sal decided she'd had enough. 'I'm sorry, Tibs,' she said with a haughty sniff, 'but I've heard your life story before. You won't think I'm rude if I say I'll be getting along, now will you, girl?' With that, she stretched her lips at Kitty in a thin approximation of a smile and strode off ahead of them.

She was quickly out of sight, but Tibs noticed that her clip-clopping footsteps over the cobbles gradually slowed down until she was walking at the same pace as they were – albeit a dozen yards in front. Close enough to shout for help, Tibs thought with a fond grin, but far enough away for her to make her point. Typical of Sal.

Kitty interrupted Tibs's thoughts with a pitiful sigh. 'I never meant to upset your friend,' she said in her soft rural burr. 'I'm that sorry.'

'Don't you worry yourself, sweetheart,' Tibs reassured her, pleased to hear Kitty talking, even if she did sound as miserable as the coalman on a sunny day. 'It don't take much to get that one going. Sal might be me mate, but even I have to admit she ain't got much patience.'

'You're right lucky, you are.'

'Me? Lucky? How come?'

'I've never really had a friend.'

'You don't mean that.' Tibs sounded shocked. 'Everyone's got friends. Someone they can turn to.'

'Not me.' Kitty shivered. 'I've never had the chance to make any, see.'

Tibs shook her head. Poor cow. They were right what they said: there's always someone worse off. 'So you reckon you've got no one to turn to? No one at all?'

Kitty shook her head.

'And you're soaking wet, love you. And it's parky enough to freeze the doodahs off of your . . . and I'll bet . . .'

'This is your last chance, Tibs,' Sal bellowed out of the fog. 'Now, are you coming or what?'

Kitty began weeping miserably. 'You'd better go. Your friend's waiting.'

'Don't be daft, and don't go fretting and crying all over the place. It ain't worth it. Nothing's worth it.' Tibs risked squeezing Kitty's arm. 'Anyway, you should be smiling. You've got yourself a friend now, ain't you? Whether you like it or not, I'm gonna look after you. We're gonna be a team see, Kit, me and you. Little Tibs and big Kitty. There'll be no stopping us.'

Good job she don't know the mess I've made of me own bleed'n' life, thought Tibs.

'*What did you say*?' Teezer – his knee swollen and aching from where Buggy had fallen on him in the shoreway and his head thick with purl – stuck his face close to the man who'd dared question his right to barge past his table.

The man recoiled. 'No harm meant, mate. I just asked you to be careful, that's all. You nearly had the lady's glass over, and . . .'

'And *I'm* just asking you to shut your noise, while I mind me own business and make me way to the front of this here theatre.' Teezer pulled himself up to his full, barrel-chested height. 'Or d'you wanna make something of it?'

As usual, Buggy couldn't resist throwing in his long-winded two penn'orth of nonsense. 'I wouldn't actually call it a theatre, Teeze. More of a big room, really. In fact, its very much like a lot of little rooms that have been knocked through and . . .'

Teezer spun round. 'Buggy.'

'Yes, Teeze?'

'You're another one who can shut up. Now go and fetch us a round of drinks, while I go and baggsy us some decent seats. And while you're about it, make sure you go down to the big bar. I don't want you messing about in the crowds up here and taking all night about it. I've got a mouth on me like the inside of a boiler stoker's glove.'

Buggy considered for a moment and came to the conclusion that he had had enough excitement for one evening. So, instead of making a song and dance about it as he usually would have, he did as Teezer told him without another word.

He turned round, shoved his way back through the boisterous crowd and trotted down the stairs to the main bar, leaving Teezer to secure a table for them near the tatty little stage at the far end of the room.

Teezer pulled out a chair and sat down just a few feet from where Jack Fisher, the new landlord, was standing surveying the room. He had no idea of the panic that Jack could feel creeping over him.

Like many similar venues, which had suddenly mushroomed all over London when it became known that the music-hall boom was creating some very rich men, the 'theatre' above the Old Black Dog was – as Buggy had tried to tell Teezer – no more than a series of rooms converted into what Jack Fisher desperately hoped was about to become a theatrical money-spinner.

The fact that the hall bore only a passing resemblance to the magnificent theatres frequented by the stars didn't seem to matter to the customers; they were as lively and as rowdy as any of the far grander music-hall crowds could be and, Jack had originally believed, as keen to enjoy the show. Almost every one of the tables that filled the high-ceilinged rectangular space was occupied, nudging right up to the stage at one end of the room and the busy, if tiny, bar at the other.

The room was decorated with luridly striped paper; there was gaudy gold paint highlighting the plaster covings and carvings dotted around the place; and the same gilt had been used to pick out the bits and pieces of moulding that only added to the faded look of the rickety, ill-matched tables and chairs. The windows and makeshift proscenium arch – created by an artful use of off-cuts purloined from a timber yard over in Shoreditch – had drapes which, even though made of tired-looking, dusty red plush, at least matched those framing the stage.

Facing the audience stood a table, which might once have been described as grand, where Mr Tompkins, the Chairman, sat surrounded by the assorted paraphernalia of his profession.

Despite the moth-eaten appearance of his evening dress that barely stretched across his bulky frame, and his shirt collar that added to the flush of his booze-reddened cheeks, Mr Tompkins presided over events with a great show of exaggerated dignity. Actually, his excessively dramatic use of the items set out on the table before him was more to do with hiding his customary inebriation than with professional pride. The objects he used with such flourish were a mirror, to keep an eye on the acts going on behind him; a clock to enable him to time the turns – with three shows a night, it was important to keep things moving – and, most essential with a rowdy hall such as the Old Black Dog, a gavel to keep order.

During the evening's first and second shows the Chairman had had to put his gavel to frequent use and, from the reaction to the opening turn of this, the third show – an elderly woman with a clever, if incredibly dull, paper-tearing routine – it looked as though this house wouldn't be much different.

The cacophony from the assembled dock workers, costermongers, labourers and the occasional well-dressed toff was deafening. And, as if that weren't enough, there were the added shrieks and hoots coming from the men's sweethearts, wives and even their babies. When the young feller-me-lads at the back of the hall started *their* hollering and whistling it was complete bedlam.

And it wasn't only the noise. There was also the smell of the place: a mingling of the noxious stink of cheap scent, the pong of fried-fish suppers that had been smuggled in under copious skirts and top coats, and some underlying rancidness that Mr Tompkins was not keen even to begin to identify. When combined they made the atmosphere almost overwhelming. If it wasn't for his need of a regular pay-packet to satisfy his taste for rum and the impossibility, with his reputation, of his ever finding employment elsewhere, there was no way on earth that Mr Tompkins would have wanted to stay in such a hell-hole.

The audience were soon baying for the first act to be dragged off and for the next one to begin. A boisterous response was only to be expected at the halls, but when the word had spread that the décor of the Old Black Dog matched the standard of the turns, the whole point of going to this tatty theatre in Rosemary Lane was that you could see the worst rubbish this side of the Aldgate Pump. In other words, you only went there to have a good laugh, a few drinks and to leave early enough to seek out some proper entertainment, either at another hall, or with one of the bargain-priced brides who frequented that part of the East End.

This, however, would have been a revelation to Jack Fisher; he honestly could not understand where he was going wrong. He pulled off his battered felt hat and shook his head, making his thick red hair flop into his eyes.

Whatever was he going to do? It had started so well. In fact, for the first few days he had had to turn customers away, they were that full, and they had all stayed to the end, drinking like fish and almost fighting to hand over every penny of their hard-earned wages. But something had gone wrong and now the punters just wouldn't stay for the whole evening, and that meant the bar takings had plummeted. If they fell any lower he wouldn't be able to pay the acts. And then . . .

It didn't bear thinking about.

He scanned the room, trying to see what the problem was and what he could do to sort it out. It looked the part all right. Well, he thought it did. Not that he'd seen that many music-halls, just those first fantastic places he had visited as a lad when his father had taken him, as a wondrous treat, all the way to Blackpool when he was a boy. Those were the ones that had fired his dreams. Then there were the ones he had seen since his arrival in London. But they hadn't had this problem.

He looked about the room, frowning, trying to see. Maybe it was something about the building.

When Jack had first come down from the north-east

and had taken over the Old Black Dog the place had been unused – save by a flock of pigeons and a whole community of rats – for almost a generation and, despite the money he had spent on trying to conceal its recent past, its downward spiral from a once grand building to a cheap riverside tavern could be seen all too clearly.

Originally built as a fine house befitting the status of a wealthy spice merchant, the building had been forcibly sold off after a notorious scandal had ruined the disgraced owner. He had been found out in a swindle, which involved a gentleman from Lloyd's and a disputed claim over whether or not the good ship *Marie Thérèse* had actually sunk off the islands of Bermuda, or, as had eventually been proved, the merchant had worked a scam. Although anchored safely downriver from the Wapping Basin, and with a fresh coat of paint and a brand new nameplate declaring it to be the more prosaically entitled *Saucy Sue*, the merchant still failed to disguise its true identity from the wily insurance investigators, who had been promised handsome commissions if they verified that a sting had been intended.

The building had then been bought by a timber-trading Scandinavian gentleman, whose wife's sister and family lived in nearby Wellclose Square. But the area had gradually become more run down – and dangerous – and the trader, his family and his in-laws had moved lock, stock and barrel to the more pleasant and safer areas close to the open fields of Rotherhithe.

Old Mary Fishguts – a woman so known because of her years of hair-splitting, penny-pinching trading with the local fleet and their pungent catches – had had no such qualms about living in Rosemary Lane when she had retired from fishmongering.

She had sunk her substantial, if stinking, nest egg into

converting the once genteel home into a rip-roaring alehouse, frequented by the roughneck seamen of all colours and all nations, every one of them eager to pass the accumulated earnings from their trips around the seven seas straight across the counter into Mary's smelly grasp.

There was no discrimination about who would be served as far as Mary Fishguts was concerned. She'd rob anyone blind.

She'd then expanded her empire by turning the high-ceilinged upstairs rooms that had previously been her living quarters into a venue for entertainments other than the usual drinking and carousing that went on down below. Keeping most of the rooms intact, she decorated them with a startling mix of cheap oriental fabrics and furnishings – all bought from Chinese and Lascar seamen down at the nearby docks, eager for extra money to spend on their shore leave, much of it, ironically, at Mary Fishguts's establishment – lending the place a truly exotic feel. There, in the upstairs of the Old Black Dog, Mary created for very little money what was supposedly a hotel catering for gentlemen – as if a gentleman would choose to spend the night in such a place. But, with the added draw of the specialist entertainment laid on by Mary – namely a highly popular combination of private bars, bawdy theatrical turns and a lush bordello – it soon became a widely acclaimed venue for men from all sorts of backgrounds, the only condition of entry being their preparedness to part with their money. With the final genius touch of introducing hot meat pies into the equation, Mary Fishguts was on to a sure-fire earner that made her into a rich woman.

When old Mary was eventually called to the great counting house in the sky, the Dog, along with its special upstairs diversions, was closed down, while her similarly avaricious offspring squabbled bitterly over entitlement to the place. Finally, after the supposedly accidental drowning of one of the brothers in the Thames and a series of blood-curdling threats among the remaining siblings, it was agreed that the place should be sold off and the money shared out equally, but by then the building was in a state of grisly disrepair.

Their greed had cost Mary's children dear, but it had given Jack Fisher a chance that he had always believed would one day be more than just a boyhood dream. As far as he was concerned, the broken windows, rotting door frames and crumbling sills didn't make the Old Black Dog a hazard to life and limb, they made it an affordable reality rather than an unattainable fantasy, which he set about repairing with the zeal of a convert, which in fact he was – in geographical terms at least.

Having arrived from the north-east of England a little over three months ago, with a bag of coins in his hand, with Rex, his elderly but fierce-looking mongrel by his side and a determination in his heart to escape from the life in the coal pits that had killed his father, Jack Fisher had decided that London and the run-down tavern would be his salvation.

As soon as the drinkers who had come to try the newly opened place had put his establishment into profit – a small profit, admittedly, but still there to be counted at the end of every day – Jack decided it was time to fulfil his ambition. And so, without a further thought, he'd sunk every last farthing he had, plus as much energy, into converting the upstairs of the Old Black Dog into a music-hall. He would have the best house in the East End and make his fortune.

Unfortunately, being brought up in a pit village

hadn't given Jack the sort of experience he needed for a career in the entertainment industry.

Of course, the new venture had only been going for a few weeks, but it should have been doing better than it was. In fact, he might as well have tried barking at a knot, so little use were his efforts to keep the crowds happy.

But where was he going wrong? People came along all right, and they seemed to be really enjoying themselves. For a while. And then they left.

Why?

The organisation was a little sloppy, he had to admit, what with the turns sometimes arriving late and Mr Tompkins usually being a bit the worse for wear, but he always did his job in the end and he was cheap. No, it was something else. But what?

As Buggy fought his way back upstairs, with a foaming two-quart jug of porter, a stoneware flask of gin and a couple of glasses clutched to his chest, Teezer's mood was reaching boiling point. He had been made to wait and Teezer hated waiting. Buggy had taken longer than anyone else Teezer could have thought of, longer than anyone had a right to. All he'd had to do was fetch a few drinks. What was wrong with the man? Mind you, the Chairman, the bloke who was meant to be organising the turns, was nearly as bad. The start of the third show was a good twenty minutes late, then they'd hooked off the first five acts almost straight away, they were that bad, but at least they had provided some sort of entertainment.

So where was the next turn? What was going on? They'd even got the young bloke with the dodgy arm to turn the lights back up. What was the world coming to? That's what Teezer wanted to know.

It was like that ingrate he'd fished out of the drink. What a mug he'd been, bothering with her. He looked down at his slime-smeared trousers. They were actually no dirtier than usual, but as far as Teezer was concerned the girl who'd had the cheek to refuse his advances had ruined a fine garment. Why hadn't he just left the stupid tart to drown? That's what the likes of her deserved.

Buggy reached the table and set down the drinks with a whistle of relief. 'Thank Gawd for that, it's like a mad-house on them stairs, people coming and going and . . .'

'Shut up, Buggy.' Teezer took a long pull of porter and wiped his sleeve across his mouth. 'If ever I get hold of that long streak of piss I'll show her what for.'

'Who's that, Teeze? What long streak . . .'

'I said shut it, Bugs. Look, the gasman's about to dim the glims again, they must have found the next turn somewhere.'

'Probably in the lav, eh, Teeze?'

Archie, the gasman in question, reached up and pulled the chain that controlled the supply to the huge, ornate gasolier – an uncharacteristically whimsical purchase made by the previous owner, Mary Fishguts, that had pride of place in the room – and the theatre was plunged back into expectant semi-darkness.

He then turned up the limelights along the front of the little stage and hissed at a battered-looking woman swaying tipsily in the wings, 'Come on, Milly, you're on. Before they get nasty. They've waited long enough already.'

'Eh?' she called, surprised to hear herself being addressed.

Archie lifted his chin towards the Chairman who was stabbing his thumb at the card he'd placed on the little wooden easel on his desk proclaiming that 'Lovely

Milly and her Musical Moments' was about to entertain them. 'You're on!'

Milly lurched on to the stage and staggered about a bit, then turned and faced the audience. She squinted into the darkness, seemingly unaware of what was going on, but then the piano struck up the opening chords of her song and it was as though Milly had been lit up like one of the new electric advertising signs.

In a slow, strangulated bar-singer's warble, made more horrible by her inebriation, she threw out her arms and began:

'All your tomorrows were ye-e-e-esterda-a-a-ayaah,
You gave up your a-a-a-ll for go-o-o-old-ah.
You traded your graces,
For satins and laces,
And no-o-o-ow y-ooooo-ou are old-ah!'

Milly's voice was too much for the audience. The cheye-eyeking, laughter and raspberries began before she'd even finished the first line, let alone the whole song. The noise from the audience grew louder and louder, until they were drowning out the singer – if she could be called that – entirely.

Well-aimed gobbets pinged into the spittoons, and rotten fruit, peanut shells and orange peel bounced off the stage and the unfortunate performer as the lads at the back began to pelt her.

'Gerroff!' they yelled. 'Go on, gerroff out of it!'

'Yeah, go on! Gerrtcha!'

Some of them were on their feet.

'Come on. Let's go down to Pickett's,' sneered a big blond seaman, on the table next to Buggy's and Teezer's. 'They have proper turns on down there. They ain't even got a minstrel show here.'

Buggy thought that Pickett's sounded tempting.

'What d'you reckon, Teeze, shall we go and all?'

Teezer turned to him and shook his head contemptuously. 'Do you know how tired I am, Buggy? How downright completely, totally rinsed through and wrung out I am? Anyway, I think Milly's doing all right. In an amusing sort of a way.'

Teezer was one of the few customers who did and by the time they'd got on to the old girl in the spangly frock, who played the musical saw while whistling a completely different tune – a neat trick but terrible punishment on the ears – Jack Fisher, from his seat by the Chairman's table, watched in despair as most of the other punters, along with his profits, left.

He threw down his hat and ran his fingers through his hair.

Even the chirrupers – the yobs who demanded money before shows in payment for keeping quiet – were no longer bothering to come round with their demands. First of all there was too much noise going on for them to make any difference, then there was complete bloody silence.

Jack Fisher was ready to tear the hair out of his aching ginger head.

The few people who were still there were more interested in playing a game of pitch and toss than in watching the stage.

Then, just as Fisher thought it could get no worse, a stern, bare-armed woman come bowling in. She took hold of one of the few remaining men by the ear and hollered angrily, 'I wouldn't mind if you was spending good money enjoying yourself. But on *this* old shit? I've seen livelier turns in the graveyard.'

Jack stared at the woman. So that was it.

It was the turns.

He'd been too stupid, too inexperienced to know any

better. How could he go about getting better ones? He had no idea. This lot had all approached him when they'd heard on the grapevine that he was opening up. Now he knew why. They probably couldn't get work anywhere else.

What was he going to do?

He'd been a fool thinking he could ever pull this off, but it was too late now, he'd spent everything he had on the place, he couldn't give up. He *wouldn't* give up. Not until he'd used up the last breath in his body.

Jack Fisher knocked back his glass of rum, pulled out a bottle from under the table and poured himself another. He'd never been much of a drinker, had actually drunk even less since he'd seen the behaviour of some of his customers, but he'd treated himself to this half-bottle tonight, which he'd kidded himself he would be drinking in celebration. He'd been sure that this bill was the best he had ever put on. There were songs, musicians, novelty acts and even comedy recitations. They'd laughed all right, but now he realised, for all the wrong reasons. He had really thought that the talking dog had amused them.

He reached down and scratched the ears of Rex, his own elderly mongrel. Maybe he should teach Rex to whistle. It was about as likely as this place being a success.

The Old Black Dog? It was more like the dead duck.

If he didn't do something very soon he'd be out of business. They'd all be off, spending their money elsewhere, in other people's pubs and halls. Maybe he should forget the turns, just concentrate on the pub. But now that their curiosity about the place had been satisfied they would be looking for something more than just another alehouse. That was something the area definitely wasn't short of.

He'd have to figure it out or he'd wind up like his old dad, God rest his soul, grafting for a governor who thought more about dumb animals than he did about his workers.

When the explosion had happened that had killed his father the owner had rushed to the pit-head. His first question, and his only apparent concern, was whether he'd have to buy new horses. Sod the poor buggers who'd been buried alive.

Jack would never put up with that, he'd die rather than live that way. He'd rather kill.

He'd gone down that place, just once, two days after his twelfth birthday nearly fifteen years ago now. His mother had said no at first, but they'd needed the money. Just as he did now. It was like descending into hell itself. He didn't know how the men managed to breathe, let alone work. To describe the stuff as dust, that you took down your lungs, was as wrong as calling a dripping tap a rain storm. He'd thought he would choke to death.

And the heat.

When he'd come back into the light he had sworn he would never go down there again, and had done anything and everything which came up to earn money so that one day he could escape.

He'd worked on farms and in mills, he'd broken rocks and served behind bars, he'd chopped logs and hauled sacks. Saving every penny, apart from the few shillings he gave his mother for his keep, so that one day he could get out of that place and go to London, the glittering place where he would make his fortune.

That's what had attracted him: the lights of London.

What a joke that was.

He tipped more rum into his glass, drank it and poured another. What did it matter if he drank away the last of the profits? He was as good as wrecked anyway. Just as he'd wrecked Tess's life by running out on her.

Tess.

He'd been such a bastard. When she'd let him have his way with her he'd as good as promised her they'd be wed one day. He'd have to write to her and try to explain. If only he could find the courage.

He shook his head and moaned pathetically to himself.

Suddenly a loud clattering of tambourines and off-key cornets came blasting up from the street below. That bloody lot from the mission again.

As if he didn't have enough on his plate, now he had the bible bashers to worry about as well. They'd taken to hanging about the front door, trying to put off the punters with their talk of brimstone and damnation. And it wasn't just the one group either, there were dozens of the buggers springing up all over the place. All going on about the new century, and the new Jerusalem, and judgement day, and who knew what else. What was it about a change of calender that seemed to bring all these lunatics out of the woodwork? Why couldn't everyone just mind their own business and leave him alone to mind his?

Archie came over to the table, a frown creasing his usually fresh-faced good looks. 'You all right, boss?'

Without even glancing up, Jack said absently, 'Makes me sick.' His northern accent was thick from the unaccustomed drinking. 'They say the halls *encourage immorality*. Immorality? The halls are nothing compared to the penny gaffs. They're the real blood tubs. It's them they want to look at. But will they? No, they'd rather bother a respectable businessman like me. They think I'm coining it. Making money hand over fist.'

Archie sat down, now even more concerned for the

man who'd become such a good friend to him.

'I've sunk everything I've ever earned into this place. Gone without food and clothes; worked every hour God sent, doing anything that came along. Never spent a farthing on myself. Even sold my old dad's watch and my grandma's wedding ring – all they'd left me – because I wanted a different life. Denied myself the comfort of having a wife and family; condemned myself to loneliness. All so I could wind up here.'

He poured the last drop of rum into his glass. 'Why should I be surprised when things go wrong, eh, Archie? Success wasn't meant for the likes of me, Jack Fisher, the son of a poor pitman.'

'I think if you could just find some different turns, boss.'

Jack spun round. 'That's what I thought. But what sort of turns? And where do I get them?'

'Anywhere except where you got this mob, boss.' Archie winced as he looked up at the stage where the Amazing Aerial Adventurer had just failed, for the fourth time, to launch himself across the remaining punters' heads on a rope suspended from the wings. 'Because, in my humble opinion, this lot stink.'

Of the handful of people left in the room the only one who seemed to be enjoying himself was Teezer. He was beside himself with laughter. It hadn't turned out to be such a bad night after all.

Kitty's night, however, had taken a distinctly sharp turn for the worse.

'I know it's not much.' Tibs smiled as she led Kitty under the dripping railway arch, past huddled piles of stinking rags, 'but this little spot in the Minories is one of the few that ain't crowded out by this time of night.'

Tibs squatted down on the ground and held out her

hand to Kitty, indicating that she should do the same.

With a resigned, shuddering sigh, she joined her. The pile of rags next to her suddenly shifted and Kitty gasped with alarm.

'You must have woke her up,' said Tibs, craning her neck to get a look at the human ragheap, then winking encouragingly at Kitty. 'Could be worse, eh, girl, we could be in the workhouse.' And, Tibs thought to herself, we could be alone out there in the dark, where girls like me get murdered and no one gives a shit.

Chapter 3

Kitty woke with a start as an icy drip of water found its way down her collar.

'You all right, sweetheart?' asked Tibs with a shudder – she wasn't only freezing, she'd been thinking again about that poor murdered girl and how, in a few days, when some other tragedy had happened or a bit of scandal had hit the streets, she'd be no more than a vague memory. That's what it was like being a tart. You counted for very little.

Kitty shook herself, then shrugged uncertainly. She'd been right to be wary about bedding down under the railway arches: it was every bit as bad as she'd feared. She couldn't imagine how she'd managed to fall asleep. She just wished she hadn't woken up. The cold was slicing right through her and her nostrils were filled with the stench of the unwashed, rag-clad humanity that surrounded her.

'I know it ain't exactly home, Kit, but like I said, it's better than going in the spike for the night. You don't even wanna know what goes on in that casual ward down the workhouse. And look, the rain started a little while ago and it's cleared all the fog away.'

Kitty held out her hands, trying to catch some heat from the dying embers of their fire.

When she and Tibs had arrived there had been fires dotted all around, but it seemed that few had managed to keep them going as long as Tibs had hers. She had kept it burning brightly until Kitty's hair – if not much else – was almost dry. But now her small blaze too had faded to little more than a heap of grey ashes. But at least it was something to look at; far better than having to make eye contact with the pitiful creatures lining the wall on either side of her.

Kitty knew about such people, of course, she had seen them in the countryside. They slept in ditches and out-buildings, and there were always a few eggs or vegetables to be had and fresh water to be drawn from a stream or a village pump. But here, in London, the streets seemed to teem with people who not only had nowhere else to go, but who had no chance of finding anything to fill their bellies other than the rotten dis-carded rubbish left at the end of the day under the market stalls.

And as for the children, Kitty *really* couldn't bear to look at them.

When she had arrived in London – was it really only a few days ago? – she had considered herself to be badly off. Then she had seen the first of the poor little barefoot mites draped in their filthy shreds, raking the streets with no expression in their eyes other than fear.

And now, here she was, just another one of the desperate, anonymous creatures, slumped in a line along one side of a dark, narrow roadway that curved under the vaulted roof of a railway bridge, so near to the wealth and comfort of the City, but so far away from any chance of ever sharing in its fortune and prosperity.

Kitty wondered if they crowded on the one side of the road like that so they could keep warm. But it didn't seem very likely. Bony bodies wrapped in rags didn't give out much heat, even if they were huddled together like piglets in a sty.

The bells of a nearby church chimed ten and Kitty realised she had been asleep for less than an hour; she also discovered why the other side of the street was left clear.

Glimmering through the slanting rain came the dull yellow light of a bull's-eye lantern, the sort carried by constables on the beat; it was accompanied by the firm, confident footsteps of a heavy, well-fed man.

The policeman himself appeared out of the gloom, his drooping black moustache and dark, bulky cape sparkling with droplets of water.

He slowed down, then stopped, adjusted the wick of his lamp and swung it slowly back and forth, illuminating the hollow eyes and scared faces of the scraps of humanity lined up along the roadway.

'I told you last night and I told you the night before,' he droned, 'you're not going to get away with using this public highway as a dosshouse. Now pick up your things – if you've got any other than lice and fleas – and clear off out of it.'

'We ain't hurting you,' Tibs snapped at him. 'And we've left the other side clear so's people can get past. So what's the harm?'

'The harm, *young lady*, is that they – *you* – are an eyesore and a public nuisance and, as an officer of the law . . .'

'As a wicked old fart, you mean.' Tibs scrambled to her feet and jabbed her finger at him. 'You can see how we're all suffering, you miserable great rabbit-pie shifter. Just look at you, too fat and lazy, and too much of a coward to have a go at that lot of ruffians up in the graveyard. Women and kids, that's your mark. Why don't you just piss off out of it and leave us alone, you mean old bastard?'

The policeman, his eyes bulging and his face flushing as scarlet as his fat, strawberry nose, enquired in a low, menacing voice, 'What did you call me?'

Usually, Tibs would have carried on with her disrespectful attack, on the principle that she could wear down the best of them with the sharpness of her tongue, or, if it came to the worst, could outrun them if they seemed to be winning the argument, but she had this half-barmy country bumpkin to think about.

She jerked her head at Kitty and said in a much softer tone, 'Don't be mean, officer. You can't expect her to carry the banner all night, can you? Look at her, she's wringing wet.' Slowly, Tibs dipped her chin, lowered her lashes and smiled shyly up at him. 'You wouldn't upset two young girls like her and me, now would you, sir? Have pity on us.'

The constable's tongue flicked across his fleshy lips. He moved closer, flashing his light over Tibs's face to get a better look. 'If you were nice to me,' he said, 'I might find it in my heart to give you a few pennies to spend on a room for the night. Think of that. A chance to get all nice and warm.'

'Sod off,' she snarled, 'or I'll be down that station so fast . . .'

'Aw yeah, and what'll you do then?' he asked cockily.

'I'll be grassing you up to your sergeant. Telling him how you take money off Limpy Mick and turn a blind eye to the betting on his terrier fights.'

'Will you now?' he asked, his confidence draining.

'So fast, you won't know your big fat arse from your old woman's skinny, bony, rotten elbow.'

He lifted his hand. 'You little whore.'

Instead of backing away, Tibs stood her ground. She folded her arms across her chest and stuck her chin in the air. 'Go on,' she taunted him, 'hit me. My feller's Albert Symes – a spiteful bastard he is, but then you probably know him. And he'd just love that, me having a nice black eye for work.'

'I've a good mind . . .'

'You, a good mind? Do us a favour.'

He took out his whistle. 'I'm warning you.'

'Go on, blow it. And you'll have every lad for miles around coming looking for a bundle. You wouldn't dare.'

He glared at her, his jaw set in impotent rage. He wanted to smack her pretty little face so badly it almost hurt. But he knew she was right. He shouldn't be patrolling these streets at night, when the likes of Albert Symes might be around. Especially not alone and definitely not at his age, and with the rheumatism in his knees playing him up again. He should be back at the station with his feet up and a cup of hot, sweet tea in his hand.

'Cat got your tongue?' asked Tibs, pushing her luck. 'Tell you what, why don't you go down Chinatown and sort out all that white slavery lark? Or that too scary for you and all, is it?'

The policeman's chin trembled. 'I've got me eye on you, young woman.' With that he walked off into the rain with as much bounce as if he'd just won a great victory.

Tibs snorted contemptuously and flipped a two-fingered salute at his retreating figure.

Acknowledging the looks of grateful admiration from her temporary neighbours, she slid back down the wall and settled herself next to Kitty. 'That showed him, eh, Kit?'

Kitty's only reply was a self-pitying sniffle.

'Don't cry, darling. It'll be getting light before you know it. Then the sun'll be up and everything'll look just sweet and dandy.'

'I feel that scared. And I'm so cold.'

'I'll see if I can find a bit more wood to get the fire

going again. How'd that be, eh?' Tibs put her arm round Kitty's shoulders. 'I'll have a lovely blaze going before you know it, then I'll entertain you with the story of how I come to be living in the smoke.'

She stood up and grinned. 'I've been up and down more times tonight than a bride's nightie.'

Kitty managed a thin smile.

'Look, I know you're tired, love, but don't nod off till I get back, will you?' Tibs bent forward, glanced to either side of her and whispered, 'And keep your voice down when you talk to me. We don't want them all knowing you ain't a local.'

'It makes me sick, Bug, d'you know that? Don't show no gratitude, some people. None at all.'

Buggy shoved a tankard into Teezer's hand and settled back into his seat. 'Who d'you mean then, Teeze? Who don't show no . . .'

'Who d'you think? That lanky mare I pulled out of the sodding river, that's who.'

'You ain't still going on about her, are you?'

'Can you blame me? She was gonna be the start of my business empire, she was. I've made me mind up, I'm gonna find her. That's what I'm gonna do.'

'You don't need her to start a business empire, Teeze. See, what you wanna do is . . .'

Before Buggy could get into his stride, Teezer raised his hand to silence him. 'Just shut up, eh? Look, the talking dog's coming on again.' He swallowed a long pull of dark stout, wiped the back of his hand across his mouth and muttered dourly, 'And I'll bet it'll speak a sight more bloody sense than you ever do.'

Tibs stamped on the big wooden crate with surprising force, splintering it into two jagged pieces. Setting down the larger part safely by Kitty's side, she gave the other bit to a group of sunken-cheeked youngsters who were sitting by the miserable remains of their pitifully small fire.

The oldest of them, an emaciated little thing of about nine – with a man's cap pulled down low over her matted hair, sores around her mouth and a cough that shook her shoulders – snatched the firewood from Tibs with a distrustful stare. Then, with a knowledge that no child of her age had any right to have, she carefully broke it into tiny pieces, in order to eke it out the best she could.

'Here,' said Tibs, holding out a cone of newspaper to one of the smaller children. 'And mind you share them out proper now.'

The child dragged itself to its feet and limped forward cautiously. It was difficult to make out whether it was a boy or a girl from its gaunt face and shabby rags, but what was obvious was that its short life had been one of poverty and deprivation: the undoubted causes of the diseased spine which hindered the little creature's movements.

Warily, it shot out a skinny hand to claim its prize.

Tibs smiled encouragingly and went back to Kitty. 'Tiger nuts,' she explained. 'I usually keep a few in my pocket for when I'm hanging around of a night. Chewing on them keeps the hunger off a bit.'

'Do you help everyone?'

'Doesn't hurt to share, does it, girl?' She gathered up the smaller splinters of wood, dropped them carefully into the embers, then sat back on her haunches and waited for them to catch. 'Who knows, I might be glad of a bit of help myself one day. And anyway, how could I, how could *anyone*, ignore them poor little arabs? Mind you, you still have to watch 'em. They're crafty.

Wouldn't think twice about trying to flimp you.'

'But they're only babies.'

'Kit, you can't trust no one.'

With the fire crackling back into life, Tibs threw on a larger piece of wood. 'If you're ill, or tired, or alone, you're weak. Makes you an easy target and anyone can pinch off you.' She held out her hands, warming them back from numbness. 'When I first come up to London I was just a little nipper like them, a green, fresh-picked pea pod from the wilds of Essex. And that was a lesson I had to learn.'

'So you really are a country girl?'

'I know it's hard to believe, but I was born right out in the sticks. The other side of Romford.' She smiled, remembering. 'Lovely out there, it was. If I close my eyes, I ain't in no dirty, stinking street, I'm paddling in a crystal-clear stream, with me frock all tucked up round me bum, singing and splashing in the sunshine. All clean and lovely. I even nearly went to the seaside once. Me mum said she'd take me. But she didn't.' She paused, staring into the flames. 'I don't think it's right, letting kids down.'

Satisfied with the fire, Tibs settled herself back against the wall next to Kitty. 'When me mum fetched me up here I never even knew where we was going.'

'How about your dad? Did he come too?'

'Me dad – if you can believe anything me mum ever told me – was a leather worker, from over Hornchurch way. But when I come along he didn't wanna know. Already had a family, see, and didn't fancy having no little surprises turning up on his old woman's door-step.'

She leaned to one side, reached under her topskirts and took out a small packet of snuff, which she offered to Kitty, who shook her head.

55

Tibs took her time sprinkling, sniffing and sneezing, then continued with her story. 'Me mum reckoned she wasn't exactly heart-broken and, at first, just carried on doing what she'd always done. Not earning much, but no one could ever have accused her of not being a grafter.'

'Where did you live?'

'With me gran. It was a one-room farm cottage and the three of us shared it with the dog, a couple of pigs and a full roost of hens, but at least it was a roof over our heads. Any odd jobs on the farm, Mum'd do 'em. And if there wasn't any, she'd sell bits and pieces around the cottage doors. She used to get a right earful from some of the cottagers, mind. They didn't take kindly to a woman with a baby on her hip and no ring on her finger.'

'It must have been hard,' said Kitty, trying to understand.

'No, not all the time. Some of it was a laugh, like when she helped out in the Romford alehouses of a market day. She was right popular there. Used to give the customers a song while she worked. Lovely singing voice she had.'

'Can you sing?'

Tibs snorted with laughter. 'Ever heard a cats' chorus? Anyway,' she went on, 'one day she was serving in the Golden Lion and she caught the eye of one of the wagoners. He took a right shine to her. Told her that with a beautiful face like hers and with that voice she could make a good living up in the big city. Said she'd love it up there, he did. And that all the lights made it like the middle of the day even at midnight, and that all the streets was paved with gold. Even said he'd give her a ride up there in his cart, if she fancied it.'

'So that's how you got here?'

'Not exactly. When Mum turned up the next morning,

with me in tow, he couldn't take her with him after all, could he?' Tibs smiled bleakly. 'Another bloke what let her down 'cos of me. But by then, Mum was right set on the idea of seeing all them bright lights, so she decided we'd walk. Well, to be truthful, she carried me most of the way, 'cos like I said, I was only a little nipper. But I'll always remember it. As soon as me gran was asleep we crept out of the cottage and sneaked by the back of the cow byre so's the farmer's wife wouldn't see us from the farmhouse. Me mum reckoned it was 'cos she was such a good worker and the farmer's wife wouldn't have liked the idea of losing her. But once I got older and wiser I reckon she'd had it away with some gear from the farm.' Tibs winked. 'Just in case, like. Well, it had just got dark, and she was telling me how we was going on this big adventure and how I wasn't to make any noise.'

Kitty nodded, drawn into the story.

'We went on for what felt like a really long time, and I was really tired and moaning. So Mum said we should stop for a little sleep. Know what we did?'

She waited for Kitty to shake her head.

'We climbed over this stile and spent the rest of the night cuddled up in a big sweet haystack. Like a pair of little field-mice we was. I always think of me mum when I smell a wagon of new-mown hay.'

She hesitated, then pinned on a smile. 'It took a few days for me to realise we weren't ever going back to me gran's. And that, Kitty, my dear, is the true story of how Miss Tibs Tyler, a country girl by birth, grew up to be a genuine cockney sparrow.'

'And you liked it, being up in London?'

'At first. 'Cos me mum was with me. She used to make me laugh. But then, when I was about seven she buggered off and left me.'

'She left you all alone?'

'Yeah.'

'How did you manage?'

Tibs shrugged, dismissing the question. 'I've always been a chirpy little thing, me. Things have to be really bad to get me down.'

'But how did you live?'

'Well, once I'd fought my way into getting a decent pitch along the shore, I tried my hand at mud-larking. That was all right for a while.'

'Mud-larking?'

'Underfed kids and battered old women toshing for driftwood; raking along the banks at low tide for coal, bits of rope and lumps of old metal. Picking up anything you can sell to the junk dealers.'

'Wasn't it dangerous by the river?'

'Sometimes, yeah. But after a few years of getting by and running wild with a gang of young hooligans down there I decided I'd had enough of it anyway. Thought it was time I got a proper business.'

'But you were still only a child.'

'Well? What age did you start work?' Tibs asked defensively.

'I was only a youngster, but I was working for someone. I'd have had no more idea about starting up a business than flying away in a balloon.'

'You grow up fast on the streets. You have to.' Tibs broke off another bit of wood and tossed it into the fire, watching as the flames threw spiky shadows across the slimy roof of the dripping arch.

'Did you really set up a business?'

She nodded. 'I did. Not that it was much of a success. I did wardrobe dealing. No rags or nothing. Only the best second- or third-hand gear.' She glanced down at Kitty's skirts. 'No offence meant, sweetheart.'

Kitty felt her cheeks flush red. 'None taken.'

'Trouble was, it wasn't that easy for a girl, especially a little dot like me. All the best stuff got grabbed by the blokes. In fact, I soon realised I'd made a real mistake. I'd given up me mud-larking pitch and I was desperate. So I started nicking stuff off of drunks and that.' She took a deep breath. 'I know what you must be thinking, Kit, but I wasn't going in the spike for no one. Then, like plenty of other girls of my age, I drifted into the life of a Ratcliffe Highway bride.'

Kitty's eyes widened. She leaned forward and whispered from behind the cover of her hand, 'Are you saying . . .'

'I'm a whore? Yeah. So?'

'Sorry, I didn't mean . . .'

'I never said I *liked* it. I just do it. I either earn money or I starve. And I've got Polly to think about.'

'Polly?'

'Just someone I help out,' Tibs said hurriedly, 'and, let's face it, being on the bash is better than some of the things I could have done.'

Kitty wanted to ask more about Polly and how Tibs could manage to care for her when she seemed to be in such a state herself; and what could possibly be worse than selling yourself for a living? But it was obvious that Tibs didn't want to discuss any of those things.

After a few moments Tibs sighed and then went on, 'You never do find the pearl ear-rings, or the gold watch when you're mud-larking, you know, Kit. Well, the likes of me don't. And at least whoring's an honest living.'

'And probably better than being tricked into doing it by a liar who doesn't even pay you for the privilege.'

Tibs laughed out loud. 'That's my girl, Kit!'

Shocked at herself for such an outburst, Kitty dropped her chin and looked away.

'Come on, let's hear more.'

Kitty shook her head. 'I don't have much to tell.'

'Course you have. How did you wind up here?'

She swallowed hard. 'My dad was sick. Real bad. And then he died. There were all these doctor's bills. Then the farmer said I had to get out of the cottage. I had nowhere to live.' She picked at the damp serge of her skirts. 'So I took a position in this big house.'

'Was it all right?'

'At first it was. I worked hard and the mistress was quite good to me, but then . . .'

'Then she found out the master was more interested in you being in his bed than in making it?'

Kitty frowned. 'It was her son, not her husband. And he said he loved me. But how did you know?'

'Just a guess.'

'He was so cruel to me.'

'What was you doing before you went into service?'

'My mother died when I was a toddler and Dad said he couldn't keep me and my brothers. I don't think he knew how. So he sent us off to live with the charity sisters.' She tugged nervously at a matted lock of her heavy dark-brown hair. 'We'd only been in the home for a few months when my brothers both died of diphtheria. But it wasn't my dad's fault we had to go to that place. He had no choice.'

Tibs nodded, but said nothing.

'Then, when I was eleven, old enough to start earning, he said I could come home. I was so pleased to get away. The nuns were kind enough, but it was terrible in there. I was always hungry and it was so cold.'

'Not much better now, eh, girl?'

'No, not much.'

'Where was this big house then?'

'Mereworth.'

'Where?'

'In Kent.'

'Kent.' Tibs wrinkled her nose. 'South of the river.'

'When I got thrown out of there, after I told the mistress her son loved me and they called me all these names, I just walked and walked until I came to that great big bridge over there. I walked right to it. Towards all the lights dancing on the water from the boats. They looked so pretty.'

'That's the trouble, girl, it's the lights what attract us all. I couldn't believe my eyes when I first saw them. I'll never forget that sight. And the noise! It made market day in Romford look like the vicar's tea party. So many people.'

'I've stayed around the bridge for almost a week. I didn't have anywhere else to go.' She lifted her chin and looked earnestly at Tibs. 'I tried to get some money somehow. Asked everyone if they had work for me. But no one did.' She turned her head away. 'I even tried begging.'

Tibs rubbed her shoulder. 'Don't upset yourself, we've all done it, love. When my mum went off like that, all I had was two farthings she'd left me folded up in a screw of old newspaper. I woke up in this filthy, horrible room in a court over in Whitechapel and she'd just vanished. I don't know if I cried more because I was all alone or 'cos I had nothing but a sodding ha'penny to me name. I just hung about the market, hoping people would feel sorry for me. But it was useless. I made less than three ha'pence and had to spend the nights walking the streets all by myself.'

'You were so young.'

Tibs nodded. 'Yeah, a baby really. Then I met this old girl. A pea sheller she was, working for the costers. Well, she smiled at me so kind, she even said she had a few coppers to spare to pay for a night's lodging for me. Promised to take me to this place where I'd have a bed for the whole night, with clean sheets and a big feather bolster. I'll never forget how grateful I was.' Tibs shook her head at her own stupidity. 'I'd fallen for the five-card trick, hadn't I. The old bag had conned me.'

'I don't understand.'

'Instead of taking me to a common lodging house,' Tibs explained, 'she took me to one of the case houses off the Haymarket. One of the ones that specialises, if you know what I mean, in youngsters.'

'A case house?'

'It's London talk for a knocking shop. A whore house? A brothel?'

Kitty's eyes widened. 'But you were ...'

'Not quite seven years old. I didn't understand all what was going on then, of course, I just knew it was wrong, her trying to get me clothes off in front of this old man.'

'What did you do?'

'I gave the old trollop such a kick she didn't know what had hit her. Had it away on me toes and wound up under the railway arches with all the other urchins.' Tibs flashed her pretty dimpled smile. 'Like I say, not a lot better now, eh, Kit? Mind you, it was summer then. Warm. And a bloody sight drier than this poxy hole. And there was this boy who sold me a boiled trotter for a farthing.'

Kitty couldn't even remember what it was like being warm and dry, let alone having food in her belly. Her stomach rumbled loudly, as she imagined the luxury of gnawing on the fatty pink meat of a pig's foot.

'Blimey, girl, you sound just like Bow Bells ringing out. When did you last have anything to eat?'

Kitty shrugged, sending a shower of dried mud from her bodice. 'I can't remember. A couple of days ago I think.'

Tibs leaned forward and looked at the children slowly chewing their way through the tiger nuts. 'I should've given them to you.'

'No, they needed them more than me.' Kitty wiped a hand across her clammy brow; she felt feverish. 'I'm all right.'

Tibs stood up. 'But you're not, are you? Just look at you.' She put out her hand. 'Now don't argue, cocker, just get on your feet and let's go. Don't let the others hear, but I've got a few coppers left in my pocket. It's a bit of a walk, but I know somewhere up the other end of Brick Lane where I can get us some cheap hot grub.' She smiled sardonically. 'You do know, don't you, Kit, that one day people'll be calling these the good old days.'

'I knew we should have gone to the terrier fight,' Buggy complained. 'They reckon that little bitch of Limpy Mick's can do twenty rats in as many seconds. We could have earned a nice few shillings on that little dog. Mind you, I ain't seen much of Limpy lately. Not since the night he went arse over tit down Pickled Herring Stairs, and me and Big Harry Wright had to pull him out of the drink. Had the right hump, he did. Can't stand getting wet, that one.' Buggy droned on, unaware that the conversation had degenerated into a monologue. 'Or we could've gone down the boxing booth. That Welsh feller, you know him, the one with the big head and the funny earholes, he's fighting tonight. Got a good chance they reckon. Would've been a good night out and a bit of easy money.'

Buggy yawned and scratched thoughtfully at his belly. 'Mind you, a game of gin rummy with me old

Aunt Mary'd have been more interesting than this lot. Don't you reckon?'

Teezer answered with a loud, whistling snore.

'Well, Teeze, you've finally proved you've got a bit of taste at last.'

As the snoring rose to a crescendo and rattled around the now almost empty auditorium, Jack Fisher dashed his empty rum bottle to the floor in despair and buried his face in his hands.

Kitty was so light-headed with hunger that when she sneezed she had to stop walking to recover her sense of balance.

'It's only a bit further, love. Come on, keep moving and it'll warm you up.'

The streets gradually became busier and Tibs had to help Kitty thread her way through the late-night strollers and traffic, as the cries of hawkers and traders filled the air.

Kitty seemed to perk up a bit as she caught the sweet smell of an Indian toffee man's stall and the mouth-watering aroma of hot chestnuts roasting over glowing coals.

'Know what I could fancy, Kit?' said Tibs, sniffing at a big copper pan of peanut brittle and wiping the back of her hand across her drooling lips. 'A nice big slab of pickled belly pork. Handsome.'

Kitty's mouth filled with juices. 'That'd do me just fine,' she said weakly.

'Half a mo', just listen to that. It's the pie-man, ringing his bell.'

Kitty's stomach gurgled longingly as a big, fat man, swathed in a long, starched white apron, appeared round the corner. On his head he balanced a tray draped with a blue-and-white checked cloth.

Tibs scampered over to him like an eager child. 'I've only got a few coppers, mister,' she said, counting out some change. 'Can I just have three ha'p'orth's for me and me mate?'

'Go on with you,' he barked, ringing his bell at her as if it were a weapon. 'You don't get round me with your pretty smiles. These pies are thruppence each and that's final.'

Tibs sighed and rolled her eyes. 'All right, but let's have a look and see if they're worth it first.'

As the man lowered the tray, Tibs's hand shot out as quick as a flash and, before he realised what she was doing, she'd lifted one of the pies, had grabbed Kitty by the hand and was dragging her along through the crowd. 'Hook it, Kit!' she squealed, her face a picture of mischievous glee. 'Move yourself!'

The pie-man was furious. A bit of a girl had duped him. Him, a pie-man for forty years, and he'd let a little scrap like her get the better of him.

Too bulky to give chase himself, 'Stop thief!' he hollered, but no one helped him. They were all too busy enjoying the spectacle of the pie-man turning blood red to the very tips of his ears, and with the added attraction, of course, of seeing someone getting something for nothing off the miserable old sod.

By the time they had rounded the corner of one of the turnings that led back towards the shadowy riverside streets, Tibs was shrieking with laughter and Kitty, if she hadn't been doubled over with a stitch, would have joined in.

Tibs leaned against the wall, waiting for Kitty to get her breath back, and snapped the pie in two. She handed half to Kitty. 'Shall we hail a cab back to our rooms?' she asked her in a mock-posh accent.

'Why are you being so kind, Tibs?' panted Kitty,

through a mouthful of deliciously melting pie-crust.

'Me old gran, love her, always used to say, it don't cost nothing to be kind. No, wait, I'll tell you her exact words: *The smallest good deed is worth more than the grandest good intention.* I started embroidering it for her on a sampler at Sunday school.' She paused, then added quietly, 'But we left before I could finish it.'

'I think what you've done for me is more than a small thing. I'd have been dead if it wasn't for you.'

'Don't fret your gizzard, girl, anyone'd do the same.' Tibs took another bite of pie, then changed the subject abruptly. 'Talking about needlework,' she said, as though they were sharing afternoon tea in the front parlour. 'I've been thinking about getting myself one of them sewing machines. Good way to earn a shilling they say. And you can buy 'em bit by bit now, you know.'

'What? In parts, you mean? You have to put it together?'

Tibs grinned happily, the effort of running and the heat of the meat pie was beginning to warm her through as if she'd been wrapped up in a big woollen coat. 'You're straight off the boat, you, ain't you, Kit? No, I don't mean in parts like that. I mean week by week. Hire purchase it's called. Sadie Gardner told me all about it. She's been able to get off the game for good now. Making a nice living without having to open her drawers for no one. Well, no one except her old man. It must be sodding heaven. Not giving her old man one. . . . Aw, you know what I mean!' Tibs held out her hand and looked up at the dark night sky. 'Sod it. It's flaming gonna piss down again. Come on, we'll find somewhere snug to tuck ourselves out of it.'

'How do you stay so happy all the time?' Kitty asked, hurrying along beside her, with her eyes squinting into the now pouring rain.

'I've got this sort of trick, I suppose,' said Tibs. 'I just forget all the things what make me unhappy. All the things that hurt. It's easy.'

Kitty didn't believe it could really be that easy, but was too polite to say so. 'I see,' she said instead. 'That's a good trick, that is.'

'It is. It's . . .' Tibs's words trailed off and she dragged Kitty to a halt.

She pointed across the street to a pub sign that was creaking and swinging wildly in the growing downpour. Tibs didn't seem to notice that, as far as signs went, it wasn't very welcoming, showing as it did the snarling, slavering chops of a huge black hound.

'That's the grog-shop what Sal was going on about. And as I never had to spend no money on that pie, we can go over and treat ourselves, Kit. To a nice drop of rum. That'll get you warmed up, that will. And I'll bet they've got a big coal fire going and all. Then, I'll tell you what, I'll get us a few bob so we can have a proper bed for the night and I'll make sure I've got enough left over to buy a pretty bit of ribbon for my little . . .' She shut up as suddenly as if her lips had been spring-loaded.

She turned to Kitty and squeezed her arm. 'You stick with Tibs Tyler, me darling,' she said with a wink. 'And you see, everything'll be just sweet and dandy!'

Chapter 4

As the sounds from the Dog grew louder, Kitty's heart beat faster, and by the time she and Tibs were standing by the pub door she was in a state of total panic. She had been momentarily fooled by this kind, laughing girl and a mouthful of hot food actually to believe that something she was involved in might not be a disaster. How could she have been so stupid?

She took a long, deep breath, blinked slowly, then said it. 'No, Tibs. Don't.' She tugged on her new friend's sleeve. 'Not this. Please. I couldn't bear thinking that you'd do this just for me.'

'I'll be all right, daft,' Tibs cut in, her voice a bit too chipper. 'And it ain't just for you, now is it? It's for me too.'

'But aren't you scared?'

'Me? What would I be scared of?' She grinned. 'Apart from the rent man. And as I ain't got no home to go to I don't even have to worry about him, now do I?'

Kitty avoided looking Tibs in the eye as she said quietly. 'You know what I mean. With what you do, aren't you scared of the Old Boy?'

Tibs rolled her eyes. 'Is *that* what's worrying you?'

Kitty nodded fearfully.

'Well, there's no need. That's just country talk.' She sounded matter-of-fact.

'But . . .'

'Look, Kit, there's no danger doing business nowadays. Well, not unless you get caught by someone's old woman, there's not.' She attempted a smile.

'It's not funny.'

'I know, but anyone around here'll tell you, the Ripper run off to America years ago. Married some rich old sort, some mad woman who'd been let down by her fiancé and was ripe for the picking. Ready to let herself be grabbed by the first bloke who'd have her. Started a new life over there, so they reckon.'

Kitty thought about the impossibility of such a dream and slumped back against the soot-ingrained wall, defeat and exhaustion washing over her like the river at high tide. 'I wish I could start a new life.'

'Tell you what my wish'd be.' Tibs pointed up at the smoke-belching chimneys that crowded every rain-slicked roof. 'I wish I could sprout wings and fly away. Right up and out of one of them bloody smelly old stacks I'd go. And I'd soar up into the sky, and float higher and higher until I was right up there in the clouds, just like a flaming skylark. Then I'd flap me wings and I wouldn't stop, not until I was right over a sweet water meadow, then I'd . . . '

Tibs's words trailed away. Dabbing at her tangled, soggy yellow curls, a smile slowly dimpled her plump pink cheeks into an image of girlishly happy innocence. 'Imagine the money we'd make if I really did start growing feathers, eh, Kit? I'd be a right sight, wouldn't I? People would pay a fortune to see something like that. Don't you think? It ain't gonna happen though, is it? And certainly not to the likes of me. But even if I don't know how to make me fortune, I do know a sure-fire, slap-bang winner of a way to get us a couple of drinks. So cheer up, stick a grin on that gob of your'n, and we can go in and get ourselves warmed up. And I promise you the Old Boy won't be in there leaning on the bar.'

Kitty was too dispirited to argue and she certainly had nowhere else to go in this strange cockney world. So she nodded glumly, pushed herself away from the wall and followed Tibs obediently into the pub.

Within minutes of stepping into the warm fug of the big downstairs bar of the Old Black Dog, Tibs proved herself as good as her word and had charmed a round of drinks for them out of one of the customers. With a hurried promise that she was just going to take Kitty's drink over to her and come straight back to him – so quick would she be, in fact, that he wouldn't even notice she'd gone – Tibs flashed him a wink and disappeared into the crowd.

Kitty sniffed suspiciously at the swift of strong ale. 'I think it's a bit on the powerful side for me, thanks all the same.'

'Christ, Kit, it's only a drop of barley wine, it ain't gonna poison you. Now knock it back and you see it'll warm you right through. Go on,' she insisted, guiding the glass towards Kitty's lips, 'get it down your neck. That's only the first of many if I have anything to do with it.'

All the time Tibs was chatting and smiling encouragingly at Kitty she glanced about her.

While it was all very well helping people out – and Tibs's conscience would never have let her leave this gormless young swede-basher to her own devices – all the good turns in the world still never guaranteed that your own luck would get any better. That was all a con that the bible thumpers put about to keep you in order. In fact, if anything, her own luck had been going from bad to worse lately and she wouldn't even have been surprised to see Albert Symes standing in the corner, glaring at her, cosh in hand, ready to teach her one of his 'lessons'.

70

Kitty had closed her eyes and, doing as she was told, knocked back the drink in a single swallow. When she opened them again it was all she could do to stop herself spitting the foul brew back into the glass.

Tibs slapped her on the back and chinked her empty glass against Kit's. 'Good drop o' gear, eh, girl? Few more of them down you and you won't know whether you're kipping under the arches or in a great big feather bed.' Then, without so much as a pause, she asked, 'Know any songs?'

From the expression on her face it was clear that Kitty thought she couldn't have heard right. 'I'm sorry, it must be all the noise in here. I thought you asked if I know any songs.'

'I did.'

'What sort of songs?' Kit finally managed to splutter.

'Well, I don't mean hymns, now do I?'

Kitty really didn't know how to reply, but it didn't matter anyway, Tibs had carried on chatting away as if they were discussing whether Kitty wanted salt or vinegar on her chips, or just a splash of both.

'Mind you, it wouldn't do no harm singing one or two of them church songs. Some of 'em have right good tunes. Stirring, like. It wouldn't do to sing none of the gloomy . . . Here.' She grabbed Kitty's arm. 'Quick. Move yourself.'

Tibs whisked her away to the other side of the bar. 'The geezer what bought our drinks is coming over. Don't go looking at him for Christ's sake. Keep your eyes down.' Then she muttered to herself so Kitty couldn't hear, 'Pity you ain't about a foot shorter.'

'Shouldn't we say thank you?' asked Kit, craning her neck to get a look at their benefactor.

Tibs's answer was to drag her further into the crowd that was milling about in the middle of the room.

'You really are fresh from the sticks, ain't you, Kit?'

'Manners cost nothing, Tibs. The sisters taught us that. It was a good lesson . . .'

'So's this,' she said and with that, right in front of everyone, she lifted her skirts almost to her knees and began singing in a loud, bawling voice, 'My old man said follow the van!' and flashing her legs in their high-buttoned boots.

Kitty watched in slack-jawed astonishment as the crowd drew back to form a circle, laughing and clapping along to Tibs's rather erratic rendition of the music-hall favourite.

She beckoned ever more furiously for Kitty to join her, but Kit shook her head in horror. Not believing in taking no as any sort of an answer, Tibs grabbed the still damp, wild-haired, mud-smeared Kitty by the wrists and whirled her round in a wild sort of polka; all the while continuing to strangle the song in an exuberant, off-key screech that bore so little resemblance to the Marie Lloyd rendition it was barely recognisable.

But despite Tibs's shaky relationship with the right notes and Kitty's hurried escape from her grasp, the crowd loved it.

Keen for more, an elderly man was urged by his pals to sit himself at the piano to try and provide an accompaniment to her quavering efforts. His playing had the effect of whipping Tibs into an even more enthusiastic performance. Kitty could only stare.

When the moment came for the impromptu accompanist to show off his solo skills during the middle break of the song, Tibs snatched off her bonnet, tossed it to Kitty and shouted, 'If you ain't gonna join in you can pass the hat round, girl! Go on, get 'em to fetch out their mouldies!'

Kitty had no intention of doing any such thing but the crowd made the decision for her. They were only too glad to contribute to the providers of such peculiar entertainment.

'What a pair!'

'Just look at 'em!'

'Big and small! Mud-covered and clean!'

'Blonde and brunette!'

As they tossed and flicked yet more coins in Kitty's direction they egged on Tibs to cock up her legs in higher and higher kicks. She was only too glad to oblige, not giving a damn that the opening in her drawers was threatening to make a show of her to anyone with half-way decent eyesight.

'Make sure you get them pennies what've rolled on the floor, Kit,' Tibs puffed, then, turning her back to the crowd she bent over and gave a tantalising flick and flourish of her skirts, showing just that bit more of her drawers to have them all cheering and whistling for more. She straightened up, flashed her eyes at the now sweat-drenched, puce-faced elderly pianist and simpered, 'Know any others, darling?'

Upstairs in his theatre, Jack Fisher leaned forward unsteadily and reached under the table for his bottle. He closed one eye to enable him to focus and stared at the shattered glass in shock. 'Who did that?' he asked no one in particular.

When no one answered him – actually, there was no one *to* answer him, as he was alone apart from Teezer and Buggy, who were now both soundo – Jack decided to go down to the bar for a refill. One more wouldn't do him any harm. Tess had never liked him drinking because she said it was a waste of money. And she was right, but just another little drink . . .

After a couple of tries he rose to his feet, almost managed to brush his floppy red fringe out of his eyes and jammed his battered felt hat down firmly to his ears. He took a deep breath. Maybe business was better down in the bar.

Maybe.

He could only hope so. He was depending on the bar profits to get in some decent acts. That's what he needed. Decent acts.

Who was he fooling? He had about as much chance of attracting decent acts to this God-forsaken hole, and for the sort of money he had left in his pot, as he had of the mine owner turning up tomorrow morning and offering to take him back to his stately bloody pile and to adopt him as his son and heir.

Still scrabbling around on her hands and knees, like a step scrubber who'd mislaid her carbolic, Kitty started in alarm as she felt someone tap her roughly on the back. She froze, the ha'penny she had been chasing between the table legs forgotten.

But, frightened as she was, Kitty's surprise was nothing compared with Jack Fisher's. Here was this odd-looking pair – one as pretty as a little doll, but certainly no singer from the caterwauling he'd heard as he'd come stumbling down the stairs, and this other one, as lanky as a boy and, by the look and smell of her, just arrived from being dragged through the Thames-side mud at low tide – and he hadn't heard such appreciation in the Old Black Dog since he'd taken the place over. Well, not since the opening night, when the fat tenor's trousers had split and it was clear to the whole audience that, despite the fog, there was a full moon shining over Rosemary Lane.

Jack coughed again.

74

Kitty pressed her lips together, took a deep lungful of air and turned her head to peer warily over her shoulder. When she saw the tall male figure in the strangely shapeless hat swaying over her she knew her caution had been warranted.

'What's your name, lass?' the man asked in a calm, if somewhat slurred, north-eastern accent.

'We never meant no harm, sir,' Kitty spluttered, her eyes pleading for mercy.

'I'm not saying you did. I just want to talk to you, that's all.'

'To me?' She tapped herself on the chest. Couldn't he mean someone else? Anyone else. Please.

'There's no one else under that table with you, is there?' he asked, with a jerky movement that had Kitty fearing he was about to get down there with her.

She shook her head and he held out his hand to her. 'I'd like to talk to you. You and your friend.'

To avoid his touch Kitty did without his help and instead scrambled inelegantly to her feet. 'I won't be a minute, I'll just go over and see what she's got to say.' With a furtive glance over her shoulder at him Kitty rushed across the bar and grabbed Tibs roughly by the sleeve.

Tibs spun round. 'What the hell?' When she saw it was Kit she leaned closer. 'Can't you see I'm busy?' she whispered. 'I'm trying to chat this feller-me-lad here, the piano-playing genius, into giving us another song without *us* having to give *him* a cut of the takings.'

'Forget all that, Tibs,' Kitty hissed back, willing her to move. 'We've got to get out of here, there's this . . .'

She saw Tibs's attention wander, saw that she was staring at something – or, more accurately, someone – standing behind Kitty's shoulder.

Kitty might not have had eyes in the back of her head,

75

but she knew exactly who was standing there: the red-haired man in the odd felt hat.

She watched as Tibs pinned on a pretty little smile, dropped a brief bob of a curtsey, then said in an almost daintily careful voice, 'Good evening to you, sir.'

'Name's Jack Fisher,' he said, carefully enunciating each word and attempting, and failing, to touch his finger to his battered hat. 'I might have a proposition to put to you.'

Quick as a flash, Tibs's smile opened up and spread as sweetly as warm syrup. She threaded her arm through his. 'Always glad to discuss a bit of business, sir, anyone'll tell you that.'

Kitty watched in horror as Tibs allowed herself to be led away by the obviously drunken man and almost screamed when she heard him say, 'And let me have a good look at those legs of yours. You might well have something there.'

As they were about to disappear through a green baize-covered door behind the bar Tibs paused, whispered something to the man, then turned round and winked at Kitty. 'I shouldn't be too long, Kit. You just make sure you wait here for me, all right? And tell that nice young barman that this lovely man said he was to give you a double rum and milk. And look out for One-eyed Sal. When she comes in, get one off him for her and all.'

With that, Tibs stepped through the doorway without so much as another backward glance.

Chapter 5

It was half past seven the next morning, the beginning of a bright, if chilly, March day, and Tibs and Kitty were standing at the big butler sink in the gloomy, low-ceilinged basement kitchen of a common lodging house in Rosemary Lane.

Although the sky outside was full of spring promise, inside the room was dank and dark, with a miserable excuse for an open fire making little impact on the almost freezing atmosphere.

The girls were doing their ablutions – managing as best they could when surrounded by pairs of staring eyes from the gloomy depths – while they waited for the huge communal kettle to come to the boil on the range in the far shadowy corner.

Tibs had produced a cracked, dried-out slither of soap from one of her petticoat pockets. She handled it as though it were of the very purest, most expensive quality and scented with the finest of French cologne, although in actual fact it reeked of something more like a sewerman would use to clear the drains.

She delved deep into her assorted layers of bodices and underthings and lathered under her arms with the tiny piece of carbolic, shivering as the cold soapy water touched her skin.

When she'd finished she passed it over to Kitty with a nod that said she wouldn't take no for an answer – Kitty *had* to borrow it, she was a mate after all – then stared up out of the small square of railing-covered window that looked out on to the street above.

'Looks nice and fresh out there this morning, Kit. Makes a change from that bloody fog.' Tibs coughed loudly as a plume of gaseous smoke poured from the hearth into the already fug-filled room, wreathing about them like rancid ribbons. 'With a bit of luck it'll be clear for a few days.'

Kitty concentrated on using as little of the soap as possible. She knew she couldn't refuse – Tibs might have been tiny but she was formidable – but it still didn't mean that she had to take advantage of her new friend's generosity. It seemed such a waste of time bothering to wash, just as it was pointless checking up on the weather. Whatever it was like, rain, hail or snow, it made little difference to her. Kitty had had a night's sleep – surprisingly good, considering that it was the first time she'd been in anywhere as intimidating as a common lodging house – and she was now dry, and cleaner than she'd been in days, but what did all that matter? Why should she care? What difference did any of it make to her?

She didn't know what had got into her last night – it was probably the shock of being hoiked out of the river by that horrible pair – but she'd come back to her senses this morning. It was all very clear to her: there was no life for her in London, no life for her anywhere as far as she could see. She'd been given a second chance, had been allowed to reconsider, and all it had done was confirm that she had been right all along. Life held nothing for the likes of Kitty Wallis and she had no intention of dragging kind little Tibs down with her as well. She would get away as soon as she could without seeming rude.

'So, what d'you fancy for breakfast then?' Tibs asked behind the cover of her hand, so that none of the other residents could hear that she was in possession of enough money to buy food.

'Nothing thanks,' Kitty said firmly. 'Funny, but I'm not hungry this morning.'

As if on cue, her stomach gurgled noisily.

'Blimey, Kit, I ain't never heard no one with guts as noisy as your'n. And I tell you what, if they make that row when you ain't even hungry I'd hate to hear 'em when you start fancying a spot of something.'

'I don't want nothing, honestly. And I have to be off soon, anyway.'

Tibs dried her arms on the hem of one of her scratchy underskirts, enquired with a look as to whether Kitty had finished with the soap and secreted it back into its hiding place. She lowered her voice. 'Don't start getting snooty with me, Kit. I told you, he was a gentleman. I never had to do nothing. So there's no need for you being all la-di-da about it.'

'I don't rightly know what being all la-di-da means, but I'm sure it's not what I'm being, Tibs.'

'So what's up then?'

'It worries me and I feel proper bad that you'd go and . . . you know, do *that*. Just for me. Just so's I can have a bed for the night and a decent breakfast. And it's not as though you even know me. We only met a few hours ago.' Kit stared into the middle distance. 'Mind you, with everything that's happened it seems a lot longer ago than that.'

'Thanks!'

'You know what I mean.'

'Yeah, course I do. I was only joking.' Tibs shoved her playfully. 'You wanna relax a bit. Have a laugh. It's good for you. You should remember that.' Then she added casually, 'And I think it's good to have a bit of a sing-song and all. Don't you?'

Kitty didn't answer her, she had other things she wanted to say. 'Tibs, I want to explain something.'

'You don't have to . . .'

'Please, it's important. What I was trying to say was that I'd rather go hungry and sleep in the gutter than have to, you know, go with men.'

Tibs looked hard at Kitty, trying to figure her out. 'You're a funny one, you know that, Kit. I ain't sure when you say stuff to me whether I should be offended or flattered half the time.'

'But I meant about the danger and the . . .'

Tibs put her finger to Kitty's lips to silence her. 'I'm gonna say this one last time. When I went out the back with that bloke last night all we did was talk. I promise you. You know, we opened our mouths and all these sounds come out . . .'

Kit's forehead pleated into a frown. 'You never had to do *anything* else?'

Tibs steered Kitty over to the range, flashing haughty looks of warning at the miserable assortment of tarts, tramps and drunks who had, like them, bought refuge in exchange for their meagre fourpences.

'I swear, Kit,' she went on, discreetly producing a screw of powdery tea and a small rock of sugar from among the rest of the treasure trove in her hidden pocket, 'not that it matters, mind, but he wasn't only a gentleman, he was really nice. He gave me that half a dollar just like that, when he told me we could keep all the money you collected and all.'

'But why?'

Tibs shrugged happily as she tipped a careful measure of tea into a battered brown enamel pot. 'I was as bleed'n' surprised as you, girl, I can tell you. It's not often you get something for nothing is it?' She winked happily. 'Pies excepted, of course. He just said we should take it as a thank you – for entertaining his customers, before you get any other ideas.' She suddenly looked thoughtful. 'Here, I wonder if he don't like girls? It takes all sorts to make the world go round, you know. Well, so they say.'

'That still doesn't explain why he took you out the back.'

Tibs took her time and spoke slowly and evenly as if explaining something complicated to an elderly aunt. 'See, he wanted to put this sort of business thing to me. What did he call it?' She considered for a moment. 'A *proposition*. That's it. A business *proposition*. And he was that nice about it.'

'You said all that. But why out the back?'

'Because it was private, that's why. I mean he didn't want no nose-ointments earwigging, now did he?'

Kitty did her best to guess at what Tibs was going on about.

'As a matter of fact it was because he was so nice that I said we'd do it.' Tibs didn't pause as she busied herself with brewing the tea. 'Anyone got any milk?' she asked without looking round. 'There's a ha'penny in it for you if you have and we only want a couple of splashes each.'

It took a few seconds for it to sink in and a few more for Kitty finally to ask, 'What did you say?'

'There's a ha'penny in . . .'

'Not about the milk.' Kitty's mouth felt dry and she was having trouble swallowing. 'You said we'd do something. *We'd* do something.'

A gaunt-looking woman sidled up to Tibs from out of the shadows. In her shaking hand she held an unhygienic-looking tin with its roughly sawn lid half opened, exposing a rust-speckled underside. 'Condensed all right?' she rasped in a tobacco-thickened croak.

81

Tibs searched through the jumble of cracked china on the big deal table that ran down one wall and picked out the two cups that looked the cleanest. She set them to one side where the woman could reach them.

'That'll do,' she said bluntly and held out a pair of dull copper farthings she'd got out ready to hand over. After her run-in with Lily Perkins, Tibs was being especially cautious about letting anyone see where she kept her special things.

Lily Perkins. The very thought of the rotten cow had Tibs grinding her teeth. She could have kicked herself for being so bloody wet behind the ears. Fancy letting herself be robbed by the likes of her. Fancy falling for that old game. If it had been someone like Kit getting herself rolled she could have understood it. But her, Tibs Tyler?

The woman slipped the two coins down the front of her dress and patted her skinny bosom. Satisfied that they were safe, she stared at Tibs, weighing up the situation. 'Say if there's any tea left in the pot?'

Tibs looked at her levelly. 'There won't be. And if you don't give us that milk a bit lively I'm gonna turn you upside down and shake that money back out of that chicken neck o' your'n, then give it a quick wring for good luck into the bargain.'

With a bad-tempered snarl, the woman glooped the thick milk into the cups, spat a muttered curse into Kitty's startled face and disappeared back into the cheerless depths of the big, flag-stoned room.

'Silly old tart,' Tibs hissed, stirring the tea with the handle of a food-encrusted knife then, pouring the steaming, dark-tan liquid on to the dollops of milk, she pushed a cup towards Kitty.

'Tibs,' Kit said as calmly as she could, 'would you please tell me what you told this man we'd do?'

'An act,' she answered matter-of-factly. 'Singing and that.'

Kitty wouldn't have been more horrified if Tibs had announced that she'd got them work digging a new canal and filling it up with buckets from the stand-pipe. 'Singing?' she gasped.

Tibs slurped noisily at her tea. 'Yeah. Good, eh?'

'Good?' Kitty supposed it was one up from what she had thought the man had proposed to Tibs. But *singing*? Maybe she was going mad. Why should that surprise her; the rest of the world certainly seemed to be well on its way along the path to lunacy.

She thought for a moment, trying to get things straight in her swirling brain, then said bluntly, 'No. Not singing.'

'Look, Kit, he's offering us a chance.'

'No. I mean it. I really can't. The only singing I've ever done in my life was hymns, and since I left the home I've not been inside a church, apart from once or twice when they let me have an hour off of a Sunday when I was at the big house.' A horrible thought occurred to her. 'Where would we be expected to do this singing? And who'd be *listening*?'

'In the Dog. And he only gets a few customers.' Tibs flashed her eyebrows and grinned wickedly. 'Anyway, you've heard the row I make, it obviously ain't our voices he's interested in. And he took a right shine to you, you know, Kit. Thought you was a real cracker.'

Tibs could only hope she sounded credible. The bloke had been plastered, hadn't even been too sure who he was talking to, let alone whether he fancied either of them or not. Typical pub owner. So much money sloshing about in his pockets that he could afford to pour half his profits down his throat, just 'cos he felt like it. Probably didn't have a worry in the world. It'd do the likes of him a bit of good to find out how it was to have a problem or two. Problems like she had.

'You're saying he thought I was . . . ' Kitty looked and sounded flustered. Men had tried things of course, but no one had ever told her she was desirable, not even *him* at the big house, even though she had said to Tibs that he'd told her he loved her. It was a strange sort of feeling and she wasn't sure whether she liked it or not. 'Don't you mean he thought *you* were . . .'

'No. You.' Tibs winked suggestively. 'And if he could see you now he'd be even more impressed. I mean, look how nice you've cleaned up.' Tibs's smile was becoming thinner by the moment, this was getting a bit too much like hard work. 'And I bet if you washed that hair of your'n it'd be lovely. Real pretty. Although,' she added, 'you're good-looking in a different kind of a way to me, of course.' She didn't want to strong it too much or Kit would know she was lying and it might frighten her off. 'But men ain't all got the same sort of taste you know.'

'Thank Gawd for that,' sniggered a fat, middle-aged woman who was boiling up something in a pan over the fire next to them. Whatever she had in the pot was giving off a terrible stink like old socks crossed with a tinge of rotten haddock.

Tibs nodded curtly at her and guided Kitty firmly across the room, away from the stench and out of the woman's earshot. 'Look, we'll go and have our breakfast and . . .'

'Thanks all the same, Tibs, but I've decided I can't take anything else off you.'

'You're not taking it off me. It's what's left out of what we earned last night.'

'Left out of what *you* earned last night,' Kitty corrected her. 'You did the singing.'

'Ne'mind who did what, they was looking at both of us. Now come on, let's go and get some food in that belly of yourn, and you'll be seeing sense in no time.'

Kitty didn't want to argue with her new friend but, hungry as she was, she had as much intention of having breakfast as she had of going on the stage. None whatsoever. But she had to admit it would have been nice to have something to eat, if only to kill the foul taste in her mouth from the rum she had drunk the night before. And as for that barley wine, she felt queasy just thinking about it.

But feeling hungry and sick were of little consequence to Kitty, especially when the price of filling her belly was not only taking money that, by rights, belonged to Tibs, but would also have meant getting involved with this new folly that Kitty had no intention of even considering.

She was going to slip away, find the Thames and finish off what she should have done yesterday. And this time she'd do it properly. She had decided exactly how when she'd been lying in her narrow cot last night, staring into the darkness, waiting for sleep to come.

She would hide under the bridge and wait for the dark, or the fog, to return, then she'd walk downstream, well away from madmen in blazing boats, fill her pockets with stones and throw herself in. There would be no one to see her, no one to stop her and, please God, no one to try and save her.

The feeling of relief at having made the decision, of knowing what was going to happen to her, almost made her forget her hunger. Her only regret was that she would have liked to have found a way to repay Tibs's kindness in helping her – even if it was misplaced – before she said goodbye. But Kitty had nothing to give anyone.

*

Jack Fisher lay on his back, staring miserably at the cracked and damp-stained ceiling of his poky little bedroom. It was way past the time he should have been up and about, but he was worn out after a night of fitful, disturbed and drunken dreams, and there was little to tempt him from under his covers in the cold, unwelcoming room.

Maybe it would have been better if he'd left himself a bit more space rather than this pitiful cubby-hole that could barely take his mean single cot and the tatty, threadbare rug. But he'd been so enthusiastic when he'd been creating the little dressing-room that led on to the stage of his theatre that he'd not given a thought to his own comfort and had happily given up over half of his own living space for his artistes.

Artistes! How could he have been so conceited as to expect that he, a lad from a pit village, could set up a theatre? What a fool he'd been even to think it. And what a fool he'd been to drink all that booze.

The hangover had first hit him when he'd tried, and failed, to raise his head from the pillow. Jack didn't have much experience to go on – in fact, this was only the second hangover he'd ever had – but he was sure it wouldn't have been possible to have one much worse than this. It was like a steam fairground had set up in his skull and all the rides and organs and side-shows were going full pelt. It was so bad that at this very moment the idea of going to sleep and never waking up again seemed a very reasonable option. If he just closed his eyes . . .

But no. He had to get up. There was something he had to do. What was it? For some reason he couldn't quite put his finger on it. Not at the moment. But there was something.

Maybe he should have a bit of a nap and it would come back to him – whatever it was – and he would wake up refreshed and ready to start another day and face whatever it was he had to do?

He would have liked to remember. It was niggling away in the back of his mind – not like the steam gallopers and the swing boats, but small and insidious, like a worm in the core of an apple. If only he could just reach out and grasp it.

He was sure it wasn't just his usual problems rearing and bucking in his brain. He'd done something. Something other than drinking a whole bottle of rum and the Lord alone knew how many porter chasers to keep it company. And he was sure it was important.

He groaned and screwed his eyes shut.

Not for the first time in the last few weeks Jack Fisher wondered why he had ever thought he was different from any other lad back home. Why he hadn't stayed in his place, where he belonged, and settled down with a nice lass from the village. And there were plenty of those after him, not to mention sturdy, sensible Tess and their 'understanding'. Then he would have gone down the mine like his dad and worked himself to the bone for a rich bastard who couldn't give a shit about anything but profit. And that was why he'd had these 'ideas above his station' as his mother had called them.

No matter how she'd begged him to stay, as she'd wrung her sacking apron between her gnarled, arthritic fingers and had wept when he had refused her, Jack had tried to explain that he'd rather die than go down that place. That he had a dream and was going off to the bright lights to make it come true. And that was that. She hadn't understood, but he'd still left her. Just as he'd left his father's grave, the girl he'd made promises to and the village, the only home he'd ever known, far behind him.

Uncomfortable with his memories, he shifted in his bed, as though he could move away from the pain of the image of seeing his mother for what she was: an old woman standing at the door of their mean little cottage, weeping for the son who was leaving her, to finish up who knew where, doing who knew what. Weeping for only the second time he could ever recall.

Compared with that pain, the one in his head now seemed of far less consequence. But there was still the aggravating feeling, that would not leave him, that he had done something – planned something? – last night.

What *was* it? It was definitely connected with this morning in some way or other. He was sure of that. But how? If only he could concentrate.

As he rolled himself cautiously on to his side, keeping his throbbing brain as still and undisturbed as possible, the sudden, head-rattling, teeth-jangling squeal of furniture being dragged heavily across wooden floor-boards came screeching at him from the auditorium next door.

Archie, clearing up from the night before.

Jack Fisher groaned in self-pity, closed his eyes tight and pulled the thin blanket up over his head. He'd worry about everything later. After he'd had a little sleep.

'See, I knew you'd eat something.' Tibs was triumphant as she wiped her greasy chops with the rough woollen sleeve of her jacket and reached across for another spoon of sugar for her big mug of tea. Why stint yourself when it was there for the taking on the counter? Even if the stall holder was giving you a slit-eyed stare, just daring you to pick up the spoon one more time.

'Hard to resist a bacon sandwich, eh, girl?'

Kitty nodded sheepishly. When Tibs had simply refused to let her say goodbye without at least having a cup of tea with her, Kitty had finally surrendered and had allowed herself to be dragged along to one of the dockside coffee stalls. The moment she'd caught the whiff of freshly baked bread and of salt bacon frying to a crisp in piping-hot fat, she'd been done for. But knowing that she was soon never going to be hungry again made Kitty feel so guilty about letting Tibs spend her money – and about taking advantage of her kindness – that she felt she had to explain herself.

'Hunger's a strange thing, Tibs,' she said in her soft country voice. 'Makes you do things. Even though you know you shouldn't. Makes you act in ways that are not quite nice. Not quite right. No matter that you know better, you still goes and does them.'

Tibs nearly choked on her tea. 'Blimey, you've turned into a proper little chatterbox, ain't you, girl? First I can hardly get a dicky-bird outta you, then you go carrying on like that.' She drained her cup and put it down on the counter. 'Here, you ain't caught the talking bug off of me, have you, Kit? That's all we need, two of us rabbiting away. We wouldn't be able to get a word in edgeways with one another, would we?' Seeing the flush of embarrassment creep up Kitty's throat and across her cheeks, Tibs shook her head and stuck her fists into her waist. 'Now don't go getting all sulky on me. I never meant nothing, did I? I was just surprised you had so much to say about . . . Well, whatever it was you was going on about.'

'I know I don't usually talk much,' Kitty said apologetically. 'But it's not that I don't have things I want to say, it's just that I've never had anyone to say them to before. Or I've been too tired. It can be a hard, lonely way of life in the countryside.'

Tibs sniffed loudly. 'It ain't much better in the East End, love. But you take things too serious, that's your trouble. Now finish your cuppa and we can be on our way.'

Kitty did finish her tea, but when Tibs tried to link her arm through hers to lead her away she stepped out of her reach and began stumbling backwards away from her. 'I've . . . I've got to go,' she stammered. With that, she ducked around the corner into Nightingale Lane, a narrow road that separated the St Katherine's and London Docks.

Tibs took no more than a split second to hurry after her. 'Oi! Kit!' she bellowed in her brash cockney growl. 'Wait for me.'

'I'm sorry, Tibs,' Kitty called over her shoulder, her lip trembling and her eyes brimming, 'I know I owe you a lot, and I let you spend all your money on my breakfast and everything, but I meant what I said about saying goodbye.'

'Course you don't.' Tibs tutted kindly and, still giving chase, held out her arm. 'Come on. Come with me, you big dope.'

'I do mean it.' Kitty began moving faster. 'I've got to be somewhere. Urgent like.'

Tibs wouldn't have it. She narrowed her eyes and lunged forward, determined to make a grab for her. 'Nobody who gets themselves in the state you was in last night has got anywhere *urgent* to go to.'

'I have.' Kitty turned round to face her. 'I have to . . .' Before she could finish, or Tibs could catch her, Kit was suddenly shoved to one side as though she were no more than a troublesome fly. She tumbled to the ground and, looking up to see what had hit her, she saw a swarthy, sallow-skinned man looming over her.

He was dressed in a dark, wide-brimmed hat, a long, black, narrow-waisted, old-fashioned sort of overcoat and had a jagged scar running all the way from his left eye right across his full mouth to his bottom lip, which lent a sinister edge to his otherwise almost handsome face. He was glowering at Tibs with so much hatred that Kitty could practically smell it.

'Albert,' Tibs gasped, pressing herself flat against the rough dock wall. 'What're you doing . . .'

'Shut your gob, you little trollop.' Albert raised his hand and she flinched like a beaten dog; all signs of the feisty little thing who wouldn't take no for an answer had disappeared like so much Thames ice melting in the first heat of spring. 'You know what I think about brides setting up and working for themselves.'

Tibs shook her head, willing herself not to tremble; she mustn't let him see she was scared. That would only make him worse. 'No, Albert, I swear . . .'

He grabbed her by the collar, twisting the cloth so tight to her throat that she could hardly breathe. 'Well, I hear different.'

Tibs tried to swallow, but couldn't. 'No, Albert,' she croaked. 'Whoever told you that, they was making it up.' She knew full well who'd been bad-mouthing her, the only tart who'd let down one of her own, and when Tibs got hold of Lily Perkins and her big, lying trap, she'd skin her fat, fleshy arse for her.

Albert pulled Tibs closer to him, hurting her, a helpless fish being slowly reeled in. There was no point in objecting. 'I'm telling you, Tibs, if I catch you I'll kill you with my bare hands. Do you understand me?'

'Please, Albert.' She was beginning to feel faint. Had to breathe.

'I said, *do you understand me*?'

She managed a nod.

Kitty, terrified, struggled to her feet. 'Leave her alone,' she pleaded. 'Can't you see she's going to pass out? Look at her. Just look at her.'

But he wouldn't. Instead, he turned to look at this person – this stupid, whining-voiced yokel – who dared to interfere with him. Him, Albert Symes!

His face crumpled with contempt at the sight of her. 'Fuck off,' he sneered in disgust, his fist drawn ready to punch her if she dared move a single step closer. 'I said, *fuck off.*'

Almost swooning with terror, Kitty hurried away.

Stopping at the bend in the lane, she hid herself in the long shadows of one of the high dock walls and watched, her eyes wide with fear and her heart racing.

She couldn't hear what the man was saying as he towered over Tibs's almost childishly tiny form, but she could see that he had at least let go of her throat.

She decided she should wait where she was until the man had gone, then go and see if Tibs was all right. And, if the worst came to the worst and he tried anything else, she'd . . .

What? What would she do? What *could* she do?

She thought frantically.

She would go and find a constable. That's what she'd do.

Albert shoved his face up close to Tibs's. 'Money,' he spat through gritted teeth. 'Hand it over.'

'I ain't got none, Albert. Honest, I . . .'

'Don't gimme that old flannel. I said, hand it over.'

She shook her head in denial. 'Albert, I swear . . .'

'What? On your nipper's life?'

Tibs shuddered. It was her worst nightmare that Albert might find out where Polly was staying. 'You know I don't see her no more,' she said, repeating her well-rehearsed story. 'You know they took her off me after I got nicked last time. You can ask any . . .'

'Poxy liar.'

'Albert, on my life . . .'

'Forget the kid, just give us the money.'

'Honest, you've gotta believe me, Albert, I ain't got a brass farthing to me name. I ain't got nothing.' She coughed dramatically, pressing her tiny hand to her chest. 'I've been too sick to work, see. It's all this fog, it must've got on me lungs. I ain't even been able to afford a drop o' jollop to . . .'

'I'll give you too sick.' As he spoke those words he jabbed her, hard, in the ribs with the knuckles of his tightly balled fist. Jabbed her again, and again.

Kitty's hand flew to her mouth and she gasped, wanting to stop him, but it was as though she'd been transfixed, a rabbit caught in the glare of the lamper's flame. She couldn't move, but she flinched as she saw the pain on her new friend's face. She watched and felt ashamed.

Then, as suddenly as he'd arrived, Albert turned on his heel and strode off towards the river, his wide-skirted coat flapping about his tightly trousered legs. He paused at the bend in Nightingale Lane, wheeled round and stabbed his finger violently at Tibs. 'Don't you try giving me no more of that shit, girl. D'you hear me? Not if you know what's good for you.'

Kitty ignored the gravel grinding into her knees as she worried and fussed around Tibs, who was sitting propped against the wall, hugging her sides and rocking back and forth, moaning softly to herself. 'I'm so sorry, Tibs,' she wailed. 'Why didn't I do something? Why didn't I help? A great big thing like me . . .'

'It don't matter,' Tibs said, wincing and gasping with every word. 'It's only me ribs and me stays have stopped him doing any real damage. I'm just bruised by the feel of it. Always makes sure he never hits me on the face, the bastard. Don't wanna spoil the goods, see.'

'He's done it before?'

Tibs nodded and even managed a thin, mournful smile. 'Aw yeah, he's done it before all right.' She screwed her eyes tight as a shaft of pain shot through her. 'Bugger!'

Kitty bit her lip. 'Tell me what I can do. Please.'

'There's nothing you can do, thanks, love, but I'll tell you what, there's something I can do. I can swear I ain't gonna work for that dirty whoreson ever again. I've had it with him. Had it. Giving him practically every penny I ever earn. Being scared he's gonna do me over just 'cos he feels like it. Using the few bob I keep for me grub to pay off the coppers again, to keep him out of the jug every other sodding week. Well, he can go in there and rot for all I care, 'cos I'm never gonna let him do that, or anything else, to me ever again.'

She shook her head as though trying to clear away some dreadful image that had found its way into her mind. 'D'you know something funny? I used to kid myself he loved me. Used to dream about how one day we'd settle down and get ourselves a proper little place to live in.' She spat fiercely. 'He'd treat a dog better than me.'

'Let me help you up off this cold stone.'

Tibs took her arm and tried to stand up, but her face creased into pleats of pain. 'Sorry, Kit, I'll have to lay down for a bit, I'm still winded and he's made me feel proper bilious, the rotten arsehole.'

Kitty pulled off her jacket and folded it gently under Tibs's head. 'You've been so kind to me, Tibs, and look how I've repaid you. If only there was something I could do.'

Tibs's expression changed, sort of sharpened. 'Come to think of it, there is,' she said slowly, levering herself up painfully on to her elbows. 'But I only want you to do it if you really mean it.'

'Whatever it is, just say. And I promise I won't let you down.'

'Good, 'cos whether you sing like a crow, you and me, my girl, are going on the boards as a double act.'

Kitty sprang away from her. 'No. I'm not singing.'

'Yes you are. You promised. And I don't reckon you're the sort what tells lies.' Tibs took a shallow, painful breath. 'But I'll tell you what, Kit, whatever else we sing it definitely ain't gonna be "Two Lovely Black Eyes".'

Kitty hung her head. 'I'm sorry,' she said, sniffing back her tears, 'but I can't. Not that.'

Tibs grabbed her arm. 'Look, Kit, this is the chance I've been waiting for. And chances like this don't very often come along for the likes of me. If there's anything I can do to get off the game and away from that cowson then I'm gonna do it.'

Kitty turned her head. 'Please, Tibs, don't ask me to do this. Anything else. Just tell me.'

'There isn't anything else. This is it. And if it means that I'm gonna have to make you feel guilty and grateful then I'm sorry, Kit, but that's exactly what I'm gonna do.'

With that, Tibs closed her eyes and moaned softly.

Kitty leaned against the wall and slid down until she was sitting on the ground next to Tibs. 'I can't.'

Tibs opened her eyes slowly and sighed resignedly. 'Stop your snivelling, Kit, there ain't no point getting yourself all worked up.' She hesitated, then said, 'Tell you what, there is something else you can do for me.'

'What? Anything.'

Tibs leaned heavily on Kitty's arm and, with a great effort, struggled to her feet. 'Just get me down Rosemary Lane and safely back to the Dog.' She clutched her sides and looked into Kitty's eyes. 'That's not too much to ask of a friend, is it, girl?'

Chapter 6

Tibs made sure that this time she had her arm firmly linked through Kitty's. There was no chance she'd let her try to get away again. The bloke at the Dog had been very clear about what he'd wanted – and what he'd be prepared to pay good money for – a double act, and if that's what he wanted, that's what he'd get, even if she had to lie to Kitty to get her there.

Big as she was, she'd be no match for Tibs, now she'd set her mind to it.

Tibs winced with pain as she hobbled along, making sure Kitty saw her, and added a pitiful little moan just for good measure. 'How do I look?' she asked pathetically, her voice coming in breathy, sad little rasps, her carefully hooded eyes a picture of pained innocence. 'All right, am I? Will I do, d'you think?'

'You look lovely.'

Tibs sighed dramatically. 'Really I'd like to have done more than just have a wash. To give a good impression, like. But I suppose I should just be grateful that Albert never hit me in the moosh.' She flashed a surreptitious glance at Kit, to see if she was laying it on a bit too thick, and figured she could go a bit further. 'I'd be in trouble then all right. I mean, who'd wanna see me with a busted lip?' She gave a shuddering little whimper and said, 'You look lovely and all by the way, Kit. Just the job.'

Just the job? Kitty looked at her suspiciously. 'What does it matter how I look?'

'It never hurts to look pretty.' Tibs's voice became brisker, more business-like, and her pace quickened so that Kitty had almost to break into a trot to keep up with her as she tugged her along the grease-slicked cobbles.

'And like I said, you could be really smashing if you fixed up your hair a bit. If you made yourself look more, you know, townified, like. It wouldn't take much.' She chanced another snatched, sidelong glance. 'I reckon I could really make something of you, you know. All it takes is a bit of powder and paint. Tell you what, let me loose on you for five minutes and you wouldn't know yourself.'

Appealing as the idea of not knowing herself might have been to Kitty, in her present circumstances she wasn't in the least interested in any sort of magical transformations. Well, not if they were merely physical. What would be the point of that? What she needed was a transformation of a far more miraculous kind. The kind that just didn't happen. She needed a change of luck.

'So, what d'you think?' asked Tibs. 'Can I see what I can do with you?'

'I haven't much interest in that sort of thing,' Kitty replied flatly.

A little thing like someone's lack of interest couldn't deter Tibs. Her agony temporarily forgotten, she pulled Kitty to an abrupt halt and spun her round to face her. 'Here,' she said, reaching up and pinching Kitty's cheeks with hard little nips. 'Let's see what we can do for now.' She stood back, with her head cocked on one side, and studied Kitty through narrowed eyes, assessing her efforts. 'Look at you! You're a proper picture.'

She shoved Kitty towards the high brick wall, where a glass-panelled door was set, engraved with the legend: Pilkington's Spice Warehouse, Manager's Office. Then she brushed Kit's thick dark hair off her face, fluffing and patting at it as though she was sorting out a feather bolster flattened by a restless sleeper.

'Go on, have a look at yourself, Kit. With a little know-how I've got them cheeks of your'n glowing as pink as a new baby's bum. Just imagine what I'd be able to do with a bit of slap.' She smiled triumphantly, her hands almost circling her tiny, corseted waist. 'Who'd be able to guess you was a turnip bonce now, eh, girl? You'll be able to pass for a real . . .'

For a brief moment Kitty had actually been carried along by her new-found friend's enthusiasm and had peered into the deeply etched glass, trying to get a glimpse of the supposed transformation. But she was immediately alerted by Tibs's ominous words. She turned slowly and looked at Tibs. 'Why should I want to pass for anything other than what I am, a simple country girl?'

Tibs held up her hands in apologetic surrender. 'Sorry, love, take no notice of me. That's me all over, ain't it? Rabbiting on and on. Never know when to hold me trap, that's my trouble. I talk so much old rubbish at times I don't make a bit of sense. Now, I promise I'll keep me gob shut all the rest of the way. How about that?'

Kitty stared hard at Tibs, trying to understand. There was something going on and she wasn't sure that if she found out what it was she'd like it very much. 'I don't know that I should go any further. I told you. I have to be somewhere.'

'It ain't far and I do need your help, Kit. I was hurt, remember?' With that, Tibs put on a brave little smile, shrugged casually as though she could dismiss any other concerns with a simple lift of her shoulders, linked her arm back through Kitty's and led her along, inwardly reprimanding herself for nearly having blown the gaff. She really would keep her mouth shut for a bit, just turn and smile every few yards, to reassure Kitty that everything was just fine, and then . . . Well, Tibs was sure she knew what would happen then, but didn't want to risk even thinking about it.

Jack Fisher whined wretchedly as Archie did his best to rouse him.

'I'm sorry, boss, I've left you as long as I could, but the drayman's downstairs. He won't deal with me. Says there's money owing.'

Under his maimed arm Archie had wedged a wet towel, which he now held out to Fisher. 'Try wiping this over your face. You see, everything'll look a sight better once you've freshened up a bit.'

Jack swung his legs out from under his rumpled blankets and sat on the edge of the bed. He took the towel and rubbed it round his neck. He said nothing, but knew in his heart that he needed a sight more than being freshened up a bit to make things look better.

What Jack Fisher needed was a bloody miracle.

Tibs had done her best to keep quiet, but she had no choice about breaking her silence when, without warning, she yanked Kitty across the street and somehow managed to walk – smack! – right into a man who was passing by in the other direction. 'I'm so sorry, sir,' she breathed, fluttering about him as though she had caused him great damage – although, from the expression on the man's face, it seemed perfectly clear that he really didn't mind a pretty girl like Tibs bumping into him any time she felt like it. 'That was so clumsy of me . . . ' Her words trailed off and she held her side, closing her eyes tight and leaning heavily against the wall.

'Not at all, my dear,' he replied with a lift of his top hat. 'Not at all. But are you in some sort of pain? Have I caused you an injury?'

Tibs smiled bravely. 'Nothing to worry yourself about, sir.'

He frowned with concern. 'Maybe you should seek medical attention?'

'That costs, sir,' she whispered, dipping her chin as though ashamed that such words had even passed her rosebud lips.

The man harrumphed and looked embarrassed. 'Of course, of course.' He reached into his trouser pocket and produced a handful of silver. Picking out two half crowns, he held them out to her.

'What must you think of me?' asked Tibs, an appalled look clouding her little heart-shaped face. 'I can't take money from you, sir!'

'Of course you can.'

She lowered her chin further still and put out her hand. 'Well, thank you kindly, sir. That's a very generous gesture, if I might say so.'

'Not at all,' he said again and began to go on his way, his eyes still fixed on her.

He should have looked where he was going.

'Ow!' This time his collision was far more unpleasant. Instead of hitting soft, feminine flesh, he had bashed into a wrought-iron lamp-post.

'Aw, careful, sir, you'll do yourself a damage!' Tibs gasped in a tiny girly voice, as she ran up to him and brushed at his elegant black topcoat, straightening him up and adding considerably to his confusion. 'Are you all right, do you think?'

'Never better,' spluttered the man through gritted teeth, not wanting to show his pain to this gorgeous little creature who was staring up at him, her face a picture of deep compassion that made her more desirable than ever. He wasn't used to such concern, not from his wife, anyway. 'Never better.'

'That's a relief, I'm sure,' she said, then inclined her head, dropped a neat bob of a curtsey and smiled coyly up through her lashes.

As the man walked off – more carefully this time, but with an infinitely redder face – Tibs held out her hand to Kitty. On her palm lay the two coins and a silver pocket watch.

'Will you just look at that!' she spat, dangling the timepiece by its chain. 'There's him, all done up like a sodding dog's dinner and it's not even bloody gold.'

'Tibs!'

'What?'

'Did you steal that gentleman's watch?'

'Yeah.'

'How could you?'

'Easy. And he can afford it.'

'But why?'

'Don't go feeling sorry for the likes of him, Kit. If he was such an innocent he wouldn't be around these parts. This ain't no time or place for proper gentlemen.'

'He might have business . . .'

'You're right there and I know exactly what sort. He's been up to no good last night, you mark my words.' She flicked the two half-crown coins high above her head, watching them as they turned over in the morning sunshine. Snatching them from the air, she hid them away in her pocket. 'Tell you what,' she went on, holding the watch to her ear, 'I'd wager that whole dollar what he just give me that he's been out gambling, whoring, smoking that stuff down the opium dens all night, and now he's gonna waltz out of here in a cab and bugger off back where he come from to his nice polite wife as though butter wouldn't melt. With a story as long as your arm about what he's been up to and who he's been chatting with down *at his gentlemen's club.*'

'It's still not right. And say someone catches you? How can you risk it? How can you be so brazen?'

'Brazen?' Tibs shrugged dismissively, weighing the watch in her hand. If she was lucky, which she certainly didn't feel, what with her ribs and now this piece of junk, Uncle might be persuaded to part with a few shillings. But certainly no more. Bugger him. 'Is that what I am?'

Kitty considered. 'More brave I suppose. I don't know how you could do it.'

'That was nothing to write home about,' she said, slipping the watch somewhere deep into her layers of clothing with the money. 'If that's what you call brave then you ain't seen very much, girl.' She steered Kitty forward and winked saucily. 'Even a scaredy cat like you could've pulled that stroke. With the right training, of course.'

'No. Not me.'

'Yes, you. I'll have you being brave as a lion in no time.'

They walked along for a bit before Kitty finally said, 'Would you mind if I asked you something?'

'Be my guest.' Tibs smiled happily, this was going well, she hadn't mentioned going off on her own for a good ten minutes.

'After he gave you the money, why did you take his watch?'

'Because I don't like being treated bad, that's why.'

'But he didn't do anything.' Kitty shook her head, not understanding. 'He knocked into you, that's all. It was a mistake. And it's not his fault your ribs hurt.'

Tibs rolled her eyes. This one was as green as a cabbage. 'It's nothing to do with me ribs,' she said, shepherding Kit round a pile of bulging hessian sacks.

'No?'

'No. I met him last night, a bit before I met up with you. Off Rosemary Lane. Did a bit o' business with him.' She paused, waiting to see if she needed to spell it out any clearer. Surprisingly, she didn't. 'Well, he never paid me, did he? The bastard. Bugger all, that's what I got off him for me trouble. And if my luck keeps going the way it seems to be he probably threw me in a dose of the other and all.'

She took out her snuff, prepared a good pinch and sneezed violently. Grasping her ribs – the snuff was a stupid mistake – she spat angrily on the ground. 'Maybe that'll teach him not to mess with the brides from the East End. Let him go with the whores from Hyde Park, or them down the Haymarket, if he wants to do business with idiots.'

'But what if he recognised you and reports you to a policeman? You could get arrested.'

'Look, last night he was roaring drunk, it was dark and, let's be honest, Kit, tarts' *faces* ain't really what they're interested in, are they. A bride is just a body to them. We ain't people or they couldn't do what they do to us. And this morning he was walking in a street where he had no right to be, with a head on him that must feel like a steam engine and he probably won't even know he's lost anything for a couple of hours till he starts sobering up. Then, what's he gonna tell anyone? I was out whoring and I got meself robbed? I don't think so, girl.'

'Are you scared of anyone?'

'Course not,' Tibs lied, as visions of what Albert was capable of doing to her when he was in a really bad temper made her flinch as though he were actually standing right there in front of her, blocking her way. with a knife in one hand and a cosh in the other. 'Fuck the lot of 'em,' she shouted, ignoring the look of surprise on a passing wagoner's weather-beaten face.

Kitty flushed scarlet. 'And you're not worried what people think, either?'

'Look, Kit, there's this moment, see, when you realise that although people might *think* they're better than you, they might even seem cleverer, know more stuff than you, but they don't. It's only that they've been to school and have been told more. We're every bit as good as they are. No, better.' She waved her free arm furiously about her. 'Let *them* try and get by under the arches. Let *them* live with no money.'

'But . . .'

'No buts. We feel just like they do. No, more than they do, 'cos we don't hide behind book learning. We are what we are. Doing what we can. The best we can. Doing what we know and getting by. Making sure . . .' She stopped speaking and pointed excitedly across the street, her face glowing with as much enthusiasm as an explorer who'd just found the source of a great river. 'Here, look, with all that chatting, see where we've ended up already!'

She hauled Kitty across the street, dodging in and out of the wagons and carts, and skipping round the piles of steaming dung and the other less easily identifiable piles of mess and rubbish that littered the cobbled roadway. 'Come on, Kit. We've made it. You said you'd see me here safely and you have.'

'I'll just see you inside, Tibs, then I'm going.'

'Yeah, course.' Tibs pushed open the pub door and shoved Kitty into the main bar of the Old Black Dog.

It was strange, but as she stepped inside, Kitty had a

105

real feeling of regret. Of loss. Soon she would be leaving this new friend of hers, this fierce little thing with the face of an earth-bound cherub and the courage of a lion. Maybe if they had met before, things might not have worked out so badly.

But what was the point of thinking like that?

'The most shocking thing is . . .' Tibs puffed, as she stood on the brass foot rail and leaned across the counter, peering over it as though the landlord would, for some inexplicable reason, be hiding down there. She looked over her shoulder. 'Are you listening to me, Kit?'

'Yes. Yes, of course.'

'The most shocking thing you'll come to realise, Kit – the *revelation* as the preacher down the mission would say – is that bad people, evil people, are so ordinary.' Tibs clambered down and wiped her hands on her skirts. 'They ain't like monsters or nothing. Not like the preachers'd have you believe. 'Cos the devil don't have horns. Oh no. When you see him he'll be wearing a posh, shiny silk topper, you mark my words.'

'Not a battered old felt hat like his?' Kitty asked, pointing hesitantly.

Tibs looked across the bar to where Jack Fisher was sitting with his head in his hands, while Archie was trying to persuade him to drink from a thick china tea cup. 'No, that ain't Old Nick's style,' she pronounced confidently. 'Definitely a topper. Now, lift your chin, look everyone in the eye and just remember, Kitty girl, you're as good as the lot of them put together. That's your first lesson.'

'But, Tibs . . .'

'Five more minutes, girl, that's all I'm asking.'

'Sod me, what's going on?'

Teezer had snored so loudly he'd woken himself up.

Sitting up suddenly, he set the skiff bobbing violently against the incoming tide.

'Buggy! Oi, Bug. Wake up and get this fire going.'

'Leave off, Teeze,' Buggy whined, rubbing his eyes with the backs of his hands. He looked and sounded like a reluctant child being dragged from his cot. 'I'm tired.'

'Leave off, you say? You're tired? I'll give you leave off. Look at that church tower.' He jabbed his thumb over his shoulder in the direction of St Anne's. 'Nearly nine o'clock. Another day's started on the river and you're still akip. If we wanna earn enough to feed our bellies and have a few bevvies in the Dog tonight you'd better get working. Now row me over to the bank. I'm going looking for that tart we dragged outta the drink last night. With them long legs on her she won't have gone unnoticed.'

Buggy groaned. Not only working, but all by himself. 'Why, Teeze? Why would you wanna do that? Why?'

'Because I, Buggy my son, am going to forget her ingratitude – water under the bridge, if I might make a pun – and with the powers of my sweet-talking tongue I shall persuade her that I might – just might, mind – have a job for her. She'll be putty in my hands.'

'We're on time,' Tibs said brightly, smiling confidently at Archie and doing her best to ignore the pain in her side.

Archie returned her smile and, tucking his broom under his bad arm, he touched his governor gently on the shoulder. 'Visitors, boss.'

'Eh?'

'Try and open your eyes. There's someone here to see you.'

Jack drank deeply from the now cold cup of tea. 'You sort them out for me, Archie, there's a pal. I just need to shut my eyes for another five minutes.'

Archie leaned closer, flinching slightly at the stench of stale beer and rum exuding from Jack Fisher's every pore. 'I reckon you'll wanna see these two yourself, boss. Two young ladies. Pretty they are and all. There's this little one . . .' he began admiringly.

'There's this little one,' Tibs cut in, tapping Archie smartly on the shoulder and stepping in front of him so that she could let Fisher have a good look at her, 'who's turned up right on time. Just like you asked her to.'

Archie grinned foolishly at her. She really was a lovely-looking girl – all dimples and bouncy blonde curls, and not afraid to put herself forward. Just the way Archie liked them.

In his dreams.

He moved politely out of her way. Since his accident he'd learned to know his place where young women were concerned. Especially young women as pretty as this one.

'Good,' said Jack flatly, dragging his gaze away from the table top.

As soon as she saw his blank expression it was patently clear to Tibs that this man didn't have a clue what she was talking about. She had to think quickly or this chance would slip from her grasp and she wasn't prepared to let that happen. Not at any price.

'Good,' she repeated. 'That's right. It is good. Good.' She was beginning to feel like a sailor's ill-trained parakeet. 'People should be on time.' She smiled brightly, turned and flashed her eyebrows at Kitty, willing her to say something sparky. To say anything. 'That's what I said, didn't I, Kit?'

Kitty remained as silent as Jack Fisher.

'Wouldn't do to be late on the first day, now would it? That's what I said, didn't I?' Tibs rambled on, trying to get the conversation going. What was wrong with this bloke? He wasn't even trying to look down her front, even though she was bending over the table so hard she was nearly folded double.

'Can I fetch you anything, boss?' asked Archie.

Tibs could have kissed him.

'More tea or something? And how about something for the young ladies?'

Jack nodded, then wished he hadn't. His head was hammering. 'Tea would be a good idea.'

'Ladies?' Archie enquired.

'Lovely,' Tibs replied, before Kitty had the chance to open her mouth. 'We're both gasping, ain't we, girl?'

'So I'll leave you to entertain your guests then, shall I, boss?' Archie hissed into his governor's ear.

'What?' Jack, bleary-eyed, unshaven and hung-over, peered up at Tibs and Kitty. What the hell was going on?

'While I make the tea . . . '

'Right.' Jack ran the back of his hand across his forehead and rose unsteadily to his feet. Supporting himself by grasping the table top, he licked his sandpaper lips and said, 'So what are your names then?'

He'd spoken so quickly, as if afraid that he wouldn't be able to finish the sentence, that the words all ran into one, but Tibs was used to drunks.

She smiled winningly. 'Tibs. Tibs Tyler. Eighteen years old and pretty as a picture. And this is Kitty . . . ' She turned and widened her eyes at Kit. 'Kitty . . . '

'Wallis,' said Kitty nervously, standing up as straight as a young recruit – just the way the hateful old housekeeper had taught her in the big house. 'Aged nineteen, sir,' she added snappily.

Jack stared suspiciously, trying to remember. 'I'm not offering you a job in the army, lass.'

Kitty blushed and Fisher looked at her more closely.

Tall and skinny, and as scruffy as a scarecrow she might be, but there was something about this girl. She was sort of attractive and sort of . . . well, familiar.

'What *exactly* are you offering again?' Tibs asked, interrupting his drink-befuddled thoughts. 'I'd like you to spell it out nice and clear for us, if you don't mind, like. I'm the one who does the business arrangements see,' she added grandly.

Kitty snapped her head round and stared at her. *Business arrangements*? This didn't sound right.

But before she could say anything, Jack was speaking again, or rather he was trying to. 'So, er, let me get this straight . . . You, er . . . '

'I know how much acts like our'n earn,' Tibs butted in with a snooty lift of her chin. 'We've got plenty of friends who work the halls, ain't we, Kit?'

Jack, for whom the penny had finally dropped, looked exactly as though someone had just lit his gas mantle. The relief of at last remembering! That was it! These lasses did a turn. Some sort of double act. And they'd been doing it – whatever it was – down in the bar. And the customers had loved it; they'd laughed and thrown pennies, and had a fine old time. He'd come down from upstairs for some reason and had spoken to one of them. The little one, if he remembered rightly, and had asked them to come in and see him in the morning. And they had.

He was far too pleased with himself to notice that Kitty's mouth had dropped open and that she was now staring at her friend in total disbelief. All he could hope was that he hadn't said anything awkward, or vulgar. He knew he wasn't used to the drink and could have said just about anything. He also hoped he hadn't promised them too much. Because the truth was, he didn't have much to give them. That bloody drayman had just about finished him off as far as cash was concerned.

He stared down at his boots. Begin at the beginning, Jack, he told himself. 'I hope that when I spoke to you last night, I didn't say anything that might have . . . well, caused embarrassment to you lasses. Or that might have given you the wrong impression.'

Tibs just about stopped herself from laughing out loud. He must have been more pissed than she realised. He couldn't remember what he'd said! Not a sodding thing. This was going to be easier than she thought. 'You was a bit tired, sir. I said to Kit here – didn't I, Kit? – that man must work so hard running this place, he looks proper worn out.'

'Tibs.' Kitty shot her a questioning look. 'I don't think . . .'

'Would you excuse us a moment, sir?' Tibs asked daintily. 'We need to discuss something. Private, like.'

He nodded, not caring this time that his blood was pumping through his poor suffering skull like a piston; he was too excited. This odd-looking pair could be the beginning of him solving all his problems. Better acts, that's what he needed, and the punters had loved these two.

Tibs pulled Kit to one side. 'Look, I know what I said about you just walking me over here, 'cos of me injuries, like' – she clutched her side without much conviction, but thought it still worth a go – 'but you've gotta help me. Singers are ten a penny. Even good singers. And as for screechers like me . . .'

'No, Tibs. I told you. I'm not going on the stage.'

'Just listen. For one minute. Please. See, Kit, when I talked to him last night he was going on about booking us as a double act. A *double* act. Not me, but *us*. The pair of us.'

111

'I told you . . .'

'Aw Kit, come on. Don't let me down.'

'I can't. I explained. I'd keep you company because I owed you a favour. But nothing else. If I'd known you were going to try and trick me . . .'

Tibs looked mortified. 'Me, trick you? Course I wasn't trying to do that. I just didn't tell you the whole truth, 'cos I didn't want to spoil things. I knew what a lovely surprise it would be, once you got over the shock, like.'

Kitty opened her mouth to question such blatant rubbish, but Tibs was already rattling on again. 'And anyway, you'll be really good. Anyone can do it. Look at me, I couldn't carry a tune in a bucket, I really couldn't, but I can still give a song. It's all about putting it over right. Like telling a story.' She gestured extravagantly with her child-like hands as she put on different expressions. 'A cheeky story. A sad story. Even a saucy story. Whatever you fancy. And if I can do it, anyone can. And that feller over there,' she jerked her thumb over her shoulder at Jack, 'reckons he can put us on the boards and make us stars.'

Kitty shook her head in wonder. 'I must be losing my senses.'

'No you ain't,' Tibs wheedled, 'you're just getting a job, that's all. A bloody good job.' And, she added to herself, one where I don't have to bend over and lift me skirts up over me head half a dozen times a night.

Jack came over to join them. 'Everything all right?' His voice was still thick from the night before, but he now sounded definitely more alert.

'Smashing, thanks, mister. And I just wanna say how grateful we are and all. Don't we, Kit? By the way,' she went on, before Kitty opened her trap and put her foot in it, 'what should we call you?'

'The name's Fisher. Jack Fisher.' He spoke to Tibs but

was staring at Kit. She turned her head away.

Jack couldn't believe it. She was shy! A tall, fine girl like her and she'd blushed as red as a robin's breast. He couldn't remember feeling so stirred since Tess had first let him kiss her.

'*Jack*. That's me favourite name.' Tibs was breathing huskily. 'But there is one little problem.

'What's that then, lass?' he asked, tearing his gaze away from Kit.

'There's this man what's been bothering me. He's got a bit, you know, keen on me and, how can I say it, his attentions are not welcome.'

'You won't have to worry about him.' Jack reached down and ruffled the ears of the scraggy-looking mongrel who seemed attached to him by an invisible string. 'Not with my Rex around.'

'Is that right?' Tibs asked, ignoring the fact that the dog looked as though it needed a bathchair. She smiled girlishly, all the while staring into his eyes with an unflinching self-possession that Kitty could hardly stand to watch, let alone imitate. It was just the way she'd been with the man whose watch she had taken. She could turn it on and off like a tap.

Jack was less analytical about Tibs's motives and happily returned her smile – she really was a pretty little thing, although his taste had always leaned towards darker girls, like this tall one . . . 'I'll make sure you're both safe and sound.' He leaned forward and said softly, 'And I've got another little pal to help me.'

Tibs flashed her eyebrows and grinned saucily. 'Who's that, then?'

He opened his jacket and pulled out a leather-covered cosh. 'No one'll bother you when you're working for me.'

'That's all right then,' breathed Tibs.

'Glad to hear it. Now, let's go upstairs to the hall and hear you sing. See what you look like up on the stage. Not too loud mind, lass, I'm feeling a bit under the weather this morning.'

'You go up first,' Tibs said with a cheerful little wave of her hand. 'Me and Kit need to discuss what tune we're gonna give you. Don't we, Kit?'

The moment Jack, accompanied by Archie and followed by Rex, had disappeared up the big staircase, Kitty turned on her heel and started towards the door. But Tibs was too quick for her. She had covered less than a few yards when Tibs threw herself across the door, barring her way.

'Please, Kit, don't do this to me. I need this chance to have a decent life. If I don't then I'll have to go back on the streets. You wouldn't want that, would you?'

'There are other jobs.'

Tibs gasped in wonder. 'What other jobs? Fur pulling? Sack sewing? The match factory? They're all lovely jobs, they are. Mind, I won't die of a dose in there, now will I?'

'That's right,' Kitty said, suddenly hopeful. 'You won't.'

'So tell me, Kit, what d'you want me to die of? 'Cos you know what you get doing them other jobs, don't you?'

Kitty shook her head miserably.

'Bad lungs. Wasting disease. Phossy jaw.' Tibs was angry, her voice cold and hard. 'You decide which is the best, Kit, 'cos me, I'm spoilt for choice.'

Kitty stared down at her boots, as tears began to trickle down her cheeks. 'Don't do this to me, Tibs. Please.'

Tibs could sense her weakening. She smiled. 'Here, did you see the way that bloke Fisher looked at you?

I reckon you could set your cap at him if you wanted.'

'I can't do it, Tibs.'

'Just come up there with me. I'll die of fright if I have to go up alone.'

'No.'

'Please?' Now Tibs's eyes were also brimming with fat salt tears. 'If I can just get the courage to sing a few lines he'll be bound to want me to do a show on me own. But I need you to be there with me.'

'I thought you were the brave one.'

Tibs dropped her chin to her chest and began snuffling miserably. 'That was all an act. I tried to be brave, but really I'm just a poor little thing and I'm that scared of Albert . . . '

Kitty sighed resignedly and Tibs realised that she might have had an easier time if she'd just told Kitty the truth in the first place. That she wanted a job, any job, where she could earn the money she so desperately needed for Polly and where she would be well out of Albert's reach. And this job might just provide both those things. 'I can't stand the thought of running into him in the street, Kit . . . '

'I'll go up there with you. But I'm not singing.'

Tibs led Kitty, trembling and sniffling, up the gaudily painted curved stairway and into the theatre. 'You sit there,' she said, shoving Kitty backwards on to the Chairman's table, 'I've just got to have a word.'

'He all the band you've got?' she asked Jack in a disappointed voice, staring down her nose at the skinny bearded man sitting at the upright piano. 'We'd be just as well with that old boy who played for us in the bar last night.'

The piano player looked offended. 'Do you think so, madam?' he asked in a haughty Russian accent. 'Well, this is not *all the band he's got*. Usually we are four.'

'That's right,' agreed Jack, mentally going through his wages bill – he'd soon have more performers than customers if he wasn't careful. 'There's four of them all right.'

'Mr Fisher asked me last night to come along this morning,' the musician continued, 'as a favour. So that you could have some accompaniment.'

This was news to Jack but he never said so.

'That's all right then,' said Tibs primly. She bent forward and said something to the man who, in contrast to his earlier sourness, had trouble suppressing a raucous burst of laughter. Next she straightened up and with a broad smile launched into a rendition of 'Ta-Ra-Ra-Boom-De-Ay!' that had the bottles shaking behind the bar and Fisher's brain rattling around his head like a pea in a colander.

Between verses, she polkaed over to Kitty and hissed at her through the corner of her mouth, 'Now don't you let me down, Kit.' Then, with a few surreptitious pinches and wide-eyed glares, followed by another dramatic threat of tears, Kitty finally joined in. She might have been miming badly, and prancing about the place like a startled pony, but she was joining in none the less. Just as bossy little Tibs Tyler had known she would all along.

Chapter 7

It was wintry for late April, exceptionally so; and, with the evening growing dark and the mist rolling in off the Thames and swirling about him in great dripping folds, Albert Symes felt damp, cold and miserable. He also felt angry. He should have been inside in the warm, getting a hot, thick stew down his neck, and looking forward to a bed with clean, bug-free sheets and the company of a willing woman. But here he was, scouring the streets and alleyways around the Ratcliffe Highway, looking for someone. And he wasn't going to give up until he found her.

One night, maybe, when he'd made his fortune he would be able to relax a bit, care more for his creature comforts, but until then he had to earn his living and that was why he was out searching the streets for that ungrateful little cow, Tibs Tyler.

When he found her he'd make sure she paid, and not only the money she owed him. She'd pay up in all sorts of ways. He'd see to that. No one made a fool of Albert Symes. Letting people think you were weak was a mistake a pimp couldn't afford to make. The girls were lazy liberty takers at the best of times, but if they caught wind of any sign of softness on his part they'd become uncontrollable and the floodgates would open for any Tom, Dick or Harry to challenge him for his lucrative territory down by the docks. Albert had to keep order, be strong, and be seen to be strong.

He pulled his worn, white silk muffler – the ever

present stolen reminder to himself that he too would one day dress in the style he deserved – tight about his throat, buttoned his old-fashioned, flared, tight-waisted coat to his neck and pushed down his dull black hat hard on his head.

Some day he would have himself a tall, shiny topper, like his so-called betters. Then he'd show them. He'd show them all. But till then he'd just have to do his best to look like a toff, even if it was a toff of twenty-odd years ago. If he'd learned little else from his wicked brute of a mother, the importance of keeping up appearances was something he'd drunk in with her milk.

He'd watched, night after night, with a mixture of relief and fear as she prepared herself to go out, donning all her tatty finery that, in the shadows of the streets around Piccadilly and the Haymarket, allowed her to pass as an upper-class whore of at least five years younger.

The fear he had felt as a small boy was knowing that he was about to be left alone yet again in that dark, dank room, with no light and paper-thin walls that did nothing to mask the terrifying screams and yells all about him – the ever present backdrop to daily life in the rookery that was his home. But he had also felt relief, knowing that for a few hours at least he was not going to be treated as a human punch bag.

But then things had changed for young Albert.

None of the neighbours – the assorted whores, pimps and drifters who peopled those slums – had been surprised when he had run into the street screaming that he had returned from an errand to find his mother burned to death. They had all agreed that the old witch must have passed out and then passed away, completely unaware that her crude bed of rags and matting was blazing around her. Even among her notoriously hard-drinking profession she was known for the amount of gin she regularly put away.

They had sympathised with little Albert, shaking their heads and tutting, even ruffling his filthy black hair, but had hurriedly disappeared back into their bug-infested rooms when it became clear that the boy had no one to care for him. No one in the rookery either wanted, or could afford, another mouth to feed.

And so it was that Albert was left to his own devices, no longer an abused and neglected child of a prostitute, but with no money for food or rent, a hungry, homeless orphan. In spite of the harshness of his previous young life, Albert was still frightened to find just how alone he was, but it didn't take him long to discover the many other street urchins and ragamuffins in his position who, despite not being half as bright as he was, still seemed to get by. Some of the cleverer ones, the ones who used their cunning, even appeared to be doing quite well for themselves. And Albert began to see all sorts of possibilities.

He watched and noted how the successful ones always put their own interests above that of others, doing whatever was necessary to succeed, with no thought of what it might do to those less brave or able. And that's what Albert did too, and it was exactly what he was doing now. Looking out for number one.

Narrowing his eyes, he chewed thoughtfully on his lip and stuck his hands deep into his pockets. They were more holes than cloth, but he had nothing else to keep out the chill, no fine, rabbit-lined gloves. Not yet. But one day he would. And he would leave this place for ever, laughing at those who did nothing to escape their stinking riverside existence, those fools with no ideas, no imagination and no determination. Not like him.

He had determination, plenty of it, and it had stood him in good stead. It had meant he always had a slice of bread and scrape for breakfast, when other kids were starving. And, as now, it had given him the strength to drive himself on, despite the bitterly cold night, to find Tibs Tyler.

He did have one trait that some, although not Albert himself, would describe as a weakness, one he could do nothing about: Albert had a temper. A temper that had so blinded him as a nine-year-old boy that he could strike a match and throw it on the bed of a drunken woman who had beaten him once too often.

Tonight the fuse of Albert's temper was growing shorter and shorter with every blank response he got from the girls. *His* girls. If they didn't start giving him the answers he wanted soon he would have to make an example of one of them.

But why bother to wait when there in front of him, on the corner of the street waiting for business, stood another one of the unappreciative mares?

He shot out a hand and grabbed Marie by the arm, twisting it so hard that she threw back her head and screamed in pain. Albert pulled her round to face him and slapped her hard across the cheek; something he didn't usually do. They earned less when they had black eyes, but he couldn't stomach her wailing.

'Sorry, Albert,' she stuttered, 'I didn't realise it was you.'

'Obviously. Now, where's Tibs?'

Marie shook her head. 'I don't know, Albert, I . . .'

'Don't waste your breath on that old toffee.' He gripped the top of her arm, his fingers digging deep into her flesh despite the thickness of her jacket, and marched her into one of the dismal, urine-reeking alleyways that ran between the high walls of the warehouses and surrounding tenement blocks.

He slammed her against the wall. 'I'm getting bored with this,' he snarled.

His face, only inches from hers, was illuminated by the sulphurous yellow of the single gas lamp at the alley's entrance; the pale light reflecting off his scarred, sculpted cheeks.

Marie felt sick.

'Now, let's start again.' He leaned even closer. 'Where is she?'

She gnawed nervously at the inside of her cheek. Her bowels felt as though they were turning to water. But she was Tibs's friend, had become so soon after she'd first met Albert. When he had vowed his undying love for her, just as he had to all the other girls he'd suckered into working for him, Marie had refused to acknowledge that she was anything like them. Her relationship with Albert was different, anyone could see that, she insisted. But it wasn't long before she was forced to admit what a fool she had been, that what she really meant to Albert was just another means of bringing in the cash.

She had thought her heart would break.

Instead of sneering at Marie, as the others had done – to cover their shame at their own past naivety – Tibs had soothed and supported her.

Such kindness had meant a lot to Marie, but she had had no way of repaying her. But she had now. Tibs was in some kind of trouble. That much was obvious, and Marie wouldn't let her down, not even if it meant taking a good hiding for her trouble. 'Who did you say you was looking for?' she asked, keeping her voice as calm as she could manage, when her arm was being wrenched out of its socket.

Albert squeezed her chin between his fingers,

pressing hard on her jawbone, forcing her head back against the wall. 'Don't fuck about with me,' he hissed, his breath coming in thick, vaporous clouds.

'Honest, I didn't get what you said.' She tried a smile. 'I must be going mutton, eh, Albert? She braced herself, ready for the blow that would probably be her reward for such impudence.

Albert looked into Marie's crudely painted and powdered face and saw his mother. His heart raced and his mind filled with loathing. 'Where's Tibs, you stupid whore?'

'I can tell you, Albert,' came a rough, wheedling parody of a girlishly feminine voice from behind him.

Still keeping a tight grip on Marie's aching face, Albert turned his head and looked over his shoulder at the dumpy figure standing under the light at the far end of the alley. He smirked nastily. 'Lily Perkins, I might have known.'

Albert let go of Marie, hooked his thumbs under his armpits, spread his long fingers across his wide, muscular chest and swaggered towards the woman who would have sold her own child for the price of a few glasses of rough-house gin – had her taste for the stuff not prevented her from ever carrying a baby to full term.

'So,' he growled, looming over her. His head was tipped to one side so that he was staring down at her from under the brim of his hat. 'You reckon you know where Tibs is, do you?'

Lily smiled carefully, all too aware that he was capable of turning like the wind. 'You should've come to me first, darling,' she said in the same wheedling voice, the one she usually reserved for punters. 'I'd have been glad to have helped you out. Glad to. And glad to have brought that Tibs down a peg or two. Always reckoned she was something special, that one. The runty little baggage.'

Some of Albert's other girls, who had all been as tight-lipped as Marie, stood across the street, staring at the sickening sight of Lily Perkins cosying up to the man whom, if he hadn't knocked most of the courage out of them, they'd have happily run through with a butcher's boning knife.

Marie hurried over to them, feeling safer with a bit of distance between her and Albert. Still shaking, she swiped roughly at the tears that were burning her cheeks. 'If that big-mouthed trollop lets on about Polly I'll bloody do her, I swear I will.'

They gave out a subdued cheer as Lily was given her turn at being shoved against the wall. Albert, not a man to waste words, poked her hard in the chest. 'Where?'

'There's no need to get rough.'

'I *said*, where?'

Lily's lips thinned with displeasure. He was supposed to be grateful. 'Further down the Highway,' she said sulkily. 'Towards Rosemary Lane. Been hanging round there for about a week now, rot her heart.' She affected an unattractive sneer. 'They reckon she's gonna try and sing, if you don't mind.'

'Sing? If you're lying to me, Lily . . . '

'I swear on my life. That conniving little mare'll be there tonight. You mark my words.' She flashed a defiant look across the street to where the others were straining to hear how much she was blabbing. 'Everyone's been talking about it.' She spat viciously. 'In fact, it makes yer bilious. It's all anyone's been talking about. And . . . ' she swung her shoulders in what she thought was an appealingly girlish way, 'so they say, it's meant to be her big night tonight. The first time on stage.' She stuck out her bottom lip, pouting like a disappointed child. 'You know, Albert,' she whined, 'I don't understand why you bother with her. Not when you've got the likes of me working for you. Not when . . .' Her words trailed away and she stamped petulantly. 'Are you listening to me, Albert?'

He wasn't. 'Nobody crosses me. Nobody. I'll give her working for someone else.'

Albert turned away and strode off towards Rosemary Lane. His pace quickened and he broke into a trot.

Lily pulled a face at the other girls. 'That's right, Albert, get a move on.' She hitched up her skirts and started after him. 'The acts are all such rubbish, they say the place'll be closing down soon. And with the way that soppy little trout squawks and squeaks she might just do the job and shut it down tonight. Albert, wait.'

Albert ignored her.

Unused to moving at any speed other than a stroll, Lily stopped running and slumped against the wall to get her breath back. 'Watch yourself,' she managed to holler after him. 'By all accounts the governor there's a right dozy sort who couldn't knock the skin off a rice pudden, but he's got a guard dog. I don't want you getting yourself hurt.'

'Gawd forbid!' mocked a skinny little woman, standing next to Marie, her face a thick mask of powder and paint that did little to disguise her advancing years. 'We wouldn't want our stinking bully of a pimp getting himself hurt, now would we, girls?'

Bartholomew Tressing touched the bottom of the cheval glass with the tip of his silver-topped cane, setting the mirror just so, to enable him to see the full effect of his outfit: the elegantly cut suit, the immaculately white tie, the beautifully lined opera cloak and the perfectly steamed and brushed silk topper.

The years, not to mention his life of ease and privilege, had been kind to him. Still handsome, despite his almost sixty years, and with regular help from his routine doses of medical cocaine, he was still full of vigour despite the increasingly progressive symptoms of his sickness.

He fancied something distinctive this evening. It was, after all, a rather special anniversary: ten years since the police and the press had finally believed that the murderer had simply disappeared, like the spectre some, at the time, had actually believed him to be. Just thinking about what fools they had been made the doctor wonder about the world. How could people survive with such feeble brainpower? They had actually suspected his own daughter of causing the deaths of those harlots. A well-bred young lady such as Celia.

But now that episode was closed, was confined to a past that might just as well have been a cheap novel he had picked up for a moment's amusement – like so much else in his life.

He stretched his lips into a becoming smile and acknowledged his reflection in the glass with a tip of his cane against his hat.

He would tell the others: tonight it was to be the East End.

Teezer shivered down into his shapeless black topcoat as he and Buggy made their way through the riverside back streets towards the Old Black Dog. 'I'm telling you, Bug, it's her. You see if she don't look familiar.'

'And I'm telling you she's nothing like her.' Buggy dismissed him. 'You say it about every sort who's taller than five foot that you set eyes on. You, Teezer, are becoming obsessed. Just because you've seen a few posters saying there's a tall one and a short . . .'

'No, Bug, it's more than that. She's been hanging around the place. I've caught sight of her a couple of times now.'

'Yeah, after you've swallowed about a gallon and a half of purl,' he muttered. 'In fact, with the amount you knock back, it's a wonder you ain't seen the Prince of Wales and the Archbishop of Canterbury into the bargain.'

'I heard that.' Teezer cuffed him – none too gently – round the back of the head. 'Now if you shut up for once and listen, instead of keep bunnying on all the time, maybe you'll learn something. Think about it.' He spoke very slowly so that Buggy could take in the lesson. 'There's you, what don't stop gobbing off all the time, and you are the worker. And there's me, what philosophises with the best of them over the world's problems, and I am the governor.' Teezer nodded, pleased with himself. 'See?'

Buggy ploughed on as though Teezer hadn't said a word. 'We'd drunk a fair bit that night remember, and . . .'

Teezer gave up with his attempts at teaching and tried another tack instead. 'Look here, Bug,' he said, slapping his hand over Buggy's mouth. 'She was tall, right? You've already agreed that?'

Buggy, wide-eyed, nodded.

'Well so's she.' He spoke quickly; even with a hand over his trap, Buggy was quite capable of mumbling his two penn'orth. 'I've been studying her this past week when she's been hanging about the Dog. And it's her I'm telling you.'

Noticing Buggy's face was turning a bit red, Teezer removed his hand.

'Well I ain't noticed no resemblance. I think you've just . . .'

'That's 'cos you're always pissed and you don't listen.'

'No, you're just trying to convince yourself, Teeze. You've been going on and . . .'

'*Me* going on?'

'Yeah, you . . .'

'Just shut it, Buggy, will you? Just hold your noise for once, and wait and see. All right?'

'You only had to say, Teeze, I mean, anyone can take the hint if . . .'

Teezer shook his head and did his best to close his ears.

Tibs fumbled around in the dingy little room beside the stage, trying to sort out some light for her and Kitty. 'Blimey, hark at her!' she giggled, as the sound of the 'serious' soprano, who was the warm-up act for the girls, came rattling through the wall. The woman's special selling point was her talking dog, which took the tenor parts, and if it came to a toss-up, the punters preferred his efforts every time.

'Sounds like a rusty nail being hammered in. But Bonzo'll start soon and drown out the old bat.'

Tibs flared a match. 'Bugger. Them sodding rats have been at the candles again.' She struggled to light the nibbled tallow. 'When we've made our fortune, Kit, we'll have proper gas lamps, eh? There, that's better.'

She turned round, shielding the guttering flame with her hand, to see Kitty huddled in the corner, her face a picture of pale terror behind the make-up that Tibs had insisted on plastering on them both before they left the lodging house. 'What's up, darling?' she asked, setting the candlestick down on the floor.

There was no furniture in the little room that had once been part of the landlord's quarters, it was simply a holding pen where the next act on the bill could wait. As the previous act was usually booed off the stage within minutes, the following turn had to be ready and waiting to get on before the audience turned nasty. 'You ain't scared of rats, are you, Kit? Not a great big girl like you.'

Kitty shook her head. 'I can't do it, Tibs. I'm sorry.' A fat tear brimmed over and plopped on to her cheek, making a watery trail through the pink powder. 'And it's not just the thought of going out there, it's . . .'

'What?' Tibs folded her arms round Kitty's waist. 'Tell me.'

'It's him. Jack Fisher.'

'I don't understand, darling.'

'He scares me. Him and that cosh and his dog.'

Tibs laughed with relief. She'd really thought Kitty was going to back out and a double act wasn't much cop if there was only of you. 'You're worried about Fisher? He's as soft as butter, that one. All his tough stuff was just a show. And as for that dog of his . . .'

'So you mean he won't look after us? What if that Albert . . .'

'Bloody hell, Kit, d'you want it all ways?' Tibs had only known Kitty for a week, but she'd never before met anyone who was so easy to manipulate in some ways, but so bloody stubborn in others. If she hadn't needed her to keep Fisher happy she'd have dragged her down to the river and chucked her back in with the sodding fish. 'Kitty, love,' she said, trying to keep the exasperation from her voice, 'course he'll look after us. He's a feller, ain't he? Never known one to resist looking after a pretty ankle yet, darling. And I reckon between us we've got the prettiest set of ankles in the business.'

Kitty closed her eyes, as though the dark would take it all away. How had she let herself be talked into this? She sighed wearily. She knew exactly how. At the beginning of this long past week Tibs had persuaded her, with the gradual sneaking power of a dripping tap, that going on the stage would be absolutely nothing to worry about. All she would have to do was stand behind Tibs, miming and jigging about a bit. And almost imperceptibly Kitty had found herself giving in. Tibs was skilful, had carried out her campaign in stages, issuing little suggestions and reminders. Putting it to Kitty – oh, so casually – that she had said how much she had wanted to repay Tibs for her kindness and to make amends for not helping when that brute had beaten her up. Then Tibs had moved on, had played on another of Kitty's weaknesses and she had allowed herself to be sucked in, seduced by the thought of the almost clean, dry bed that Jack Fisher was willing to pay for – *every night* – in the common lodging house.

Then there was the food. This time Kitty's sigh was pathetic. She'd had plenty of that all right – almost as much as she could eat. Every day.

It had all made sense at the time, but now here she was, paying the price. Not only going on stage, but for all she knew, putting herself in danger from some sort of madman. Maybe two.

It was just like the nuns had told them in the home. No one ever gets something for nothing. You always have to pay in the end.

At the front of the stage the room was gradually filling up with its nightly quota of jeerers and critics. The appalling standard of the acts was still enough of a novelty to ensure that, for the first half-hour anyway, the room would be full, and Fisher had given himself an added advantage by opening up a full hour before any of his local rivals. But once that hour was up, even the most hardy of audiences would begin to thin and more sophisticated entertainment – well, entertainment which was intentionally funny – would be sought. It was that time of the evening that Fisher had grown to dread. But tonight he would stun them all with his double act. He'd get them on early on the bill, then have them back on to finish the first half, and back again to open and close the second.

The girls were going to knock the punters' socks off!

Teezer wasn't happy. He was meant to be here getting a good look at the girl in the new double act, but the seats were nearly all taken. What was the point if they had to sit right at the back? 'This is your fault, Buggy,' he fumed, ripping off his hat. 'You made us late.'

'My fault? But Teeze, it was you what insisted on going to old Bob's to get yourself a shave and a haircut.'

'Buggy . . .'

'It was. You said you wanted to look neat and tidy, so's when you found her she'd think you was all respectable and . . .'

Teezer held his head in his hands. 'Buggy, for Christ's sake just shut up. I will *try* and get us a seat, while you make yourself useful for once and go and get us two pints of wallop. And don't be all night about it.'

As Buggy was forcing his way down the stairs, fighting through the crowds going up to the theatre, Bartholomew Tressing was just arriving at the pub door with two companions he had brought along from the London hospital.

'Any old clay pipes, mister?' begged an eager bare-footed child of about six.

'Pipes, Tressing?' enquired Cameron Hunton, the younger of his colleagues.

Tressing said nothing, but just looked down at the

fair-haired boy with a sort of detached, mild curiosity.

'One never knows what these urchins will ask for next,' Lucian Mayerton, the other member of Tressing's party, offered in reply.

'Go on mister,' persisted the waif. 'We only wanna blow bubbles. We've got a bit of soap and we . . .'

Tressing's hand suddenly shot out from under his cape. He swatted the child aside without so much as a glance and swept open the door. 'Do you intend joining me?' he asked his two companions in his faultlessly cultured tones. 'Or would you rather stay out here in the gutter?'

Hunton was about to reply, but Mayerton's urgent if silent gesture made it very clear that he thought it better if they simply followed Tressing inside.

Albert Symes's arrival at the Old Black Dog was a far more furtive affair. He made his way along the street, ducking in and out of the shadows, moving with the practised guile of a man used to looking over his shoulder.

When he was a few hundred yards from the Dog he stopped to check his pockets. Bone in one; knife in the other. Albert always liked to be prepared.

On stage, Bonzo had just launched into a yelping encore from *The Barber of Seville* and, surprisingly, the audience were still amused.

As she watched him perform from the little side room Kitty urged him on, praying that the smelly, slobber-jawed mutt had a canine repertoire that could last at least another couple of tunes. Another couple of hours, maybe. Until closing time, preferably.

Tibs, who was standing beside her, was equally nervous, but for different reasons. This was the chance that she had to make work. She needed it to be a success. More than Kitty could ever know.

Archie, who was in there with them keeping an eye on his lights, could sense the mounting anxiety. 'Anything I can do for you girls?' he asked. Despite the caterwauling on the stage and the raucous cheers from the audience Archie spoke in a professionally low whisper. He had only been working with Jack Fisher for a few months, but he was a quick learner.

Tibs smiled at him. 'No thanks, Arch,' she whispered back. 'But thanks for asking.' Then, as she turned back to watch the ghastly performance on-stage she had a brainwave. She'd get Archie, with his dodgy arm, chatting about it – quietly of course – and that would take Kitty's mind off her own worries. She'd show the great tall thing that there were people worse off than her. Far worse. 'How d'you get that crippled arm then, Arch?'

In the candlelight Tibs didn't notice the fleeting expression of pain that crossed his face.

'Had an accident or something, did you? Or was you born with it?'

'Only got it quite recently as a matter of fact.'

'And Jack Fisher still give you a job?' Tibs sounded more surprised than sceptical.

'No. The boss took me on right at the beginning. As a chucker out. I've never really been one for fighting or anything. But I've always been strong.' He paused. 'I always was strong, I mean.'

'You still are,' Tibs said encouragingly.

Archie shrugged. 'Maybe.'

'Anyway, it was a way of earning a living without having to queue on the stones every day.'

'The stones?' It was the first time that Kitty had spoken.

'I was a casual down the docks. You all crush forward when they come to pick the teams. Treat you like animals, they do. Specially at times like these when there's not much work about.'

Kitty didn't fully understand, but she got the idea. 'And that's how you got hurt? Chucking out?'

He nodded. 'Two days after the opening. There was this drunk. Shouting the odds about how he could force down another dozen pints. He was upsetting some of the other customers. I went over to him and he stuck a knife right under me arm.' Archie turned his head away.

'Cor, bad luck, eh, Kit?' Tibs said. 'But good luck he never done you in, eh, Arch?'

'I don't remember that much of what happened after that; I lost a lot of blood, see, and passed out.'

'Probably a blessing, what with all the terrible pain you must have been in.'

'The boss was really good to me. Helped me.'

'But no one would have just left you, surely. Not when you was being attacked,' Tibs said pointedly, glancing at Kitty to see her reaction. She was gratified to see her looking thoroughly ashamed.

Archie laughed ruefully. 'If most people's reactions are anything to go by, the way they laugh and call me names, then I reckon the boss is special. And I'm not just talking about mouthy kids either. Adults are as bad.

But it wasn't just the fact he was nice to me and let me keep my job, he took me to the hospital that night, you know. Paid for the hansom and the treatment and everything.'

'Did he?' Tibs raised an eyebrow. Fisher must have a few quid to be able to splash it about on the likes of Archie. 'That *was* kind of him.'

'He's a good bloke. There's not many that would have let me keep working here, not when I can't chuck out no more. Mind you, it's not been that long since I got hurt. Maybe one day . . . '

'Yeah, maybe one day.' Tibs was beginning to feel sorry for making him tell his story. It obviously upset him.

'But, you know, I keep busy. I find odd jobs. Working the lights, cleaning up.'

Tibs swallowed hard. The poor sod. A big, nice-looking feller like him, reduced to odd jobs.

'And he let me keep my room up in the attic. Not much smaller than the boss's own, you know.'

'He sounds very kind,' Kitty said softly.

'I won't hear a word said against him,' said Archie.

Tibs, keen to keep the conversation steered away from Kitty and her problems, was about to ask him how he managed his ablutions, but Archie was saved from such personal revelations by the crowd who had started booing.

Bonzo had apparently run out of steam and the audience out of patience. A curl of orange peel had found its target in the soprano's considerable cleavage and she had started screaming. The effect on Bonzo was instantaneous. He lost control of his bowels, knew what his mistress's reaction would be and leapt into the audience, scattering tables and chairs as he went.

Archie rushed out and twisted the gas tap at the side of the stage that brought up the house lights.

Tibs, grinning with glee, watched the mayhem from the wings.

Kitty tapped her on the shoulder. 'How could you ask him those things, Tibs?'

'What things?'

'Couldn't you see how humiliated he was?'

Tibs shrugged dismissively, although she actually took what Kitty said to heart. She knew she had a big mouth on her at times. And she really hadn't meant to be so rude to the poor sod.

Tressing, who had just come up from the bar downstairs, entered the room and observed the confusion with detached calm.

He led his two companions to a table, flicked his handkerchief over the rickety wooden seat and sat down. Lucian Mayerton, his colleague of many years, looked perfectly at home in the grubby surroundings, but Cameron Hunton, a more recent acquaintance from the hospital, was rather more awestruck.

'Aren't we somewhat overdressed?' he asked from behind the cover of his hand as a barrage of peanut shells flew past him.

Tressing shook his head. 'Why lower standards? And anyway, compared with some of the blood tubs I've visited in these parts this, my dear Hunton, is a palace.'

Hunton wasn't convinced. He looked around him, noting the rough-looking men and women with their jugs of ale and greasy-looking fish and chips wrapped in sheets of old newspaper. They were slapping their thighs, throwing back their heads and roaring with laughter. And there was more, some of them were touching one another. He was horrified by such openly wanton behaviour.

He puffed on his cigar and took a sip of whisky. 'Lower orders are getting above themselves, if you ask me. People such as us being squeezed, while these dullards enjoy subsidised food, laze around rather than work, accept money from the Relieving Officer and rush out on railway excursions to Herne Bay every Sunday, or block up the roads with their damned safety bicycles. Smoking, drinking, gambling and fornicating. I've even heard talk of them using these damned public libraries.

It's as though the Fall of the Roman Empire is being re-enacted before our very eyes. I blame all this on the hysteria about the new century coming along. New Jerusalem. I ask you. The whole world's going mad.'

Tressing turned his head and flashed a brief glance at his companion. 'Shut up, Hunton, I'd like to watch the show.' With that, he lifted his chin and twisted back to face the stage where Tibs and Kitty had just appeared.

Hunton's face was a fair match for Kitty's – both of them had cheeks blazing with embarrassment.

'Look at her, will you, Bug?' Teezer pointed animatedly at Kitty who was shuffling on behind Tibs. 'I told you, it *is* her. And if it's not then I'm a flaming Dutchman.'

Buggy rolled his eyes. 'I reckon you'd better get out your clogs then, mate,' he muttered. All he could think was that Teezer must've had more purl before they'd come out than Buggy had realised. Admittedly, they weren't very near the front and Teezer's eyes weren't exactly as sharp as a hawk's, but surely even he could see that it wasn't her. It was obvious. Not only did this girl have more meat on her, but she was far prettier and her face had a nice sort of pink colour to it. She was glowing. And her hair was all shiny and nice. In fact, if she wasn't such a lummocking great thing Buggy could have been quite taken with her.

As Mr Tompkins, the music-hall Chairman – a vision of cod-gentility – scanned the room, anxiously seeking out possible missile launchers who might be targeting him, Tibs yanked Kitty to her side.

'Smile, for Gawd's sake, Kit. You look like you've been flaming-well pole-axed.'

Albert, who was standing at the very back of the room, shook his head in disbelief. Lily Perkins had been telling the truth for once in her lying life. Even with the strange effect of the limelight there was no mistaking it. That was Tibs up there on the stage. His Tibs. Earning money for some other man.

He'd kill him. He'd kill the pair of them.

But despite his temper, Albert was no fool. There were too many people around for him to take any chances. Anyway, he was in no particular hurry. Let the disloyal bitch earn a bit extra – he'd have that off her as well. He'd let her get all nice and comfortable with her new life. Let her be off guard and then he would strike.

He slipped out of the theatre and down to the main bar. He'd seen enough for his purposes.

Chapter 8

As Mr Tompkins scanned the baying crowd for potential antagonists he spotted Archie, dragging a toppling stack of chairs along the side of the room. The sight of the odd-job man triggered something in his memory. What was it? Mr Tompkins looked about him. The card on the easel, announcing the next turn. It hadn't been changed!

This place really was a shambles. He signalled frantically to Archie, who immediately abandoned his chairs – the newly arrived group of sailors would just have to sort themselves out – and rushed over to swap the brightly painted card on the announcement board.

Satisfied, or rather, placated, Mr Tompkins raised his gavel, brought it down with a crash, which both terrified Kitty and alerted the audience, and introduced them in the mock-refined tones of his profession. 'And now, ladies and gentlemen, we have here tonight for our delight and delectation . . .'

'Get on with it!' yelled one of the sailors, who had taken a chair and seated himself right by the front of the stage.

Mr Tompkins merely raised a suspiciously perfectly arched eyebrow – Tibs was sure he used a pencil on his facial hair, no one that old was without a bit of grey in his mutton chops – and continued, 'A brand-new double act. They are Mistresses of their Music. Doyens of their Dance. They are, in short . . .'

'That big 'un ain't very short!' cheye-eyed one of the sailor's shipmates.

'. . . the very latest act! All the way from San Francisco!' With that, Mr Tompkins sighed with the weariness of a disappointed man – he should have been at a civilised venue such as the Alhambra, not a rough old gaff like the Dog – raised his whisky glass to his lips with one hand and crashed his gavel down again with the other.

The piano struck up and Tibs gave Kitty a little pinch above the elbow. 'This is it, girl,' she warned, 'now don't you let me down.'

Staring into the wall of darkness that the glare of the limelights created before them Kitty was mesmerised, a vole held by the stare of a stoat, and as Tibs launched into the opening lines of 'Shabby Genteel', she found herself singing along, just as they had rehearsed. Her voice might have been pitched unnaturally high to keep up with Tibs's warbling, wavering soprano, but she was singing none the less: 'Too proud to beg, too honest to steal!'

They hadn't even got as far as the chorus and Jack Fisher already had his head buried in his hands. After having kidded himself for a whole, stupid, head-in-the-clouds week, even he had to admit that whatever else their oddly matched pair might be, it was clear that they weren't going to be his salvation. They didn't only sound terrible, they looked it. Instead of the lively, prancing girls he'd expected, they were standing there as if they'd been paralysed. The punters were beside themselves with laughter.

'Bring the talking dog back on,' hollered an elderly, ruddy-cheeked man, apparently unperturbed to be pressed up hard against the group of young seamen. 'It had a better voice than that lanky mare!'

'But you have to admit she's better looking,' chipped in one of the sailors.

'Depends on your taste, sonny,' said the old man wistfully, eyeing the youngster beside him.

The sailor frowned. Not sure he'd quite caught the other man's drift.

'I even preferred the paper tearer they had on the other night,' offered a woman sitting behind them, with a baby clamped to her breast, 'and she was a right load of shit. Worse than that old bag with the musical saw.'

Teezer, hearing the growing buzz of discontent about him, took a long draw of porter, wiped his mouth with the back of his hand and nodded towards the stage, where Tibs was doing her best to carry on, but Kitty wasn't even pretending to do anything other than stand there, transfixed with shame.

'Do you know, Buggy, you was actually right for once? She ain't nothing like that sort I rescued. Not a bit like her at all.' He craned his neck to see why the din coming from the front of the room was becoming increasingly aggressive. He jabbed his thumb at Kitty's lean frame without a glance. 'That one up there's a very big, manly type of a girl. Nothing like my young lady at all.' He half rose to his feet. 'What's all that going on up the front then?'

What was going on was a fight that had broken out between the young sailor and the florid-faced man who had been bold – or stupid – enough to have made a grab under the cover of darkness for the mariner's groin. A fight always had entertainment appeal and when the alternative was something as horrible as what was going on up on the stage there was no contest.

Used to being in charge, Teezer ordered whoever was listening: 'Oi, someone get the gasman to turn up them glims so we can have a proper butcher's at them two scrapping.' He climbed up on his chair, balancing himself by clamping a hand firmly over Buggy's head. 'I'll give odds on the young 'un,' he grinned.

The four-piece band were as keen as everyone else to see what was going on – they had the welfare of their instruments in mind. This type of brawl had a habit of escalating with alarming speed and anything might be used as a weapon, even a piano. They all stopped playing and rose to their feet, leaving Tibs to go it alone like a strangulated sparrow. Her lamentable warbling soon petered out and she stomped to the edge of the stage in enraged, tight-lipped silence.

She stuck one hand on her hip and used the other to shield her eyes from the stage lights at her feet. 'Do you mind?' she bellowed, but even her fog-horn of a throat couldn't carry over the row. She turned on her heel, grabbed Kitty by the arm and steered her towards the wings. The last thing she heard was someone shouting, 'Are you gonna get the house lights on or do you want a good hiding and all?'

Someone did eventually turn the lights up, but it wasn't Archie. Anxious for the girls' safety in a roomful of half-drunken men and women, all eager for entertainment, which at that precise moment seemed to mean seeing blood being spilt, he'd ushered them out of the theatre and down the back stairs to the alley that ran along the side of the pub.

It was still very cold, and all Tibs and Kitty had on were the ill-fitting costumes made of some cheap, flimsy material that Jack Fisher had produced for them that morning.

Archie eyed the odd-looking pair with concern. There was Kitty, tall and broad, if still far too thin for her height, shivering and trembling like a gawky baby bird that had tumbled from its mother's nest. And Tibs, despite her façade of loud-mouthed bravado, a beautiful, warm-hearted little thing, with her pussycat eyes and her lovely blonde curls, so small and feminine. His heart went out to them both, and to Tibs in a way that had him feeling as confused as a schoolboy experiencing the first nervous stirrings when it occurred to him what the differences between men and women actually meant. 'We'd better get you two inside,' he said, trying to keep his tone casual and a smile on his lips. 'You'll catch your death out here.'

Tibs's eyes flashed. 'After the way they treated us?'

'I don't mean back upstairs. Come in the bar and get warm. Have a drink. It'll be almost empty in there now. They'll all have gone upstairs to see the punch-up.'

Right on queue a loud cheer went up, followed by a sharp smack, then a chair came flying through the high side window, just missing Kitty, who shied away, her eyes wide and rolling like a frightened thoroughbred.

Tibs shrugged. 'All right then, Arch. We might as well get something out of it. I don't suppose our wages are gonna amount to much.' She looked at Kitty. 'Come on, girl, get moving.'

Kitty said nothing, she just let Tibs lead her away.

Archie was right, the big downstairs bar was almost empty, apart from a few huddles of battered-looking old drunks leaning against the walls for support. The bar staff – Joe, a young but big Irishman, who doubled as a chucker out since Archie's accident, and Florrie, a dumpy, middle-aged woman whose hefty bosom burst out from either side of her stained, once starched apron – had left the remaining customers to their own devices, while they went upstairs, Joe to see if his help was needed and Florrie to have a bit of a laugh.

Archie lifted the flap in the counter and poured the three of them a large measure of gin, which he topped up with water from a muslin-covered jug.

Tibs and Archie were leaning on the bar, sipping at their drinks, and Kitty was standing close by, staring at her feet, when Jack came storming in. 'We might as well give up. It's more like a boxing booth than a theatre up there, and even that manky excuse for a Chairman's gathered his stuff together and walked out.' He slapped down a handful of copper coins on the scratched mahogany counter. 'Here, take this. You're obviously not up to the job and you're certainly not going to make the money I thought you would, so just finish your drinks, pocket your wages and then, if you've got any brains, clear off before that mob upstairs turns really nasty and decides to take out on you whatever it is that's got in their pipe.'

Tibs looked at the miserable pile of coins. 'But this'll barely pay for our beds for tonight. There's only . . . ' She began counting.

Jack gestured with a lift of his chin for Archie to pour him a drink, then said to Tibs without looking at her, 'If you wanted more money you should have tried harder, lass.'

She was slack-jawed with indignation. '*Try harder*? You bloody hypocrite. You knew I weren't no flaming Lillie Langtry when you took me on.' She jabbed a finger at Kitty. 'And that she *certainly* weren't no Marie Lloyd.'

Jack turned to Kitty as though he was about to say something, but she immediately looked away. He took a step towards her, was about to take another, when an alarming crash reverberated through the building.

Jack's head shot back as he stared up at the ceiling. 'What the hell was that?'

'Someone trying to dismantle the stage?' suggested Archie.

Forgetting his other worries, Jack made for the stairs. 'Archie, get up here with me,' he shouted over his shoulder.

Tibs stuck her elbows on the bar and rested her chin on her fist. 'Me and my big ideas,' she said, as the din above their heads increased to a wild crescendo. 'Remember what I said about me not being able to carry a tune in a bucket?'

Kitty nodded miserably.

'I should have listened to meself for once.' She swallowed the remainder of her gin, stood on tiptoe, reached for the bottle and poured herself another. 'All I'm fit for is a life on the streets.'

'And I'd have been better off at the bottom of the river.'

Tibs spun round and confronted her. 'Don't you *dare* say that, Kitty Wallis. Don't you dare.'

Kitty looked away, unable to meet her gaze. She had never wanted to be here, had only ever wanted to repay her new friend's kindness and then disappear back into the night where she had come from. She had wished, time and again, that she could get away and never set eyes on the Old Black Dog ever again. But it was true what they said: be careful what you wish for, it might just come true.

Now it had. They were never going to have to come inside this building again, because as far as Jack Fisher was concerned they were finished. And now they had nothing. And this kind, plucky little thing, who had been through so much but had still taken the time to help a stranger, was probably in worse trouble than she'd been before.

This wasn't what Kitty had wanted. Not what

she had wanted at all.

'Listen to me, Kit,' said Tibs, pouring herself another drink. 'We're gonna have to do something about this. Do something a bit lively. We're gonna have to use our loaf. 'Cos I'm telling you, I ain't gonna wind up kicking the bucket in some pigsty of a stew down the Seven Dials. And you ain't gonna drown yourself neither. Right?'

Kitty gnawed at her lip. If only she could think of a way out for Tibs, that would be something. 'You could get a job as one of those shop girls,' she said. 'That seems a nice clean type of work.'

Tibs snorted. 'Yeah, slave labour for no money. No thanks. I knew someone who did that for a while. Young Marie. They made her live in this horrible little room with a load of other girls, right up in these flea-bitten attics above the shop. Made the lodging house look like some fancy toff's hotel, so she reckoned, and they had the cheek to keep back most of her wages to cover the rent. And the old slop they used to give 'em for their so-called meals. Treated worse than dogs, she said they was.'

'Better than dying under a slimy railway arch,' Kitty murmured. Then – she couldn't stop herself – she began to weep.

Tibs didn't notice her tears. 'That wasn't all,' she went on, staring into her gin. 'She was also expected to be *nice* to the owner of the shop whenever he felt like it. At least she gets paid for doing it now she's working the Lane.' She sipped at her drink and said quietly to herself, 'But Marie ain't got Polly to worry about, has she?'

Jack climbed up on the stage and stared about him. The place had gone mad, with practically half the audience fighting, while the other half watched and offered their advice and encouragement. Behind him, the Amazing India Rubber Man had actually launched into his act as though nothing was happening. He was surprisingly deft, as it happened, balancing on his hands while wrapping both legs behind his head. He didn't appear to notice the incongruity of doing his act in front of a throng of men and women who were more interested in smashing seven kinds of bells out of one another than in whether he could stick his toe up his nose.

Jack ducked as a chair flew past him. It knocked the contortionist flying sideways, causing peals of appreciative laughter from the table where both Bartholomew Tressing's companions were now thoroughly enjoying their evening out – thanks in no small measure to the amount of port they had managed to polish off between them.

Dr Tressing himself was sitting calmly, observing the spectacle of the masses taking one another apart. Almost languidly, he beckoned to a boy, the younger brother of Joe, the Irish barman, who was scrabbling about the floor searching for coppers that just might have rolled from the pockets of unwary brawlers.

The boy looked about him, searching for who the man might be signalling to. There was nobody obvious. He glanced back at Tressing, tapped his chest and mouthed, 'Me?'

Tressing nodded.

He thought for a moment, then went over to the table, making sure he was just out of reach – you could never tell with toffs.

'Is that the owner? That man over there?' Tressing asked the scabby-kneed child.

'Why d'you want to know?' the boy answered cautiously.

Tressing held up a shilling. 'That's why.'

The boy hesitated for a moment, but the coin tantalised him. It was enough for him to buy a whole big paper twist of barley sugar – just for himself – a couple of meat pies and have plenty left over to waste on toot down the market. 'Yes, sir,' he said, straightening up as though on parade. 'That's him. That's Jack Fisher.'

'Give him this note and the shilling's yours.' Tressing scribbled something on a gold-cased pad, ripped out the sheet of paper, folded it in two and held it out to the boy.

'I'll do it if you give me the shilling now.'

A trace of anger clouded Tressing's face and a muscle twitched in his jaw. He slapped the coin into the boy's hand.

'I'll take it over to him right away, sir.'

Hunton, now really in the swing of things, was grinning like a monkey. 'Have you heard what Dolly Bosanquet had to say about errand boys?'

Tressing, weary of Hunton's sudden perkiness, raised a bored eyebrow. 'No, but I'm sure you're going to tell us.'

'They're like postcards, so easy to send and so cheap that everyone likes to have one handy!' He paused long enough to laugh at his own wit, then went on, 'I say, Tressing, d'you suppose this Fisher fellow can read?'

Tressing didn't reply, he just wondered why he had been rash enough to invite this tedious man along to the next meeting of the Occultist Circle. Then a hint of a smile flitted across his lips. He knew full well why he had asked him. It would be amusing to see how the fool would react.

Jack Fisher could read, and when he saw what was in the note he pulled the child up on to the stage beside him. 'Point out the man who gave this to you, Sean.'

'That's him, Mr Fisher. The one with the posh clothes and the two pie-eyed mates.'

'Good lad, Sean,' Fisher said, his brow pleating into a frown. 'Now you go over and tell him to come out and meet me on the landing.'

The boy looked reluctant.

'What's wrong?'

'He's a bit, you know, Mr Fisher. Strange like.'

'I'll keep an eye on you, Sean. Don't worry.'

Tressing immediately joined Jack outside the auditorium, at the top of the stairway where the din from inside was muffled by two heavy swing doors. The landing was lit by a pair of hissing, popping gaslights, which sent long shadows up the scarlet-painted walls.

Jack looked the finely dressed man up and down, warily appraising the person he was dealing with. 'Your note said you wanted to speak to me.'

Tressing smiled and nodded his approval. 'A man who gets straight down to business. I like that.'

'Business, you say?'

'The two girls. The tall one and her partner. They interest me. I'd like to meet them.'

'I'm no pimp,' he glanced at the signature on the note, 'Mr Tressing. And if that's what you think you've got the wrong idea. But if it's girls you're after there are plenty around these parts. You don't need to come to me.'

Tressing didn't let his surprise show, but he'd have laid money that this shoddy-looking specimen would have sold his own sister for the right price. 'It's Dr Tressing, actually,' he corrected him, 'but you misunderstand me, Mr Fisher. What I think is that they have the makings of an interesting act. They could be very successful with the right management.'

Jack narrowed his eyes suspiciously. He was confused. Was this Dr Tressing some sort of rival from another venue? These theatrical types called themselves all sorts: Professor and Maestro and what have you. But if he was, then what on earth did he want with those two? 'You saw them,' Jack said. 'And you heard them. They can't sing. They were terrible.'

'Ah yes, but they have something about them, something hard to define.' Tressing hesitated, thinking about how truly marvellous they had looked together and what fantasies had filled his jaded mind.

'I don't understand what you want.'

Tressing, his face a studied mask of indifference, shrugged carelessly. He had to be careful. He didn't want to seem too eager or he might frighten off this naive young northerner. Having noted the man's shabby clothes and thin-soled boots, Tressing decided on his approach. 'As I said,' he drawled in his refined high-society tones, 'I believe they have something special. Something from which you could make a great deal of money.'

'You do, do you?'

Tressing nodded casually. 'Maybe I could, er, let's say, invest a little money in the show. Get the girls some decent costumes. Some voice training.'

Now Jack was really puzzled. What was this man up to? Why would he be offering to invest money in those two? What was the catch? He needed time to work this one out. 'I'll think about it,' he said bluntly.

Tressing blinked back his astonishment. The man had made it clear that he wasn't prostituting the girls, but he was offering him legitimate money, for God's sake. 'Very well,' he said briskly. 'Perhaps we'll speak later.' With that, he swept through the double doors with a flap of his coat-tails and returned to his table.

Tressing pulled out a chair, sat down and glared at the stage, where the Amazing India Rubber Man was skulking about the stage with an exasperated scowl distorting his already ugly face.

'You had as much luck with the young ladies as that fellow had with the audience, eh, Tressing, old chap?' chirped Hunton with an inane snigger.

Tressing just stared ahead, watching as the Rubber Man picked up his mat and mouthed something obscene at the battling mob below that, by rights, should now have been applauding his talents.

Mayerton, hiding his amusement at Tressing's failure to meet the young women he had assured them would be joining them for supper – at least – took the opportunity to have a sly dig at Hunton. He had never had much time for physicians, considered them cowardly namby-pamby prescribers, too feeble to cut off a limb or open an abdomen in order to sort out a problem in a manly sort of a way. He half turned to face his unsuspecting colleague. 'You think Bartholomew's lost his touch, do you, Cameron?'

Hunton nodded happily, pleased, as a newcomer to the august circles of the London Hospital, to be in on the banter. 'I certainly do, Lucian. I'd heard you were a devil with the fair sex, Tressing, a real lady-killer.' He looked at Mayerton and grinned broadly. 'He must be spending too much time abroad, if you ask me. Losing that English charm I'd heard everyone talking about.'

Tressing felt the heat and colour in his face. He stood up. 'If you'll excuse me, *gentlemen*, I'll be a few moments. I'm sure you can find something to amuse you in my absence.'

*

Jack, who had spent the last five minutes alternately panicking and fuming about Tressing's suggestions, took a deep breath, raked his floppy fringe from his forehead with his fingertips and shoved open the heavy doors. There was nothing else to do. He had no choice. He had come all the way to London to make his fortune and this was probably his very last chance to make a go of it. He had to speak to Tressing, because if this carried on for another week he wouldn't have a pub left to worry about.

Shoving past the few remaining customers, who were standing around in noisy arguing knots, Jack knew he was doing the right thing. As he walked over to the table, he practised what he was going to say and how he was going to say it. He'd be humble. He could manage that. If it meant saving his business he could manage anything.

But when he reached the table he was at a loss. Tressing wasn't there. Damn it. He should have jumped at the chance when the man had mentioned investing in the show. Never mind losing his pub, he must be losing his grip. He took a deep breath, stuck on a smile and said to the two men who'd been with Tressing, 'Your friend gone home, has he?'

Hunton looked up at him through bleary eyes. 'No. Just popped out for a breath of fresh air, old man. Don't think this part of the show was to his taste.'

Jack glanced over his shoulder and winced at the rather elderly, toga-draped 'classical' dancers who had made the inconceivable decision still to come on after the Rubber Man had stalked off the stage. The world really had taken leave of its senses. Did the stupid old hens honestly think he was going to have the money to pay them when he had all this damage to repair?

If he even bothered to try.

But he had to bother. This was all he had.

Swallowing his last grain of pride, he folded his arms and, sounding as smooth as he could, said to the two men, 'I was a bit taken aback by what your friend had to say earlier and I might have come over as being a bit rude, so maybe I can buy you gentlemen a drink to make up for it.'

Neither Mayerton nor Hunton needed any persuading; both accepted his offer.

'So,' Jack began, as he poured them each a large measure from the bottle he'd brought to the table. 'Your friend, Dr Tressing, is interested in my double act.'

Hunton snorted into his glass, sending a fine spray of port into the air. 'Interested? That's putting it rather mildly. I'd say he found the idea of those two charming ladies together – how can I put it politely? – rather stimulating.' He grinned at Mayerton. 'Isn't that right, old man?'

Mayerton agreed, but decided to keep his own counsel.

'I must admit,' Hunton continued, 'I found them rather stirring myself, if you see what I mean. But for Tressing it was more than that. The story is that the fellow's been ill, you see. And the illness has, let us say, weakened him somewhat. Even heard rumours from one chap that he'd gone Uranian! Bit of a nancy boy tendency surfacing. But no. Your girlies have interested him. Definitely.'

Mayerton shook his head in wonder. The drink had turned the man from a bore into an idiot. If Tressing could hear him passing on all this gossip about him. And to a pub landlord . . .

Jack hadn't actually understood half of what Hunton was going on about, but he nodded regardless. He needed money and these people had it. 'He mentioned something about investing in the show. Is he some sort of manager, or does he own another music-hall?'

Hunton seemed to find the idea wildly amusing. 'No. He's a doctor.'

'What, at the hospital?'

'At the London, actually,' Hunton informed him proudly. 'Same hospital as me.'

While his colleagues were inside with Jack Fisher, Tressing was outside, standing as far away from the light as he could manage, which wasn't difficult in the seedy, ill-lit East End street. He reached inside his jacket pocket and took out a small engraved case. He opened it and, with shaking hands, snapped the top off a small glass phial. He drew its contents into a hypodermic syringe, tapped the barrel and plunged it into the crook of his bared arm.

Within moments, Tressing was back in the theatre, his mind artificially alert, his eyes bright and hard. He didn't return to his seat immediately, but stood in the doorway watching Hunton prattling away to the landlord as though they were old friends. Intrigued, he moved closer and was infuriated to hear what the dull-witted physician was saying.

'. . . not just any doctor, mind. A really famous surgeon. In fact, he's recently received an award from the United States of America. Not the first, I might add.'

'That's enough, Hunton,' Tressing said, suddenly appearing at his side. 'You don't want to bore the chap.'

Hunton had the grace to shut up.

'My companions and I will be going now, Mr Fisher. But I presume you joined our table in order to tell me you've made up your mind about my proposal.'

Jack rose to his feet. 'That's right, Dr Tressing,' he

said. And I've decided to accept.'

Tressing nodded. 'I'll speak to you soon, and we can discuss how much you need and the changes to the act.'

Fisher frowned. 'Changes? But why?'

Tressing raised an elegant eyebrow. 'I'd have thought that was obvious to a professional such as yourself, Mr Fisher. Now, if you'll excuse us.'

As Tressing left, with his two companions in tow, Jack sat back down and wondered exactly what it was that these men – not only Tressing and his pals, but the men who had applauded them down in the bar – could see in those two girls. They were attractive enough young lasses, but nothing really outstanding. He rubbed his hands over his eyes. He was exhausted. Maybe that was why he couldn't think straight. But what was important was that Tressing was impressed; impressed enough to spend money on them.

But how much? And when, exactly, were they going to discuss it? When was *soon*?

Jack leapt to his feet. He'd catch up with Tressing before he disappeared into the night and ask him. At least knowing that might let him get a decent night's sleep.

Jack was standing in the pub doorway, looking left and right, trying to catch sight of his unlikely benefactor, when a man in an old-fashioned, flare-waisted coat stepped out of the shadows. 'Jack Fisher?' he asked.

'What's it to you?'

'I'd like to introduce myself. The name's Albert Symes. You might have heard of me.'

'I don't think so,' said Jack impatiently, looking over the man's shoulder for a possible glimpse of Tressing.

'I look after Tibs Tyler.'

That got Jack's attention. The girls had said there was

a man Tibs used to work for, a violent type of a bloke, who had been worrying them. He'd guessed then, and was now sure he was right, that this Albert Symes was a pimp.

'And I think we should have a little talk about it. Don't you, Jack Fisher?'

Jack nodded. This was all he needed. The moment things seemed to be looking up, someone was going to come along and try to pinch half his double act. 'Good idea, Mr Symes. I've just got a bit of business to attend to inside, then I'll see you out here in, what, two minutes.'

'In the alley next door, I think,' Albert said with the smugness of a bully who had decided he had a victim neatly in his clutches. 'Oh, and make sure you come alone, Jack Fisher. I'll be waiting. And watching.'

Back inside the pub, Jack wondered what to do next. If he tried taking his chucker out, or even Archie, as reinforcements, Albert might just turn tail and leave before they could sort anything out. But from what Tibs had said, Symes could be a really nasty piece of work.

He was hoping that a bit of bribery might do the job of persuading him to let Tibs stay on, although how he was going to pay any sort of a bung was another matter, but he'd worry about that later. All he knew was that he couldn't let Albert just muscle in and take Tibs away. But he didn't fancy getting himself beaten up for his trouble.

With only minutes to think about it, Jack came up with the closest he could get to a solution. He rushed up to his room, woke the elderly Rex from his doggy dreams of chasing rats and buckled on a ferocious-looking studded collar that Jack had inherited from a far more vicious animal once owned by his father. He took the dog's hairy muzzle in his hands and stared into his sleepy, liquid brown eyes. 'You, Rex, are about to play the part of a savage guard dog. Try and get it right, eh, lad?'

Jack stood at the top of the alley that ran along the side of the pub, with Rex kept firmly behind him, his intention being that the old mongrel would be his secret weapon.

'You took your time,' complained Albert.

'I had something to do,' replied Jack, moving his legs together so that Rex could, if necessary, slide by him to get to his quarry – Symes – at the other end of the walk-through.

Albert, whose eyes were accustomed to the gloom, immediately caught sight of the dog that Lily had warned him about. 'So I see.' He delved deep into his poacher's pocket and produced his own secret weapon – a pink, juicy ham bone which he threw on the ground. Rex, rather than leaping for the pimp's throat, wagged his tail and fell on the succulent morsel.

Albert grinned with amusement as he watched the supposedly fierce animal almost purring like a pussycat over the butcher's scraps – he'd have done himself a better service if he'd kept his eyes on Jack.

Without a thought for the consequences, Jack pounced forward and punched Symes – crack! – right on the nose with one fist and then – smack! – right on the jaw with the other.

It was difficult to tell who was the most surprised as Albert's nose began to bleed like a scarlet fountain: Jack, as the pain seared through his knuckles, or Albert who, thanks to Lily Perkins, had had Jack down as a coward; or the dog at being woken up, dragged outside and then being thrown a ham bone as if it were his birthday.

For all his talk and promises to the girls, Jack had never so much as laid a hand on anyone before. But he wasn't going to let someone, anyone, take away this chance. And throwing the punch had exhilarated him. 'I've heard all about you, you spineless bastard,' he sneered, waving the cosh that up until then he hadn't even considered using.

Albert glared at Jack as he dabbed at his bloody face with his sleeve.

'Well, you're facing a man now, not some little lass you can knock about. So you'd better watch yourself, because I'm letting no one touch those girls. No one. So fuck off. I've got an establishment to run.'

Albert's lip curled in contempt. 'You stupid . . . ' He shook his head. 'You've no idea, have you? You'll be sorry you ever laid eyes on that treacherous little trollop by the time I've finished with you.' He lifted his leg, swung back his heavily booted foot and took a shot at Rex, who squealed and scrabbled away from him.

Astonishingly, the old mutt actually managed to avoid contact with Albert's toe and, as intoxicated by his success as his master had been, growled ferociously at Albert, left his precious bone and trotted off to stand by Jack's side.

Jack scratched behind the mangy creature's ear. 'Good lad, Rex,' he praised him. 'Good lad.' Then, with a lift of his chin, he pulled his hat down smartly and said down his nose, 'I'll be saying good-night then, Mr Symes.'

When he went back into the bar, with Rex by his side, Jack was glowing with achievement. This was how it felt when things were going well. He swaggered over to the girls, who were deep in conversation at one of the little side tables. 'I'm sorry about what I said earlier, about you trying harder.'

157

Tibs frowned at the half-daft expression he had on his face. 'Forget it,' she said, wondering what was going on.

'I don't want us falling out. We should sit down together and discuss a few things.' He was about to say something else when he looked down and suddenly went quite pale. He shoved his hands behind him and began backing off. 'Don't go away, I'll be back in no time. No time at all.'

'What was that all about?' Tibs shook her head in wonder as Jack reversed across the bar towards the back stairs that led up to his room.

'Didn't you see?' breathed Kitty, grabbing Tibs by the arm. 'He had blood on his hands.'

'Course there's blood on his hands,' said Tibs more abruptly than she'd meant to. 'Didn't you hear the row up there? It sounded like a flaming slaughterhouse. But it's our necks I'm worried about, not some drunk's. I wonder what he wants?'

'I don't know if I care.'

'Well, I bleed'n'-well do. I've just got used to having our bed – our clean, dry bed – in the lodging house paid for every night and to having two decent meals a day. And I must say, Kit, I rather like it. I ain't gonna just let it go like that.'

'Aren't you?' Kitty asked cautiously.

'No, I ain't. I'm gonna kid him somehow. Find a way to make him let us carry on for a while. At least until I come up with something else. The thought of going back to Albert ain't exactly sweet, you know, and that's me only other option. And don't look at me like that, Kit. I know you ain't taken to all this, but you ain't exactly got much alternative either. I mean, it's this or going back to kipping with all them other poor buggers on the streets again.'

*

158

Jack scrubbed furiously at his hands. If the girls only knew it, his anxieties were very similar to theirs. The momentary thrill of beating Albert had gone and he was wondering what Tess would have to say if she could see him now.

She was always so careful, so steady. And here he was, punching people on the nose, running a clapped-out music-hall and planning to throw good money after bad. Money that wasn't even his. Given to him by a man he didn't even know. And a doctor of all people.

He felt frightened and confused, to say the least.

'So, Jack,' Tibs said, with far more boldness than she felt, 'you've got something to say, have you?'

Jack pulled up a chair and sat down. 'We have to work out what's wrong. Try and sort it out.'

Tibs rolled her eyes and said sarcastically, 'Have you thought about selling hot meat pies. They always go down well.'

'I meant with your act.'

'You gave us the elbow, didn't you?' Tibs's mouth was dry as sandpaper. Had she overstepped the mark?

'No, that was just me shooting my mouth off. We're going to change the act.'

'Are we now?' Tibs kept her voice calm, but her pulse was racing.

He nodded. 'That's right. I've had some ideas put to me.'

'And they are . . . '

'We'll talk about them,' he said with another nod, 'soon.'

'It had better be very soon,' ventured Tibs. 'I mean we can't just sit around waiting for you, you know, Jack. Much as we like you. We have had other offers you know.'

Kitty opened her mouth to speak, but Tibs kicked her under the table and she said nothing.

'I'm sure you have,' agreed Jack, going along with what he could only hope was a blatant lie, 'and I promise you it'll be very soon indeed.'

'Good. Now if we can have our lodging money for the night.'

'I'll just get it from behind the bar.'

As Jack was messing around with the cash box he looked up and called across to them, 'By the way, girls, I don't think Albert whatever-his-name-is will be bothering you again.'

Tibs frowned. What did he mean by that?

Chapter 9

It was getting on for nine o'clock and Albert was just about ready to give up for the evening. He had been searching the streets for Lily Perkins for two cold days and nights without so much as a sniff as to where the stupid cow was hiding, and it was definitely getting on his nerves. Not only did he not like being defied, but he was spending so much time away from his business lately, chasing after one trollop or another, that it was beginning to interfere with his profits.

He'd been looking for her that far afield – as far as Bethnal Green – that he hadn't had time to collect the takings off his other brides and he knew what they were like when they had money in their greedy little hands. They'd go spending it all on gin and bloody ribbons, and he'd have to waste even more time giving them all a good whacking to get them back into some sort of order.

Albert ran his hand over his jaw. And that was sodding painful as well. He didn't take kindly to being on the receiving end of violence.

It was all Lily Perkins's fault. He'd just about had enough of her. Why hadn't she told him about Fisher being so handy with his fists? At least he could have been prepared, and have sorted out the business over Tibs there and then, but now that still had to be cleared up as well.

If she wasn't careful he'd get shot of Lily for good. It wasn't as though she'd be missed. All right, most of his customers weren't that fussy, especially when they'd had a few, but she was getting too haggard even for the rum-pickled old seamen who hung about the dock gates and wasn't exactly coining it for him. There was plenty of fresh meat about for him to pick up.

What amazed Albert was how Lily had got wind that he was after her. Who'd tip *her* the wink? He couldn't imagine who'd even think of helping that one. But the lousy tart definitely seemed to know he was looking for her. Well, he would personally make sure that there was something she didn't know: Albert had a little surprise planned for Lily Perkins, something to repay her for his cuts and bruises.

When he eventually found the manky whore.

His attention was suddenly diverted by the sound of footsteps, a woman's footsteps. They were coming his way.

He ducked into the doorway of a nearby shop.

Peering out into the darkness, he waited until she came close to the pool of yellow gaslight spreading out around the lamp-post. Albert's luck was in at last. It was Marie.

As she stood among the broken chairs in the empty theatre – the Old Black Dog was doing strictly down-stairs, bar-only business this evening – Tibs smiled brilliantly. It would have taken a shrewd individual to guess that, actually, she wasn't completely thrilled by Jack's new idea. Or rather, the idea that his new backer, whoever he was, had come up with. She was, in fact, secretly appalled by the prospect.

Not only was she going to have to think up yet more ways to persuade Kitty that she had to *Please, stick around for just a few more days, Kit. Please. Till I get myself sorted out, like,* but somehow she was going to have to make her go up on the stage, open her mouth and sing again. And it certainly wasn't going to be easy, especially not now Jack and his benefactor had come up with this hare-brained scheme.

But Tibs wasn't going to let him, or Kitty – especially Kitty – sense even a hint of the reservations that were rattling around her brain. 'Just look at you,' she enthused, straightening the military-style gold frogging on the front of Kitty's jacket. 'You look exactly like a young hussar.' She paused, then let out a tinkling, girlish giggle. 'Whatever one of them is when he's at home!'

Kitty just stood there, staring.

Jack didn't look too happy either.

After listening to Dr Tressing and having had a few drinks, Jack had come up with what he'd thought was a brilliant idea – although the idea was, in fact, very much Tressing's own, but that man had the knack of bamboozling you into believing whatever he wanted you to.

The big idea was that the girls' straightforward double act should be changed into a novelty item. That Kitty should become a male impersonator, like Vesta Tilley, and Tibs would play the part of 'his' girlfriend.

Female cross-dressing acts were certainly taking big money in the halls and, with the added titillation of the artiste having a female companion, Jack had convinced himself – with Tressing's help – that they couldn't fail.

But now he had physically laid out the money, which Tressing had advanced him, for the hiring of the professional-quality outfits – man-about-town, cockney urchin and this showy army uniform for Kitty; and a single flouncy pale-pink creation, with matching parasol and picture hat, for Tibs – his anxiety had returned ten-fold.

It still seemed a terrible risk, even if he was being

subsidised by Dr Tressing. He couldn't help it, when he began to reckon up how much he had already wasted he could just imagine what Tess would have had to say about such wanton profligacy. But Tressing, whose money he was spending, probably didn't even care. Not only was he loaded, but, if Jack was honest, the man seemed more than a bit potty, or *eccentric* as it seemed to be called when you were posh.

But if Tibs and Jack were dubious about this latest venture, Kitty could only be described as totally horrified by the very idea. When Tibs had persuaded her to try on the uniform *just for a lark*, she had objected, but Tibs had, of course, managed to get round her. Then, when Jack Fisher had let the cat out of the bag, not knowing that Tibs was keeping the male impersonation as a kind of vile surprise, Kitty had gone into shock.

Since meeting Tibs less than a fortnight ago her life had spiralled out of control and plunged down into increasing madness. It now seemed impossible that she had simply wanted to end her life by plunging into the ice-cold waters of the Thames. That was far too simple a punishment for whatever she had done to wind up in this position. She was being tortured, was in some sort of purgatory, just as the nuns had predicted when she hadn't scrubbed the stairs at the home as clean as they had wanted, or had dared to talk in the freezing dormitory after the candles had been snuffed, or had committed any number of other sins on an almost hourly basis.

It was as though when Tibs had found her she had briefly shaken off some terrible dream and the sun had found its way into the sky, but then she had fallen asleep again and entered some other, far worse, sort of nightmare world, the logic of which failed her completely.

The three of them, Kitty, Tibs and Jack, were just

standing there, as though time had decided to give itself a rest, when Archie shoved open the double doors with his shoulder and dumped his shovel and broom on the floor. He was intending to start sorting out the mess that the near riot of the night before had left in its wake. But when he looked up he didn't see the damage or the dirt, all he saw was a vision in palest rose, her blonde curls framing her tiny heart-shaped face. He swallowed hard as he felt his body stirring. 'You look beautiful,' he blurted out, before he could stop himself.

'That's really nice of you, Arch,' Tibs told his back as he turned and fled from the hall. She flashed a grin at Kitty. 'See, Kit, he reckoned you looked beautiful.'

Kitty didn't even have the will to disagree. She was a marionette and Tibs was working her strings.

Jack Fisher took a deep breath, a single step forward and said, 'I'll throw in a room.'

Tibs narrowed her eyes. 'Room?'

'Of your own.'

'What sort of room? We'd want something decent, you know.'

'Look, lass, I know you've been staying in that common lodging house in Cable Street. Anything'd be better than that.'

How wrong you are, thought Tibs and Kitty, for once in complete agreement.

What Tibs said, however, was somewhat different. 'You're right there,' she lied.

Marie was doing her best to smile. When Albert had dragged her into the shop doorway she'd thought her heart would stop, but she knew she mustn't show him she was scared, it only made him worse.

'What are you doing around here?' he snapped. 'This ain't nowhere near your patch.'

Think, girl, think, she urged herself. 'I was going to see my auntie,' she said. 'She ain't been very well.'

'Where does she live, this auntie?'

'Near here, in Hoxton.'

Albert stared deep into her eyes. 'How much you earnt?'

She gulped back the bile that was rising in her throat. 'Fifteen bob.'

'Is that all? In two days?'

Marie squirmed. Hers was a small world, where word soon got around when there was trouble. She'd not needed to be warned twice. She'd been hanging around this strange manor, keeping out of Albert's way, so that she wouldn't have to answer any questions about Lily Perkins. That was all she needed, putting herself on bad terms with that vicious cow. The problem with that plan, however, was that it meant she'd only been able to work in fits and starts, whenever she'd been sure that there was no one else around doing business. If the local girls had caught her at it they'd have beaten her up for trespassing. But at least they might not have cut her face, which was something that Lily was almost guaranteed to do – especially to a bride almost twenty years younger than she was and a sight more attractive.

'I'm sorry, Albert,' she began slowly, 'but you see . . .'

Before she could say another word, Albert shoved her out of the way, leaped past her like a scalded cat and was making his way up the street as though the seat of his pants was on fire and he was looking for a horse trough to douse the flames. What on earth was going on? Not realising what a coward the man actually was, Marie couldn't begin to think what might be able to scare Albert Symes.

'Does your mother know you're out, miss?'

Jumping at the sound of the strange man's voice, Marie turned and found herself squinting directly into the glare of a constable's bull's-eye lantern.

A copper. That was it. Albert must have seen him coming.

'Yes, officer,' she croaked. Even though she wasn't known around this way, she still had the prostitute's fear of being pulled in and getting stuck with yet another stretch inside, or a fine she had no hope of paying. If he was just playing with her and had actually seen Albert standing with her in the doorway, he'd just presume she'd been doing business and she'd really be for it.

'It was me mum what sent me out. To fetch some milk from a neighbour,' she began. 'But I . . . ' She started to sniffle miserably. 'I, I dropped the jug and I'm scared to go home 'cos I know she's really gonna tell me off.'

'Well, better that than hanging around dark streets at this time of night, young lady. You don't want to go getting yourself in some sort of a scrape, now do you?'

The constable, Martin Leigh, was a man with daughters of his own and knew what type of trouble young women nowadays were capable of getting themselves into. Wasn't Mrs Leigh always telling him? Over and over again . . .

'Now off home with you, before you go getting yourself mistaken for a . . .'

'For a what, sir?' Marie asked innocently.

'Never mind that,' he blustered. Why couldn't he have come across something nice and simple like a burglar? 'Just trust me, you'll be better off getting a tongue lashing from your mother than hanging around here.'

'Why sir?' Marie wasn't just taunting the man for the sake of it – although it did give her a certain amount of satisfaction to aggravate someone who would more usually be giving her a hard time – but she was giving herself time to make sure that Albert was well out of the way. She almost laughed to herself; this had to be a turn-up for the book, her trying to keep a copper talking. Wait till she told the girls about it. 'I don't quite get your drift.'

'And you don't want to neither,' he snapped. 'Let's just say there's hanky-panky what goes on round here and you don't want to know about it. Now go on, off home.'

With that he shooed her away as though she were a cat reluctant to venture out on a frosty evening.

Constable Leigh shook his head and clapped his hands over the sides of his head. He must need a squirt of Mrs Leigh's special jollop down his ears. He could have sworn that the little girl he had just packed off home to her mother muttered something about him buggering himself.

Jack decided to be quick off the mark. The idea of letting them have a room was obviously the right bait. Even Kitty, who had, up until then, remained entirely aloof from the conversation, had widened her eyes at the mention of having a place of their own. 'Come with me, lasses, and I'll show you.'

He led them next door to the narrow three-storey building that butted directly on to the slightly higher wall of the Dog, an almost derelict house that had been part of the deal when he'd bought the pub.

He took a few moments opening the rusty lock, then gave the door what he thought was a surreptitious kick. With a drawn-out creak it fell slowly off its hinges. 'I'll get that fixed,' he said, hurriedly lifting it to one side. He stepped into the hallway, turned up the wick in the

168

lamp he was carrying and led them in single file – there was no room for more than that – up a flight of stairs.

'This it?' Tibs asked, her obvious disappointment hanging in the air like a bad smell on a hot day.

'I'll admit the downstairs is a bit rough, like, but this room on the middle floor,' he shoved open a peeling, wonky door, 'isn't too bad. Not too bad at all. I was thinking of doing up the whole place as lodgings, when I get the time.' And the money, he thought. 'But I reckon you two lasses could make it very cosy.'

'Cosy!' sneered Tibs, flashing a surreptitious look at Kitty, as she ushered her into a cobweb-ridden, dust-coated space of about twelve feet by twelve. 'It's a rat trap, that's what it is.' She pulled her skirt up to her ankles. 'Listen, you can hear 'em scuttling about all round the place.'

The three of them listened.

Fisher pulled off his battered felt hat and scratched his head. 'You could get a cat in. There's always plenty of strays about the streets.'

'You must think I only go as far as Thursday.' Tibs snorted derisively. 'You'd need something more than a stray to sort these buggers out. They sound like they're wearing hobnailed sodding boots.'

'I'd throw in a bit of money for the cat's meat.'

Tibs said nothing, she just looked at Kitty and shook her head for her to do likewise.

It was a bit of an impasse, as Jack too held his tongue, not wanting to sound too eager.

But he couldn't keep it up. He had to hook them and reel them in. 'Five days' cat's meat each week, I'd pay for,' he said casually. 'You two will have to cough up for the rest.'

'And look at this,' Tibs went on, flicking aside the tatty sheet suspended on a length of twine that

169

separated the room into two separate compartments.

Jack sighed, a defeated man who'd played his final card, foolishly believing he'd been holding a trump. 'If you're not interested . . .'

'I never said that,' Tibs consoled him. 'Bit of fly paper, a bedstead and a mattress. A nice *clean* mattress,' she emphasised. 'And who knows. It might do us.' 'There's not much storage space,' she added, kicking at the orange box and the single upended market basket that served as furniture.

Jack Fisher put his hat back on his head, handed Tibs the lamp and said flatly, 'I'll leave you two to think about it.'

As they listened to him making his way down the stairs, Tibs and Kitty looked around at the peeling, lurid, green-distempered walls. There wasn't a hint of cheer about the place. A sudden gust of wind came whistling down the chimney, sending a heavy swoosh of thick, damp soot spilling into the hearth and out on to the bare floor-boards at their feet.

'There's dust and dirt everywhere,' said Tibs loudly. 'Filthy! And, like I said, nowhere to store anything.'

She paused, waiting until she heard Jack step out into the street, then she leaned close to Kitty and whispered, 'What d'you think?'

'I can't believe it,' she breathed back.

'Nor can I. It's bloody wonderful, ain't it? And I reckon he'll be a right soft landlord.' Tibs went over to the window, wiped the grimy pane with the hem of her underskirt and peered down at the street below.

'A place of our own.' Kitty sighed, joining her. 'It's like a dream.'

'I just hope Albert don't find out about it.'

'Is he really that bad?' asked Kitty.

'Worse, darling. Far worse.'

170

Although Albert had spent the past forty-eight hours searching the streets and alleyways of the East End for Lily Perkins it was, ironically, as he was running away from a portly, middle-aged copper – and if Marie told anyone about that he'd give her a hiding she'd never forget – that he ran smack bang into her as she came stumbling out of a gin palace in the Bethnal Green Road.

'Lily!' he roared.

Her hand flew to her mouth, but she immediately dropped it to her side, knowing that she had to look bold, at ease, had to pull herself together. 'Hello, Albert,' she wheedled, stretching out to touch his cheek.

'Shut up.' The words came out flat and cold, just like the first blow.

He waited until he had pulled her into the pitch darkness of a disused building used only by vagrants – all unconscious with meths and such-like by this time of night – before he struck her a second blow, this time using a piece of lead pipe wrapped in a length of foul-smelling sacking.

If she hadn't opened her mouth and started that bloody screaming, maybe he wouldn't have hit her again. And again. . . .

He paused just long enough to catch his breath – the fat cow had struggled, of course, but at least she hadn't bled very much – then he stepped out on to the street. He took a deep lungful of air, wiped his hand on the sacking and threw it on to a pile of rubbish in the gutter.

He straightened his shoulders and re-tied the worn silk scarf at his neck. He was well pleased with his evening's work. That was one overripe old trollop who'd be off the streets for a few weeks; that'd teach her a lesson. Now it was the other little whore's turn to get a bit of discipline.

But as he strode off into the night he was in no hurry to get to Tibs; he was more interested in finding himself something to eat and he'd need a few days to collect up his earnings. Then he would rest up for a while, have a bit of a think about things, about how he could make the most out of the situation. That's what he'd do. He'd bide his time. Do it right and let her worry for a bit. Tibs knew he wasn't happy with her and must be really fretting about when he'd finally decide to pay her a visit.

It made Albert smile just thinking about it.

Chapter 10

Kitty, with an unusually cheerful expression on her face, was standing by the now clean window of the room that she and Tibs had been sharing for a whole week. She was looking down on to the busy street scene below. 'It's such a lovely afternoon, Tibs. Chilly still, but really bright. Why don't you get up and enjoy what's left of the day, before it gets dark?'

Tibs rolled over, pulling the covers up to her chin. 'I know how pleased you are, Kit, us having this place, but do you have to chirrup and twitter away like a sodding skylark all the time? I need me sleep.'

'It's not just having this place, Tibs. It's . . . '

Tibs sighed loudly. 'What?'

'I can't really explain it.'

'Well, while you're trying to figure it out d'you mind being quiet? If I'm gonna do me best for this new act tonight I've gotta be rested.'

Kitty nodded silently and returned to her observation of the bustling business of Rosemary Lane.

There were a few tarts hanging around and trying their luck – mostly unsuccessfully, but their work would pick up later. For now it was the supposedly respectable trades that were busiest, although for the inhabitants of the tough dockside neighbourhood respectability came a long way down the list of what they considered important in life. Many of them had a second, or even a third string to their professional bow and were usually involved in something that was at least a small step towards the wrong side of the road.

But despite the varied opportunities which could present themselves in such an area, and all the ingenious connivings that went on to take advantage of them, times were still hard in the East End and there were some who would never manage to make much of a living for themselves, no matter what they were prepared to do.

Kitty watched sadly as one tiny girl, weighed down by a big wicker basket full of watercress, thrust out her hand to passers-by, imploring them to buy her wares. Her heart really went out to the poor child, as she thought how desperate she herself had been only a short while ago. Life could be so unfair at times.

She had just about made up her mind to run downstairs and give the child some of the food that Jack had got Archie to bring in to them when a smile slowly appeared on Kitty's face. She had realised what the child was up to.

She was deliberately seeking out specific people to approach – sailors fresh off the ships. While they had no obvious use or need for salad vegetables, their sentimentality, fuelled by long months at sea away from their own wives and families, meant, more often than not, that she was given at least a shiny farthing for her trouble. Sometimes she was given far more. And she kept the cress.

Kitty's smile expanded into an impressed grin. Tibs was right, they obviously learned how to survive at an early age in this uncompromising part of the world.

So taken was Kitty with the antics of this enterprising young scrap that she didn't even notice the man pushing a high-wheeled cart with a huge, belt-driven whetstone strapped on to it. But she heard him all right.

'Knives to grind!' he hollered at the top of his tobacco-thickened lungs. 'Fetch out your knives to grind!'

This was followed by a piercing, rolling blast on a set of bamboo pan pipes, recently acquired from a Lascar seaman, whose alarmingly long, curved dagger the grinder had honed to murderous sharpness.

Tibs groaned pathetically and pulled the bolster over her head. As if that din weren't bad enough, a handbell now joined in the general crashing and clattering from below.

'Muffins for sale!' the handbell ringer proclaimed. 'Nice fresh muffins for sale! Get some in for your tea!'

'What the bloody hell . . . ' Tibs flung the pillow to the floor, scrambled out of bed, shoved Kitty to one side and flung up the window making the box sash rattle. 'Will you shut up down there, you noisy bastards. Can't you see I'm trying to get me beauty sleep?'

Tibs threw herself back on the bed. 'I'm fagged out, Kit,' she wailed. 'Like an old, worn-out dish rag, I am. Practising the new act night and day for a whole sodding week, and now this bleeding row. Our big night tonight and I have to put up with this. Why don't they all just shut up?'

Ignorant of her pleas, the bells of nearby St George's rang out their five o'clock chimes, making Tibs scream with fury. 'Is this a bloody plot against me or something?'

Kitty laughed out loud, a rare, surprisingly pretty sound, which had Tibs sitting up in bed so fast it was as though someone had pulled her lever. 'Don't you start and all, Kitty Wallis.'

'Now you're wide awake, Tibs, you might as well get up. And it wouldn't hurt if we had just one more practice, would it? I don't want to go getting it wrong and risk losing this lovely place of ours.'

*

Fifteen minutes later Tibs still wasn't up exactly, but she was at least sitting on the edge of the bed and her earlier grumpiness was entirely forgotten. She was watching, fascinated, as Kitty pulled on her soldier's uniform and then stood herself in front of the cracked and speckled full-length glass that Archie had found for them, admiring the results.

Yes, shy, forlorn Kitty was actually admiring herself.

And she had every right to, thought Tibs. She looked good. Just like an assured, handsome young man. Her posture had improved too. She was no longer slouching, ashamed of her height, but stood tall and proud, with her back straight, her chin lifted high and her eyes shining.

'You look right pleased with yourself,' said Tibs, finally hauling herself to her feet and wriggling straight into her stays. She turned round for Kitty to lace her up.

'You know, Tibs, I feel pleased.'

'I'm really glad,' gasped Tibs, as Kitty tightened the laces. 'But I've been thinking, after all the trouble that Jack's gone to to make sure we get a good audience for tonight – putting up them posters everywhere and promising all them free drinks – we can't let him down by not even bothering to do something with that hair of your'n, now can we.'

'What do you mean?' Kitty's new confidence had suddenly ebbed. 'Something?'

Tibs pulled down the layers of her costume, which she had dragged over her head, and adjusted her bosom inside the bodice. She frowned thoughtfully at Kitty's hair and shoved her on to their single wooden chair. She weighed the thick dark waves in both hands. 'Scissors or tongs?'

'I don't know.' Kitty sounded as alarmed as she looked.

'We'll try the tongs and see how we go, shall we.' It was a statement rather than a question. 'Tonight's too important for you to go getting all squeamish on me.'

Tibs shifted the kettle off the fire – their single source of heating, cooking and water-boiling – and gave the coals a good poke. 'I reckon that should be hot enough,' she said, shoving the rust-pitted hairdressing tool into the embers.

They were soon glowing a dull red and Tibs, using her underslip to protect her hands, took them from the fire and tested their readiness by touching the ends to the sheet of newspaper that served as their table-cloth.

The paper immediately caught light.

'Tibs!' yelled Kitty, flapping at the flames.

'You're all right,' Tibs said, calmly extinguishing the blaze by slapping the kettle down on it. 'Just hold still, I don't wanna go burning your ear'ole.'

Kitty's hair sizzled and crackled.

Now she really looked worried.

'We've gotta get rid of most of it somehow or other and curling it up tight will make it look shorter. It'll be smashing, you see. A beautiful mass of tight little curls. Mind you, right proper short hair's all the go now you know. So if you're concerned about me burning it . . . How about if you let me cut it all off? Have it all done with.'

'Carry on with the tongs,' said Kitty, resigned as ever to Tibs's powers of persuasion.

Tibs carried on. 'D'you know, Kit, I still have to pinch meself when I think how we've fallen on our feet with this double-act lark and Jack giving us this place. Beats kipping under the arches, eh, girl?'

Kitty nodded, scratching furiously at her legs. 'If we could get these bugs to move house it'd be perfect. They've got right up under my trousers already.'

'Hang on. With all the excitement about tonight I forgot.' Tibs put her torture instrument down carefully on the hearth and dug into the pocket of her coat that was hanging on a nail on the back of the door.

She pulled out a brown, ribbed bottle and handed it to Kit. 'I nipped over the road yesterday afternoon and bought us this. Guaranteed to get rid of the little bleeders, it is.'

'So that's where you were,' Kitty said, although they both knew that even if Tibs were blindfolded and had walked backwards it still wouldn't have taken her nearly three hours to wander along the street to Mr Robinson's chemist shop. But it wasn't Kitty's business where Tibs had been and as she was volunteering nothing more, Kitty kept quiet.

'Quicksilver and egg whites, all mixed up,' Tibs said, clearly set on changing the subject. 'Jack told me about it.' She grinned as she wrapped another length of Kitty's shiny dark hair round the metal tongs. 'He wouldn't want you being all uncomfortable, now would he?'

Kitty ignored Tibs's insinuation and instead took her turn at changing the subject. 'How do you use this stuff then?' she asked, studying the label as though it were the latest ha'penny instalment of a torrid melodrama.

'All you have to do is dip a feather in it, and paint it all round the bed and windows and round the door. That sees the little buggers off. But if not, then it's back to the Krokum Powder, even if it is a load of old rubbish what makes you sneeze as bad as a potful of pepper. Let's just hope Jack knows what he's talking about, eh? And a cat. That's what we need and all. He was definitely right about that. And I'm gonna keep him to his promise about paying for the cat's meat.'

'You're really good, Tibs. You sort everything out.'

'I wish I could.'

Kitty twisted round and looked up at her little friend's uncharacteristically serious face. 'What's wrong?'

'What, apart from the bugs, the rats, the lack of sleep and this being the first night of a big act that's either gonna make or break me chance of ever getting off the streets, you mean?'

Kitty smiled. 'Apart from all that.'

'Nothing. Now stop fidgeting around and sit still, will you, or I'll wind up pulling all your hair out and you'll finish up as bald as a billiard ball. And nobody wants you to look *that* much like a bloke.'

'There's something else, Tibs, I know there is. And I'm not interfering or anything. But whatever it is, it'll be all right. You wait and see. I promise.'

Tibs smiled ruefully. 'I thought I was the one who was meant to look after you.'

Kitty laughed, pulled back her shoulders and saluted. 'It must be the uniform.'

Archie had got his routine off pat. All week he'd been practising, using every spare minute when he wasn't doing things for Jack, or fixing up the girls' room for them.

Since losing the use of his arm, he had tried to repay his boss for being generous enough to keep him on by making sure he always did his job as well as he possibly could. But this time he had an extra incentive.

Tibs.

He wanted everything to go perfectly for her sake, as well as Jack's. So, as soon as the warm-up act had bowed and left, Archie was ready. After a quick check that all the limelights were working along the front of the stage, he plastered a smile on his chops, trotted out on to the boards and treated the packed audience to a quick wave, and Mr Tompkins – who'd been persuaded to return with the promise of a pay rise in the *very* near future – to an encouraging thumbs-up. He then proudly changed the title card to the one introducing Tibs's and Kitty's first piece. Tonight it promised to be 'The Young Soldier is Bid Farewell featuring Miss Tibs Tyler and Miss Kitty Wallis, the Pulchritudinous Pair!'.

He then dashed back into the wings and turned down the tap to dim the big central gasolier.

This was it. They were on. Their big moment had come.

As Kitty swaggered boldly, marching and pointing, and Tibs simpered shyly, twisting her parasol and lowering her lashes, the whole audience went wild, cheering and clapping and whooping with pleasure, their enthusiasm fuelled by the generously measured free drink they had each received on admission.

Then, as Tibs began to dab dramatically at her stage tears, clasp her bosom with grief and warble her song of her undying love for Kitty, her beau, the coins rained down all about their feet.

Teezer, who'd parked himself right by the Chairman's table and had the best view in the house, nodded sagely at Buggy as he flipped a shiny threepenny bit that landed right by Kitty's gleaming knee-length riding boot.

'I was right all along, Bugs,' he said with a loud sniff. 'That's definitely not my girl.'

Buggy folded his arms. 'Never?' he said sarcastically. 'How d'you make that out then?'

'I'll tell you how. I'd bet my last sprazzy that this one's wearing queer drawers. I mean, just look at the way they're carrying on up there.' He nudged Buggy hard in the ribs and winked. 'Mind you, I can't say as how it'd put me off the pair of them. How about you, Bug?'

He was saying all this just as Jack Fisher was passing by on his way over to Tressing's table. Teezer's words pulled him up short. Queer drawers? Jack didn't understand a lot of cockney slang but even to a chap from a little village up in the north-east it was quite clear what this Londoner was on about.

Jack turned to face the stage. He saw Kitty tall and erect, standing to attention with a rifle on one arm and Tibs's dainty little gloved hand resting on the other.

They were like that?

It was a complete revelation to him. He honestly hadn't realised. It had never even occurred to him.

But regardless of what they were and who they preferred to . . . well, who they preferred, the cheers weren't dying down. If anything, they were getting louder. If their next song went down as well with the crowd as this one and the word got round – as it somehow seemed to in this business – it looked as if they were going to earn him plenty of money after all.

He couldn't help feeling sorry though. It was a shame. He'd taken more than a bit of a shine to Kitty and as he looked about him it seemed that so had many other men in the room. And the sight of pretty little Tibs in her feminine pink frills and Kitty in her sleek, boyish turn-out was – how had Tressing's pals put it? – *pleasing* every man in the house. In fact, they were practically dribbling at the very sight of them.

It was almost midnight when Tibs and Kitty eventually got back to their room next door. The audience, cheering until the rafters rattled, had refused to let them leave the stage until Archie, after the girls had given yet another encore of 'Champagne Charlie', had, to the accompaniment of loud boos and hisses, pulled the curtains and turned up the house lights.

The crowd continued to demand more – stamping their feet and clapping their hands – not realising that the girls, beaming at one another and filled with the exhilarating flush of success, had already hurried off down the back stairs and up to the safety of their room. It took some time, but Mr Tompkins, who wanted to get home himself, convinced them all to go downstairs and spend the rest of their time – and what money they had left, of course – in the bar.

Some of them didn't have much over to spend; having got the taste for rum with their first free drink, they'd shelled out all too freely and then, having been carried away with the mood, they'd showered the stage with what was left of their hard-earned cash, the very cash that Tibs and Kitty were now counting out on their table.

Tibs had just let out a long, low whistle of amazement at the sight of the final stacks of coins, when One-Eyed Sal popped her head round the door.

'As Mr Tompkins might say, girls, magnificent you was. Truly magnificent. A right pair of stars. But you'll have to start locking that street door or you'll have all the stage-door Johnnies coming up here after you.'

Tibs kissed her friend warmly on the cheek. 'I can hold me own with any of them fellers next door, thanks, Sal. It's that Lily Perkins I've gotta be careful of now. If she finds out I've got money in me hand the rotten cow'll try and rob me. But I'm telling you, I'd kill her before I let her get away with it again.'

'Talking about fellers next door,' said Sal slyly. 'I was standing up the back having a nose,' she winked extravagantly, 'slipped in after the lights went down of course. And I saw this posh-looking bloke with his two mates and I'm telling you, Kit, his eyes was out on stalks, really goggling at you, he was. And as for you,

Tibs, well, that cripple bloke's tongue was practically hanging out like a puppydog's when you was prancing about on the stage.' She laughed unkindly, not noticing Tibs's darkening expression. 'I reckon you could be in there.'

'He ain't no cripple, Sal,' Tibs said, wiping off the thick layers of powder and rouge with a flannel dipped in the china basin set in their rickety washstand. She also thought, but didn't say: *no more than you are, with that one eye of your'n*.

Sal, never one to be overly sensitive, ploughed on with her theme. 'So how'd he get that bad arm then?' she demanded. 'Here, he rides a safety bike, don't he? I've seen him. You do know you can get all sorts of *problems* doing that, don't you. It's unnatural, see. They get what they call Bicycle Face. Bicycle Foot. Even Cyclist's Hump. Well, that's what they reckon. I bet that's what caused his arm.'

Tibs scrubbed roughly at her lipstick. 'Stop talking such shit, will you, Sal. Just leave it alone, eh?'

Sal didn't. 'And you know what it does to a feller's bits and all, don't you?' She flashed her eyebrows suggestively at the crotch of Kit's masculine outfit that was now lying inertly across the back of the chair. 'Sitting on them hard saddles squashes 'em all up like. And makes 'em talk funny. Should never be allowed on the roads, if you want my opinion. And what with these trams all over the shop nowadays. They frighten me, never mind the horses.'

Tibs bit her tongue. Sal was a good mate, the last person she wanted to argue with, but she could really get on your nerves once she got going. 'How's that sister of your'n, Sal?' she asked, deliberately changing the subject – something in which she'd had to become an expert. 'Well, is she?'

'What, our Elsie d'you mean?'

'Yeah.'

'Don't let me start on her! Poor cow. Fancy being married to him *and* losing your home? That's what I call bad luck. Got breath on him like an old sock on a hot day, he has.' Sal shuddered. 'He knocked her up again, you know. And you'll never guess what she said to me.' She didn't wait for the answer. 'I'll tell you: if she couldn't get rid of it she'd top herself by drinking lysol. And we all know what a terrible way *that* is to go, don't we?'

'How did she lose her home?' asked Kitty, peeling off the tight undershift that she'd worn to flatten her bosom. Having just become a person with an address to call her own, she didn't fancy making the same mistake as this Elsie woman.

'Slum clearance is what they call it. Knocking all the Old Nichol down.' As she spoke, Sal used her single, experienced eye to give Kitty's body the once-over. If she was just a little bit fatter she wouldn't be half bad. And with that tight uniform showing off her legs . . . No wonder all the fellers were panting and slobbering like dogs outside a butcher's shop window.

'Over Bethnal Green way,' explained Tibs, taking the opportunity to get a word in. 'Towards Hoxton.'

'That's right. Building new places over there, they reckon. Decent homes, but for ordinary working people.' Sal snorted in disbelief. 'If you think *that'll* ever happen . . . You see, it'll be the next bleeding century and they'll *still* be living with me, I'm telling you. I don't mind having our Elsie, of course, but having that bloody Bobby under me feet . . . Honest, it's bloody purgatory. But thank Gawd she's only got the three kids still with her, eh? Gardens they reckon they're gonna put round them new places. Gardens! What's the use of sodding gardens?'

Tibs continued changing back into her own shabby clothes, nodding every now and again in an encouraging way at Sal to show she was keeping up with the monologue.

'When he went missing before – her Bobby, I mean – he reckons he'd got himself shanghaied down the docks, if you don't mind. Shanghaied my Aunt Fanny. If you ask me, he had it away on his toes 'cos he couldn't stand our Elsie and all her bloody rabbiting. She can't half bunny, can't she, Tibs? Last time he went among the missing he had her believing he'd been off fighting in Africa. Africa? He don't even know where it is. He's such a bloody Tom Pepper. Tell you what, I wish he *would* bugger off to sodding Africa.'

'I dunno about Elsie, Sal, I reckon you could talk them Africans into surrendering.' Tibs shook her head and tutted kindly at her old friend. 'And don't look at me like that. Come on, now me and Kit's changed I'm gonna treat the pair of you to a slap-up supper.'

'Blimey, what's this in aid of?'

'All of this is down to you, Sal. It's because of you we're here tonight. Now, I'm gonna take you to this place up by Aldgate. I went past there once when I had nothing in me pocket, and I couldn't even get any business 'cos it was snowing out and everyone who didn't have to be out was inside in the warm, all snug and cosy while I was freezing me arse off. I smelt this wonderful smell and I pressed me nose against the window. Great, greasy chops they was eating, and steaming-hot pies. There was jellies and moulds and trifles all stacked up on the sideboards. And big wheels of cheese. I nearly fainted at the sight of it.'

Sal's stomach grumbled loudly. 'When was this then, Tibs?'

'Couple of winters ago. Christmas Eve it was. Honest,

I was that starving.' She looked at Kitty, remembering how hungry she had been that night when she'd bumped into One-eyed Sal. 'When I saw all them people tucking in I couldn't believe how much food they had between them.' Her eyes lit up. 'There was one bloke with a whole stuffed heart on his plate. And this woman, she had a great big apple dumpling, all covered in thick custard. That's what I'm gonna have.' She paused and thought about the rubbish she had sorted through at the back of the restaurant, desperate to find something to eat, and how the man had chased her away as though she was no more than a filthy gutter rat.

'I saw Cook, up at the big house once,' said Kitty. 'She was making custard. It smelt really good, but I've never tasted it. Not for myself.' She dipped her chin as she felt herself colour. 'And I've never been to a proper eating house before neither. I'm not sure I know . . .'

'Don't you worry, Kit,' said Sal, nudging her in the ribs. 'There's a first time for everything.'

'You're right there, me old love,' said Tibs with a giggle. 'Come on, let's go and give ourselves a treat.'

As Kitty and Tibs left their clean, cosy little room, Albert Symes was sitting glowering in a miserable, dingy hovel less than a mile away, that he had rented from a tall Dutchman he had met in an alehouse. Albert had a place of his own in Whitechapel, but he liked to keep a few steps ahead of the game by not having anyone know where he might be found at any particular time.

He had had this place for almost a week and would probably be gone from there without a trace in less than a fortnight, but it suited him for now; it gave him somewhere private to plan his revenge on Fisher and Tibs. Particularly on Tibs. But he hadn't yet worked out exactly what he could do to cause her the most aggravation. And that was what he wanted. Because although he had hated Fisher hurting him like that – his jaw still ached when he woke up in the mornings – it was almost excusable. Blokes getting violent was what blokes did.

But what Albert couldn't stomach was having whores taking liberties with him, although he wasn't surprised by it. They were all the same: worthless, useless, liberty takers. Just like his mother.

Jack was standing in the pub doorway, taking a breath of cool night air before he and Archie got stuck into the clearing up. If they were going to have another full house like this tomorrow they would be too busy to leave the sorting out until the morning.

He heard the girls' door being opened and the sound of female voices, laughing and joking. He stepped back inside and pulled the pub door to, leaving it open just a crack so that he could see out into the street.

Despite the sulphurous yellow smoke pouring from nearby chimneys, Jack had a clear view of Kitty and of Tibs's loud one-eyed friend, as they waited for Tibs to finish fiddling with the imaginary lock she had decided, after Sal's warning, should be there for the benefit of anyone who was listening.

'There,' exclaimed Tibs loudly, 'all locked up, safe and sound. Any stage-door Johnnies are gonna have to kick it right off its hinges if they wanna get in there. And deal with me bull mastiff what's sleeping on the stairs.' She linked one arm through Kitty's and the other through Sal's. 'Off we go then, girls.'

As Jack watched Kitty walking past the doorway, tall and lean – but still so feminine – he couldn't help thinking of what those men had said about her and Tibs. He wasn't exactly used to looking out for such

187

behaviour, in fact, it was something that was only ever whispered about in the village where he came from, in connection with two elderly women who lived on a nearby farm. When he had asked his mother about the rumours he had been given a swift swipe round the legs with the copper stick and told to wash out his mouth with soapy water. After that he had decided it was wisest to dismiss such talk as the dirty imaginings of growing schoolboys' fevered imaginations. But maybe he should have listened and learned a bit more.

'Hello, darling. Bar still open, is it?' The cooing female voice dragged Jack back to the present.

He opened the door wider and saw one of the local brides, a young woman he sort of recognised, standing there with a smile on her face and her hand on her hip.

'I'm Marie,' she said. 'Remember? You've said hello to me loads of times.'

'That's right,' he said, although he was sure he'd never known her name. 'Marie.' Then, without thinking, he added, 'Fancy coming upstairs?'

'Theatre still open, is it? I thought the show'd be over now the stars have left.' She smiled and jerked her thumb at the crudely painted posters of the 'Pulchritudinous Pair' that were pasted all along the street's rough brick walls. 'I saw 'em walking off just now. Right happy they sounded. And good luck to 'em I say. They deserve it.'

'I didn't mean up to the theatre.' Jack's voice was low. 'I meant up to my room.'

Marie's eyes brightened. It wasn't only Tibs's lucky night, it was hers as well. The landlord of a pub wanting to do business. He must be rolling in it.

Kitty and Tibs hadn't even reached the end of Rosemary Lane when they were accosted by a group of serious-looking people all dressed in sombre black clothing. One of them, an elderly man with a long grey beard, waved a copy of the Old Testament in Tibs's face.

'What's going on, Sal?' asked Kitty, backing away and averting her eyes from their piercing stares.

Sal sniffed inelegantly. 'This mob reckons the world's gonna come to an end at the New Year.'

'But why is he picking on Tibs?'

'He's picking on all of us.' Tibs spat at the man's feet. 'Because,' she said venomously, 'these *ladies and gentlemen* are members of a wonderful bunch what call themselves the Mission of the Millennial Pioneers. And they are offering to help us miserable sinners by delivering our souls. And I've just about had enough of 'em.' She stuck her finger almost in the man's face and hissed, 'Now why don't you go off and do what I told you to do the last time you tried to save me? Go down the river and take a running jump.'

The man rolled his eyes heavenwards and began muttering in a strange, babbling language. The rest of the group joined in.

'Here we go.' Tibs sighed. 'More old nonsense.' She poked the man in the chest. 'Starting on us 'cos you can't find no evil gamblers playing Pitch and Toss or Crown and Anchor, are you?'

The bearded man lowered his eyes and glowered at Tibs. 'I have seen the pictures,' he boomed, pointing at the posters advertising the girls' new act. 'I know what lewdness goes on in such places.'

He turned to Kitty, who shuddered under his gaze. 'Dressing as a man. An abomination! Reject your ways. You are doing it for the demon money, but what price your soul?'

'No, you've got it wrong, mate,' Tibs said with mock-friendliness. 'We work the skin off our arses 'cos we love it. Now bugger off and, if you ain't gonna jump in the river, go and hang around some other hall instead, eh?'

'Our brothers and sisters, disciples all, are planning to visit every public house and music-hall in the East End, Lord be praised. We urge you to accept our offer . . .'

'What's that then?' asked Sal, looking him up and down contemptuously. 'A new black frock and a long white beard?'

One of the women stepped forward. 'No. We are offering you all a free passage to Australia where, on the chimes of midnight as the new century begins, the righteous shall be lifted in the hands of the Almighty. Aloft they shall rise and into Paradise they shall be received.'

'Would that be Paradise Row then?' slurred Teezer who happened to be staggering by at that very moment.

'No,' Buggy corrected him, with a loud, rumbling belch. 'Paradise Alley down by the Cut.'

Undaunted, the bearded, self-proclaimed messenger of the Lord continued, 'When the old world is destroyed on the eve of the century we shall begin again in the New Jerusalem.'

'What, the convicts been busy building over there, have they?' Sal asked, joining in the joke.

Tibs was getting fed up. She was supposed to be taking her friends for a treat, not arguing the toss with this miserable mob of bible bashers. 'They're the same lot what caused all that trouble a few years back. You remember, Sal, down at the Empire. You are, ain't you?' She stared at them accusingly. 'What d'you get out of bothering honest people who're just trying to earn a living?'

'We are simple people doing God's work.'

'Aw yeah? Why're you staring at my tits then? To see

if you can see me Holy Spirit? Or are you checking to see if I've got me spare banjo tucked down there? If you really wanna do some good, you wanna get down Nightingale Lane and sort out them bastards what mess around with little boys of a night. That's what you wanna get yourself all hot and bothered about, not hard-working girls like us. You should think about them poor kids.'

'And you should think on your own words. Be warned. You are lost. Be found or your children will suffer as surely as those small boys. Condemned to the eternal flames by the sins of their harlot mothers.'

Tibs laughed, but Sal saw the fleeting shadow of fear that crossed her friend's face.

'Take no notice of him,' Sal scoffed. 'His lot don't even give you a drop of soup like that other lot down the proper mission.'

Tibs shook her head in disgust. 'They don't even play the sodding harmonium, I'll bet. Yet just look at 'em. Holier than bloody thou, thinking they've got the right to give decent people like me all their old shit.'

'Please, Tibs.' Kitty looked afraid. 'You shouldn't swear at church folk. I'm sure it must bring bad luck or something.'

'You expect me to be worried by all their old toffee when I've had a life like mine? Do me a favour, Kit. This lot ain't got a clue about real suffering and having to do your best just to get by, or even treating people with a bit of respect. If you ask me, they know bugger all about anything.'

Tibs's words might have been bold, but she didn't feel very brave.

Say the world really *was* going to end and sinners – no, put it straight – *whores* like her were going to be punished? What would happen to Polly then? Would she be punished as well? Would an innocent child really have to pay for her mother's sins?

Jack lay awake, listening to Marie's gentle snores. He didn't feel right. In fact, he felt ashamed. He'd used her.

All right, it was her job, going with men for money. But he had never been with a prostitute before. Worse, he hadn't even really wanted her. Not her. He had wanted someone else. Someone who cared more for another woman than she ever would for him.

Marie moved languidly in her sleep, her thigh brushing against his.

Jack felt himself stir.

He closed his eyes and took a deep breath.

What was the point in denying himself?

Chapter 11

Despite another exhausting evening performing on the boards at the Old Black Dog – three separate shows plus encores – Kitty was wide awake. But it wasn't the heat of the sultry July night that was disturbing her sleep, or even the noises from the river. She couldn't rest simply because she felt so good.

She flipped over on the lumpy mattress, making the big brass bed she and Tibs shared rattle and shake against the wall, and sighed happily. 'Who would ever have thought things would work out so well for us, eh, Tibs?' She stretched luxuriously, tensing and relaxing her long limbs.

She was so much stronger than she had been that night – nearly four months ago now – when she had first met Tibs and now, instead of cowering and crouching, she moved with the ease and enthusiasm of an excited puppy. Regular meals and the exertions of their stage act had transformed her into a firm-bodied young woman with a hearty appetite and a ready smile – a picture of youthful good health.

'There I was, up from the country with not a friend in the world, ready to end it all, and now look at me.' She rolled over again, until she was facing Tibs.

Kitty's contented smile vanished. She levered herself up on her elbows, staring down at Tibs in the pale light that filtered through from the gas lamp outside the half-open window.

She reached over and lit the candle they kept beside

the bed in a jam jar to protect it from the rats. 'What's wrong, Tibs?' she asked, pinching out the match. 'You look so sad.'

'Do I?' Her voice was light, but she couldn't hide the pain.

'Yes, you do. Right upset. I've seen you look like this before. When you think no one's watching you.' She hesitated for a moment, unsure how much she should say. 'I never ask where you go off to, because it's none of my business, but would you just tell me this – are you in trouble, Tibs?'

She shook her head against the pillow. 'No.'

There was the sound of scuffling and Tibs reached down beside the bed, picked up her boot and aimed it at the skirting board. It sailed across the room and landed with a thud. The scuffling stopped. 'Bloody rats.' The emotion was blocking her throat, so that she could barely speak.

Kitty took Tibs's little hand in hers. 'Are you poorly?'

Tibs felt the tears brimming and the words forming in her mind. But was she really ready to say these things? Ready to do something that might be dangerously stupid?

But if she couldn't trust Kitty she might just as well give up. 'I've got something to tell you, Kit,' she began. 'Something I want you to know, but you've gotta keep it a secret.'

'Of course. But you don't have to tell me anything.'

'I want to.' She sniffed hard and blinked back the tears. 'I've got a little girl, Kit. There, I've said it.' She raked her fingers through her hair, pulling the loose blonde curls off her face.

Kitty said nothing, but she'd suspected for a while that Tibs was hiding something like this. She had said there was this Polly she was caring for and then Kitty had heard her saying things to One-eyed Sal.

But Kitty hadn't interfered. Tibs must have had her reasons to keep it private. Maybe she hadn't married the father and had felt ashamed that her child was a . . . Well, was officially fatherless.

'And where she's staying,' Tibs went on, throwing back the covers and swinging her legs round so that she was sitting on the edge of the bed, 'it ain't exactly what anyone'd want for their kid. There's this woman, see, Mrs Bowdall.'

'Does she mind your little girl?'

Tibs didn't answer her question, but stared down at the floor, looking at a world that Kitty could neither see nor understand. 'She used to take in mangling,' she said instead. 'That was when she only minded one or two little ones. Now she's got a house full of nippers and babies, and she takes in washing and all.' Tibs paused. 'All them stories you hear about baby farms and babies being murdered, Kit. It frightens the life out of me. And I'm sure some of the kids there have got the croup. You ought to hear their little chests, love 'em. They sound like old men and women. I don't want my Polly getting sick.' Tibs began weeping softly.

'Why don't you keep her with you?'

'I did at first,' Tibs said, scrubbing roughly at her eyes with the back of her hand. 'But Albert Symes, the no-good bastard . . .' She shook her head angrily. 'As Polly got older . . .' Her words faded as she fought against the tears. 'Some of the things he hinted at. I thought then I should be trying to get Polly out of the way, but I never got around to doing anything about it. I had this mad idea that I could work hard for a few more months and earn enough for us both to run away. Then things changed.'

'You don't have to tell me any more if it's upsetting you.'

It was as though Tibs hadn't heard her. 'He threatened me. Said he'd heard how hard I'd been working and if I didn't start bringing him more money he'd take it out on Polly. I always reckoned it was that bastard Lily what told him, you know. She was always jealous of me. I could kill her. If Albert don't lose his temper and kill the dirty, stinking trouble-maker first. Everyone hates her, Kit, everyone.'

'Tibs.' Kitty folded her arms round her friend's shoulders. 'You poor little thing.'

'And I'm sure that old hag, that Mrs Bowdall, drugs them tiny babies what she minds. So's they don't bother her.'

'What did Albert think happened to Polly?'

'I told him I sent her off to the countryside to stay with her dad.'

'So why didn't you?'

'What?'

'Send her to the country.'

Tibs smiled mirthlessly. 'He couldn't be a lot of help from Dartmoor, could he?'

Kitty's eyes widened. 'He's in the prison you mean?'

Tibs nodded. 'They ain't too keen on letting their guests pop in and out to take their kids out for an afternoon stroll.'

'How long is he going to be in there?'

'A long time. They pulled him in after he got caught creeping this big house down Devon way. This bloke what worked there disturbed him and my feller hit him a right wallop over the head.'

When Tibs saw the colour drain from Kitty's face she added hurriedly, 'He never killed him or nothing. And, thank Gawd, it was only a footman what he clobbered, so they wasn't too hard on him. He got fifteen years, mind. Ten of 'em hard labour.' She shook her head, remembering. 'Still, should be grateful, I suppose, if it'd been the master of the house I reckon they'd have topped him. It was more'n fortunate they never tumbled all the other jobs he done.'

Tibs smiled and said with a fond lift in her voice, 'He always was a lucky bugger, my Michael. And not a bad sort of a feller. Real skilled cracksman.' She buried her face in her hands. 'I bet his wife don't half miss him. Just like I miss my little Polly.'

They sat there, with Tibs weeping pitifully and Kitty holding her.

'This is ridiculous,' Kitty said eventually, slapping her hand on the bedclothes and sending up a puff of dust. 'We'll just bring her back here with us. There's plenty of room.'

Tibs dropped her hands from her face and shook her head urgently. 'No, Kit. It's not safe. I don't even go to see her as often as I want to 'cos I don't want Albert following me. If we brought her back here he'd find out in no time.' She dried her eyes with the hem of her nightgown. 'If only I had a bit more money.'

'How would that help?'

'I could at least get her somewhere a bit decent to stay.' She blew her nose noisily on a ragged cotton handkerchief. 'I was gonna ask you before, but I didn't want to have to explain why I needed the money.'

'Ask me what?'

'What d'you think about us going round the bigger halls like some of the other turns? They reckon in the newspapers that some of them earn a bundle.'

Kitty was silent for a long, drawn-out moment, not wanting to hurt her friend. 'If you're honest, Tibs, do you really think we'd be good enough to start touring those big places? We're quite new to all this.'

Tibs shrugged. 'I suppose.' She sighed, resignation clouding her tear-stained face.

'Yet, I mean,' Kitty added hastily. 'Soon we'll be able to do shows all over the place. They'll be fighting for us to appear.'

'D'you reckon?'

'Of course I do. Jack'll be going mad to keep us exclusive to the Dog.'

'Hark at you. *Exclusive!*'

Even if Kitty hadn't known about Polly it would have been obvious that Tibs's giggling trill was put on, an act.

'You're really worried about your little girl aren't you?'

'Course I am. There's Albert hanging over me like the bad fairy at the bloody christening, then there's Mrs Bowdall – aw, Kit, if you could see that place – and then, well, kids need their mums. Even if they are old whores like me.' Her tears began to flow again. 'And like I said, there's all them stories you hear about baby farms . . .'

Kitty had to say something to try and pacify Tibs, to make things at least seem better. Although she actually had no idea what a baby farm was, had no inkling of the scandals and crimes that had been committed by the supposedly kindly women who were paid to look after people's children for them, rather than treating them as cruelly as stray dogs, or even, in some terrible cases, even murdering them.

'You don't want to take any notice of what people say about them places, Tibs. You know what people are like. It'll all be old wives' tales.'

'If only I could earn a bit more money.'

'Would it really help?'

'Doesn't it always? It gives you freedom. Gets you protection. Buys you chances. Opportunities. I dream about it, you know, being able to get Polly somewhere really nice to stay.'

'How much more do you need?'

Tibs shrugged. 'I'll be honest with you, Kit, I know we're raking in a fair whack here, but it's not as much as I thought we'd be getting. On a good day I earned more on the street than I do in two nights on the stage. Admittedly, I had to risk diddling Albert out of most of his share, but it was a risk worth taking.' She lifted her chin and looked Kit directly in the face. 'If we don't do the other halls, or a miracle don't happen, I'm gonna have to give up this lark and go back on the game. Not round here though. Not near Albert.'

'You're honestly thinking about doing that?'

'To tell you the truth, I haven't thought about much else.'

Kitty took a deep breath and picked at the tatty lace on the petticoat that served as her nightie. 'You know that posh gentleman? That Dr Tressing?'

'What about him?'

'He asked if he can . . . ' She faltered, looking for the right words. '*Hire* us to go to a ball.'

'A ball?'

'Yeah. In a few months' time. With him and a party of friends.'

'What did you say?'

'Nothing. I was too frightened.'

'I know I kid you about being scared, Kit, when you're big enough to knock the block off most fellers' shoulders if you put your mind to it, but I'll agree with you on this one. That so-called gentleman is a bloke what really puts the willies up me.'

'But if he'll pay really well. Up front and everything. And as soon as we say ye . . .'

'If we say yes.'

'He'll pay us some of the money right away, so we can get something to wear. And the rest he'll give us on the actual evening.' Kitty hesitated. 'I was thinking – after what you said about money – if we did it and it goes all right we could offer to do it for other gentlemen.'

Suddenly, the window was shoved right open and a man's leg appeared over the sill. A deep, snarling voice came out of the darkness. 'Do *what* for other gentlemen?'

Tibs leapt to her feet, shoving Kitty, who had almost collapsed with shock, roughly to one side and placed herself firmly between her and Albert who was now standing in their room. The last thing she wanted was Albert seeing how scared Kitty was. He was the sort who thrived on people's fear.

'What the bloody hell d'you think you're doing here?' she demanded.

He took the few paces needed to cross the little room at a nonchalant stroll. 'I said, do *what* for other gentlemen?'

Tibs was shaking deep inside her, but she'd be damned if she'd let the rotten bastard see he could rattle her. 'Piss off out of it, Albert, or I'll tell Fisher.'

Albert laughed nastily, as he wiped his hands on the bedspread, getting rid of the grime from where he'd shinned up the drain-pipe. 'That northern idiot don't worry me. I've got the measure of him now.'

'And I've got the measure of you and I ain't having nothing more to do with you, Albert Symes.'

'I've been watching you, Tibs. Watching and waiting. Biding me time. I've seen how you've been coining it. Getting all the blokes so worked up with your singing and dancing up on that stage. Making 'em all wish they could have you. Well, I'm gonna give 'em all a treat, ain't I? You're back where you should be, working for me.'

Tibs tried a dismissive snort. 'Do what?'

'You heard. You're back on the game. Her and all.'

'You can't talk to us like that,' said Kitty in a low, calm voice.

Tibs spun round. Have you taken leave of your senses, her expression demanded.

Albert reached past her and grabbed Kitty by the wrist. He moved so quickly that Kitty hadn't a chance of pulling away. 'If you don't fancy doing as you're told, just think about what I did to Sal when she upset me.'

He let go of Kitty's wrist, grasped the neck of her petticoat with one hand and pushed her hard, back on to the bed, with the other.

The thin, worn material ripped into a frayed zigzag, exposing her breasts and making Albert grin with delight.

As she tried to cover herself with the bed covers Albert wrenched them away. He leered down at her. 'Don't spoil the view, darling,' he breathed, clearly enjoying not only the sight of her flesh, but also her obvious uneasiness. 'And don't even think about trying anything, Tibs, or I'll have to ruin that pretty face o' your'n.' He reached in his pocket and pulled out a long thin blade.

Tibs gulped, hoping desperately that Kitty wouldn't do anything stupid like starting to cry. He'd really enjoy that.

'You might have ragged old underthings,' he said, running the tip of his finger slowly around Kitty's nipple, 'but I've seen all that fancy new clobber the pair of you have been wearing. I'll be able to pass you off as half-decent sorts. Go for the dearer end of the market.' He bent forward and touched the tip of his tongue to Kitty's breast, and laughed out loud as she cringed.

'And what with the way you two act up on the stage I reckon we might get some specials and all. There's those who'll pay well for having the two of you together.'

'How d'you mean the two of us together?' Tibs asked, trying to distract him from Kitty. She was holding up well so far, amazingly well, but if he pushed her just a bit further she might burst into tears or get hysterical. Then who knew what he might do. Albert took great pleasure in the weakness of others, but especially in that of pretty young women.

'What d'you think I mean, you silly whore? Now do me a favour and stop playing little Miss Innocent, eh, Tibs. I know you brides all wear queer drawers. And as for you . . .' He leered at Kitty, who stared straight ahead at the wall, refusing to meet his gaze, 'you wouldn't like nothing happening to your new little friend, now would you?'

Tibs was eyeing Kit closely, watching her squirm as she fought back the tears. Any minute now and Tibs would have no choice, she would have to do something. Cause some sort of distraction.

Why did this have to happen? Why now? Why this?

She was just about to take the sickening step of offering Albert a quick knee-trembler on the landing outside – anything to put off the potential fireworks if Kitty lost control – when she was saved, not by the bell, but by someone downstairs bashing on the street door.

'Come in,' Tibs hollered. She stared Albert in the eye, defiant and angry, but inside she was praying that it wasn't just some other madman who'd decided to announce his arrival with a polite rat-tat-tat on the door jamb. They'd have to get a lock put on that door one day, but for now she just thanked her lucky stars that they hadn't got round to taking Sal's advice just yet.

They all heard the front door open and someone

shouting up the stairs. 'You all right up there, Tibs? It's only me, Archie.'

'Thank Gawd,' Tibs murmured.

'Sorry to disturb you,' he went on, his words echoing along the uncarpeted passageway, 'but I was just locking up next door for Jack when the dog started whining at the fence. So I listened for a bit and I thought I could hear noises.'

Tibs could have kissed him – and Rex as well for that matter. 'Thanks, Arch,' she called, running over to the door and flinging it open. 'It was just a rat wheedling its way up the drain-pipe. You know how they come out of the sewers on hot nights like this.' She turned round and glared at Albert. 'Here, Arch, tell you what, you wouldn't mind coming up and having a quick look round in here, would you? It sounds like it might be one of them horrible big manky ones with mange.'

'Course I wouldn't mind.' The sound of Archie taking the stairs two at a time was Albert's cue to leave and Kitty's to wrap herself in the bedclothes.

Albert dived over to the window, began to climb out, then turned and hissed over his shoulder, 'I'll be back for your answer, you two. And let's just say it had better be yes.'

After Archie had bashed around the room – flushed with pleasure at what he insisted were vastly exaggerated thanks just for scaring away a common old rat – the girls wished him a grateful good-night. Then Kitty banged shut the window, while Tibs wedged a chair firmly under the door handle and lit some extra candles. They finally got back into bed, cuddling up close, despite the muggy heat.

'Tell that Tressing we'll do it, eh, Kit? I need that money.'

203

'I'll make sure I talk to him the very next time he comes in.'

'I can only hope Albert ain't found out where Polly's staying,' Tibs said quietly.

'He won't have. Or he'd have mentioned it to upset you. But I think it would be good to try and move her anyway.'

Tibs smiled at her. 'You were right brave tonight, you know, Kit. With what he did to you. And him having the knife and everything. You did well.'

'It's because of you, Tibs. You've changed everything for me. That's why I want to help. I just wish I'd met you years ago.'

'Even though I make you sing up on the stage?'

'Even that. I know I hate the thought of getting up there, doing the songs and dancing, but once I'm in my costume and I'm doing it . . . It's not something I really like, but it's so much better than anything I've ever had to do before. You can't imagine what my life used to be like.'

'No. I bet I can't,' Tibs said. She could have added, *If only you knew the half of what I've been through, love, you'd think you had it easy.* But Kitty was a kind sort of a girl, it wasn't her fault she was a bit clueless.

'You told me about Polly, Tibs, now there's something I want to tell you.'

'You don't have to tell me anything.'

'I want to. That night, when I bumped into your friend, Sal. I'd tried to drown myself.'

Tibs snorted affectionately. 'You great daft lump. Sorry, I don't mean to laugh, Kit, but you was dripping wet from head to foot, and covered in river weed and mud. It was a bit bleed'n' obvious, wasn't it?'

'Maybe.' She hesitated. 'And there's something else too.'

'Here, you don't have to go spilling all your secrets to me, Kit.'

'I told you, I want to.'

'If you're sure.'

'I am. Remember what you said about Polly's dad, hitting someone over the head?'

'I ain't likely to forget that, girl, now am I?' Suddenly intrigued, Tibs sat up. 'Here, you ain't been bashing no blokes over the bonce, have you, Kit?'

She nodded, ashamed.

'Blimey, you're a dark horse. I thought you was like a little mouse. Or a big mouse, should I say.'

'I am usually, but it was when I was at the big house. And I didn't get thrown out. I ran away.'

'Kitty Wallis, you told me lies!'

'No. Not exactly. I just never told you the proper truth. See, the master, he called me to his room, to fetch some water for his bath and . . . ' She lowered her voice and whispered, 'He said his son had been bragging to him that he'd *had me* and that he told his dad he should have me too.' She turned her head away. 'He'd told me he loved me, Tibs. Then he said that to his dad.'

'Aw, Kit, I'm sorry.'

'I dropped the water bucket and started to cry, and his dad, he grabbed me.' She jerked her chin towards the window. 'And touched me, like *he* did just now.'

'What did you do?'

'I whacked him over the head with his chamber pot.'

The shock of hearing Tibs burst out laughing had Kitty suddenly indignant. 'You don't understand, I hurt him. To get him off me.'

'How bad?'

'Bad enough.'

'Sod me! You mean you killed him?'

Kitty was horrified. 'No! But I gave him a nasty bump

205

on his forehead. And he went mad, said he'd get me put away. So I just ran. I've been really scared he's going to find me and tell the police.'

Tibs laughed again. 'You big dope.' She pinched Kitty's cheek, then patted it affectionately. 'Look, you've got nothing to worry about, Kit. Trust me. No one would even recognise you now. In fact, what have either of us got to worry about? We'll go to this ball thing, whatever it is, charm some rich old men, earn our fortunes, become ladies of leisure, bring Polly home to live with us and . . .'

'And what?'

Tibs pinned on a thin smile. 'And then we'll all live happily ever after, of course.'

'I know you're only putting on a brave face, Tibs. I know how worried you are. I'm going to speak to Jack again. Make sure he realises what Albert's really like. And get him to put some proper locks on for us and all.'

'Kit, you don't understand . . .'

'Yes I do.'

'You mean well, but don't overstep the mark, eh, darling? This is a tough world I'm involved in. A right tough, horrible world. Just leave sorting it out to me, eh?'

Kitty looked hurt, but Tibs couldn't help that. Jack Fisher might have been a well-meaning, decent sort of a bloke, but now Tibs knew him better she had doubts, serious doubts, that he'd be any more use than Kitty, or even a whole doorful of locks, in dealing with the likes of Albert Symes. Not now Albert knew where they lived.

Albert hung around the alley that led through to the back of the Dog, waiting for the nosy bastard with the dodgy arm to shut Fisher's yapping mongrel away for the night and lock up the place, then he slunk back into the now deserted Rosemary Lane. He stared up at the dilapidated narrow house next to the pub, focusing on the first-floor room he now knew was shared by Tibs and that tall sort she'd taken up with.

She interested him; wasn't half bad, even attractive in her own sort of a way, although he usually preferred his women a bit smaller as they were easier to control. Not that you'd think it, as far as that little mare Tibs was concerned. She definitely seemed to have other ideas.

Tiny as she was, she was a real fighter and, by the look of it, she was encouraging this other one to be the same. It made him want to spit, women thinking they could have one over on him. But they'd soon see the error of their ways, once he'd *explained* the situation to them. And maybe that gammy-armed runt would see sense and all – if he didn't put up too much of a struggle.

But the important thing was to get that pair where he wanted them – right under his thumb. A bit of novelty always meant getting a nice few quid extra off the punters and then things would all start getting back to normal, back to when birds did as they were told and kept their traps shut, and he, Albert Symes, got the loot.

That first moment of sensation, as the drug entered his vein, was really the only peace that Tressing now experienced; such was the condition of his disease-racked mind that he no longer even considered his use of the stuff to be aberrant. It was just his way of life.

The ritual over, Dr Bartholomew Tressing dropped the paraphernalia of his addiction into a silver kidney dish that stood on a beautifully carved and polished rosewood table by his side, slumped back into the depths of his leather wing-backed chair and gave himself over to his morphia-enhanced dreams.

Much of his reverie, as was now usual, featured his twisted imaginings as to what he might do to young Kitty Wallis.

If only Kitty, innocent country girl that she was, had known a fraction of what was being thought about her she would still not have believed it. Not only did she appear in both Tressing's and Albert Symes's tainted thoughts, but Jack Fisher also had her firmly on his mind. 'Night, Archie, and thanks for looking in on the girls next door,' he called down the stairs. Then, seemingly as an afterthought, he added, 'Leave Rex down there when you come up, will you, Arch? In case there's any more noises.'

'All right, boss.'

Jack quietly closed his door and turned round to look at his cramped, uncomfortable room.

Stretched out on his narrow bed was Marie – the real reason he didn't fancy having Rex in with him. She had been waiting for him, lying there, with her auburn hair spread out on the ticking pillow-slip and with her frock pulled up almost to her knees, as inviting as any red-blooded man could want.

The trouble was it still wasn't her that Jack wanted, despite having her up here with him as an almost regular arrangement over the past few months. He knew he shouldn't be so weak, but he had needs just like any other man and when she turned up of an evening, smiling and soft and warm . . .

And what would she think of him if he just sent her away?

Sighing wearily, he pulled off his hat and tossed it on the rickety chair that doubled as his bedside table, then slowly began unbuckling his belt.

As he put his hand to unbutton his fly, Marie smiled

up at him, pleased, apparently, to be there. She was a nice kid: bright, willing, almost pretty in a slovenly sort of a way.

But it was Kitty he wanted. Wanted so much he could taste it. He'd never felt like this before. Ever.

From almost the first time he'd seen her, the day after she and Tibs had done their turn in the bar and he'd drunkenly asked them to come the next day for an interview. An interview! What a pompous sort of a sod he had been then. But he'd known right away how she'd made him feel. And that feeling had made him realise that all his relationship with solid, reliable Tess had ever meant to him was a chance to have his first cack-handed fumblings up a woman's skirt. Then, as the years went by, he had used her as no more than an outlet for his purely physical frustrations. He'd never come anywhere near loving her.

Poor Tess. He'd treated her shabbily. He'd have to write to her. He owed her, at the very least, an explanation as to why he'd run away like that. Just, he decided, as he rebuttoned his trousers, like he owed Marie some sort of explanation as to why he was about to throw her out.

'Look, lass,' he began, 'I know what I said earlier . . .'

Marie, her eye on his now tightly buttoned fly, lifted her shoulders in a dainty shrug and stood up. 'But you've got something better to do.'

'No. I . . .'

'It's all right.' She snatched up her moth-eaten velvet cape from the floor and slung it about her neat little neck. 'I don't need it spelling out, do I?' She laughed ironically. 'Not that I could read anything if you *did* spell it out.'

Marie was determined not to let her disappointment show. She had thought, during these past months, that her relationship with Jack might somehow be different, even develop into something that might, one day, become respectable.

But now she knew she'd been kidding herself and she wasn't about to let him even begin to think she could be that idiotic; that she had had the slightest thought that she was any better than any other two-bob trollop he could use or throw away as the fancy took him.

It was too shameful. Like the time she'd got it into her head that she could better herself by becoming a shop girl, when all along, all she was was the bastard daughter of a whore. She'd been born rubbish and would stay rubbish. That was her lot in life.

Why be simple-minded enough to kid herself that things could ever change? Fairy-tales and happy endings were for kids. And if anyone knew that better than Marie she'd hate to hear the poor cow's story because it would probably break her heart.

Chapter 12

It was Saturday afternoon and the new matinée that Jack had introduced because of the soaring popularity of his – *his, Jack Fisher's*! – hall, was almost over, and 'Sweet and Dandy', as Tibs had decided they now should be known, were just finishing their big finale.

Tibs, who had been out all morning and hadn't seen anything of Kitty until she'd dashed into the wings at the very last moment, still doing up the pink sash that clinched her tiny waist, was trilling her way through the final lines of 'I'm Only a Poor Little Rich Girl'. Her voice was far less excruciating since Tressing had paid for a voice coach. She sashayed across the stage, twirling her parasol, swishing her skirts and flashing saucy, knowing looks at the audience, then stood to one side to 'admire' her dashing young blade of a soldier – Kit parading up and down in a suitably military fashion – while the coloured smoke bombs that Archie had produced from somewhere or other went off around them in loud, nose-prickling bursts.

The effect, though spectacular from the audience's point of view, was usually rather alarming for Kitty, who had to dodge back and forth as though she were actually in battle dodging explosives, but tonight nothing could upset her. She had taken control and organised everything for her little friend, and she felt truly pleased with her efforts. Just a few short months ago she wouldn't have dared do what she'd done today.

It was strange, but having to look after Tibs made her

braver than if it were only herself she was sticking up for.

As she marched past Tibs, Kitty transferred her wooden rifle to her other shoulder and whispered out of the corner of her mouth, 'Everything's going to be just fine, Tibs. You're not to worry any more. I had a talk with Jack today and told him how we're really worried about Albert. And he's going to keep his eyes open.'

She did some neat marching steps that showed off her long, shapely legs in the skin-tight breeches, then turned, saluted and offered her brightest smile to the cheering audience. 'And I've said to that gentleman, that Dr Tressing,' she went on under her breath, 'that we're going to the ball with him. Ten pounds each he's gonna pay us. For just going out dancing. Five pound each up front.' She was grinning fit to burst. 'If I had brains I'd be dangerous!'

Kitty was so pleased with herself that she didn't understand the expression that swept across Tibs's pretty little face. What Kitty read as admiration and surprise was actually panic-stricken alarm.

Tibs forced herself to smile at the audience, but her mind was racing. Whatever had Kitty done? Say Jack realised that Albert was planning to take his stars away from him? With the money Jack must be earning he'd probably risk doing a whole lot more than just keeping his eyes open. But Jack would never be a match for that vicious, evil bastard, Albert Symes.

Tibs acknowledged the calls and hollers of appreciation with mechanical waves and nods. It wasn't only dangerous for her and Polly having Jack – a man so out of his depth it was frightening – involved in all of this, it wasn't exactly safe for him either. And if Jack was involved then Archie certainly would be caught up in it all as well . . . As she curtsied modestly to the cheering audience, Tibs felt dread creeping slowly up her spine.

Kitty, oblivious of what she'd done, lifted her chin, saluted and winked again, acknowledging their adoring admirers. Then, spotting Jack at the back of the auditorium, she gave him a special smile and a wave of thanks.

With the universally optimistic hope of the lovelorn, Jack felt his heart lift. She'd waved to him! And you could ask anyone, that definitely wasn't a mannish sort of smile and wave. They were the gestures of a woman. A real woman. When she'd come to see him earlier, asking for his protection, he'd been sure he'd noticed all sorts of little signals that she'd taken a fancy to him; signals that it took a real man to recognise. And he'd been right.

Why had he ever listened to that drunken gossip of a purl-man about her and Tibs in the first place? All it had done was waste time. He grinned happily to himself. He'd soon make up for that.

Kitty gave a final lunge at the crowd with her rifle – that had them cheering all over again – and turned triumphantly to Tibs. 'You should be really proud of me, Tibs. And yourself. It's all because of you that I've been brave enough, and sensible enough, to sort this all out.'

Jack pulled off his hat, stared into the little square of looking-glass that stood on his mantelpiece and examined his reflection. Should he shave? No, that would take too long. If he wasn't careful he'd miss them. On a lovely afternoon like this they'd be bound to have plans to go out somewhere before they had to be back for the evening show. With a quick flick at his unruly red mop, Jack jammed his hat back on his head, took a deep breath, a final look in the mirror and said out loud to himself, 'Nothing ventured, nothing gained, Jack old lad.'

Kitty and Tibs were sitting on the bed in their room next door, taking off their stage make-up.

As Kitty scrubbed at her cheeks with a damp rag – the remnants of what had once, not that long ago, been her only petticoat – she twittered away at Tibs like an over-active goldfinch. 'It's all going to work out just right, Tibs, you see.' She twisted round, her face shining. 'And I've kept the best till last. Wait till you see this.' She got up and rummaged through the pocket of her peplum-skirted jacket that hung on the jam-packed clothes rail that Archie had set up for them in the now seriously overcrowded room.

'Look. Look what that Dr Tressing gave us.' She held out her hand to Tibs. On her palm sat ten shiny sovereigns. 'I told you he was going to give us half on account.'

Tibs's eyes widened.

'He said we were to get ourselves some thin muslin frocks. For the ball. Everyone's going to be wearing special clothes or something and the top dresses are going to be there waiting for us.'

'Kit,' Tibs began warily. 'A fiver each is a lot of money. To be truthful, I didn't think he'd ever really come up with that much. But now he has I don't want you getting carried away.'

'Don't worry. It'll be just fine, I told you. I've worked it all out. We can get something cheap off the barrows, spend a little bit on ourselves – you need cheering up – then you can keep the rest for Polly.'

Before Tibs could say anything there was a loud rapping on the front door. She gasped in panic, but Kitty merely jumped up with a cheerful grin. 'Put the money away somewhere safe, Tibs. I'll go down and get rid of whoever it is, then we can go to the market and treat ourselves.'

She skipped down the stairs and flung open the street door. 'Jack.'

'Hello, Kit,' he said, far more loudly than he'd intended, pulling off his hat and feeling his cheeks colouring at his clumsy behaviour. What was wrong with him? He was nearly twenty-seven years old and he was acting like a bloody schoolboy. 'I, er, came round to see you about this, er, Albert business,' he stammered. 'And I wondered if I could come in for a while. To discuss it.'

'Well . . . ' she said, stepping outside and pulling the door to behind her. She didn't want him going upstairs and seeing how messy it looked with all their clothes and things everywhere. It was like the sisters had taught her, an unkept home is a bad reflection on a woman's soul. If only she'd tidied round a bit. 'It's not really convenient at the moment.'

'Maybe you'd rather come in next door, for a drink, or a cup of tea, like.'

He grinned happily. 'Just to have a chat about, you know, things.'

'I'd love to.'

'You didn't let me finish, Jack. I'm sorry, but I've already made arrangements with Tibs. And I was just getting changed . . . '

'I can see.' Jack nodded and backed away in stumbling, embarrassed haste. He stared at her tight military trousers and the braces that were dangling from her waist to her knees, and the open neck of her soft white shirt that showed off her long, willowy neck. It was bloody confusing. Here she was, a beautiful, desirable girl, but she looked every inch the self-possessed young man who wouldn't disappoint his girl.

'I can't let her down, Jack,' she said, unconsciously echoing his thoughts

'You don't have to explain,' he burbled. 'I understand. You're busy.'

'It's just that I promised her.'

'Don't worry. I'll speak to you later.'

He fled back next door to the pub, sat himself in one of the window seats and called for the barman to bring him a jug of porter.

He must be losing his grip. Whatever was wrong with him? When she'd come to him, going on about that Albert Symes again, he'd seen her as so vulnerable. So feminine. Now he was just bewildered by her.

He nursed his drink in his hands without touching it, looking through the thick engraved glass at the blurred outlines of passers-by.

Then the familiar forms of Tibs and Kitty appeared, tall and tiny, 'Sweet and Dandy'.

He knelt up on the bench, peered through the clear glass at the top of the window and watched them go off arm in arm.

'You all right, boss?' asked Archie, joining him at the seat.

'What?' snapped Jack.

'I've just finished the clearing-up upstairs. All ready for the next show.'

'What a fool.'

'Sorry, boss?'

'Nothing.'

Slowly, Jack climbed off the bench and sat down, staring unseeingly at the beer-stained table before him. It seemed those men might well have been right after all. But whether Kitty was involved with Tibs or not, she certainly wasn't interested in him. That much was clear. He buried his face in his hands and groaned. He'd even mentioned Kitty when he'd finally written to Tess.

He'd told her why he'd left the village, and how he hadn't told her before he'd gone, because he'd feared she'd have mocked his big ideas, as she was always such a sensible sort of girl where money was concerned. Perhaps the guinea he'd enclosed would please her. It would definitely please her more than the bit in the letter where he went on and on about this girl he had taken a fancy to.

Sensible, careful Tess. She'd think him a real fool.

He didn't even want to think about what she'd have to say if she knew what he was about to spend even more money on.

He was going to find Marie. It was August Bank Holiday and he didn't fancy being alone. He'd pay her enough to stay the whole weekend if he felt the need. He could afford it.

He downed the remains of his pint and held the jug out to Archie, lifting his chin to indicate his desire for a refill but not for conversation.

He felt his face redden as he recalled what he'd written. He'd practically claimed that Kitty was his girl. He groaned again and stared down at his boots.

Silently, Archie took the empty glass to the bar, shaking his head at this inexplicable turn of events. Something had upset his boss and that meant that Archie was upset too.

'Are you sure about this?' Tibs asked for what must have been the tenth time.

'Of course I am. I told you. We'll get something cheap off the market to wear to this ball thing. They're only meant to be sort of undergarments after all. So Dr

217

'Tressing'll never know because he'll never see them.'

Tibs raised a cynical eyebrow. 'Course he won't.'

'Then we'll have just a little treat for ourselves and you take the rest for Polly.'

'I don't half appreciate this, Kit, but if it's all right with you, I'll buy the undershift and keep the rest of my share. You get yourself something.'

'Don't be silly,' Kitty said, squeezing Tibs's arm and steering her firmly onwards. 'You need a treat. And anyway, things'll be easier from now on. Now I know about Polly I've decided I'm going to start giving you half of what I earn every week.'

'No, Kit, you can't.'

'Oh yes I can. I can do whatever . . .' Kitty stopped suddenly. Slowly looking about her, she sniffed the air, trying to locate the source of the tantalising scent of freshly baked bread. 'Come on, Tibs. If I don't get my hands on a nice crusty loaf it's going to drive me mad.'

With the loaf – minus one knobby end which they immediately ripped off and shared – tucked securely under Kitty's arm, the girls made their way to the corner grocer's in Cannon Street Road.

The pleasure of being able to choose what she wanted was still a wonderful novelty for Kitty and she dragged Tibs along with her enthusiasm.

As they stood beneath the fly papers that curled down over the white marble counter, Kitty's order for two ounces of butter became a quarter, then two ounces again, then increased to three. If they hadn't begun to earn themselves a sort of local celebrity – or weren't such a good-looking pair – they might well have found themselves being thrown out on their ear. But the shopkeeper, butter pats in hand, was pleased to indulge them.

'So, we'll make it three ounces, eh Tibs?'

'Have three ounces and have them as my treat,' said the middle-aged grocer, smiling tolerantly. When it got out that music-hall stars – well, budding stars – were coming in the place it wouldn't do his custom any harm. And he'd make sure that the word got round all right.

'Thank you, sir,' breathed Tibs, nudging Kitty in the side before she could protest. 'That's right nice of you, I'm sure.'

He dipped the wooden paddles in a basin of water, patiently shaped the piece of butter he'd cut from the big block and wrapped it in grease-proof paper.

'And how about six ounces of broken biscuits while you're at it?' suggested Tibs. 'Might as well push our luck while it's in, eh, Kit?' she whispered out of the corner of her mouth, while still somehow managing to smile at the grocer.

Giggling like twelve-year-olds, the girls made their next stop the pork butcher's, where they bought four plump faggots, hot and steaming from the big silver urn at the back of the shop.

'This is what I call a treat,' Kitty beamed, burying her nose into the grease-soaked brown paper parcel.

'You've not seen anything yet, my girl,' said Tibs, now completely infected with the rare fun of spending money on herself. She guided Kitty along the street until they came almost to the end, where it met the Commercial Road, and pulled her across the street to a makeshift stall set up on a narrow handcart.

'If you thought the smell from the Jewish bakers was good, get your hooter to work on this.'

Kitty breathed in deeply. She had smelt the mouth-watering aroma of spices, hot frying apples and batter before, but she'd never actually eaten an apple fritter.

Once she tasted the delicious morsel dipped in fine, cinnamon-laced sugar she thought she would never want to eat anything else ever again.

'What a life, eh, Tibs?' she sighed, wiping the sugar from her lips with the back of her hand. 'Like I said, who'd have thought we'd ever be this lucky?'

Tibs, her fritter uneaten in her hand, nodded but said nothing. She was thinking about how much Polly loved the taste of the hot, sweet apples.

'How about if we get going with doing up our room a bit, Tibs? Getting it nice, so we won't be ashamed if we ever have, you know, visitors. For a start, there's that horsehair sofa in the pawnshop where Jack gets our stage clothes. I know it would be really cramped, but we could manage. You must have seen it. It would look just right and I'd bet we'd get it for next to nothing as we're such good customers.' Kitty swallowed her final morsel of fritter, wondering if she could really manage another.

'Kit.'

'Mmmm?' she mumbled, her mouth full.

'I know you're thinking about getting the place nice for my little one . . . '

Kitty was surprised and a bit ashamed. Polly wasn't the visitor she had had in mind – she had actually been thinking about Jack – but she didn't say so.

'But don't go wasting your time and money. There's no point. It just ain't possible for me to bring her round to ours. Not with Albert knowing where I live now.'

'I told you, I've seen Jack about him.'

'Thanks for trying to cheer me up, Kit, and for everything you're doing. But I won't bring her round. Just in case. But you mustn't think I don't appreciate it though.' She smiled wryly. 'It's just that I'm not right used to people being nice to me. Or to Polly.'

'Well, you'd better *get* used to it. I told you, Tibs, you leave it all to me. I'm going to look after you, just like you looked after me when I needed it. You wait and see, we'll have Polly there with us one day. One day soon. And even if we don't get the sofa yet, we're going to make that place a proper little home for her when she does come. And Uncle's is as good a place to start as any.'

When Jack had first taken Kitty and Tibs to the pawn-shop to buy clothes for their act, Kitty had been astonished. Not only by being bought things, things that were almost new, but by 'Uncle' – the name cockneys gave to pawnbrokers – himself.

He appeared to Kitty to be at least a hundred years old. Small and bent over, he had skin as thin and yellow as fine parchment and was dressed in a style that was the height of fashion when Queen Victoria had been a slip of a girl.

Then there was the place itself. There had been nothing like it in the countryside where Kitty had been born and raised. It wasn't very wide, not much wider than their little room, but as they walked through the crowded, dusty shop, it seemed to Kitty that it went on for ever. It was like entering a cave that led deep into a mountainside. In fact, it was a cave, an Aladdin's cave, filled with some of the most remarkable things she had ever seen: a moulting stuffed bear with bared fangs and razor claws; parcels of fine, dust-clogged lace; a tatty ostrich feather fan; odd, patched boots; a fly-specked print of a group of rather bored-looking women about to be ravished by muscle-bound men in classical costume and, dominating the place, every kind of garment that could be imagined.

They were everywhere. In piles and on racks, hanging from doors and ledges, and wrapped in brown paper and stacked behind the grimy counter on row after row of shelves – a special service at a small extra cost to preserve the privacy of the pledge's owner.

Kitty had become used to the shop now, but she still loved to root about, to find the unredeemed pledges that Uncle had decided should be sold off, never knowing if she was about to uncover a glass dome sheltering a beady-eyed owl, a Sunday-best suit, or a table-top mangle.

She held up a length of cream-coloured fabric. 'We definitely ought to get this runner,' Kitty said, adding it to the bundle of bedlinen she had draped over her arm. 'It's really pretty. All threaded through with pale-green ribbon. It'll look lovely on the mantelpiece.'

Tibs examined the lace work and smiled up into Kitty's excited face. She felt as miserable as sin, but Kitty appeared so happy it seemed mean not to let her enjoy herself. 'It's lovely, Kit.'

'And how about this gilt-framed looking-glass? I've always liked this type of thing. The mistress, when I worked up at the big house, she had them all over the place. 'And,' she grinned, adding in a bad imitation of Tibs's rough cockney growl, 'a right bugger to clean they were and all.'

'Hark at you!' Tibs said, digging her matily in the ribs and doing her best to join in the fun. 'No one would ever know you was a yokel.'

Kitty suddenly plonked her pile of spoils on to Tibs and dived into a wooden crate that was half hidden behind a huge stack of books. As she stood up she was waving a pair of matching wooden frames as triumphantly as a warrior displaying the victor's banner. 'Look at these, Tibs. They'll be just the job.'

'What for? Lighting the fire?'

'No. For our pictures. We could get proper photographs done and Jack could hang them up in the bar. There's that photographer's studio near the London

Hospital.' Her eyes were shining.

Tibs shook her head in surprise. 'I don't know what's got into you, Kit, but you seem chirpier than a cageful of finches.'

Kitty dropped the frames back into the box. 'What I want is you to be happy, Tibs.'

Tibs sighed. Her troubles weren't Kitty's fault and the great soft thing was doing her best. 'Course I'm happy,' she said with a thin smile. 'Now how about if we see how much he wants for this?' She pointed to a stack of Windsor chairs in various sizes and states of repair, pulled one off the top and sat down on its rickety seat, testing its strength. 'It'd be a nice change to have a chair each to sit on, instead of sharing just the one.'

Kitty's face lit up. 'You're right. And if we pushed the clothes rail right into the corner there'd be plenty of room. And d'you know the other thing I'd love one day? Wallpaper.' She said the word as though she were describing the most sumptuous luxury. 'And do you know what else I was thinking?'

'No. Tell me.'

'When the winter comes we're going to be able to afford coal every day.'

'That'll be . . .' Tibs's words and her expression froze. She eased Kitty aside with a brisk, ''Scuse me a minute, Kit.'

'Oi, you!' She grabbed hold of a bare-headed man with hair that looked as though it had been cut with a blunt knife and fork, who was making his way towards the door.

Kitty craned her neck to get a look at what was going on. She had noticed the man earlier, just after they had come into the shop. He'd been talking quietly, no, more secretively really, to Uncle. Now Tibs was talking to him and she seemed really annoyed.

Kitty moved a bit closer, not to listen, but in case Tibs needed help. She had let Tibs down once before and had no intention of doing so again.

'Don't you go getting no ideas, Bill,' Tibs hissed at him. 'Do you hear me? I'm not having the likes of you doing me over. Or anyone else for that matter. That's one place that's out of bounds to you and your thieving mates. Got it?'

The man shrugged morosely. 'Never had a bad thought about you and your gaff in me head, girl. I never . . .'

'But you knew I had a place?'

He shrugged again. 'S'pose so.'

'And you can keep your gob shut about what you heard her talking about buying and all,' she said, jerking her thumb over her shoulder at Kitty. 'Now clear off, or I might tell Albert you was bothering me. Go on, piss off out of it.'

The odd-looking man slunk away like a whipped dog.

'Who was that?' whispered Kitty.

'Spiky Bill. He lives with Dutch Bet in one of the lodging houses in Ship Alley. You know, where all the foreigners doss. I feel a bit sorry for him to tell you the truth, living with her. But you have to watch him, he'd do anything to get another bottle of rum to keep that old cow quiet.'

'I couldn't help it, Tibs, but I heard you mention Albert to him.'

Tibs hesitated, staring at the door as Bill closed it behind him without a sound. 'Well, I wanted to frighten him off. And if I'm so bloody scared of Albert Symes I reckon Spiky Bill has to be and all.'

Jack didn't go looking for Marie until much later, not

until he'd tortured himself by watching the girls do their first two performances.

They were pleasant-looking enough apart, particularly young Tibs if it was an obvious sort of prettiness that interested you, but when they did their act together . . . They had the same effect on him as they seemed to have on every other man in the audience. But it was Kitty who drew him. She was special. Really special. And it was driving him mad.

Eventually, frustrated, disappointed and, he admitted it, lonely, Jack left before the final show began and went to find Marie.

When he found her she was with a fresh-faced young sailor at the end of one of the dark alleys around Dock Street, favoured by the local brides when they didn't have a room for the night and the railway arches were too full. She was standing so close to the man that at first, Jack had thought she was alone.

As his eyes grew accustomed to the shapes in the shadowy darkness he stood there at the opening to the alley watching, with mounting desire, as Marie moved the flat of her hand up and down the young man's thigh, each time getting tantalisingly closer to the button flap of his fly.

Jack waited until the very last moment – just before it would be too late to interrupt – to call to her, 'Are you busy there, lass?'

His voice was husky with desire, but Marie recognised it immediately. She swung round and treated him to a broad smile, then said something hurriedly to the confused-looking seaman before leaving him standing there alone as she trotted off to join Jack at the top of the alley. 'Hello, Jack,' she breathed.

'Thought you might fancy doing business in a bit of

comfort and having a guaranteed customer for the next couple of days. Over the Bank Holiday, like.'

Marie's eyes opened wide. 'What? You, you mean?'

He nodded.

'Hang on.' She ran back to the sailor, said something else to him and didn't even flinch as he shoved her aside and rushed off into the night with a mouthful of curses that would have had Jack, a grown man, blushing if he could have understood his broad Highland accent.

'What did you say to him?' asked Jack with an amused smile.

She screwed up her nose and said carefully, 'I sort of told him you were me old man. And that you've got this horrible disease . . . '

There was a long moment's silence, then Jack laughed loudly, throwing back his head and showing his strong, even teeth. 'That'll teach him, messing with other men's wives. Now, how about a drink before we go upstairs?'

'That'd be smashing.' Marie, unused to anything even remotely like a treat from her usual customers, was beaming with pleasure.

'Let's go to the Anchor.' He tipped his head towards a nearby pub. 'I can see what the opposition's up to.'

Marie was almost beside herself. He was taking her into a pub where he had to buy the drinks!

'Look, I know what happened that other night when . . . '

'Please, Jack, don't. There's no need for any explanations. I'm just glad to be with you.'

Jack smiled and patted her hand. 'You're a good lass. Maybe, after we've had our drink, we'll go and get ourselves a bite of something to eat off one of the coffee stalls by the bridge. How about that?'

Marie felt a glow of pleasure warming her through like a hot toddy on a cold winter's night. She probably wouldn't have felt quite so flattered, as Jack steered her across the street towards the din that was pouring out of the grubby-looking half-timbered building, had she realised his real motive for treating her so well. The truth of it was that Jack didn't want anyone seeing him taking Marie up to his room. Not that he had anything to be ashamed of as far as she was concerned – after all, she wasn't like some of the addled old toms who worked the dockside streets. No, it was something else. Jack just didn't fancy people seeing him taking *anyone* up there. Particularly not the girls and specifically not Kitty. So he was going to hang around for an hour or so, until Kitty and Tibs were safely back next door, and even Archie was all tucked up in bed and snoring.

'Don't make any noise,' Jack hissed tipsily into Marie's ear, as he fumbled around with the padlocked door. 'Or Rex'll start barking.'

Marie tapped her lips with the side of her finger. 'Not a word.' She giggled happily.

If Jack hadn't had the last two rums he'd ordered, in his efforts to spin out their visit to the Anchor, and then finished the quart bottle of porter that they'd taken with them to wash down their beef and oyster pies, he might have been sober enough to have spotted the figure standing across the street, watching the door of the Old Black Dog, a woman, patiently waiting for Jack Fisher, the landlord, to return home.

Chapter 13

The next afternoon a small group of men, taking advantage of Jack's unexplained absence, had sneaked upstairs with their drinks so they could get a free eyeful of the girls putting the final touches to their new show - *Sweet and Dandy's Saucy Seaside Sensation* – that they were putting on for that evening's special Bank Holiday performances.

The pianist, trying to hide his exasperation, had just stopped Tibs in mid-warble for what seemed about the tenth time – her singing might have improved, but it still definitely wasn't among her best selling points – and was trying to explain, in as nice a way as possible, that maybe she could dampen down the high notes a bit and try going for a more even type of assault on the poor blameless notes of the song in question.

While Tibs stomped her foot and wagged her finger at the piano player, the unofficial audience decided it was time to sort out getting in another round. Teezer counted out some money from the pot the men had earlier contributed to and looked round enquiringly at his companions. 'Same as before?'

They all nodded.

'Right. Go down and get us another round, Bug,' he said, tossing a handful of coppers at him across the table. 'I'll wait up here and keep an eye on the girls to make sure their drawers don't fall down or nothing.'

'Dirty bugger,' grinned Bert.

A purl-selling competitor of Teezer's, Bert had been

only too glad to accept his rival's proposal that they forget their usual battle for trade and both go into the pub for a few hours' respite from the blazing August sunshine.

'You, Bert, do not fully understand the situation,' Teezer responded pompously.

'That girl up there should be his by rights,' mocked Buggy, as he scraped the coins into the palm of his filthy hand.

'What was that?' demanded Teezer.

'Nothing, *sir*,' mumbled Buggy sullenly, then added as he slouched off out of earshot: 'Maybe if you stayed sober for a couple of days you'd remember what a sack of old bones we – *we* – actually dragged out of the river that night. *And* that you've already said a dozen times how it definitely wasn't her. And maybe then you'd stop bleed'n' going on about being done out of a blinking fortune every time you get pissed.'

'This weather's as clammy as a two-bob tart's corsets,' Bert said, unknotting the red-and-white spotted handkerchief he wore round his neck and wiping it over his sweaty face.

'If you ask me,' said Harry, a younger man who assisted Bert in his purl boat, much as Buggy did Teezer, 'it ain't the weather what's getting you hot under the collar, it's the sight of them pair up on the stage.'

'I must admit, Harry, my son,' replied Bert, 'that there is something strangely appetising about them two. Do you reckon, Teezer, that they're, you know, a pair of whatsisnames?'

'That's what we all wonder,' chipped in a fat, grinning man who'd just joined them, uninvited, at the table. Usually jealous of their privacy, they were all too sticky to complain. 'And this weather makes a man's thoughts turn to all sorts of things,' he went on, with a lascivious lick of his lips and a spreading of his great fat legs, so that he could rub at his fleshy groin.

'I don't know,' said Teezer, suddenly bothered by the amount of space this flabby stranger was taking up, 'London has a heatwave as regular as my old gran's clock and everyone's still surprised when it happens.'

'Tell you what, how about if we get a party together?' said Harry. 'We could go off somewhere, for a beano, like. That'd be just right on Bank Holiday. You know, getting out in the fresh air for a bit . . .'

'For a bit of what?' asked Bert, nudging Teezer in the ribs.

'I only . . .'

'Don't tell me, Harry,' Bert interrupted his young worker. 'You want us to go to Alexandra Park.'

The young man bristled with indignity. 'I never even suggested it.'

'Don't make me laugh, Harry, I've got a split lip.' Bert rolled his eyes at Teezer. 'We all know your game, don't we, Teeze?'

'What game's that then?' asked the fat man. 'What do we all know?'

'Not that it's any business of your'n,' Teezer answered on Bert's behalf, 'but Harry here's brother runs a carting business over Alexandra Park way. And he gets a cut, don't he, if he lays on customers for the racing track.'

'No, I don't,' protested Harry sulkily. It was bad enough having Bert on at him all the time, without someone else's governor getting in on the act. 'It was just an idea.'

The fat man nodded. 'Sounds all right to me.'

Harry nodded enthusiastically. 'Yeah, it's a right good idea. Come on, let's have a whip round. If we all put a few more coppers in the pot we'll have enough for a really good day out.'

Bert looked at Teezer and winked conspiratorially before shaking his head at his young worker. 'Not likely, son. I mean, we don't wanna miss Sweet and Dandy, do we, Teeze? Here, heads up, the little 'un's started singing again. Now that is a lovely sight. Will you just look at them bosoms on her. She's bloody magnificent!'

'Bugger magnificent bosoms,' butted in a man who had just appeared at the top of the stairs, knocking the drinks-laden Buggy sideways in his effort to get over to one of the tall windows that lined the room, 'you wanna get a look at this.'

'Oi!' complained Buggy, licking the spilt beer from the back of his hand. 'What's your hurry, Jim? Got kippers for tea?'

'Kippers?' snorted Jim, shoving the window open. 'This is better than kippers. This is as good as a plateful of roast beef, mate. You look down there, there's only a riot. And we've got ringside seats.'

'Never!' sneered Teezer.

'Honest. You have a butcher's.'

Teezer sauntered over to the window to see for himself what, if anything, was going on.

'Here, he's right you know,' Teezer confirmed, giving the signal for them to crowd round for a look.

Teezer was soon jostling with the others for space.

'How'd it start?' asked Harry, straining to see over the fat man's shoulder.

'It was one of them unemployed meetings,' Jim said with the smugness of one in the know. 'All nice and orderly it was at first, but what with it being Bank Holiday, there was a lot of people on the streets that was kind of merry. And you know how easy things can get out of order. Well, they started joining in with the march. For a laugh, like. Then someone threw the first punch and now, well, you can see for yourselves. It's a right old turn-out. And once the words gets round there'll be no stopping them.'

'Hit him back! Use your fists, you great Jessie!' Teezer hollered at full volume to a bewildered young man who'd just been cracked over the head with a chair leg and was now slumped against the door of the warehouse opposite.

'Yeah!' joined in Buggy. 'Have him back, you dopey bastard. Punch his lamps out for him!'

'Oi, you lot. Do you mind?' shouted Tibs from the other end of the room. 'We never said nothing when you come up here for a crafty look – without even paying for the privilege, might I add – but you can at least keep the bloody noise down.'

'Our bit of noise won't make no difference,' Jim called over his shoulder. 'Soon there's gonna be enough noise down there to drown out a full choir and a pipe organ accompaniment.'

As if on cue, the sound of hobnailed boots racing across cobbles rang out, followed by the smashing of glass and a loud, animal-like whooping and hollering that rose to a terrifying crescendo of screams, whistles and yells.

Forgetting their rehearsal, Tibs and Kitty jumped down from the stage and, joined by the pianist – who was more than happy for a break from the wear and tear on his ear-drums – ran over to the window to have a look for themselves.

The first thing Tibs saw was the little watercress girl. She was cowering against the wall staring at the man who had been knocked down. Barrelling along in her direction was a crowd of hobnail-booted men, apparently being pursued by an as yet unseen enemy.

'She's gonna be trampled,' gasped Tibs. 'Can't someone do something?'

'Leave off,' puffed Teezer. 'What d'you think we are, stupid? They'll trample us and all if we go down there.'

'Don't move, darling,' Tibs called down to her at the top of her fog-horn voice. 'Don't move. I'm coming down to get you.'

'Don't be silly, Tibs.' Kitty grabbed her little friend by the arm. 'They won't be able to see you among all that lot; you'll get flattened.'

'But, Kit . . .'

'Don't worry, I'll go and get her.'

Before Tibs could protest, Kitty was already half-way down the stairs.

Tibs went to run after her, but Bert took hold of her arm. 'It's better for Dandy to go, darling,' he said with a suggestive leer. 'She's meant to be the feller, after all.'

'She's more of a man than you lot'll ever be,' yelled Tibs, shaking him off, and to the sound of the men's lecherous, mocking laughter and their shouts of 'I told you so!' she rushed off to find help.

She couldn't find Archie – he was out the back, letting Rex loose and making sure that the outhouse where the bar stock was kept was secured – so instead she went to get Jack, even though he'd left a note saying he wasn't to be disturbed under any circumstances.

Tibs rapped urgently on the bedroom door until it opened, just a crack, and Jack Fisher, looking dishevelled and hungover in his combinations, peered out at her. 'This had better be good.' His voice was thick with sleep.

'I'm sorry, Jack, there's real trouble down in the street and Kitty's gone out and . . .'

Jack reached back, snatched up his trousers and closed the door behind him with a brisk slam.

Tibs was sure she heard a woman's voice call after him, but said nothing. She had more important things on her mind than who Jack was shtupping.

'It's that little girl who sells the watercress,' Tibs explained as she dashed down the stairs, trying to keep up with him. 'She's over the road by the warehouse and Kit's gone out to . . .'

Before she could finish, Jack was gone. Out of the side door that served the backyard and that he and Archie used as their private entrance, and into the street.

'. . . fetch her,' finished Tibs. She locked the door behind him, sat down on the floor and began to mouth a silent prayer that Kit and the child would be all right, and that there would be no trouble anywhere near Mrs Bowdall's.

'Are you all right?'

Tibs looked up, her eyes brimming with tears, to see who was speaking to her. It was Archie. He was peering at her through the letter-box.

'Yeah,' she sniffed, 'I'm all right. It's just that Kit's outside, over the road and . . .'

'I'll go and get her.'

Tibs leapt to her feet and threw open the door. She wrenched him inside with surprising strength. 'No, Arch, please. Not you as well. Jack's gone already.' She rested her head against his chest and the tears really began to flow. 'Stay here with me, please. I don't wanna be alone.'

Jack had to fight his way across the street to reach Kitty, where she was crouched over, sheltering the terrified kid with her body from the press of the surging, bellowing mob that surrounded them. 'It's all right, Kit, it's me. Jack.' He put his arms around her, holding her tight, protecting her and the child.

They stayed there, jammed hard against the wall, as the crowds spilled past them, making their way along the street and down towards the river.

After what seemed like an age the noise at last began to recede, and cautiously Jack straightened up and looked about him. 'Thank the Lord for that,' he murmured, taking in the welcome sight of the mere few dozen youngsters who'd been left milling aimlessly about.

But he suddenly stiffened as he heard, in the distance but definitely there, the faint but ominous sound of heavy boots, and it was growing louder. 'Are you up to making a run for it before that next lot turn up?' he asked quietly so as not to alarm the child.

Kitty nodded.

'Right then, come on, lass.' Jack scooped the little girl into his arms, took Kitty by the hand and sprinted across the street.

He'd barely touched the door with his knuckles when it was flung open and Tibs had seized the child from his arms. She and Archie rushed her off to the safety of the theatre upstairs, leaving Kitty and Jack to lock up after them.

'Thanks, Jack,' Kitty said, her voice quavering. 'I can't tell you how grateful I am.'

'There's no need to thank me.'

She stared down at the floor, wanting to say something, but not sure what or how.

'You're not hurt?' he asked.

'No. I'm fine.'

'Sure?'

She nodded.

'I'm pleased.'

She raised her eyes and looked closely at this man who had just taken such a risk to help her. 'Are you?'

'I am.'

*

235

Albert Symes heard about the riot second-hand, from Violet, one of his girls who, fleeing from the violence and the fighting, was unlucky enough to run smack into another kind of trouble – her pimp. Terrified what Albert would have to say about her not working her pitch on a Bank Holiday, she began babbling away, telling him how scared she was, what horrors she'd seen, how she'd had to run for her life, and could only pray that he would accept it all as a reasonable excuse. When she saw the smile begin to play about his lips she could have passed out with relief. He'd believed her!

But she was mistaken, Albert wasn't sympathising with her, he was thinking about how he was going to earn some extra money. 'Come with me,' he snapped, grabbing her by the arm. 'We're gonna find the others.'

This was an opportunity not to be missed. Albert knew that when men had their blood up their passions needed cooling and there was bound to be good business to be done. He'd seen it often enough when he'd taken his girls to work the bare-knuckle bouts and the dogfights. The men practically queued up for their services.

All he had to do was work out where the conflict would wind up and that wouldn't be too difficult. A mob mentality took over on these occasions and the crowds moved around the streets like a living creature hunting out its prey. He'd then marshal his girls into the nearest pub and Bob was as good as his uncle. He had no worries about the girls refusing. They were more scared of him than of any riot.

He might even take this occasion to explain to Tibs that this was the day she was returning to the fold; and it'd be a good opportunity to introduce that lanky mate of hers to his firm at the same time. That northern bastard who ran the Dog was bound to be too busy protecting his precious boozer and his own skin to worry about what happened to a pair of tarts.

He smiled nastily to himself. They could more than make up for the earnings he'd lost since Lily had been *indisposed* and not well enough to do business recently. Bless her.

That wouldn't be a bad day's work. Not a bad day's work at all.

But while Albert's plan might have been simple, it still had a flaw. Not everyone was as keen as he was for the riot to continue.

Just as he was doubling back through the side streets around East Smithfield to get to the rear of Rosemary Lane – no matter how keen he was to get to Tibs and that skinny great bean-pole, he had no intention of getting caught up in the throng in the main roads – he heard the sound of police whistles coming from the direction of the Tower. It wasn't that close, but he could hear it all right, and much as he knew the law didn't exactly relish getting involved with a crazed rabble and would probably keep their distance from the actual fighting, he still couldn't afford to take any chances of getting a tug, not with his previous form hanging over him.

Shit. He kicked furiously at a passing dog, sending it yelping and limping on its way. Whenever that rotten little cow Tibs was involved he seemed to wind up with some kind of bother, and he was getting just about sick and tired of it.

He spun Violet round and spat angrily in her face.

The upstairs of the Old Black Dog was now full of customers staring down at the heaving crowds swarming around in the street below. Downstairs was all locked up and certainly safe enough, but the view was useless. Up here, the full panorama of events could really be appreciated.

The only ones not looking out were Tibs and Archie, and the little watercress seller, whom they had sat up on the counter of the small theatre bar at the back of the room. They were fussing and petting her, feeding her with lumps of rock sugar that the barman used in his hot toddies, and the fizzy pop that was intended for making port and lemon.

Kitty and Jack, after having made sure that the child was all right, had joined the others at the crowded windows, although Jack had had to remind some of the more eager spectators that it *was* his pub and he was entitled to a view. As strangers to the area, he and Kitty watched with amazement as the scene unfolded below.

'Here they come again!' went up the cry as a gaggle of boys, who looked barely twelve or thirteen years of age, surged around the corner.

'Look at 'em,' Bert said solemnly. 'Not even as old as young Harry here.'

'He's right,' agreed Jack, 'they're only kids, some of them.'

'They might only be kids,' Teezer said, 'but, believe me, we're used to their sort around here. You watch, and don't be surprised if all their sodding families don't turn up to join in. Women included. So, youngsters or not, belive me, they're to be taken seriously.'

Kitty craned her neck. 'Look at that lot coming along now. They're in some sort of uniform.'

Buggy sucked his teeth. 'You was right about taking it serious, Teeze. It's the Brigade from over Poplar way. This has gotta mean trouble.'

'Why?' Kitty asked, staring down at the strangely dressed young men in their button-sided, bell-bottom trousers, held up with heavy-buckled belts, and their white stocks tied at their throats. Each was wearing a plaid cap, which he had perched at an angle on the back of his head, showing off his peculiar, unflattering haircut, with its shaved sides and dead-straight fringe that had been oiled and combed flat over his forehead.

Not fancying one of Buggy's monologues Teezer, still staring out of the window, took up the explanation. 'Because they, darling, are the Plaid-cap Brigade and they hate the Highway Larrikins, who are the gang of Herberts what reckon they run this manor. And you see those belts?'

Kitty murmured in confirmation.

'They double as weapons. And those daft-looking trousers? Well, they're hiding knives in their socks under them. And I wouldn't advise laughing at them donkey-fringe haircuts, neither. Getting that done means they've been accepted as part of the gang. One of the real hooligans, as they like to call them in the newspaper. It's like a badge, see, means you've got up to some nasty bit of nonsense and have been allowed to join with the other little bleeders.'

This time Kitty could only stare down at what was no longer a crowd of garishly dressed children, but an army of threatening, lawless brutes.

'And see them stocks they've got round their necks?' Buggy said with awe in his voice. 'You know what they use them for?'

'I do,' breathed Harry. 'They use them to garrotte their victims.'

'And their girls,' added Buggy. 'They're as bad. They'll gouge your eyes out as soon as look at you.'

'Can't the police do anything?' Kitty asked, looking over to Tibs for some sort of sane answer in all this madness.

Tibs, having emptied the bottle of lemonade and finished up most of the sugar, was now stoking up the little watercress seller with the doorstep-sized cheese sandwich that Archie had planned on having for his tea before the show and a foaming glass of cloudy brown ginger beer. She shook her head and smiled fondly at her country-bred friend. 'The law ain't exactly popular round here, Kit, and if previous experience is anything to go by they'll be doing everything they can to keep well out of it. In fact, I'll lay odds they won't get no nearer than Dock Street, up by the Tower.'

Teezer turned round to say something to Tibs, but then, instead, said to Kitty, 'Here, did anyone ever drag you out of the Thames?'

Kitty shook her head and blinked wildly. She looked at Tibs and back at Teezer. 'Why would you say that?' she asked nervously.

Just at that moment another group appeared. With much roaring and bellowing, they poured out of side alleys and clambered over walls.

'Look, Teeze!' roared Buggy. 'It's the Highway Larrikins! They've set up an ambush!'

Teezer forgot all about Kitty and, despite his earlier warnings about the horrors of the gangs, he cheered in triumphant glee at the sight of his 'home team' arriving. 'They'll skin the arses off them fairies from Poplar!'

With the unexpected entrance made by their enemies, the Plaid-cap lads began running about in wild disorder, their agitated rabble spilling haphazardly towards Tower Bridge.

'Look at that one!' Teezer pointed excitedly at an unmistakably unconscious youth. 'He's tripped over and hit his head on the tramline. Look at all that blood.'

'That would never have happened if it wasn't for these trams,' said young Harry smugly. 'They're not natural, see, what's the matter with horses and carts, that's what I want to know. I mean, if you take my brother's trade, that's a decent sort of a way to earn a living, but he reckons that when the new century comes all they'll allow on the roads are these motor cars. Everywhere, they'll be. And there's gonna be so many fumes, none of us'll be able to breathe. But if we all keep to horses, like in his business . . .'

'That's enough about your brother's business, thank you, Harry,' said Bert, pushing himself away from the crowded window.

He took a deep breath and wiped his kerchief round his sweat-drenched face and neck. 'We've got business of our own to worry about. Now come on, there's bound to be quite an audience for this little lot down by the bridge. If we slip out the back and make our way to the river we can row right out to the middle, away from all the fighting, and sell as much purl as we can make. The crews on the boats are bound to be thirsty with all this going on.'

Harry looked dubious.

'We'll have a good view of all the fun,' Bert encouraged him.

'And be just in line for all the half-bricks they're gonna be throwing,' added Teezer grumpily.

'Just think of all that lovely money,' said Bert, rubbing his hands. 'See you later.'

'Teeze?' said Buggy slowly, as he watched Harry trotting off after his governor.

'Yeah?'

'D'you know what Harry said, about all the trouble there's gonna be when this new century comes? Us not being able to breathe and all that?'

'Yeah.'

'Well, d'you reckon it's true?'

241

'If you don't shut up, Buggy, and let me finish this drink before we get ourselves down to the sodding boat and start working you'll soon find out about not breathing. And it won't be nothing to do with no motor cars.'

The main trouble-makers might have moved down towards the riverside, but there were still hordes of youths, admittedly not as organised as the gangs, but just as intimidating to anyone who came within missile-throwing distance of them. They cluttered up the street in noisy huddles, threatening and shoving and swearing at passers-by. Making sure that everyone could see that they were hard enough to be out there and that they were just as capable of causing damage as any tartan-hatted hooligan.

They were still there when the evening light began to fade and the lamplighter turned up. They laughed and jeered as he cursed to find that he had no work to do, as all the gas lamps had been broken, smashed with stones or well-aimed coins.

He shook his head with a weary sigh. Bugger. He'd not only earn nothing that night, but worse, he had to decide whether it was too dangerous to stay out on the streets or go home to the wife and all the bloody boot mending she'd have him doing.

Some bloody choice.

Archie was also faced with a dilemma. He was pouring the little girl yet another glass of ginger beer and trying to think what to say to Tibs. When she had leaned against him like that, holding on to him and asking him not to leave her, he had thought he was going to explode with pleasure. But, thrilled as he had been, he shouldn't kid himself that she did it for any other reason than that she was scared out of her wits.

242

But say he was wrong? Say he missed the opportunity of showing her how he felt about her? But then, say he went and said something out of place? Something that really put her off him, maybe even more than his dodgy arm must do. But he still felt that he had to take his chance.

He took a deep breath. 'Don't worry, Tibs, it'll be all right. It was the same on the streets last year, if you remember. The hot weather came along, people got all worked up about not having jobs, the kids got bored and then, by the time the water shortages had carried on for a few weeks, it all went off like an anarchist's bomb. But by midnight it'll all be forgotten, you wait and see.' He smiled warmly, hoping against hope that he wasn't going too far. 'If they don't all get too thirsty beforehand and clear off to find an alehouse that'll serve them.' He pointedly avoided looking at her as he added, 'You don't have to be scared, Tibs. Not with me here to look out for you.'

'Thanks, Arch, you're a kind man.'

With those few words, Tibs had Archie's heart racing.

He was trying to stop himself from grinning like a fool, and wondering what on earth he should say next, when Jack came over to join them at the bar to fetch himself a drink. Kitty was trailing behind him, unable to get that man asking her about the river out of her mind. As if the riot weren't frightening enough. 'Are you planning on opening tonight?' she asked Jack, her voice unsteady.

'I suppose we'll have to see how it goes,' he answered.

Kitty could feel herself trembling. 'I see,' she said, and turned round and went back to see what was going on in the street.

Jack opened his mouth to call after her, but Archie

tapped him on the shoulder. 'Mind if I have a word, boss? Private like.'

'All right.'

To Jack's surprise, Archie ushered him to one side, out of Tibs's earshot and said quietly, 'I might be talking out of turn, boss, but you're a stranger round here. I don't think you realise what that lot down there can be like. When they're all worked up like that they're capable of anything and I reckon opening up tonight would be too dangerous for the girls.'

Jack raised his eyebrows and considered for a moment. 'Maybe we'll open later.'

'Please, boss, think about it carefully, eh? I really don't reckon it's such a good idea, you know.'

Now Jack was flabbergasted, it just wasn't like Archie to be so determined to get his own way. 'All right. I'll think about it carefully.' With that he went back to the window and stood by Kitty. He wanted to talk to her, but she was staring down at the street, her eyes wide with fear. Archie was probably right and Jack certainly didn't want to do anything that would put the girls in danger. Especially Kitty.

While Jack watched Kitty, thinking how lovely she looked standing there next to him, Archie was observing Tibs trying to pacify the child who was now sobbing miserably into her grubby little hands. 'Don't upset yourself, Flora,' she said gently. 'The nasty men'll all be gone soon.'

'I ain't crying 'cos of them,' the child sniffled.

'What's up then, sweetheart?' Archie asked her. 'You can tell me.'

'Me mother says I have to be home by nine. And I just heard the church bells go.'

'I'll bet she worries about you,' Tibs said, thinking

how anxious she was about her own child's well-being. 'I know I'd be right fretful if I had a pretty little girl like you and didn't know where she was.'

Flora dropped her hands into her lap and looked up at Tibs through her knotted, greasy fringe as though she had taken leave of her senses. 'She ain't worried about where I am. She's waiting for me to bring home the money I've earnt. She has to have her grub and a drink, see, before she goes down Whitechapel to work the queues outside the penny gaffs.' She began weeping even more pitifully. 'But now I ain't gonna get home in time and I ain't earnt no money. She's gonna muller me.'

Tibs and Archie exchanged glances. Whitechapel. So her mother was a bride, working one of the toughest areas of the East End. Far worse even than Rosemary Lane. They both knew how far a woman would have to sink to work that sort of rough trade – and how she might react if she couldn't get her hands on the money to buy whatever sort of Dutch courage she needed to fortify herself for her night's work.

'Don't worry, little 'un,' said Tibs. 'I'll give you some money. And I'll get you home. We'll be there in no time at all, and . . .'

'No,' Archie said firmly. 'I'll take her.'

If Archie hadn't chosen to carry the little girl through the comparative safety of the back streets he might well have seen an incongruously well-dressed group of three men stepping down from a hansom, as their driver, following the warnings of two policemen in nearby Leman Street, refused to take his cab any closer to the rioting. Although it had to be said there was only one of the men who actually thought that it was anything like a good idea to be in this area and heading for the Old Black Dog.

'Look, Tressing,' began his colleague, Cameron Hunton, making sure that he kept a firm hold on the cab door, 'much as I'd like to have the pleasure of seeing those charming young ladies going through their paces again, I think I'll leave it for another night if you don't mind.'

Tressing raised a greying eyebrow. 'Really?'

'Yes, I won't come any further. It's all beginning to feel rather too dangerous, if you know what I mean.' He stroked his moustaches and laughed with false bravery. 'I do believe those police officers were right.'

'A few hooligans make you fear for your life, do they, Hunton?'

'No. No,' he blustered. 'It's just that situations such as this, well, they make a fellow aware of the terrible things that go on in these neighbourhoods.' He looked about him at the tall, grim buildings. 'And how these people live.'

'You weren't so concerned before, Hunton.'

'I know, but you see, well, it's like this, I feel I might as well be in darkest Africa.'

Lucian Mayerton, Tressing's other companion, didn't exactly feel comfortable himself, but he grinned at Hunton's unease. 'You spent time out in Africa, didn't you?'

Hunton nodded nervously. 'In the army. And I'll tell you this for nothing, I know as much about the lives of the ignorant cockney creatures who live hereabouts as I do about the natives in the wilds of the Sudan. And I can't say I care to learn much about either.' He was growing increasingly agitated. 'I think I might just tell the cabman here to take me back to the club.'

'Well, would you mind hurrying up about it?' grumbled the driver, who wasn't all that thrilled to have his vehicle within missile-throwing distance of the gangs. Not that he expected *gentlemen* like these three to be bothered by his opinion.

He was right. The men took no notice of him.

'Respectable England has no place here,' Hunton went on, as he looked along towards the Minories, the road that led to the safety of the City and beyond, terrified that he might come face to face with the crowds who were making such blood-curdling noises. 'You know why they're so ugly and deformed, I suppose?' Now he was gibbering. 'I was reading a paper in one of the journals just the other day and . . .'

Tressing didn't look at him, but simply asked, 'You consider them ugly, do you?'

'Yes, I do. Of course. According to the author of the monograph, the one I was reading, it is the result of them coupling with their own children. They all do it, you know.'

Tressing turned slowly to face him. 'And you think such behaviour wrong?'

Hunton's monocle popped out of his eye, and bounced up and down on its cord against his chest. 'Of course I do!'

Tressing said nothing, he merely raised his top hat, turned on his heel and walked determinedly towards Rosemary Lane, leaving the two men standing by the cab, apparently not caring that he would have to negotiate his way through the crowds they could all clearly hear, if not see.

'He's behaving strangely, you know,' Hunton said with a shake of his head.

'Strangely?' muttered the driver to himself. 'Barmy, more like.'

'Not that I know him as well as you, Mayerton. Although I'd heard a lot about him at the hospital, of course, but I only actually became acquainted with him when I approached him about joining his Eastern Occultist Study Circle.'

Lucian considered his words for a moment, then said, 'They have some interesting parties, so I've heard.'

'I don't know about that, old fellow,' Hunton said hurriedly, screwing his monocle back in. 'I simply expressed a healthy interest in taking part in an improving pastime, studying ancient philosophy and so on, as I believe it to be a fascinating amusement, a diversion, something to occupy the long evenings when Lavinia is in the country.'

Mayerton smirked knowingly. 'Of course it is, old fellow. Maybe the next time Marjorie is in the country I should come along for a bit of studying myself.'

Embarrassed, Hunton merely grunted in reply.

Mayerton lit a cigarette, took a long slow draw and smiled thoughtfully into the darkness. 'I can't help wondering what goes on in that mind of his, you know.'

'I agree. He's brilliant, of course, no question of that. But his enthusiasm at times makes him seem quite . . .'

'Mad?'

'I never said . . .'

'You didn't need to. I've known him for years and I can tell you he's becoming gradually more eccentric by the day. He suffered, of course, when he lost his family. But the opium pipe and the morphine needle have become rather too good friends to him, if you understand me.'

'A temptation for all too many in our profession I fear.'

'But not all of us succumb,' Mayerton said disdainfully.

'No, no, of course not. Of course not.'

Throwing his almost unsmoked cigarette to the ground, Mayerton opened the cab door. 'Come on,

Hunton, let's be off. I feel a bit too much like a target at the best of times when I walk past these alleys. No point tempting fate, eh?'

Mayerton hauled himself up, with the immensely relieved Hunton following fast on his heels. 'St James's, driver,' he said up into the hatch. 'And don't take too long about it.'

With a click of the driver's tongue and a jingle of harness, the hansom pulled away.

'Won't Tressing mind us going off and leaving him alone like this?' asked Hunton, unable to disguise the relief in his voice. 'It feels quite awfully dangerous out there.'

Mayerton rested his head against the studded leather interior and smiled knowingly to himself. 'Nothing scares Tressing, old boy.'

Ten minutes later Tressing was rapping on the door of the Old Black Dog with the end of his walking cane, apparently oblivious of the jeering crowds that were circling him menacingly. He felt the sharp whack of a rock hitting his shoulder and calmly turned round to face his assailant. As he did so, he slowly and deliberately drew the handle of his stick from the main shaft of his cane, exposing a long, thin stiletto blade.

His attacker, a lad who had moments before been so brave, was, like most bullies, a coward when confronted. He reeled back with a muttered insult regarding Tressing's sexuality and disappeared into the fold of the now howling mob.

With the slightest of sneers, Tressing returned to the task of making himself heard.

After what seemed to him an annoyingly long time, Jack eventually opened the door and took the doctor firmly by the arm. 'Quick, inside.'

Tressing, amused by the man's obvious concern for him, but not very happy with the informality of being dragged in, looked down his nose at Jack. 'Thank you so much for your concern, Mr Fisher,' he said, brushing at his sleeve, 'but I assure you I do not allow hooligans to worry me. What does bother me, however, is that I have invested in your theatre, but I see there is no show this evening. I must say I am disappointed.'

'There's been trouble, Dr Tressing.'

The doctor's brow pleated into a disbelieving frown. 'If you consider this slight disturbance to be trouble . . .'

Jack, coming from a long line of mine workers who prided themselves on their manhood, felt wrong-footed by this toff impugning his courage. He felt his throat flush scarlet. Damn it, he was blushing. He cursed his redhead's colouring, as he tried to think how he could restore his reputation with this strangely aggravating man.

The answer came to him almost immediately, one that would solve another problem into the bargain. 'I'm not talking about those idiots out there,' he said boldly. 'I'm talking about a different kind of trouble. The girls are being threatened.'

Tressing's frown deepened. He wasn't a man who tolerated anybody interfering with his property. And as far as he was concerned his investment in the show meant that the girls were exactly that. 'By whom?'

Jack considered his words. 'Tibs's previous employer.'

Tressing didn't need any further explanation. 'And what do you propose to do about him?'

Jack was thinking on his feet, but he was doing all right. 'I wondered if you could put a few more pounds on the table. A bit extra, so I can pay for some muscle. We've got the young barman and Archie, of course, but as nice a feller as he is . . . '

'Give me a few more details, then leave it to me. I'll speak to some people I know.' Tressing reached inside his beautifully cut topcoat – worn regardless of the evening's increasingly sultry heat – and took out a silver case.

Despite the din coming from just the other side of the door he lit himself a cigarette and tossed the match to the floor with dismissively casual languor. 'Well?' he asked, blowing a stream of lavender smoke from his haughtily arched nostrils.

Jack flashed a wary look at the door as though it might shatter at any moment and let in the now doubtlessly alcohol-fuelled mob. They'd be capable of a sight more damage than a disgruntled audience. And then there was Marie to worry about. She was still stuck upstairs in his room. He could only hope she wasn't thinking about going into the bar to find him. That was the last thing he wanted, especially as he'd been sure that when he'd gone into the street to fetch Kitty and the child he'd seen more than simple gratitude in her eyes.

'I'm becoming bored, Mr Fisher.'

'Let's go upstairs and talk about it.'

'No. Tell me now. I don't like to wait around. If there's a job to be done I like to get on with it.'

Jack's eyes widened. 'You're planning on going back out there?'

Tressing snorted dismissively. 'And why not?'

Jack shook his head. This man was crazier than he'd thought.

Upstairs, Kitty had given up looking out of the window. It was all too depressing to see the pleasure the gangs were taking in the simple, mindless destruction of whatever they could get their hands on – including each other. Although the men still seemed fascinated by it all and were offering running commentaries, full of bluff and bravado.

'I wish we could go next door, Tibs.' Kitty sighed wearily. 'I've had enough of all this. I'd like to climb into bed and pull the covers up over my head, go to sleep and forget all about it.'

'I don't think I'll get much sleep tonight.'

'I was forgetting all about poor Archie. I wonder how he's getting on out there with young Flora.'

'Kit, I want to ask you something.'

'What?'

'Look, what with Albert turning up and with all this bother, I'm that unsettled. It's got me really worried. I'm gonna go and check on Polly tomorrow and I wondered if you'd come with me.'

'You want *me* to go with you?'

'If you don't fancy going out on the streets, 'cos of the trouble . . .'

'No. It's not that. I'll do whatever I can to help. It's just that I thought you never liked anyone knowing where she was staying.'

Tibs took Kitty's hand in hers. 'Kit, you're my friend and if anything ever happens to me I want someone I trust knowing where she is.'

Bartholomew Tressing was just passing the pedestrians' entrance to St Katherine's Dock, having suffered no more than verbal abuse as he had kept his sword stick drawn, when a woman stepped from out of the shadows of the gateway.

It was Lily Perkins.

He swiftly sheathed the blade and raised an enquiring eyebrow at her.

'Hello, darling,' she said, astonished by the luck of coming across a toff during a street riot. Although, it had to be said, if she hadn't needed the money so desperately she'd much rather have been getting her head down having a kip somewhere; her body was still screaming with pain from the beating that Albert had given her. 'Fancy doing business with the only girl brave enough to work on the streets tonight? 'Cos that's me. Game for anything I am, lover.'

Tressing looked her up and down. She was an addled mess: dirty and fat, and even though she was painted with so much powder and rouge that her wrinkled face and throat were clogged with the stuff he could still see that she was covered with bruises.

The idea of taking her amused him.

He seized her by the arm and jerked her towards him.

'Here, you're right excited, ain't you, ducks? All this fighting got your blood up, has it?' She smiled, showing stained and broken teeth. 'I've met gentlemen like you before.'

Tressing narrowed his eyes and carefully placed his stick against the wall. 'Not like me, you haven't.'

'Aw, I have, darling. Believe me. Take my friend, Albert, he likes a bit of rough stuff.'

'How rough?' His voice thick with lust, he put one hand to her throat, shoving her viciously against the unforgiving bricks, while he hurriedly dragged open his fly buttons with the other.

'You're hurting me,' she complained half-heartedly, her mind more on the money she'd be getting than on the grip he had on her throat. But when her gaze dropped to his open fly, to see if she needed to give him a hand to hurry him along a bit, she couldn't suppress a sneering giggle. 'Is that the best you can do, darling? You ain't gonna be very rough with a Johnson as limp as that, now are you?'

Had Lily not been so busy staring down at Tressing's

flaccid penis and making comments about his inadequacy, she might have seen him snatching up his stick and drawing the sword from its shaft. But, what with the injuries she'd suffered during Albert's attack, she probably wouldn't have been able to get away from him anyway.

Chapter 14

The sparrows were barely beginning to clear their throats when Tibs gently lifted the bedclothes, making sure she didn't disturb Kitty, and got up.

They'd only been in bed a little while – since Archie and Jack had escorted them back to their room, once they were all satisfied that the rioters had packed it in for the night – but sleep was out of the question and she was far too agitated to lie there staring up at the cracks in the ceiling.

No matter how she tried she just couldn't stop fretting about how far last night's rioting might have spread and whether Polly had been in danger. Then there was the worry of what on earth use Jack and Archie would be in keeping Albert away from her, and then, from sheer desperation, she began to wonder if she shouldn't just pack it all in, go and get her little girl, clear off somewhere where nobody knew them and just wait and see what happened next.

Unfortunately, she had a very good idea what would happen next: near starvation, then the workhouse.

She stepped into the dress that she'd tossed over the chair only a few hours before, twisted her thick blonde curls into a tight knot and pinned it neatly at the back of her neck.

She went to the wash-stand and splashed some water over her face, then stared unseeingly at her reflection in the glass.

Jack was physically strong enough to fight off a

woman-beating coward like Albert, Tibs had no doubt about that; and Archie, even with his bad arm, was a big man and could probably give him what for in a fair fight. The trouble was, Albert didn't fight fairly. And Tibs really wasn't convinced that either of them was any sort of match for his malevolent brand of cunning.

Checking that Kitty was still asleep, Tibs peered round a corner of the curtain and saw the beginnings of a beautiful summer's day. But although the sun was rising in a clear, blue sky, it was shining down on a street littered not only with the usual steaming piles of horse shit, but with broken bottles and an assortment of other grim reminders of the mindless battles of the day before.

She sighed and rubbed the heels of her hands into her eyes.

A bit of fresh air and a cup of tea was what she needed. But first she'd see to the pretty young marmalade cat that Archie had got them to see off the rats.

At least that was one little girl she could take care of.

Out in the tiny yard at the back of the house Tibs took down one of the wooden skewers of cat's meat from the hook outside the door, just about able to summon up enough energy to brush away the swarm of buzzing flies and bluebottles. The cat materialised as if by magic, winding itself round and round her legs, and purring like a clockwork toy.

'I dunno, puss,' she said as she thumbed the cubes of horse meat off the stick for the now ecstatic creature, 'you're happy for a farthing. Wish it was as easy for me.'

'Wish what was as easy, Tibs?' It was Archie, peering over the fence from the pub yard next door. He was bottling up, getting ready for the inevitable crowds, who would be keen to make up for the drinking time and the shows they had missed the day before and, just as important, to brag and compete shamelessly with implausibly brave stories of their part in the riots.

Archie tried again. 'Anything I can help with?'

'Take no notice of me, Arch, I'm just feeling a bit sorry for meself today, that's all.' She snapped the skewer in half and stared at the splintered ends, then looked up at him. He had such a kind face. 'I never told you properly yesterday, Arch, but it was right good of you taking that little one home. Right brave and all.' She dipped her chin. 'I was worried about you, you know. You was gone for ever such a long time.'

Archie shrugged. 'It wasn't nothing. I just made sure we went round the long way so's we wouldn't bump into none of them blockheads beating hell out of one another.'

'Still . . .'

'And I was glad to do it. I love kids, don't I. Wouldn't see 'em hurt for the world.' He tapped his crippled arm as though it didn't belong to him. 'If it wasn't for this I'd have liked to have had some of me own one day.'

Tibs stepped towards the fence. 'And what makes you think you won't?'

'Who'd want me?'

'Archie . . .'

'It's all right, Tibs. Now it's just me feeling sorry for meself.'

Tibs tried a smile, but it didn't happen. 'We'll have to join one of them unions they all go on about in the bar. They reckon they sort everything out for you.'

'Yeah, having your life sorted out, that'd be good, wouldn't it.'

They stood there for a moment, looking everywhere but at one another, both wanting to speak, but neither sure what to say.

It was Archie who eventually broke the silence. 'You should have seen where that little girl lived, Tibs. It was one of them courts they've been saying they're gonna knock down.'

'Which ones d'you mean? One-eyed Sal reckons they're always saying they're gonna knock 'em all down.'

'You know, the well-known ones that all the toffs got worked up about. When the Ripper did in all them brides.'

'Surely you don't mean them ones opposite the London Hospital?'

'Yeah. Them bug-holes. And I'm telling you, she'd be better off living on the streets. And I mean that. A bloody sight better. The stink of that place.' He shuddered. 'I ain't no shrinking violet, Tibs, but they're unbelievable. Especially in this heat. D'you know they've got open cesspits in the basements?'

'Wonder they ain't all got the fever.' Tibs shook her head. 'You're right, Arch. The streets are better than that.'

'And there's up to eight to a room. You can imagine what goes on. And with the kids there and all.'

'Christ, Arch, you see some bad enough things around here – I know, I've done some of 'em meself – but that's like something you hear about the old days. It's nearly bloody 1900, not 1800.'

Archie laughed without pleasure. 'I never thought I'd reckon Rosemary Lane was posh.'

'And fancy that little dot coming all the way from Whitechapel every day. I thought her mum just did the business round there, but lived over here somewhere.'

Archie shook his head. 'No, they live there all right. I asked Flora about it. She said her mum sends her over this way 'cos of the trade from the docks and the City types. Still, at least she's with her mum, eh? That's something. Even if she is living over an open sewer and her mother's a boozy old crow who looks like she could go twenty rounds in a boxing booth, she's still kept the little mite with her. When you think how some kids just get dumped.'

Tibs swallowed hard. 'Yeah. When you think.'

Archie gripped the top of the fence. 'You sure nothing's up, Tibs? You're looking right peaky.'

She nodded silently, unable to speak.

'I don't wanna speak out of turn, Tibs, but Jack said something about someone bothering you and I want you to know that I'd kill anyone who ever hurt you. You've just gotta say.'

She lifted her chin and smiled through her tears. 'There's a long list, Arch. But if you like, you can do me a favour and start with that ugly mare, Lily Perkins.'

Archie stiffened. 'What, Lily Perkins who used to work the streets around here, you mean?'

'Used to? The rotten cow still does, as far as I know. She's just been keeping her head down 'cos she knows I realised it was her what robbed me, the no-good bleeder.' Tibs sniffed loudly and wiped her nose on the back of her hand. 'Although One-eyed Sal reckons it's because she got herself a good hiding off of someone and her face is all busted up.'

'Tibs . . . '

'Yeah?'

'The drayman just told me, when he was doing the deliveries like.'

Tibs frowned, not understanding what Lily Perkins had to do with some bloke from the brewery. 'What're you going on about, Arch?'

'They found her last night. After the riot.'

'They what?'

Archie wished he knew how to say things better. 'She's dead, Tibs.'

'Lily Perkins?'

He nodded. 'You might as well hear it from me. The talk is . . . ' He paused. 'She was murdered. Brutal and all, apparently. Throat cut and all carved up.'

Archie vaulted over the fence to help her, as she folded up like a paper fan and dropped to the ground in a heap. He wasn't quick enough to catch her before her legs gave way, but before she passed out cold he heard her say, faintly but quite clearly, that Albert Symes had gone too far this time.

Albert Symes – the man Jack had said was after Tibs – was a murderer?

Bartholomew Tressing pushed past his sour-faced butler, threw his topcoat on to the mahogany hall chair and strode purposefully across the black-and-white tiled floor towards the grand staircase which rose from the centre of the sumptuously furnished entrance hall. 'A wounded drunk,' he snapped, without looking round at his servant. 'Grabbed hold of me at the hospital last night. If that blood won't come off, burn it.'

'Listen, Marie,' Jack said, buttoning his shirt, 'I don't want you getting the wrong idea, lass. I let you stay the extra night because of all the trouble out there. But it was just business. All right?'

Marie threw back the bedclothes and began picking up her clothes. 'All right.' Her voice was low, unsteady.

'You knew all along . . .'

'I said it was all right.' She wouldn't cry. She wouldn't. She'd known it was going to be like this again. 'I was about to get going anyway. I've got things to do. Lots of things. Always busy, me.'

Jack almost handed her a sovereign, but changed his mind and put it on the pillow instead, then he went over to the window, keeping his back to her while she got dressed.

All he could think of was the way Kitty had looked at him yesterday, when he had put his arms around her to protect her . . .

He heard the sound of someone coming out from next door. Throwing up the sash, he leaned out. It was Kitty. She and Tibs were going somewhere. 'Morning, girls,' he called down to them. 'Bit more peaceful than last night, eh?'

Kitty smiled up at him. 'Morning, Jack.'

'Going out?' he asked. 'Anywhere interesting?'

Tibs, who had been fiddling distractedly with the door, looked up at him in alarm. 'No. Just out.' She turned to Kitty and said something he couldn't hear.

Kitty replied, turned to give him a little wave and then, without another glance in his direction, she hurried off arm-in-arm with Tibs.

Jack, his face now solemn, lowered the window.

'I'll be going then, Jack,' said Marie.

He twisted round to face her. She was a picture of misery.

What was the matter with him? Couldn't he get anything right as far as women were concerned? He wanted to say something to Marie, something to make it all right, but he couldn't help himself, he had to turn round and catch a final glimpse of Kitty before she and Tibs disappeared round the corner.

Dear God, this was driving him mad.

He didn't even notice Marie as she picked up the money, slipped out of the room and closed the door quietly behind her.

*

As the girls walked along, neither of them said much, Tibs because she was so concerned with making sure they doubled back on themselves every five minutes so they couldn't be followed and Kitty because she didn't have a clue what she *could* say.

She had tried asking Tibs a couple of questions about Lily Perkins and what the police would be doing about it, but when Tibs had snapped at her not to be so stupid and why would the police be worried about finding out who murdered a whore, Kitty thought it best to keep quiet.

She was soon distracted anyway, by the gaudily dressed women who seemed to be lining just about every one of the unfamiliar streets.

Kitty might no longer have been as naive as she had once been – she'd have had to have been blind not to notice the brides who swarmed around Rosemary Lane every night and Tibs had never made any pretence about her own past – but this place, this had her wide-eyed with amazement. There were just so many of them. These women were everywhere.

And then there was Frederick Street, a narrow turning lined with squalid-looking terraced houses, with an underlying stench that had their nostrils twitching and their eyes prickling.

Tibs stopped outside a particularly mean-looking hovel. 'Before you say anything, I know it's a dump.'

'It's not that . . .'

'I can see from your face what you think. And I know every other gaff round here is a case house. But before we go inside, I don't want you to think too badly of me. I've had no choice, Kit.'

'I don't think badly of you, Tibs.'

'Course you do. I think bad enough of myself. Believe me, I've hated only being able to afford this for her, but

I just don't know what else to do. It was this or having her with me on the streets, where anything could have happened to her when I was working. Or letting them take her into the workhouse and I wasn't having that. But even if I could have afforded the best in the world, that bastard Albert would still have been hanging over me like a bad debt.'

Kitty squeezed her arm. 'I know you've done your best, Tibs. Just like my dad tried to do the best for me. Sometimes people can't . . .'

Before Kitty could finish trying to pacify her friend, the door was thrown open. 'What d'you want?' growled a ferocious-looking woman from out of a fug of stale, tobacco-tainted air. Her hair was a mess of grey corkscrews, matted in wild frizzes all over her great round head so that she looked just like an elderly, pipe-smoking Medusa.

'Aw, it's you is it?' She narrowed her bloodshot eyes and cleared the phlegm from her throat with an unpleasant rasping sort of sound. 'I thought you might be them interfering old trouts from the Relief trying to get their noses in again.'

'I've come to see Polly, Mrs Bowdall.'

'Not to pay me?'

'That and all.'

She considered for a moment. She was happy enough to take the little whore's money, but she wasn't too keen on having her routine disturbed by visitors – especially unexpected ones. 'Who's she?' she asked, stabbing her pipe stem at Kitty, stalling for time to think.

'This is me cousin, Minnie.'

Mrs Bowdall scratched at her sagging belly and stared up at the dark-haired bean-pole of a girl who towered over the little blonde. 'I can't see much family resemblance.'

'On me mother's side,' answered Tibs flatly and took a step towards the doorway.

The wide form of Mrs Bowdall filled the frame. 'It's not exactly convenient at the minute.'

Tibs frowned. 'Well, it is for me. Come on, Kit.'

'I thought you said her name was Minnie.'

'It is,' Tibs snapped, jerking Kitty over the doorstep. 'We call her Kit for a laugh.'

'She's out the back,' Mrs Bowdall called after them. 'Helping me with the laundry. She loves doing that, bless her.'

Kitty tried to hold her breath as she followed Tibs along the rancid passageway and through to the scullery at the back of the house.

'Hello, Polly, my little angel.'

The small girl, who was struggling to turn the enormous cast-iron handle of a massive wooden-rollered wringer, jumped at the sound of her voice.

When she saw Tibs, kneeling down on the dripping-wet flagstones holding out her arms to her, the child threw herself at her mother.

Tibs pressed the child's red, chapped fingers gently to her lips and touched her dull, knotted hair. 'You been helping Mrs Bowdall with the laundry, have you, darling?' she whispered, determined not to cry in front of her baby. 'Ain't you a clever, big girl.'

Chapter 15

As they turned the corner out of Frederick Street, Tibs suddenly stopped dead in her tracks. *'You'll have to go now,'* she snarled. 'Who the hell does that old witch think she is, telling *me* to go?'

'She said it was upsetting the other children, Polly having her mum there.'

'Bollocks,' spat Tibs.

Kitty didn't know how to reply.

'I'm sorry, Kit, I ain't having a go at you, but you know as well as I do that bastard couldn't wait to get rid of us so she could get them poor little sods all working again.'

'Tibs . . .'

'Leeches like her know they've got girls like me over a barrel. They do what they like and charge what they like. And always just that bit more than we can really afford.' She dragged her fingers down her cheeks. 'I can't stand the thought of Polly having to stay in that place no longer, Kit. I've got to find a better life for her. And I can't bear seeing her scratch like that. I know we all get cooties, but did you see her little head? It was raw. She should have rag ringlets with pretty bows, not scabs and bloody sores all over her.'

Kitty took a deep breath. 'Tibs. Let's go back. Let's go back and get her. Take her home with us. You can wash her hair, like you did mine. And we'll get some Miranda Paste for her hands. It's only a shilling a box. I've seen it in the chemist's shop window, and . . .'

'*Only* a shilling?'

'We'll find the money for it somehow.'

'How?'

'I know you used to earn more, Tibs, but soon, you see, we'll be earning plenty. We're going to that ball thing, remember. And we've got half that money already. And that's only the first of it.' She threw up her hands in exasperation. 'Tibs, listen to me. I know you're worried about Albert, but Jack says it'll be all right and I trust him. He'll look after us. Come on, we'll go back and get her.'

'You don't understand. You don't know what he's like.' Tibs's chin dropped, and she spoke as if she were remembering something far away. 'I don't understand how she even survived, the way I was living. So many babies die. You hear about it all the time. Girls, not much more than kids themselves, carrying them for nine months, and then . . . Nothing. Maybe it would have been better if . . .'

Kitty grabbed her by the shoulders and shook her. 'Don't, Tibs. Don't ever say that. Remember how you saved me. How you made me see it was better to be alive.'

Tibs's eyes were misted with tears. 'She's gonna be old enough to go to school in a year or so. And, d'you know what, I'm gonna find the money for her. She's gonna do it properly. Have every chance. Every chance I can give her. She's gonna have books, and pretty clothes, and shoes, and . . .'

'She'll have all of that. And more. You see. I know she will. You'll make it all happen for her.'

'How? How can I make it happen? I'm always saying how I'm gonna take her to the country one day. Let her smell the flowers and see the hills and the grass. Even thought about taking her hopping. But I know Albert would find out and stop me. I can't even take her to the sodding park in case he sees me.'

'We'll take her to the park,' Kitty said, folding her arms around Tibs and holding her close. 'I promise we will. Please, Tibs, don't worry. I told you, Jack'll look after us.'

'I wish I could believe it.' She began to sob as though her heart would break. 'I wish Albert would drop dead and leave us alone.'

Just then, a man stopped beside them. He winked at Kitty, looking her up and down. 'Doing business, are you?'

Kitty shook her head at him in disgust. 'Why don't you bugger off?' she yelled into his face. 'We're decent girls, if you don't mind.'

The man laughed as though Kitty had cracked the funniest joke he'd ever heard. 'Oooh! Fussy are you? You skinny-arsed bitch.' Then he leaned closer. 'Here, don't I know you? Haven't I seen you two? I know, you're them, what is it? Sugar and Spice. No, wait, I've got it, Sweet and . . .'

'I don't know what you're talking about,' Kitty said, hurriedly dragging Tibs away. 'Come on, let's get you home and don't worry, I'll work out what to do next.'

Albert, who was lurking in a nearby doorway watching them, smiled nastily to himself. So, she was keeping the kid in Frederick Street. What a dump.

Marie had been gone from Jack's room for barely ten minutes when there was a knock on his door.

Jack, who had flopped, fully dressed, back on to his bed and had been trying to get his thoughts together, rolled his eyes wearily and hauled himself to his feet. 'Please, Marie,' he muttered to himself, 'don't drag it out. I'm sorry, but it's bad enough without all this.' He pulled open the door, ready to spin Marie some sort of line to get rid of her, but his mouth fell open.

It wasn't Marie. It was Tess. *His* Tess. Tess from back home.

Albert stepped out of the doorway, slumped against the wall and lit a cigarette. He drew the smoke deep into his lungs and watched the girls rushing off in the direction of Rosemary Lane.

Silly tart. Fancy thinking she could keep anything from him once he'd set his mind on it. Maybe if she hadn't been so cocky with him he'd have been a bit nicer to her.

He knew one thing: she'd be wishing she had been nicer to him once he got hold of her. He was going to wipe the smile right off that pretty little dimple-cheeked face of hers for good.

He laughed out loud at the thought and ground the finished butt hard under the steel-rimmed heel of his boot.

The sound of approaching footsteps had Albert on the alert. He levered himself away from the wall and looked up and down the narrow street. He didn't fancy being spotted by another pimp, who might start asking difficult questions about what he was doing hanging around someone else's patch – someone who might be carrying a cosh, or worse, someone who might have a pistol tucked inside his waistband.

He couldn't see anyone, which was a relief, he'd never liked explaining himself, especially when there might be pain involved.

Albert relaxed and took out another cigarette; he was enjoying himself, savouring the image of Tibs begging him to stop, then imploring him to finish her off.

He had just flicked the spent match into the gutter

when a hand touched him lightly on the shoulder. He spun round, his eyes wide. 'What the hell . . .'

'Albert Symes?' the person asked.

It wasn't really a question.

The next morning Archie was, as usual, out the back, getting on with his work, when he heard a sound coming from the yard next door. He looked over the fence and smiled. It was Tibs, exactly who he'd been hoping to see.

He watched her for a moment, thinking how lovely but serious she looked, as she concentrated on pegging out the washing, and felt a silly, but pleasing, thrill of achievement because she was using the line that he, Archie Hutchinson, had strung up for her. 'Morning, Tibs,' he said at last.

She looked up, nodded and offered him a thin, strained smile.

'Jack said you went out with Kitty yesterday. Have a nice time, did you?'

Tibs jumped as if she'd been wired up to the electric light and only just saved the wet petticoat she was holding from falling on to the dusty flagstones.

'Jack said we went out, did he?' She sounded flustered. 'Well, we didn't. We just went for a walk. All right?'

Archie held up his good arm in surrender. 'I'm sorry, Tibs. I didn't mean to pry or nothing.'

'No, Arch, I *m* sorry. Things have just been a bit, you know . . .' She shrugged.

Archie nodded. 'You must be shocked, I suppose. By that . . . ' How could he put it nicely? 'By that *friend* of yours getting done in like that.'

'Me? Upset over Lily?' Tibs's eyes were like saucers. 'I don't wanna sound hard, Arch, and I wouldn't wish me worst enemy to go the way they're saying she went, but

I can't honestly say I'm that sorry she ain't around any more. When you see how some have to suffer, that bitch was well down my list of who I spend me time worrying about.' She rammed the peg down hard over the wet petticoat and picked up a blouse, shaking out the surplus water at arm's length. 'Yes, Arch, there's plenty more deserving of me sympathy than her.'

'Like little Flora having to come all the way over here to sell her watercress?'

'Yeah, just like her.' Tibs nibbled at her lips, as images of the scrawny, frightened child, and of her own little Polly, swam around in her tear-blurred vision. She wouldn't cry again. She wouldn't. It was all she seemed to bloody do lately.

Archie ran his fingers through his hair. He hadn't got off to a very good start. How was he going to say this so it came out right? 'It don't sound like you've heard the other news, eh?'

'What's that then?' She took a peg off the line and gripped it in her teeth.

Archie took a deep breath. 'They reckon there must be some sort of, er, maniac or something on the loose.'

'Maniac?' She threw the wet blouse to the ground and rushed to the fence. 'Archie, where are you talking about? He's not hurt . . . ' How could she say the words?

'I'm sorry, Tibs, I didn't mean to frighten you . . .'

'What? Just tell me.'

'It was over by Frederick Street.'

Tibs felt her world falling about her, then spinning away, out of control. Surely Albert hadn't found out that Polly was with Mrs Bowdall. He couldn't have. He just couldn't. Because if he had, then . . . Aw, no. Please God, no. 'Archie. Tell me. Please.'

'It's that Albert Symes.'

Her blood froze. 'Archie. What's he done?'

'He ain't done nothing.'

'So what . . .'

'One of the brides over there. She found him. In an alley, he was. Dead as a doornail.'

'Dead?'

'Cut to ribbons and his throat slit. Just like Lily Perkins.'

Tibs took a step back.

'Like you were saying, I know it's a terrible way to go. But I thought, well, after Jack mentioning you being bothered by him and what you said about him yesterday I thought you'd be glad he was out of the way. You are glad, aren't you, Tibs? Tibs?'

Tibs looked at him and blinked. She *had* said Albert's name to Archie, she remembered, before she'd passed out. And Jack had told him to keep an eye out for him. And now . . . He'd been cut to ribbons. That's what he'd said.

No, it was ridiculous. Not Archie. He couldn't have. He wasn't like that.

'Are you all right, Tibs?'

Her only reply was a brief nod, then, ignoring the heap of wet washing at her feet she turned on her heel, hitched up her skirts and ran from the yard.

'Be careful if you're going out, Tibs. They're saying it's just like what happened to that poor girl they found back in the spring,' Archie called after her. But she didn't hear him – she was yelling at the top of her voice for Kit to wake up and get dressed.

'So, will it be all right then, Jack?' Tibs's eyes were pleading. 'She wouldn't be no nuisance or anything if you let me bring her back here to live with us. I promise. She'd be ever so quiet. And . . .'

'And we need the other room,' Kitty butted in, nearly

271

as excited as Tibs, 'so we can make the place nice for her. A proper home, with a sitting-room and everything. She's a lovely little thing, you wait and see.'

Jack was feeling confused. He had been sitting quietly alone in the bar, supposedly going over the weekly figures, but actually trying to figure out what the hell he was going to do about Tess, when these two had burst in like a pair of whirling dervishes.

First Tibs had started rattling on about a little girl – *her* little girl, from what he could make out – and then Kitty, usually so reserved, had started demanding he give them another room. Well, not demanding exactly, but she was certainly being forceful all right. What was going on?

'How is it you never mentioned this kiddie before, like?' he asked, scratching his head. Having Tess around and seeing what she had turned into – or what she had really been like all along, maybe – had made him suspicious. Maybe the girls were working on a scam, planning on taking in lodgers next door, or even setting up some sort of case house on the quiet.

Tibs glanced sideways at Kitty, who encouraged her with a nod. 'Albert,' she said, as though that explained everything, then stared down at her feet and added, 'I was too scared to bring her here in case he found out. It wasn't just me the bullying bastard was threatening. I couldn't risk him knowing where she was.'

'We went to see Polly yesterday,' Kitty began.

Jack felt like cheering. That's where they went, to see this nipper of Tibs's. And that's why they were so secretive. 'You went to see her, did you?'

'We did. And it was a terrible place.' Kitty shook her head at the memory.

'And that's why I want to bring her here. Back home with me, where she belongs. Please, Jack.'

'There's plenty of room next door, of course, although it'd take lots of work to sort it out,' he said slowly. 'But why aren't you worried about this Albert any more?' Jack couldn't help wondering if Tressing had said something to the girls about him keeping Albert out of the way. For reasons Jack really didn't want to think too much about he didn't much like the idea of Tressing having too much to do with them.

'He can't hurt her now,' said Kitty in a dramatic whisper. She leaned forward and with eyes opened wide she breathed, 'He's been murdered!'

Later, as Jack knelt on the bench in the bar, craning his neck to see out of the clear top of the window, watching the girls race off along the street to fetch the child, he wondered how on earth he'd managed to hide his reaction at the news of Albert's death.

He knew Tressing was a strange one, but surely he couldn't have had anything to do with it?

No. It was a ridiculous idea. And it wasn't as if murder was that rare in the East End slums where life seemed to be so cheap. In fact, when he thought about it, he'd only been here a matter of days when that girl had been found carved up like a slaughtered animal, just a few hundred yards away, up by the Royal Mint.

And anyway, Jack had worse problems than worrying about the death of a man who, from what he'd gathered, was capable of committing just about any sort of crime you cared to mention, murder included no doubt. He'd have wound up on the gallows anyway, more than likely.

It was probably just someone settling an old score. A score they'd all be far better off knowing nothing about. When Jack came to think about it the world was a better place without the likes of Albert Symes.

What he really had to sort out was his own life. He wanted to know exactly what Kitty thought of him and then to do something about Tess.

Tess.

Now there was a problem.

She wasn't much like the person he'd remembered. Granted, she had always come across as a sensible if slightly stern type of a girl, but now he saw her quite differently. She was a hard-faced, caustic-tongued woman. Yes, she'd probably suffered when he'd left the village – no one would care for being left behind like that – but she seemed to have got over it soon enough and had married the first lad with decent savings who'd asked her.

But the marriage hadn't lasted. Within a month the new bride had become a widow. The pits had claimed another group of lives. And now she was determined to find yet another new start in life. And good for her. But what concerned Jack was that he – or rather his money – seemed to figure quite prominently in her plans.

He pulled off his battered old hat, raked back his hair and sighed.

Why did life have to be so bloody complicated, that's what he wanted to know.

Chapter 16

It was Saturday morning, only a week since Polly had been brought back to the house, but she was already looking like a different child – clean, far less anxious about being sent back to Mrs Bowdall's and growing happier with each day that passed.

'You know, Kit, I've never been much of a one for mornings before,' said Tibs, as she gently stroked the head of her golden-haired daughter, who was sleeping contentedly between them. 'But now I really look forward to waking up. Even after doing three shows a night it's a pleasure opening my eyes and seeing this little angel, and knowing that that bastard's not waiting down some alley, ready to pounce on me and ruin everything.'

Kitty got out of the bed, careful not to disturb Polly, stretched and yawned. 'Any plans?' she asked, pouring some water from the jug into the wash-basin.

Tibs nodded. 'With this lovely weather holding up I thought Polly could do with some fresh air. And I want to get her a few bits and pieces, so I can chuck away them horrible rags that old cow had her in. So, how about coming down the market with us?'

'If you're sure you want me to come.'

'Course I do. Why d'you say that?'

'You've been a bit . . . I don't know how to say it.'

'Say what?'

'I feel silly.'

'*Kit*.'

She shrugged gloomily. 'I thought you might not want me around any more.'

Tibs crawled off the bed and pulled Kitty over to the window. 'What the hell are you talking about?'

'I know you've got a lot to think about, but you've been sort of different.'

Tibs touched her gently on the cheek. 'Kit, I'm sorry, love. But, you know, what with Polly coming home . . .'

'And Albert being killed?'

Tibs flapped her hands casually. '*Albert being killed*? Why would that worry me?'

'All right, all right,' called Archie, 'I'm coming. What's wrong with everyone this morning, eh, Rex?' he said, grabbing the growling dog by the scruff of his neck. 'People bashing on the door, trying to get in the bar and it's not even ten o'clock, and you acting like you was some big old guard dog after a burglar or something.'

Archie pinned Rex firmly between his knees, while he unbolted the door with his good hand. 'Oh, it's you.'

Dr Tressing took off his hat and moved forward to step inside, but Archie stood his ground, blocking the doorway.

'Mr Fisher's out,' he said, tempted to let Rex go. The dog didn't like this bloke and nor did he for that matter. He knew Jack had needed his backing and had been glad he'd come up with the money for him, but there was something about him that Archie just couldn't stomach.

'It's not him I came to see. Now move aside and let me in. And tell Miss Wallis,' he paused, 'and Miss Tyler I wish to see them.'

Archie felt relieved at honestly being able to say, 'They're out as well.' Then added less truthfully, as he'd spoken to Kitty only a few minutes ago, 'And, before you ask, no I don't know where, and I can't let you in 'cos I'm going out and all.'

Kitty and Tibs walked along with the sun on their backs, each holding one of Polly's hands. Tibs pointed out a twittering starling perched on the bar of a lamp-post and a dusty weed growing up through a crack in the gutter to her wide-eyed child, who was taking such delight in the simple childhood pleasures that her mother had, until now, been unable to give her.

Then, when they turned into a small street off Cable Street and Polly gasped out loud as she caught sight of the colour and bustle of the busy market, Tibs could have cried with joy at her child's happiness – and regret at the time they had lost. 'You don't remember this, do you, darling,' she said. ' 'Cos you was a tiny little thing when I used to bring you here. I'd carry you around in my arms, snuggled up to me, like a baby bird all warm in her nest.' She waited for Polly to repeat what had become her favourite phrase.

'Tell me again what I was like?'

'You was my little princess and I'll never ever let anyone take you away again. Not ever.' Tibs kissed the top of Polly's head. 'Now come on, let's go and see what we can find for you.'

The three of them moved from trader to trader; one minute sorting through piles of bright ribbons and the next considering the quality of the dull bundles of 'hardly worn' flannel petticoats that, in only a month or so, they'd be layering up under their top clothes to keep out the chill.

By the time they had walked from one end of the market to the other and back again – just to make sure they hadn't missed any treasures in between – Tibs and Kitty were laden with bags of second-hand children's clothes, a pair of little red button boots that looked almost as good as new from the shoe doctor and three fat, juicy pears to enjoy after their supper.

'I reckon we deserve a nice cuppa before we get off home, don't you?' said Tibs, lifting her chin at the coffee stall. 'And a big cup o' milk for me baby.'

As they sipped at their drinks Polly watched, warily at first, peeping from behind her mother's skirts, but then laughing happily, as a gang of boys arrived at the market hanging on to the tail-board of a cart, the Blakeys on the soles of their boots sparking and cracking as they dragged their feet over the cobbles.

'Taking passengers now, Alf?' hollered a ruddy-faced costermonger at the driver. 'Make sure they pay their fares, won't you!'

The carman twisted round and, seeing the boys, flicked his whip angrily at them. They immediately let go and fell in a laughing heap to the ground. But they were soon on their feet again, starting on their next bit of mischief, circling and taunting the man who had just parked his garishly painted ice-cream cart by the refreshment stand.

'Hokey Pokey, farthing a lump,' they yelled, jumping up and down as they recited their rhyme. 'The more you eat, the more you trump!'

'Bloody street-Arabs,' Tibs chided them, but at the same time tossed them a silver threepenny piece. 'Go on, get yourselves a farthing lick each,' she went on, pointing to the stack of thick glass returnable cones that the ice-cream came scraped into. 'And don't be so bloody rude to grown-ups in future.'

Tibs turned round to pay for their drinks – she had refused to allow Kitty to pay for anything today – when someone called her name.

She looked over her shoulder and saw Archie, puffing

and blowing as though he'd just competed in the hundred-yard dash.

'I found you,' he gasped.

Tibs bent down and said something to Polly, then ushered her towards Kitty. 'Take Polly over there a minute, will you, Kit?'

'Where?' Kitty was completely taken by surprise. Tibs had been so protective of her little girl since they'd fetched her home that she barely let her out of her sight and was forever running in and out of the pub to go next door and check on her, even though she was sound asleep in bed, with the young barman's clucking old Aunt Sarah keeping an over-protective eye on her.

'I dunno, Kit,' she said distractedly. 'Show her the barrel-organ man's monkey or something. Just take her, eh?'

'All right.' Kitty nodded and led Polly away.

Satisfied they were out of earshot, Tibs turned to Archie and said firmly, 'What's wrong with you? You're panting like you're being chased. Not got someone after you, have you?'

He wasn't sure what to say. He'd come to warn her about Tressing, but the man hadn't actually done anything he could really point to. It was just this feeling he had. And while Archie certainly didn't want Tibs to think he was interfering, or, worse still, that he was raving bonkers accusing a doctor of something Archie couldn't even put his finger on, at least he now knew she was safe and well.

'Well?' Tibs demanded.

'Nothing really. There was just this weird bloke hanging around, that's all. And I wanted to make sure he wasn't, you know, bothering you.'

'What bloke? What're you talking about?'

'One of them . . . stage-door Johnny types,' he -

improvised. 'Never left no flowers though.' Archie looked about him for a distraction. 'Nice sunny day for September, eh, Tibs?'

Tibs stared at him. He was certainly acting strangely. But was that really any reason to think he might have had something to do with Albert being done in? It was hard to credit it, the attack was so savage. But he had said, bold as anything, that he'd kill anyone who hurt her.

She looked round to check on Polly, then hissed at Archie, 'What's really going on?'

Archie looked startled. 'Going on? I told you. Nothing. Fancied getting out in the sunshine, you know, having a bit of a walk and I thought – kill two birds with one stone – make sure Tibs is all right at the same time.'

'I hardly think a stage-door Johnny's gonna come looking for me down the market, now is he?'

Archie shrugged. 'I was just worried. Sorry if I over-stepped the mark.'

'And I'm sorry to interrupt.'

Tibs twisted round. It was Kitty. She was holding Polly's hand safely enough, but she was looking really harassed. 'I know you're talking, but . . .'

'What?' Tibs snatched Polly up into her arms and held her close. 'What's wrong?'

'I sort of told Polly we'll take her to the seaside. It just sort of . . .'

'Tomorrow!' piped Polly excitedly.

Tibs felt relief wash through her. 'That's a smashing idea,' she said, squeezing Polly tight. 'We can go over to the beach at Greenwich.'

'Greenwich!' Polly squeaked with pleasure.

'No,' said Tibs. 'We'll go to the proper seaside. We'll go to Southend. I've not been there for years.'

Polly didn't know what any of this meant but it sounded a lot better than mangling in Mrs Bowdall's scullery. 'And Uncle Archie can come!'

Archie shrugged. 'Your mum won't want me coming along, Poll.'

He was right, Tibs didn't much fancy the idea of having a man who might be capable of such violence going on an outing with her child, but before she could come up with a way of saying so, without accusing him of such terrible things in front of Polly, Kitty had settled the matter.

'Of course we do, Archie,' she said, flashing a smile at her friend. 'Don't we, Tibs?'

'Well,' he said, ruffling Polly's hair, 'it looks like I'm invited.'

'And we'll invite Uncle Jack and all,' said Tibs with what she hoped was a carefree laugh. 'Safety in numbers, eh, Kit?'

It was nine o'clock the next morning and Jack was like a dog with two tails at the prospect of going on an outing with Kitty. Not that he'd ever been to Southend, but they could have been going down the mine and he'd still have been thrilled. The only fly in the ointment of this glorious morning was Tess.

There she was, sitting on the edge of the bed – where she had taken to sleeping, while he was forced to camp out on the floor – with her back stiff, her lips pursed and a look on her face that could have curdled milk.

'And where do you think you're off to all dressed up like a dog's dinner?'

'I've had a wash and a shave, Tess,' he said, fastening his collar stud. 'I'm not wearing white tie and bloody tails.'

'And there's no need for that kind of language, Jack

Fisher. You're not talking to one of your cockney guttersnipes now you know.'

'I'm going out for the day.'

'Wasting more money, I suppose.'

'Tess, I offered to give you your fare home on the train. I'm even prepared to stump up for second class. What more d'you want from me?'

She laughed unpleasantly. 'This is fine behaviour, this is. You could send me a guinea in a letter, just like that, but now all you're offering me is a few pounds, and you expect me to be satisfied and to disappear out of your life for ever.' She looked him up and down. 'But then, that was before you got involved with your fancy new friends.'

Jack sighed in desperation. 'You can't be happy being stuck up here in this poky little room.' Then he added under his breath, 'Even if you have taken my bloody bed.'

'I'm not, but then I'm not exactly thrilled at the prospect of you going out spending money on rubbish either. But I don't get much say in it.'

'We've gone over all this too many times to need to say it again, Tess, but I'll say it this once more. I'm prepared to give you money. I wouldn't want to see any widow woman going short, but I'm sorry, I'm not prepared to give you half of everything. I've had to work hard to achieve all this. Had to put in all the hard graft and take all the risks. I'm not just going to give it away.'

'You made me promises, Jack Fisher. And I want more than just a few pounds for my trouble. Coming all this way, making a fool of myself by begging for what's rightly mine.'

'Are you saying you want me to marry you?' The words nearly choked him.

'Don't be ridiculous. I'm entitled to half because I'm the one who gave you the strength to start saving in the first place. You'd have been nothing without my encouragement. Nothing. I took real trouble over you.'

'I don't remember it that way, actually, Tess. The way you talk, you make it sound as though I was some sort of plan you were working on.'

'What else were you? And what thanks did I get? You cleared off and left me once you'd got what you wanted. And I'm not just talking about the money to open this place. I gave myself to you, Jack Fisher.' She sneered. 'And don't look at me like that, I know I never meant anything to you. You never meant anything to me either, to tell you the truth. You were a means to an end. I was going to have a respectable life with a decent bit put by in the bank, but you dumped me. And now you've wound up messing around with all this nonsense and mooning after that tall great thing next door.'

'*What*?'

'You don't think I stay up here all the time, locked away like a guilty secret, do you?'

'You mean you go out?'

She smiled nastily. 'That's got you worried, hasn't it, lad? If you must know, I've been standing at the back of the theatre every night, watching the goings-on of that pair of harlots. Can't say I'm that impressed. But then I'm not paying for the privilege like all those fools. What a waste of money.'

'I don't believe it. After everything I said. And you promised . . .'

'Like you did, Jack. Remember? Tell you what, maybe I should introduce myself around as the girl you said you'd marry.'

'You wouldn't.'

'Wouldn't I?' She paused, taking pleasure in his

discomfort. 'You'd better get going, Jack, or you'll be late for your fancy piece.'

Next door, Tibs was working herself into a state about having Archie tagging along – one minute wanting to go and tell him he couldn't come and the next telling herself not to be stupid. The trouble was, she so wanted the day to be a happy one for Polly that everything was getting on her nerves. She was even distressing herself about what she should or shouldn't be taking with her and had wound up with a valise stuffed with enough gear to keep her supplied during a fortnight's trip to lands with any climate known to man.

'What're we gonna take for you to bathe in, Kit?' she wailed, flipping through the outfits on the clothes stand.

'Bathe in?' Kitty sounded horrified. 'I don't think I want to bathe.'

'We probably won't even go in, but just in case.'

Polly didn't know what bathing was, but as with most things her mum talked about she made it sound like fun, so she wanted to do it, whatever it was. 'Just in case, Kit,' she said, copying her mother.

'Yeah, just in case,' joined in Tibs. She stabbed her thumb over her shoulder at a pale-pink, ruffled two-piece she had tossed on to the bed. 'I've got me costume from the seaside routine.' She suddenly grinned. 'I know what you can wear.'

'I haven't got anything.'

'Yes, you have.' Tibs dived into one of the boxes of clothes that now littered the room. 'You've got your second-best set of unmentionables. And with this long-sleeved chemise of your'n you'll be a proper bathing beauty, won't she, Poll?'

'Yeah!' squealed Polly.

'No, Tibs, I don't . . .'

284

'It's only just in case. Now put 'em on. Go on, Kit. And take your other set of underthings with you. You can put them in my valise. And we'll take our towels. And you can use this to trim your hat.' She threw a length of ribbon at Kitty, and laughed happily as it fluttered across the room. 'I can't tell you, Kit. This is like a bloody dream come true.'

It wasn't even half past nine when they all met up outside the pub, but it was already stifling and the street was ripe with the choice medley of stinks and pongs that had hung about like a low-lying mist since the heat-wave had first begun. But from the expressions on their faces as they stood there, all spruced up for their big day out and smiling fit to burst, anyone would have thought that Rosemary Lane smelt of violets and sweet lavender.

Tibs had on a white lacy dress, clinched at the waist with a scarlet satin tie, and Polly, also in white, had emerald-green ribbons tied in her hair, while Kitty's frock was cream, with a contrasting sash of the deepest royal blue. To complete their outfits all three wore straw boaters, as did both the men – Jack having borrowed his and Archie's slightly ill-fitting ones from members of the band.

Tibs looked at Archie in his newly pressed suit and freshly polished shoes, chuckling at Polly, who was bouncing around as if she were on springs. It seemed impossible that someone who looked so kind would be capable of doing anything so violent. And surely not just because she'd mentioned she wanted Albert out of the way? But confused as she felt, Tibs was certain of one thing: she had Polly being there to think about now. And she was her priority.

Archie looked up and saw Tibs watching him. 'Er, hadn't we better get a move on?' he said, self-consciously holding on to his bad arm. 'Fenchurch Street station'll be crowded on a lovely day like this.'

'We'll do better than that, Archie,' said Jack, slapping him on the shoulder. 'When the girls were kind enough to invite me along yesterday, I made a few enquiries and I came up with these.' He pulled off his boater and took out five tickets that had been tucked inside the band. 'We're going along to the Old Swan Pier and we're getting ourselves on a paddle steamer.'

Being on the boat was a rare treat. There was a small, neat dining-room, serving freshly cooked food, with real cotton cloths and little vases of flowers on every table; a proper barber shop and another selling sweets; and even a miniature bar with a single curved counter, where a large proportion of the men – including Jack and Archie – seemed to have gathered for 'just a swift one' to quench their thirst 'what with all the heat'.

Like most of the other women, Tibs and Kitty stayed outside, enjoying the refreshing breeze. With Polly tucked safely between them they stood at the rail, sniffing the increasingly salt air and staring down at the foaming water being thrown up by the massive paddles of the *Missie Lou*, as she made her stately way down the Thames towards the open mouth of the estuary.

'This is better than being stuck in the Lane, eh, Kit?' Tibs took a deep, appreciative breath. 'Tell you what, I'd do this for fourpence an hour and wouldn't even want extras for doing Sundays.'

'It's smashing all right.' Kitty closed her eyes, and felt the fine spray cooling her face. 'The freshest air I've smelt since I came up to London.'

'And it's nice, just us three being out here together.'

Kitty glanced at her. Tibs had seemed more relaxed since Jack and Archie had gone off for their drink.

Maybe she'd done the wrong thing saying Archie could come along; perhaps Tibs had felt that Jack shouldn't be left out. But surely Tibs would have said.

'I'll have to be careful though,' Tibs went on, her voice low and serious.

'Why's that?' Kitty asked.

'You know how small I am,' she whispered to her friend, so Polly couldn't hear. 'If we get shipwrecked, you'll have to promise to hide me somewhere.'

'I don't understand.'

'You've read the penny dreadfuls, haven't you?'

'One or two.'

'Well, I don't wanna get mistaken for one of them little cabin boys and have the crew all gobble me up when they get desperate, now do I?'

Kitty, realising she'd been had, rolled her eyes and tutted. 'Glad to see you're back to your normal barmy self.'

Tibs laughed happily and gave Polly a squeeze. 'You wanna see me really back to normal, Kit? Hold on to Polly's hand for me and watch. It was a stroke I used to pull on Tower Bridge.'

Tibs kissed Polly on the cheek. 'Mummy's just gonna play a little game,' she said, then peeled off one of her gloves and hid it deep in her pocket.

'Just follow me, Kit, but don't let on you're with me. Got it?'

Kitty nodded and did as she was told.

About half-way round the boat Tibs stopped. 'Here's a bit of carriage trade if ever I saw it,' she hissed out of the corner of her mouth. 'Now, just stand back and learn.'

Kitty, with Polly by her side, watched as Tibs leaned on the railing and stared down into the churning waters.

'Oh, my glove,' she wailed in a girly little voice, then looked pointedly over her shoulder at the well-dressed man she had just targeted. She batted her eyelashes helplessly at him and held up the hand still wearing the cheap cotton glove.

'Brussels lace.' Her lip trembled. 'A gift from my late mother.'

Lowering her gaze, she stared pitifully at the deck. 'I'll never be able to afford to replace them. It'll break my father's heart.'

'We'll have to see about that,' said the man taking off his topper. Within moments he was encouraging his companions to throw coins into his hat.

Tibs protested.

He protested more strongly.

She protested again and pressed her gloved hand to her throat as he presented her with one pound, eleven shillings and fourpence.

'I hope that will enable you to buy another pair,' he said with a refined hint of a bow, then added more furtively, 'May I escort you inside to the dining-room for luncheon?'

Tibs slipped the money into her bag. 'Sorry, sir,' she simpered, looking up at him through her lashes. 'But my father wouldn't approve.' She dropped a dainty curtsey and added in her more usual cockney growl, 'And he'll be joining me as soon as he's finished in the lav.'

The man didn't flinch, he merely bowed again, replaced his topper, turned on his heel and was about to to walk away when Tibs said, just loud enough for him to hear, 'And I don't suppose your old woman would approve either for that matter.'

He strode off without another word.

Tibs returned to Kitty, glowing with success. 'Did you

see his face?' She twinkled. 'Looked just like he had a brick in his hat.'

'Tibs!'

'What?'

'You should be more careful. Who knows what he might have done.'

'I knew. And anyway, it was only a laugh, and what was he gonna do on a boat full of people? I can look after myself, you forget that.' She picked up Polly and swung her round. 'And I can look after my little Polly Wally Doodle and all. Can't I, babe?'

'You look like you're having a good time.' It was Archie. 'I asked Jack if he thought it'd be all right if I bought these for Polly.' He held out a cone of paper. 'It's a few sugar mice from the sweet-shop.'

Tibs took them, but her face had become stony. 'Maybe I'll give 'em to her later.'

'I'm sorry, I only thought . . .'

'You don't want her being sick all over the boat, do you?'

Kitty stared at Tibs's rudeness. Whatever had got into her?

'Here we are, sweetheart. Our first proper outing together.' Tibs cuddled her daughter to her side and laughed at Kitty, who had to make a wild grab for the rail as the paddle steamer docked with a jolt against the pier. 'Whitechapel-on-Sea.'

Jack took off his boater and scratched his head. 'It must be this daft hat and the stiff collar I'm wearing. I'm not used to them, especially in this heat. But I could have sworn you said Whitechapel.'

Tibs smiled. 'That's what they call Southend, don't they.'

'Do they?'

'Yeah. See all them people?'

He nodded.

'Apart from a few locals, they'll all be Londoners. Nearly every one of them.'

'Attracts visitors like Blackpool, I suppose.'

'Dunno, Jack, I ain't never been there.'

'That makes us quits then. I've never been here. So how about if you and Archie show us two out-of-towners what this place has got to offer and I'll tell you if it matches up?'

Tibs cast a furtive glance at Archie and considered for a moment. 'You want us two to show you round?'

'Can we go, Mum?' Polly pleaded. 'Please. Please.'

She looked down into her child's face. Tibs really didn't fancy spending the day with Archie, but if that's what Polly wanted how could she deny her?

What Polly actually wanted, what she *meant*, was that she was desperate to get away from the suffocating press of people, apparently all determined to disembark at the same time from the *Missie Lou* in case the stalls sold out of toffee apples, whelks and chipped plaster ornaments.

'All right, Jack, you're on,' said Tibs, holding on to Polly with one hand and taking Kitty's arm firmly with the other. 'Follow me and I'll show you all the sights.'

They started by hiking around the muggy town, looking at the rows of shops and restaurants, and marvelling at the crowds. They were used to the East End being packed, but the people there were usually doing something – working, fighting, or passing the time of day – but here everyone seemed to be just milling about doing nothing much at all except eating one kind or other of greasy-looking food.

Quite soon, the novelty of being part of the strolling,

sweaty, masticating throng began to pall, and even the stepping stones, laid across the High Street to protect the bottoms of ladies' skirts, that had at first fascinated them – especially Polly, who had used them as a hopscotch pitch – could no longer distract them from the almost suffocating heat, and they made their way back to Marine Parade and the cooling relief of the sea breezes.

'Blimey, I wish I could take me stays off,' Tibs whispered to Kitty, who nodded in sincere, if frazzled, agreement.

'And I wish I could take off this collar and get a bit of grub down me,' said Jack with a wink.

'Oi, you!' Tibs said. 'You weren't meant to hear that first bit, it was girls' business. But them pies don't look half bad.' She pointed to the gleaming display window of Schofield and Martin's, the self-styled 'high-class grocers', where a pyramid of glossily crusted and fluted pork pies had pride of place.

Jack didn't need two chances. He'd considered, for a very brief moment, taking them in to Mitchell's Quality Chop House and Dining-Rooms for a fry-up, or meat and two veg, but the idea of being stuck inside on a day like this, while all dressed up like a suet pudding about to be steamed in the pan, was too horrible to bear. He was in and back out of the shop with a bag full of pies before anyone could argue.

He handed them out and they all began eating.

'I'll have to have a drink,' puffed Tibs, spraying crumbs down her front. 'Me mouth's as dry as the bottom of a parrot's cage.'

She shoved a damp strand of hair out of her eyes with the back of her hand. It stuck to the side of her face as if it had been pasted there. 'How about if we stop here?' she suggested, flopping against the wall and pointing wearily to a street vendor selling lemonade from a big silver urn.

'That'd be just right,' gasped Archie, running his finger round his neck to try and loosen his stiff collar. 'I'll get 'em if you'll help me, boss.'

Archie paid while Jack handed round five glasses of the cold, cloudy liquid.

'Do you think young Polly here might have had enough of walking about the shops?' Jack asked cautiously.

Polly looked over the rim of her glass at her mum, willing her to say yes.

'I reckon she has,' said Tibs, 'but I thought you all wanted to see the town.'

'We did, didn't we, Kit?' Jack said hurriedly, not wanting to spoil things by sounding unappreciative. 'But maybe . . .'

'It ain't much fun when it's sweltering like this, is it?' Tibs took her glove from her pocket and wiped her brow. 'How about if we go on the sands?'

Polly had her boots and stockings off and was in the water, while Tibs was still asking her if she'd rather paddle first or have a donkey ride.

Polly didn't much like the look of the bad-tempered beasts carting the hot, bawling children up and down the beach, but the water and the muddy sand squelching up between her bare toes – she had never felt anything like it.

'Keep to the edge!' shouted Tibs, although Polly was less than two feet away from her. 'Gawd, I'm tempted to join her, Kit.'

'You can't!'

Tibs was about to show Kitty that yes she could, when an overbearing woman came barging past them, with a sweating young constable – complete with helmet and heavy tunic – by her side. 'That's her, officer!' she shrieked in the shrilly, excitable tones of the deeply shocked. She pointed her parasol at a woman of about twenty years of age, who was standing in the water cooling her feet.

'Look, there! Exposing her flesh! Arrest her!'

The overheated constable dragged himself down to the shoreline and approached the young woman. 'Sorry, miss,' he said sheepishly – the girl was very pretty – but it is an offence for you to . . . ' He coughed nervously. 'Expose certain areas of your flesh.'

'Me ankles, d'you mean, darling? Or these?' With that she lifted her skirt and flashed her calves at the now bug-eyed policeman.

Jack, Archie and all the other men on the beach, and quite a few of the woman, showed their appreciation by clapping or whistling, or generally cheering her along.

'Cockney scum! I knew it!' The woman pushed past the officer and made a grab for the girl, whose reply was to stick out her tongue and give the woman an almighty shove, sending her crashing backwards into the salty waves. Then she hitched her skirts higher still and made a run for it along the shoreline, splashing and laughing as she went.

The now completely flustered constable did his best to help the woman to her feet, but she wasn't taking that sort of familiarity from a young whipper-snapper like him. 'Take your hands off me, or I'll report you to your sergeant!' she bellowed, whacking him about the head with her sopping-wet parasol. 'Now get off after that harlot,' she ordered him, 'or they'll all be wearing bathing suits on the sands before we know it. This isn't the continent you know.'

Tibs couldn't resist it. 'Good job Mummy never

tucked her frock in her drawers, eh, Polly?'

'Sssh!' Kitty had to restrain herself from putting her hand over Tibs's mouth. 'She'll hear you.'

'Good, she was meant to. Ugly, toffee-nosed old bitch just don't want no one enjoying themselves, does she. Mind you, you can understand it when you look at her. Looks just like the bashed-in back end of a bloody tram.'

'Tibs!'

'Well, cheeky old cow, you'd think we was all common or something.'

Tibs folded her arms and stared defiantly at the dripping-wet woman who was now fighting off her harrumphing tweedy husband's efforts to assist her in her floundering attempts to rise to her knees in the waves.

'Have you got me valise with the bathing things in it, Jack? We're going in.'

'Here we go.' Tibs helped Polly up on to the platform of the bathing machine marked LADIES AND CHILDREN ONLY and opened the door for her to step inside. 'Now you hold my hand tight while the man winches it down the slope, Poll, then we'll get changed and have a right laugh in the waves.'

Kitty clung to the side. 'I'm not sure about this, Tibs.'

'They don't take you that far out. And you're so flipping tall anyway.'

'It's not that.'

'And the canopy folds down if you're worried about your modesty.'

'I don't know.'

'Blimey, Kit, we'll have to get you back in your uniform, you're turning back into a flaming mouse.'

'Is Auntie Kitty really a mouse?'

'Sometimes she is, Poll. Ooops mind, we're moving.'

Tibs grabbed Kitty by the arm and, before she knew it, she was inside the shed-like interior of the machine, being ordered to strip down to her second-best set of unmentionables.

'Come on, Archie. How about it.'

'I didn't bring anything to wear.'

'I'm going in my long-johns. No one can see us, you step straight down into the water according to Tibs. It'll be a laugh.'

'I won't if you don't mind, boss.'

Jack looked at him standing there, like a small boy called up by the teacher to be punished for something he didn't do. It must be that arm of his again. He was that embarrassed about it. It was a real pity, a big handsome feller like that feeling so bad about himself. 'If you're sure, lad.'

'I'm sure.'

But Jack only had it partly right about Archie. He was, as always, concerned about his arm, but now more so than ever. Because he had decided his arm was the reason for Tibs being so off with him. Why else would she not want her or her little girl going anywhere near a useless thing like him? He just wished he hadn't let her know how much he liked her. She must feel so awkward with him hanging around. But if he wasn't too pushy, maybe she'd let him just be a friend.

'You don't mind if I go in, like?' Jack asked him.

'Course not. I'll go and have a scout around.'

'Good idea. Find a good shellfish place. We can't go to the seaside without having a shrimp-and-winkle tea, can we?'

As Archie walked away, off the sands, he could hear the sound of Tibs shrieking with laughter and of Jack calling after him, 'See you by the bandstand at the pier entrance in about half an hour.' Archie felt too choked to look round.

It was actually over an hour later when they eventually found Archie leaning against the bandstand waiting for them. 'I've got this for the little one, if that's all right,' he said, handing Polly a little cloth sailor doll.

'Say thank you,' said Tibs flatly. 'Now put it down while I dry your hair off.'

She rubbed furiously at the ends of Polly's ringlets, stuffed the towel back into her bulging bag and handed it, without a word, to Jack. 'There. Now, what can we do next? I don't feel you've seen very much.'

She saw Jack's face drop as he envisioned being made to traipse around yet more airless, crowded streets.

'Don't worry, Jack. No more shops. I was thinking of somewhere far more interesting. Wait till you see this, Poll.'

Tibs led them down a road beside the Britannia pub to a small fairground by the Marine Gardens. 'Look up there,' she said and pointed triumphantly to a wooden structure that rose 110 feet above them. 'Only opened last year. Sal told me about it.'

'You've not seen Blackpool Tower, lass,' snorted Jack smugly.

'And you've not seen the Observation Tower once it gets moving.'

'Is it safe?' asked Kitty, watching the platform, packed with people, as it began to revolve slowly and then rise jerkily, but inexorably, towards the flag-topped summit.

As the platform came to a shuddering stop, everyone stumbled to one side, including Kitty who, of course, had been persuaded by Tibs to go up with the rest of them. She staggered against Jack who, putting out his hands to save her, caught her about the waist.

They looked at each other for a long, gulp-making moment, before Kitty, fumbling about with her boater and her dignity, pulled herself upright and brushed down her skirts. 'Sorry,' she said from under the brim of her now straightened hat.

'Why?' asked Jack. 'I enjoyed it.'

'Look, look at that!' Kitty shouted a bit too loudly and pointed haphazardly at the sights of Southend-on-Sea laid out below them like paintings on a picture postcard.

Tibs was tempted, but her friend was too easy a target for teasing, so instead, she went to her aid. 'Look what Auntie Kitty's showing you, Poll,' she said. 'Look down there. There's the Marine Gardens. See all the people whirling round and round on the dancing platform? And look at the chairoplanes and the scenic railway. And all the pretty flowers and trees. And the swan boats and the rifle ranges. And there's the coconut shy and the fortune teller's tent.'

Polly, clutching her sailor doll, looked down, not understanding, but, being with her mum, loving it all.

'And there's a pony-riding track and all sorts of other things. What would you like to do when we get back down there?'

'I know what I want to do, Archie,' said Jack, determined to include him.

'What's that, boss?' he asked.

'There was a shop in, what was that street called? That one down by the front.' He pointed.

'Er . . . '

'Marine Parade,' cut in Tibs. She rolled her eyes at Kit. 'There's one or two shops down there actually, Jack. Which one did you have in mind?'

'The photographer's. I was thinking, those frames

you got from the pawnbroker's. We've not done anything about them.'

It didn't take much to persuade Tibs that they should go into Dawson's Photographic Studios; she loved the idea of having her picture done with Polly, but Kitty was more reticent.

'It looks a bit posh,' she said uneasily.

'So? We're as good as anyone, ain't we? And so's our money.'

'Tibs is right,' said Jack, 'and I'm paying. This is my treat. So go on, in you go, and let's see you smile.'

Kitty needed more convincing than that, so Jack asked the others to go inside while he had a word with her.

Within ten minutes, Kitty walked into the studio.

Smiling!

It was soporifically warm in there. The photographer refused to open any windows in case the potted palms and draperies – just two of his many and varied props, which ranged from the classical to the downright exotic – were disturbed by the wind and so might prevent him from capturing the true artistry of his compositions.

But Tibs didn't care, she loved it, posing first alone, with a whole range of columns, backdrops and different hats, then with Polly and then with Kitty. Next, Kitty was cajoled by Jack – with surprising ease, thought Tibs, after all that fuss – into having her own solo portrait done.

Jack then suggested that Tibs might have one done with Archie.

Archie squirmed. '*Jack*.'

Tibs looked levelly at Archie and said, 'I don't think so, Jack. It's getting too hot and uncomfortable in here. And Polly's getting tired. Come on, Poll, let's go and wait in the fresh air while Uncle Jack sorts it all out with the man.'

Kitty frowned as Tibs led Polly outside. Couldn't she see how hurtful she was being?

'There, that's all done,' said Jack, tucking the receipt inside his hatband. 'He'll send the pictures to us within the week with a bit of luck.' He put his boater back on and surveyed the now cheerless-looking group who surrounded him. It was all going too well for him to let this happen. 'Right, now how about a ride on one of those brakes opposite that pub over there?' He squinted his eyes and shielded them with his hand against the still strong afternoon sun. 'The sign says it's, let's see, an hour's round trip to Shoebury.'

Kitty went to say something, but Tibs got in first. 'An hour's too long.'

'Well,' he suggested, casting around for what other attractions had caught his eye. 'Let's go on the pier instead. We could go on that Electric Tram ride. That only takes five minutes. Or we could have a stroll along the lower deck and watch the fishermen. Or even have a look at the Pavilion. See what sort of show they've got on.'

'Look, Jack. It's been a long day. Polly'll be getting fretful.'

Jack looked at Kitty, who shrugged for want of a better comment to make. 'Maybe we'd better be getting home,' he said. 'But before we do, let's round it all off with a nice shrimp-and-winkle tea.'

'Maybe,' muttered Tibs, tempted by the idea. 'It'd be a shame to go home without a bit of shellfish.'

'That's what I said to Archie,' Jack said, encouraging him with a smile. 'And you went off to find a good one for us while we were in the sea, didn't you?

'That's right, I found a really good place.'

'Well, it had better not be too dear,' sniffed Tibs.

'I'm glad Tibs asked us to come back on this earlier boat,' said Jack, leaning on the rail next to Kitty. 'I'm as whacked out as young Polly.' He looked along the rows of people either side of them, all standing admiring the glorious colours of the setting sun. 'And we'd have missed this smashing view if we'd have caught the later one.'

'Jack,' said Kitty quietly. 'Where's Archie?'

He laughed fondly. 'Having his hair cut if you can believe it. I just hope the boat don't start rocking or he'll wind up looking like a convict.' He took out a cigarette and took his time trying to light it against the breeze. 'I was disappointed Tibs didn't want her picture done with him.'

'Were you?'

So Jack had noticed how Tibs was behaving towards him as well.

'I was. It would have been a good excuse to have had one done with you.'

Kitty felt herself colour. 'I'd have liked that,' she said quietly.

Jack grinned and flicked the spent match over the side and into the water. He turned to face her. Maybe he could risk just a little peck on the cheek.

'Jack,' she said.

'Yes, Kit.'

'While Tibs is taking Polly to the you-know-where . . . '

'Yes?'

'Will you tell me something?'

This was getting promising. 'You name it, lass.'

'Have you noticed anything sort of, well, strange about Tibs lately?'

Bugger! 'Well, she does seem a bit on edge. But I suppose it's having young Polly with her. Having to make up for all that time they lost together. We all waste too much time in our lives.' He lifted his chin towards the horizon and blew a plume of smoke into the air. 'I mean, just look at that sky. It's beautiful. But how often do we bother to look at the sunset? To look up at the sky when we're walking along the street.'

'If we all did that,' said Tibs, who had just come up behind him, 'we'd wind up stepping in great steaming piles of horse shit.'

There wasn't much that either Jack or Kitty felt they could say in reply to that, so they just stood there, looking awkwardly about them.

It was with relief that Jack saw Archie appear among the crowds.

'Well, Archibald,' Jack said, flicking his cigarette butt the same way as the match. 'That is a very smart haircut.'

'Glad you like it,' said Archie, then he leaned forward and said to Polly, 'Did you like them sugar mice I got you?'

She nodded enthusiastically.

'And do you like liquorice comfits?' he asked. 'And bull's-eyes?'

Polly's eyes widened at the thought of these new delights. 'I don't know.'

Archie looked at Tibs for permission to take her to buy them.

'She's had a lot to eat today,' she said frostily.

'Sorry,' he said. 'I shouldn't have mentioned it.'

'I don't suppose one more bag of sweets would hurt,' said Jack.

Polly smiled and held out her hand, ready to go with Archie, but Tibs wasn't having it. 'Don't be naughty,

Poll. Uncle Archie'll be getting tired of you hanging round him all day.'

'She's all right,' he said.

Tibs looked him directly in the eye. 'I'll tell her what to do, thank you very much.'

'Hang on, Arch, why didn't you wait with me to see the girls in?' Jack pulled off his boater and gave his head a good, hard scratch.

Archie stopped in the pub doorway and turned round to face his boss. 'I just wanted to go in and see if Joe's been managing without us, that's all.'

'Come on, Archie, this is me you're talking to, not a drunken sailor.'

'It's Tibs.' He sighed.

Jack nodded. 'She's upset you.'

'No, not really. It's me. I was stupid enough to think she liked me. But now . . .'

Jack was beginning to wish he hadn't asked. This was more like women's sort of talk. 'We've all made mistakes with women, Arch. But what makes you think she doesn't like you?'

'It's obvious, innit?' Archie slapped angrily at his arm. 'It's this, of course.' Then he shoved open the pub door and let it slam loudly behind him.

Jack followed him in, but he didn't stop in the bar. He went straight up to his room, where he had woman trouble of his own.

He was dreading seeing Tess, but he knew he couldn't put this conversation off any longer and he also knew exactly what he was going to say.

He pushed open the door and just stood there, staring.

She was sitting on the bed with his tin box – *his private tin box* – going through his things.

She looked up, apparently unperturbed at being caught. 'I thought you'd be back later.'

'We were tired.' He stepped inside to get a closer look. 'What do you think you're doing?'

'I've long since given up pretending I've got any interest in you, Jack Fisher – I've got no interest in any man, to be honest. Why be a housekeeper for no pay?' She snorted unattractively. 'But I do have an interest in what's mine by rights.'

'But why are you . . .'

'I told you, I want my share of the money and I was just going through your papers to find out exactly how much that comes to.'

Jack snatched off his boater and his stiff collar and dashed them to the floor. 'To think I've felt guilty about you all this time.'

'Not guilty enough to come back and marry me.'

Jack hung his head. 'I will get the money sorted out as soon as I can. You've looked through those papers, you know how much I had to lay out to get this business started. And the debts that've mounted up. But I'll find a way. Now will you just go?'

She stretched out on the bed and smiled up at him slyly – a snake judging its strike. 'Soon, Jack Fisher. Soon. In fact, as soon as I get the money in my hands. But don't take too long about it, will you, or I might start forgetting myself and go opening my mouth to that lass next door.'

Chapter 17

With a clatter of hooves and a jingle of harness the hansom pulled up by the flaring torches lighting the entrance to an impressively grand white stucco building in St James's.

Tibs lifted the corner of the blind. 'This must be it,' she said, tilting the stiff white address card that Tressing had given them towards the light.

Kitty said nothing. She just ducked her head, so that she could see through the window. She stared up at the massive neo-classical façade of columns and pediments standing out starkly against the velvet of the winter sky, closed her eyes and gulped.

Tibs pushed open the door and stepped down on to the street. 'It ain't gonna fall down and wallop you on the head, Kit. Now come on.' She pulled her coat tightly round her, covering up the thin muslin dress.

'Bloody glad he gave us the money for a cab,' she said through chattering teeth, as Kitty sheepishly joined her on the pavement. 'Coming out on a November night wearing just these little things, we'd have froze our bits off. You know, all I hope, Kit,' she went on, as she concentrated on sorting out the exact fare, 'is that Joe's old Aunt Sarah makes sure my Polly don't kick off the blankets and that she keeps plenty of coal on the fire. It's sodding bitter tonight.'

She counted out the coins into the cabman's hand and he snatched them from her, furious at not being given a tip. 'Pissing cheek,' he spat, cracking his whip over his horse's flanks. 'Trying to act like ladies when anyone can see they're just a pair of whores.'

'What was that?' asked Kitty, as the cab pulled away in a shower of sparks from the startled hackney's metal-clad hooves. 'What did he say, Tibs?'

'Nothing,' she said hurriedly. She didn't want to risk losing out on the evening's pay just because Kitty got scared by some loud-mouthed old goat of a driver. She wanted that money. Although, she had to admit, she wasn't as desperate for it as she had been a few weeks earlier when Jack had first agreed to them having the night off to go to the ball, because, just this morning, he had announced he was giving them a rise.

Tibs smiled as she mounted the broad sweep of steps, thinking how full of himself Jack had been when he'd told them; how proud he was at what he'd achieved at the pub and how he'd managed almost to sort out his finances at last. He had, however, been surprised that they were still going. He'd thought that if he gave them the rise they would give up the idea of the evening with Tressing. But although Tibs didn't exactly need the extra money now, she still wanted it. It would be Christmas soon and she was going to make up for all those other Christmases, make it a day Polly would never ever forget.

Jack had really tried to persuade them not to go and had even gone as far as telling them that there was something about Tressing he didn't like. He should have added that there was something about the man that not only made his flesh crawl, but that had him seriously questioning whether the bloke was actually all there. But Jack didn't want to risk making too much of a fuss and falling out with him. If they had a row and Tressing stormed out of the place, he could still just come back whenever he felt like it. No, that was no good, Jack wanted to get rid of him properly. And that meant getting the money together to pay back the IOU – which, with a bit of luck, he would be able to do very soon. And with the debt repaid there would be no excuse. Jack could bar him from the Old Black Dog for ever.

Tibs reached the top of the steps and looked over her shoulder to see where Kitty had got to.

She was still hanging around on the pavement.

'For Gawd's sake, Kit, get yourself up here or you'll freeze to the bleed'n' spot.' Tibs turned back round to find herself being snootily appraised by a liveried doorman. 'And what d'you think you're bogging at?' she demanded, sticking her nose in the air. 'We're guests, we are. Of Dr Tressing.'

The man smirked. 'I might have known.' Then added sarcastically, 'Madam.'

'Oi! You!' Teezer leaned drunkenly in his chair, tipping it alarmingly on to its back legs. 'Over here!'

Archie shielded his eyes with his hand and peered out into the darkness of the auditorium.

'Over here!' hollered Teezer, snatching Buggy's matches and striking one in front of his face.

Spotting the unpleasant sight of Teezer's fat, beery mug, illuminated by the flare, Archie put the name card announcing 'Miss Tilly Thomas and her Tantalising Tunes' carefully on the easel, tapped himself on the chest and mouthed 'Who me?' in the vague direction of where the flame had been.

'Yeah, you,' Teezer shouted back over the band who had just launched into the introduction of 'I May Be a Poor Little Rich Girl but I Know what a Copper is Worth'. 'I wanna word.'

Reluctantly, Archie picked his way through the tables

306

in the gloom, whispering his apologies to the customers as he threaded his way over to where Teezer and Buggy were sitting.

'We've got a complaint,' slurred Teezer.

'You and the rest of the audience,' muttered Archie under his breath.

'We came here to see Sweet and Dandy, not some fat old tart squawking like a parrot and waggling her wobbly, flabby old arse.'

'I'll go and get the boss,' said Archie, almost as fed up with taking complaints as he was with the fact that Tibs was doing anything to avoid his company. 'But I'm telling you, he's as unhappy as you gentlemen that they ain't appearing tonight.'

The interior of the private club was even more nerve-rackingly impressive than the façade and even usually perky, mouthy little Tibs was momentarily lost for words.

At first they just stood there in the wonderful warmth, staring about them at the glowing braziers and candles that threw shadows dancing against the walls and the almost cathedral-height ceiling.

There were servants everywhere, gliding around the huge entrance hall with silver trays laden with drinks. But instead of the powdered wig and breeches worn by the doormen they were dressed in flimsy white drapery that barely covered their nakedness.

Tibs opened her coat, looked down at her own white dress and let out a little sigh. So, they were here as bloody servants – she might have guessed.

Kitty hadn't seemed to make the connection. 'Look at those outfits,' she whispered behind her hand, lifting her chin at a group of costumed guests who had just appeared from one of the side doors. 'They look just like those Alhambra posters for *The Arabian Nights* that they pasted on the warehouse opposite the pub.'

'Lovely,' said Tibs flatly, thinking of carrying all those glasses and the weight of the bloody silver trays.

'Tibs! Look at him,' Kitty gasped, pointing to a man who had appeared at the top of the sweeping staircase that led to the galleried upper floors.

He was dressed in a shimmering floor-length robe, which fell in fine jewelled pleats from a golden breast-plate. On his head he wore an eagle's head mask fashioned from iridescent green and gold feathers.

'Blimey, Kit, he's only coming over to us.'

'What'll we say?'

'How about good-evening?' As soon as they heard his deep, hypnotic voice, they knew it was Bartholomew Tressing. 'This way, Miss Wallis, Miss Tyler.'

As they followed him through one of the doors leading off the hall, Tibs puffed out her cheeks and shook her head. 'You wait and see,' she whispered. 'It'll be the sodding kitchen. I just know it.'

But it wasn't. It was a dressing-room.

In it, there were matching gilt and brocade chairs, a cheval looking-glass, a table covered with powders and scents, and a carved double wardrobe which the doctor opened.

He took out two extravagantly embroidered gowns that wouldn't have looked out of place in ancient Egypt and held them at arm's length, judging the sizes, before handing one to each of them. 'You can leave your own things in here,' he said. 'You won't be needing anything you are wearing.'

'Not even our drawers?' asked Tibs sourly. She wasn't worried about shedding her underwear – the place was gloriously warm and she'd never been keen on stays anyway, not since One-Eyed Sal had first insisted she should lace herself into them when she was about fourteen years old – but she was angry at having wasted good money on the thin muslin shift for which she now had absolutely no use, except for maybe hanging over the window to keep out the flies and bluebottles.

Tressing raised an amused eyebrow. 'Actually, undergarments would spoil the effect of the clothing and it is, after all, a costume ball.'

'So I can see,' she said, looking him up and down. 'But if that's what you really want – and we agree to do it – it'll be an extra Jacks. For each of us, mind.'

Kitty didn't know whether to be more shocked by Tressing wanting them naked under their outfits, or Tibs having the front to ask for yet more money.

'I mean it, it's a tenner or we're off. And you can think yourself lucky we ain't asking for more.'

'You shall have it. I'll leave you to change.'

'Now.' Tibs, having guessed, quite rightly, that even in costume his sort wouldn't risk leaving his personal effects where some light-fingered servant might help himself, held out her hand.

Perfectly calmly he slipped his hand between the folds of his costume and took out his wallet.

As soon as he left, Kitty propped one of the chairs under the door handle, turned her back modestly on Tibs and slowly, reluctantly, took off her clothes.

'I'm sure you can see through these costumes in the light.'

'Good job we'll be wearing masks then, eh, Kit? They'll save our blushes.'

When she was dressed, Kitty walked over to the mirror to look at herself.

'Let's have a butcher's,' said Tibs, nudging her to one side. 'Blimey! We're flipping gorgeous. And just look at them,' she said, poking Kitty's bosom that was bulging over the top of the beaded bodice. 'You don't look much like a soldier boy now, darling.'

'Tibs. I'm not sure about this.'

'Don't you start fretting and carrying on. They won't be able to see a thing out there.' Tibs pulled one of the chairs over to use as a ladder and set about fixing Kitty's feathered head-dress and mask in place. 'It's almost pitch dark, apart from a few candles and fires. And just think what a nice change it all is from wearing trousers.'

Tressing, who was waiting outside the door, led them through to a dimly candlelit room, where all they could make out at first were shapes moving around in the gloom, some deep rumbling music and an almost overwhelming scent of incense.

'Behold, the Room of Ritual,' Tressing intoned in a slow, breathy gasp that made Tibs want to giggle. 'Watch and prepare for the mysteries.'

Gradually, as their eyes became accustomed to the darkness, they saw a scene unfolding before them that had Tibs digging Kitty in the ribs and snorting, as she did her best to stop herself from laughing out loud.

'It's like the Old Testament stories,' whispered Kitty as a man who, except for an enormous black leather codpiece, was dressed entirely in the red satin of a cardinal, chased a woman – naked apart from a breath-takingly tight corset and buttoned-up ankle boots – across the room, switching at her bare buttocks with a riding crop.

'Don't look very much like the Bible them mission lot go on about outside the pub,' sniggered Tibs, as she spotted a group of kneeling, semi-naked, masked men, who were chanting an incantation, beseeching the Great

God Pan to join them. 'More like a flaming orgy if you ask me.'

'I think I'd like to go home,' Kitty said, her voice betraying the fact that she was on the verge of tears. 'Please, Dr Tressing.'

Tressing ignored her. Grabbing them both by the upper arm, he pulled them roughly over to a circle of men, who were sitting round a low table, throwing dice and laughing raucously.

'Oi, watch it!' snapped Tibs, as he let her go. She rubbed her flesh where his fingers had dug in. 'That bleed'n' hurt.'

Still Tressing acted as though he hadn't heard a word. He pushed Kitty forward.

'Gentlemen of the Circle, here is my chosen goddess for the rituals. She will be known as Cyrees. She will keep company only with me, but this handmaiden' – he dragged Tibs forward – 'will gladly make her favours available.'

'Bloody handmaiden? Favours? Cheeky bleeder,' Tibs whispered from the corner of her mouth. 'Why ain't I a sodding goddess?'

'Tibs. I don't like this.' Kitty stared, saucer-eyed, at the leering men. 'What does he mean by *company*?'

Tibs never got the chance to lie about what she thought he meant, because Tressing suddenly announced, 'I will now introduce Cyrees to the others.' With that he whisked Kitty away, while one of the gamblers swung Tibs round and plonked her unceremoniously on his knee. 'Come and bring me luck, my little handmaiden, and I'll see you are rewarded.'

Tibs smiled happily to herself, this was more like it. She could earn herself a good few quid from these mugs and if they kept drinking at this rate she wouldn't have to do too much in return. She just hoped Kitty would be all right. She twisted round to see what was happening to her, but just as she saw Tressing pushing her into a curtained alcove, the man pulled Tibs back round by her hair and covered her mouth with his.

'This ain't so bad, is it, Bug?' Teezer poured himself another measure from the half-bottle of rum that the landlord had so kindly given them – Jack had learned about keeping good customers happy – and grinned at the scantily clad young woman on the stage, who was doing eye-poppingly athletic things with her body. 'In fact, I find it rather entertaining.' He elbowed Buggy in the ribs and winked. 'No wonder the newspapers are getting themselves all worked up over the Naughty Nineties, eh, kidder?'

Jack too stared at the stage. He supposed the girl was diverting. Very, when he came to think of it. He'd certainly caught on how to be a bit more discriminating in the acts he booked, and since Sweet and Dandy had taken off he'd been able to afford them as well. But he had no interest in the show tonight, even though one or two of the turns had made it clear they would be more than willing to oblige him for a few extra bookings and a bit of a bonus as the girls were away. He hadn't even been tempted, not only because Tess was upstairs like a spare part at a wedding, but because what Jack wanted was to have Kitty here with him and he was finding it very difficult to concentrate on anything much at all except what Dr Bartholomew Tressing might be up to with her.

All he could console himself with was the thought that soon he'd be in a position to pay him off and get rid of the mad-eyed old debaucher. And it couldn't be soon enough.

*

'Glad I decided to take up your invitation, old man.' Lucian Mayerton sipped his champagne and glanced about him as he jiggled Tibs up and down on his knee and rubbed her leg absent-mindedly through the flimsy material of her costume, as though she was no more than a lapdog that he was stroking. 'Bit livelier than you'd led me to believe though.'

'I . . . I never understood from the lectures I attended,' spluttered Hunton, his eyes bulging as they followed the rhythmic movements of Mayerton's hand, 'that Tressing's Occultist Circle was quite so . . .'

'Don't worry, Hunton,' Mayerton said, transferring one hand to Tibs's breast, as he leaned forward to throw the dice with the other, 'I won't go blabbing to Lavinia. If you promise not to say anything to Marjorie.'

Cameron Hunton knocked back the rest of his drink and took another from a passing servant girl. He nibbled his lip, hesitated for a brief moment and slapped her hard on the bottom.

The serving girl momentarily winced, then smiled seductively and thanked him for his attentions. Tibs took the opportunity to snatch a drink for herself, which she swallowed in a single gulp, but unused to champagne, she almost choked on the bubbles.

'One thing that does concern me,' Hunton continued, ignoring Tibs's coughing and spluttering as though she wasn't there, 'is Tressing's apparent taste for mixing with rather low women. That's a sure way to,' he lowered his voice, 'contract some of the more, let us say, unpleasant conditions.'

Mayerton laughed heartily, clapped Hunton on the shoulder and ran his other hand under Tibs's dress, right up to the top of her naked thigh. 'Too late for that, old boy.' He grinned.

Tibs wriggled away, not sure how much more of this

she was game for without knowing how much he was prepared to stump up for the privilege. But his hand merely became more insistent.

Hunton frowned. 'Not sure I follow you.'

Mayerton laughed again, amused by Hunton's innocence – he wasn't used to fellow professionals being so naive. Still, he was only a physician. It was the sawbones, such as himself and Tressing, who were the real men of the world.

'Remember we had that little discussion about – now how can I put this delicately? – Tressing's mental state?'

The other man shifted uncomfortably. Talking about a colleague's personal life wasn't really on, but he had to own up to a certain curiosity about the man. 'Yes,' he admitted slowly, pushing the dice towards him. 'Your throw.'

'Well, what d'you think killed his wife and children?' Mayerton's free hand had now found its way down Tibs's bodice and he fiddled with her nipple as though he were fine tuning a dial on a piece of hospital equipment.

Tibs said nothing, she didn't even squirm this time. She wanted to hear what this bloke had to say as much as his mate did.

'I don't know, but didn't his daughter die in some strange sort of circumstances?' He moved closer and said behind the cover of his hand, 'Killed herself, according to some rumours.'

'The circumstances, my dear Lucian, were stranger than you think. She killed herself in a police cell.'

'*She did what*?'

'She'd been driven mad by . . .' he dropped his voice so that his companion could barely hear, 'syphilis.'

'Never!'

'I'm telling you. The whole family had it. Passed on by . . . Well, you know by whom. The youngest, a boy, had it at birth. Died horribly by all accounts. That's what drove the wife from reason.'

'Shocking!'

Tibs thought the same. *Syphilis* . . . She had to get away. Get to Kitty.

She tried moving, but the man grabbed harder at her breast. She bit her lip to stop herself crying out. 'Can I just go to the . . .'

'No more shocking than that daughter of his dying in front of a young constable in the East End,' Mayerton went on, completely ignoring her, as he did all servants and employees except his valet. 'At a police station near the docks, apparently. I knew the chap who was acting Police Surgeon at the time. Jackson. A decent sort. Based with us at the London Hospital. He was called in to, let us say, verify matters concerning the likelihood that the girl could have been capable of committing certain acts.'

'Acts?' Hunton couldn't disguise the prurient tone of his question.

'Acts that, at the time, were associated with a beast rather than a young lady.'

'I don't . . .'

'It was about ten years ago now.'

Hunton still didn't follow.

'The Whitechapel murders.'

'*You mean the Ripper*?'

He nodded. 'And in his opinion she was capable, in that she had midwifery skills and, more convincingly, that she was completely mad. The syphilis had got to her too.'

'How?'

'It isn't only slum dwellers who couple with their families.'

Hunton's hand flew to his face in horror, knocking his mask completely skew-whiff.

Mayerton paused for a long moment, rubbing and pulling more urgently at Tibs's breast, as he remembered some of the more bizarre rumours that had over the years been associated with Dr Bartholomew Tressing, and while Hunton wished he'd never heard of the man or his damned Eastern Occultist Circle.

'Terrible business,' Mayerton said eventually. 'Terrible. I saw the so-called death certificate. Signed by Tressing himself, if you please. I know for a fact that he was ready to commit the girl. Jackson went to the trouble of seeking out the least dreadful place to send her, but even the private places . . . ' He shook his head. 'She was at least saved from that.' He paused again, before adding darkly, 'She knew too much, if you ask me.'

He swallowed the remains of his drink and snorted with incredulity. 'You might not believe this, but Tressing was a leading light in the Anti-Vice League at the time – while he was visiting every kind of whore in every corner of London. Mind you, you've heard the stories that that particular habit is on the wane. What with the amount of, let us say, *medicine* he takes nowadays, he apparently finds it rather more difficult to perform. If you ask me, one of the reasons he set up this little society was a way of seeking new thrills in the hope that it might, er . . . ' He coughed politely. 'Let us say, *stimulate* his jaded appetites.'

'How did it not become public?'

'Tressing has quite a gift for being untouched by scandal. An example. At the same time as the Ripper business was happening in Whitechapel you'll remember there was that body-buying business going on.'

'I was actually still doing my time in Africa.'

'Of course. Well, the police investigating the murders uncovered it. It was based at the hospital. Ruined some of our colleagues, but despite what everyone believed about his involvement, Tressing came out of it untouched. Not only that, while the police were rounding up his friends he was over in America collecting an award for his services to surgery. He seems to have spent quite a lot of time over there during the past fifteen years or so. Every time there's any trouble, in fact. Quite remarkable.'

'How can you bear to be near the man?'

Mayerton smiled coldly. 'He amuses me.' Then, without a word, he shoved Tibs off his lap and on to the floor, pulled up her costume, pushed her over on to her knees and straddled her. 'Now for the handmaiden's reward.' He laughed, thrusting himself into her.

'Seems funny without the girls around,' said Jack, putting the cash box on the counter and looking at the photographs of Tibs and Kitty that he had put up behind the bar. 'I've got used to them being about the place.'

Archie leaned on his broom and glanced at the clock. The pub had been closed for nearly a quarter of an hour. 'What time are you expecting them back then?'

Jack shrugged as he carried on piling the evening's takings into neat stacks. 'I don't know how long these things go on. I've never been to a ball.'

'Me neither,' said Archie. 'And I don't suppose I ever will.'

'Not our sort of thing, eh, Arch?'

'No.'

'Fancy a drink?'

'I'll pour them, boss.' Archie eased his way past Rex, who was snoring quietly by the brass foot rail, and took two glasses from the shelf. 'Beer or a short?'

'Hang on a minute, Arch.' Jack held up his hand and then, muttering under his breath, he recounted the piles of money. He looked up and grinned. 'A short, please, Arch, and make it a double. I think I've got something to celebrate.'

Jack tapped his glass against Archie's and smiled happily to himself. At this rate he would soon be able to settle everything; he already had enough for Tess and soon he'd have no debts, no dues, no Tressing. The Old Black Dog would be his, just his.

And maybe, if his luck kept in, Kitty would be his as well.

Kitty hardly dared to breathe, terrified that any movement would wake Tressing, even though he was lying on his back with his mouth open, snoring like a pig. But she so wanted to move his arm, it was stretched across her middle and just the touch of it was making her feel sick. Carefully, she lifted the corner of the heavy drape shielding the alcove and peered out into the gloom, praying silently that Tibs would be coming to find her.

But it was no good, Tibs wasn't coming.

With tears gathering in her eyes, Kitty let the curtain fall.

'Another one, boss?' Archie pointed to Jack's empty glass.

Jack considered for a moment. 'No thanks, lad,' he said, scooping all the money back into the cash box. 'I've got a bit of business I need to sort out upstairs. But you help yourself. And maybe call up to me if you hear the girls come in.'

*

Mayerton moaned to himself and rolled off Tibs, leaving her lying on her back, with her dress rucked up around her waist.

She could almost have kissed him with relief; not only had he finished with her at last, but, after what she'd overhead, Tibs was desperate to find her friend.

Rising unsteadily to her feet, she pulled her clothes down to cover herself. 'I'm going for a piddle,' she blurted out, and before Mayerton had a chance to object made a dash for the alcove.

Taking a deep breath, she pulled back the curtain with a single tug, ready to scratch Tressing's eyes out if necessary, but when she saw he was lying there sound asleep her heart sank. She was too late. He'd already had Kitty. Doing her best to smile reassuringly, Tibs lifted Tressing's arm so she could sit up.

As her friend helped her down from the divan, Kitty started sobbing.

'Ssshh, it's all right, love. Don't let's disturb him, eh? Come on, we'll get you off home so's you can have a nice wash and a good night's kip.' She took Kitty firmly by the hand and led her across the room. 'Tell me,' she said, almost casually. 'What happened?'

'He was smoking some stuff in this water pipe thing and then he started . . . ' Kitty lowered her voice as they pushed past a writhing heap of bodies, 'touching me. He put his hand right . . . ' She closed her eyes and shuddered. 'But then he just fell asleep. I'm so glad you came for me before he woke up. I couldn't have stood it if he'd done anything else to me.'

'That's all he did?' asked Tibs, steering her into the dressing-room. 'Touched you with his hand?'

'All?'

'You know what I mean. He didn't . . . ?'

Kitty shook her head.

'Thank Gawd for that.' Tibs had been dreading having to tell her friend about Tressing's disease. 'And if he's been smoking what I think he has,' she said, kicking the door closed behind them and tossing her mask to the ground, 'he'll be asleep for a good while yet and with a bit of luck he won't even remember whether he's done the business or not. Which means,' she said, stepping out of her dress, 'we won't have to pay him back the money and be left with just an old mop to suck on for our trouble.'

'He can have the lot back for all I care.' Kitty pulled off her costume so roughly that she ripped one of the seams. 'He said things to me. They scared me.'

Tibs tried another smile. 'Well, we knew he wasn't the sort who only likes discussing the weather, now didn't we, girl?'

Kitty started putting on her underthings, throwing them on anyhow as long as she got them on quickly. 'I don't mean just saucy talk. I've got used to that from the men at the Dog. This was different.'

Tibs stood there with her costume in one hand and her drawers in the other. 'What sort of things?'

'Really horrible. How it's so easy to get rid of things. People. People that are in the way. And worse.' She stared down at the ground, her hands shaking. 'What he'd like to do to me. I'm scared, Tibs. I'm scared he'll come after me.'

Tibs's face and throat flushed with anger. 'I won't be a minute, Kit, I've forgotten something back there.'

'Don't leave me, Tibs.'

'I promise I'll be no time at all. You just wait here. Wedge that chair under the doorknob like before and I'll let you know when it's me outside.'

Pulling the muslin slip over her head, without even bothering with her underwear, Tibs dashed back into the ballroom. As she edged quickly along the wall, trying to keep in the shadows, a man grabbed her and pulled her to him.

'And which character have you come as?' he asked, leering at her breasts through the fine, almost transparent gauze.

'I've come as this girl who kicks drunken old bastards what can't keep their hands to themselves right in their privates. Now fuck off,' she hissed and shoved the man away.

'What did you say?'

Tibs stuck her fists into her waist and jutted out her chin. 'I've had just about enough of men scaring me and making my baby's life a misery. And I ain't having some jumped-up toff frightening me mate neither. All right? Or d'you wanna make something out of it?'

The man, none the wiser, decided quite sensibly that if he wanted to keep his testicles intact, a simple nod was his best option. The good doctor always did have strange tastes, but he could keep this one for himself.

Tibs peered round three sets of the heavy drapes before she found Tressing. He was still drugged senseless and didn't even flinch or moan as she expertly dipped his wallet and took one of his visiting cards. She was about to relieve him of his money for good measure, but stopped herself when it occurred to her that he would immediately blame Kitty.

If she'd had time, though, she wouldn't have minded going back for that bastard Mayerton's wallet – it was probably lying under the table where he'd thrown most of his clothes – but she wasn't going to risk it. And anyway, revenge was a dish best eaten cold. She knew where he worked; what he did. She'd have her day with Lucian Mayerton. Just like she was going to with Tressing.

Tibs slipped the wallet back into his robe, slid down off the divan and made her way back to Kitty.

She'd get something on the pair of them.

Archie might have killed a bloke and that was wrong, especially when Tibs thought about how he'd killed him. But Archie had done it for all the right reasons. He'd got rid of Albert just like a rat catcher makes the world a safer place by getting rid of flea-carrying vermin.

It was ironic, but it was what Archie did that meant she could have her child with her without having to worry about the bogeyman lurking in every alley and shop doorway – and she would always be grateful for that – but it was also having Polly with her that meant Tibs would always have to be wary of him. Pity it had to be Archie who'd done it.

But these bastards. These were different. Everything they did, they did for themselves. There was Mayerton, who was too ignorant even to acknowledge she was a human being; all he was interested in was his own gratification. And as for Tressing . . . Well, he was something else. There was no other word for it: he was evil.

Jack opened the cash box and let the coins pour in a stream on to the bed. 'That's it, Tess, every single penny. Take it and go. I want to get on with my life.'

Tess lifted up the blankets, careful not to disturb the money, and got out of bed. She fetched her bag from the chair and began to count the coins into it. Eventually she said, 'You've kept your side of the bargain at last, Jack Fisher. So I'll be gone by the morning. Don't you worry yourself about that.'

'That can't be Joe's Aunt Sarah back, surely?' whispered

Tibs. She was staring out of the window, wearing only her underclothes, trying to see who was knocking on the street door at this time of night. 'We've only just stuck her in a cab.'

The knocking continued.

'Bloody hell!' She stood on tiptoe, craning her neck. 'Get it, will you, Kit, or they'll wake up Polly.'

Kitty just stood there. 'Say it's Tressing? Say he's come to and realised I've gone?'

'He was unconscious, Kit, he couldn't . . . Aw, all right, give us me coat and I'll go.'

Tibs hurried down the stairs, doing up her buttons as she went, and opened the door just a crack. 'Yeah? Who are you?'

'My name's Tess. Tess Hawtry.'

'You've got the advantage over me, darling, now if you don't mind . . .'

She tried to close the door, but Tess was too quick and too big for her. She shoved it back on its hinges and stepped inside the hallway.

'What d'you think . . .'

'I'll just come inside for a moment if you don't mind. It's cold out there. Not as cold as up in the north-east, mind.'

'Listen, I dunno what you want, but . . .'

'I've come to have a word with that great tall thing who lives here,' she said, trying to push past Tibs. 'So if you'll just excuse me. *Miss.*'

Kitty appeared on the stairs. 'Is everything all right, Tibs?'

'And there she is. The lovely Dandy.' Tess smiled maliciously. 'I've come to say that if you're stupid enough to want a man, then Jack Fisher is yours.' Her smile became a grin. 'You haven't got a clue what I'm talking about have you? He *loves* you.' Tess said the word as though it were poisonous. 'You know, it's interesting seeing the look on your face. I always wanted to see what a fool looked like close to.'

Chapter 18

It was early evening, with just a few days left until Christmas and over a month since the night of the ball. The sky was a strange, leaden yellow, signalling the snow that had been threatening to fall all day, and Tibs was standing at a coffee stall in the shadow of the Tower, with her gloved hands wrapped tightly round a thick china mug of scalding tea, but despite her heavy coat, hat and shawl she was still shivering. The wind blowing across the river was bitter.

But she had to be there, she had made a decision: enough time had passed since she had taken Tressing's card for there to be no chance of linking anything that happened now to that night, so, with not quite an hour to go until the first show, instead of being in her room getting ready, Tibs had slipped out to meet someone.

She had been relieved to find that the stall holder and Spiky Bill – the man she had come to meet – were the only people there. Bill was the last person she wanted anyone to see her talking to. He was a criminal known for his greed, his cunning and his complete lack of scruples. 'Honour among thieves' wasn't a saying that had much meaning for him, but his greed gave him courage to steal and the woman he lived with gave him the need.

When Tibs had seen him coming towards her over the bridge, hunched against the cold, looking about him as though he were being trailed, she had asked herself if she really was mad enough to be using the likes of him to do this job for her, but it was too late for that now.

'So, Bill,' she repeated, her patience wearing thin, 'you just go over there, crack his crib and take what you like. And I guarantee, he's loaded.'

Spiky Bill digested this with a frown. 'And you just wanna know what sort of place it is?' he said, his voice low so that the stall holder couldn't hear. 'There's nothing you want me to nick for you? Just see if there's anything *interesting* about it?'

'That's right,' she said, nodding at him. This was harder work than she'd imagined. And finding out if there was something odd about the man that she could use against him just by looking at his house didn't make as much sense as it had when she'd planned it. 'Look, d'you want this job or not?'

He held out his arms in submission. 'Course I do.'

'Well, get on and do it then. And don't go getting no ideas about farming it out to no one else, so you can stay in the warm in the boozer. I'm not having you sending Limpy Mick or any of your other useless mates in your place. Right?'

Bill looked offended. He placed his hand on his heart. 'I swear, on me old grandmother's life, Tibs.'

'Bill, you ain't got a grandmother.'

'Look, it's started snowing,' Bill said, changing the subject. 'Give us the address of this bloke's drum and you can get back home before the weather gets too bad.'

After a final moment of hesitation the now swirling snow decided her. 'Here,' she said, thrusting a card into his hand.

'You'll have to read it to me, won't you,' he said, rolling his eyes at Tibs's stupidity.

Tibs had long since gone back to her room to get ready, but Bill was still at the stall, busily working his way through a steaming baked potato and chatting to the owner – he could afford to treat himself with a job like this dropping in his lap. 'Don't suppose you do much business on a night like this, eh, Jim?'

'Not really, Bill,' replied the gloomy-looking man.

'Why don't you get off home then and set yourself up all snug with that missus of your'n?'

Jim shuddered at the thought. 'You just answered your own question, mate. I'd rather be out here with me tea urn and taters and chatting to you than be stuck indoors with her bending me ear'ole all night about her old witch of a sister's lovely sodding home in Bow and how we should move out there. Bow! What does she think, that me mother's sold her mangle? How can I afford to move to Bow? I ain't the sodding Prince of Wales, am I? Now, let me treat you to another cuppa and you can tell me all about what that little darling wanted with the likes of you. And I promise I won't let on to Dutch Bet.'

Bill grinned, baring the few teeth he still had left in his head, wiped his mouth on the newspaper that had wrapped his potato and tossed it over his shoulder. 'Sorry, no time, Jim, I've gotta be off before me glue pot comes unstuck. And as for me talking to Tibs, if you're brave enough to tell my Bet about it – if you're brave enough to tell her *anything* for that matter – then you're welcome, 'cos you'd be a braver man than me.' He swung a small hessian sack over his shoulder and winked. 'See you later, eh, Jim?'

'Yeah, see you, Bill. Be lucky.'

'I always am, thank Gawd.' Bill wasn't kidding either. He was lucky all right. He was about to turn over a doctor's gaff. In bloody Belgravia!

Bill pressed himself flat against the wall of the house

and banged one boot against the other, knocking out the snow that was packed into the ridges of the soles. Even though there were only lights on in the porch – which probably meant no one was in – he didn't want to risk slipping on the window ledge and making a noise. He just hoped he'd picked the right room to break into.

He figured that if anyone was at home then there'd be servants in the basement kitchens; and any one of the dining-rooms, drawing-rooms or sitting-rooms, or whatever these toffs called them, on the ground and first floors could be in use at this time of night – or so Tibs reckoned, Bill wasn't used to screwing this type of place. So, even though it had meant a bit of a slippery climb, he'd gone for the second floor, the bedrooms.

Bill let go of the thick branch of the chestnut tree that had been his ladder – he was always amazed at how sloppy people were about security, not that he was complaining, mind – took a jemmy from his sack and inserted it expertly into the frame. It took no more than the pressure of a single hard shove downwards to have the window loosened. The wooden internal shutters were even less trouble. A tap with the side of his gloved fist and they gave way.

He held his breath, this was always the nerve-racking bit. Was there anyone in there?

There were no lights on in the room. A good sign.

He lowered himself to the floor and whistled softly as his feet sank into the luxuriously deep pile of a very expensive carpet. 'Nice,' he breathed. 'But don't get carried away now, Bill. Be a professional. Let your eyes get used to the dark, have a quick shufty around in here, then get yourself up to the top and work down.'

With the jemmy still in his hand – it served as a weapon as well as a tool – Bill went to work.

He moved stealthily about the room looking for

saleable bits and pieces, and for anything *interesting*, as Tibs had put it. Not that he had any idea what she had meant, of course, but perhaps he'd know it when he saw it.

This really was the poshest room he'd ever been in. It was bulging with stuff he could shift with no trouble at all – including that carpet – but he had to be selective. It was no use piling himself up with so much gear that he wouldn't be able to leg it if he had to.

Bill grinned to himself. He could always pay another visit. Maybe he should start specialising in this sort of gaff.

He picked up an ashtray. Lovely. Silver by the look of it. He weighed it in his hand. Heavy too. He dropped it into the sack.

After adding a jade paperweight, a carved ivory stud box and a pair of gold cuff-links to his haul, Bill pushed the shutters to, to cover the still open window, and went over to the door.

He opened it slowly and looked along the landing.

All clear.

Then he made his way along to a flight of narrow stairs at the end of the hall that he guessed led up to the attics.

He presumed that they would contain the servants' quarters, but that they might also prove to be a nice place for the doctor – God bless him, whoever he was, for having such tasty gear to nick – to stash any extra special valuables.

Bill was in for a shock.

Gingerly, he stepped inside the first room and, holding his breath, waited a moment. Definitely empty. He breathed again and immediately a terrible, familiar stench hit his nose and throat.

What the hell was it?

Then he remembered. He'd been just a little boy, and he and his family had all gone down with the fever. They had been taken to the hospital ward. That was the smell. The carbolic and something else they used to clean the place. It made him want to gag, as it brought back those memories.

All his family had gone into the fever hospital, but Bill had been the only one to come out again.

'No time to start getting all maudlin, Billy boy,' he muttered to himself and rummaged through his pockets until he found the candle he had brought with him. He had to have a good look at this. He reckoned it would definitely count as interesting.

As the match flared and the wick burst into a yellow and blue flame, what Bill saw in the shadowy candle-light made him wish he hadn't bothered.

He threw himself back against the door, dropping his sack and spilling his haul across the scrubbed wooden floor-boards.

There, on the other side of the room, were three glass-sided coffins, each containing a dark-haired woman.

Setting the candle down on a strangely hinged wooden table, Bill gathered up his collection with shaking hands and stuffed it back into his sack.

With sweat beading his forehead he took up the candle and walked over to the dreadful caskets.

Had he not been worried about being discovered, Bill would have laughed out loud with relief. They weren't dead bodies, they were sodding wax models! One of them even had the peculiar hinged lid that they all had on their torsos propped open on a little hinge.

He plucked up the courage to peer inside. Again, it wasn't a wise move.

Blimey O'Reilly! There, like the mess on a slaughterhouse floor, were all her organs, picked out in vivid, stomach-churning colours.

But it was easy to see how he had been fooled. As they lay there, reclining provocatively on their piles of plump red velvet cushions, with their gleaming raven hair falling in loose curls about their creamy white shoulders, naked save for a single strand of pearls at their throats, they looked uncannily real.

Bill thought, very briefly, that he might open the coffins and help himself to the necklaces, but he couldn't bring himself to touch them. Even though it was now obvious they were models, they were still too realistic for comfort as they languished there, immodestly exposing themselves.

With a shudder of distaste – even Bill had his standards – he took a quick look around the rest of the room and saw cabinets and shelves full of bottles of liquids and powders, and then – bloody hell!

Bill moved forward for a closer look. He was right. There was a whole row of jars full of bits of bodies.

He put his hand to his mouth as he felt the bile rise in his throat.

If there was any treasure knocking about up here then the doctor could keep it. He was going back downstairs a bit sharpish.

He snatched up his sack, snuffed out the candle and hurried back down to the floor below.

The first room he went into was a library.

Disappointed, he almost turned round and walked away, but then he noticed several books spread out, open, on the table and saw some very classy-looking gold-edged pages glinting lavishly in the firelight.

Firelight.

Shit! There must be someone in after all.

'Keep calm, Bill,' he whispered to himself. 'Them

books look like they could be worth a few bob. Have some of them.'

He picked up one of the books and his mouth fell open.

'Sod me!' he said far louder than he'd intended.

He turned the book this way and that, staring.

He picked up another and flipped through the pages. How on earth could anyone . . .

He swallowed hard. He didn't like this stuff. He didn't like it at all. It wasn't normal.

He dropped the book on the table and stumbled backwards to the door. He'd had enough of this place. He'd work his way back to the room where he'd broken in, shoving anything portable that he passed into his sack and pockets, and have it away on his toes before he come across anything else *interesting*.

Just as he stuck his leg out of the window he heard a noise from the street below, then muffled footsteps trudging up the snowy path. Shit!

With the blood drumming in his ears, Bill ducked back inside. Leaning close to the shutters he peered down, praying that whoever it was would hurry up and come in so he could get out of the bloody place.

As the figure drew nearer to the porch, Bill shook his head in amazement.

Surely, it couldn't be. Not in Belgravia.

Bill would have been even more shocked had he known that while he was creeping about upstairs, directly below him in the drawing-room the owner of the house was sitting in a wing-backed leather armchair.

The only illumination in the room was a heavily shaded lamp on the side table by the chair. In the pool of light around its base were a leather strap, an empty glass phial with the top snapped off and a hypodermic syringe.

Somewhere in his head Tressing could hear a bell ringing.

He frowned, as his fuddled brain was disturbed by the noise. He was already angry. At Fisher. How could that simpleton think he could buy him off? Could treat him as if he were settling an account with a vulgar tradesman? Him, Dr Bartholomew Tressing. Fisher wouldn't get away with it.

And that girl, that damnable Kitty. Who did she think she was, refusing him like that when he'd asked her – *asked* her! – to come to his house?

He'd show Fisher and he'd show that pathetic slut.

The ringing started again. What was going on?

It finally occurred to Tressing that it was the doorbell and that he had deliberately given his staff the night off.

He rose to his feet, infuriated by the stabbing pains in his head, and went to answer the door.

Tibs and Kitty had finished for the night, but rather than going straight to bed as Kitty had done, Tibs insisted on seeing home Joe's old aunt, who had been looking after Polly, in case she slipped in the snow.

With the old woman safely indoors, Tibs still didn't go home. Instead, she went to the corner of Ship Alley where, as agreed, Spiky Bill was waiting for her.

'Tibs,' he began, shaking his head, 'I don't know what to say.'

'Just hurry up will you, Bill? It's sodding freezing out here and I wanna get to me bed. And I don't want no lies or no old fanny. Right?'

'You asked me to see if there was anything interesting.'

'Yeah.'

'Well, it was interesting all right.'

'How d'you mean?'

'It was strange. Definitely not normal.'

'Blimey Bill, you ain't exactly normal yourself, but it don't really tell me much about him or his house, now does it?'

'There was this hospital thing.'

'Hospital?'

'All these bottles and bodies.'

'*Bodies*?'

'Well, bits of bodies, and these wax model things that you could open up and look inside at all the giblets. Bloody disgusting it was. Nearly had me fetching up the tater I had for me tea.'

'Bill, the bloke's a doctor. That's what they do. Look inside bodies. Now, I am getting very cold and more than a bit fed up, so how about if you . . .'

'And there was all these books.'

Now Tibs was getting angry as well as cold. 'Just 'cos a bloke can read . . .'

'Not reading books. Well, not all of them. Some of 'em had these pictures. People with not a stitch on.'

Tibs rolled her eyes. 'Bill, they was probably medical books.'

'Medical? Well, if they was, I can't think what they was meant to be curing. You should have seen 'em, Tibs. I like a bit of sauce as much as the next man and round the docks you can see plenty, believe you me. I've even bought one or two pictures meself. Here, don't mention that to my Bet, will you, Tibs?'

'Bill!'

'All right. All right. Well, like I was saying, if you want the truth what they was doing in them pictures made my stomach turn right over. I'm telling you, they wasn't the type of pictures your average sort of a bloke would get any pleasure from. Bloody criminal, they were. I just hope that girl's all right.'

'What girl?'

'I was just about to creep away when I saw that young Marie. The one who works the Lane of a night. Honest, Tibs, he let her right in the front door. A bride, as bold as bloody brass, like he was having some posh lady-friend round for a sodding tea party.'

Christmas Day had arrived, and Tibs and Kitty were sitting round the table that Jack and Archie had set up in the downstairs bar of the pub.

Archie was leaning on the counter, smiling as he watched Polly playing on the floor; Kitty was watching Jack sharpen a lethal-looking carving knife on a butcher's steel and Tibs was watching Kitty.

Since that strange, northern woman, Tess, or whatever she called herself, had visited that night, Kitty's attitude towards Jack had developed in a way that Tibs was finding touching, but also highly amusing. And Jack was lapping up every little bit of fuss and help that Kitty had dropped his way.

With Polly so happy as well it would have been a perfect day, had it not been for Tibs's unease over Archie. But she wouldn't let that spoil things for Polly. She was going to make this day special if it killed her.

'It's no point waiting for One-Eyed Sal any longer,' Tibs said, looking at the big round clock over the bar. 'You can bet she's got herself caught up at some party or other and don't know even know what day it is, let alone what time.'

'If you're sure.'

'Yeah. Go on, Jack, get carving.'

She beckoned to Polly, who was staring in wonder at the china doll that Archie had bought to go with the sailor boy he'd got for her at Southend. 'The smell of all this grub's making me belly think me throat's been slit from ear to ear.'

Realising what she'd said, Tibs glanced furtively at Archie to see his reaction to her talk of cut throats. He didn't even flinch.

'If you're sure,' said Jack and turned to Archie. 'Want to do the honours?'

'Don't look at me, boss,' he said, tapping his bad arm. 'I have trouble cutting me dinner up.'

This time Tibs stared openly at him. Trouble cutting his dinner up? It hadn't occurred to her before. How could he have done all that to Albert? Crafty, snidey, violent Albert who you couldn't even surprise in a dark alley because the artful bastard would always be there before you. It must have taken brute strength and surely more dexterity than a man with only one good arm could ever have?

'You all right, Tibs?' asked Jack, waving the big knife around like a pirate captain showing off his cutlass. 'I'm not taking your job away, am I, lass?'

'What? Er, no. No. You do it, Jack.'

Jack was just dishing out the fat slices of goose, when Sal began bashing on the pub door, yelling to be let in.

'All right, girl,' called Tibs, 'we ain't ate your share.' She turned and winked at Polly. 'Not that we wouldn't have if you'd been any later, mind.'

As Tibs slid back the bolt, Sal came rushing in, her hair flying wild and loose behind her, as though she'd got out of bed and had set straight off on the hundred-yard dash. 'It's Marie,' she wailed, dragging her fingers down her face. 'Ivy from up the Anchor just told me. They're burying her the day after tomorrow.'

'Burying her, Sal? What on earth . . .'

'She's been mullered.' Sal pointed at the groaning table. 'All carved up, she was, just like that Christmas goose. Just like that other bride and like Albert.'

Tibs could barely breathe. Marie was dead.

'It's like the Old Boy's walking the streets again,' Sal moaned into her hands.

'What?' asked Jack, trying to keep up with the madness.

'It's what people round these parts called the Ripper.' Sal grabbed a glass from the table, swigged it back and slumped, defeated, on to Tibs's chair. 'But this wasn't done round here. They found the poor little mare's body over in bloody Belgravia.'

The day after Boxing Day had dawned as cold, grey and desolate as the huddle of shivering brides felt, as they walked away from the bleak graveside, slipping and sliding on the snow, wondering which of them would be next to feel the cold steel across her throat.

Kitty was standing with Jack, too shocked to weep.

Tibs touched her on the arm. 'Kit, I've got something I've gotta tell you.' She looked at Jack. 'We won't be a minute.'

'Take as long as you like, girls. I'll go and have a cigarette.'

Tibs drew Kitty aside and led her close to a snow-laden yew tree – protection from the wind and from prying eyes and ears.

'I'm sorry to do this to you, Kit, but if I don't tell someone I don't know what's gonna happen.'

'You can tell me anything, Tibs, you know that.'

Tibs nodded, but wasn't really sure that she believed it. 'Someone I know saw Marie going into a house. A few days before Christmas.'

'And?'

'The house was in Belgravia.'

'But that's where they found her.'

'Kit, it was Tressing's house.' She chewed on her bottom lip, staring into the middle distance as though there were something only she could see. 'And you heard what they're all saying, Marie was done in the same way as Albert and that girl they found up by the mint. And there were other girls. Last year. All the same. It's him, Kit. He's the one.'

'You'll have to tell the police.'

'I can't. The bloke what saw her was turning the place over.'

'So what difference . . .'

'I'd told him to do it. And he ain't the sort to go to the law. Believe me. But even if I could force him, I know what he's like, he'd put all the blame on me somehow. I just know he would.'

'You'll have to slow down, Tibs. I don't understand. Why did you get this man to break into the house?'

'I wanted to get something on Tressing.' She shook her head. 'What is it they say? Mind what you wish for, you might just get it. And I've got it all right. Aw, Kit, this is all such a mess.'

'But if he's not stopped someone else is going to get hurt.'

Jack called Kitty's name. She looked over her shoulder and signalled that she wouldn't be long.

'The only choice I've got is me saying that I saw her. But if I go to the police, what are they gonna think, a known bride grassing on a posh doctor? It'll go wrong and Tressing'll take it out on Polly. I've already done enough to that poor little darling to last a lifetime without risking making things worse.'

'Look, Tibs, I'll tell the police that it was me who saw her going in there.'

'You can't. And what use'll the police be anyway? All they're interested in is aggravating girls who're just trying to earn a living.'

'We've got to do something and we haven't got any other choice. We both know you can't get involved, but I've never even been in a police station before. They've got nothing on me. Now, I'm going over to tell Jack and Archie. We'll get some extra locks on the way home and they can put them on the doors.'

'Maybe we should ask Jack or Archie to go.'

'What would they be doing in Belgravia?'

'What would you be doing there?'

Kitty shrugged. 'Meeting a stage-door Johnny?'

'It's too dangerous. Jack won't let you do it.'

'Tibs, I'm not that little mouse any more. I do what I want to do. What I think's right. And this is right.'

Chapter 19

Kitty stared at her uniformed reflection in the looking-glass. 'It doesn't seem right us doing a show so soon after Marie . . .'

Tibs put her hand gently on Kitty's shoulder. 'Listen, love, I reckon Marie would have understood. Especially after you going to the police like that. She'd have been proud of you. You was right brave doing that.'

Kitty shook her head. 'I don't know, Tibs.'

'And we've gotta do it for Jack. He's been so good to us, giving us all last week off. He must have lost a fortune.'

'I still . . .'

'Look, I'm not being hard, Kit, but the world has to keep turning and this is a once-in-a-lifetime thing, when all's said and done. The end of the bloody century. We can't not do a show. It wouldn't be right.'

'I suppose we do have to pay back Jack for everything he's done for us.'

'And it'll be a good start to the New Year. A chance to brush all the old rubbish that's happened over the past few years right out the door.'

'I suppose so.'

'I know so. Just think how things are working out for us at last. Marie would have been pleased about that, wouldn't she?'

'She would. She was a kind sort of a girl. Everyone liked her, didn't they. I know Jack's been right upset about it all.'

'And now the police know all about that Tressing bastard because of you, and we don't have to worry about him no more. He's the sort who'll have friends on the force. Important friends. And he'll be long gone now he knows they're after him.'

Kitty looked a bit brighter at that thought.

'And Polly's safe and sound, back with me. I've got a job where I don't have to take me drawers off no more and Jack's given us that rise. So don't let's tempt fate, eh, Kit, by getting the hump on a night like tonight. And it's only the one late show we're doing.'

Kitty smiled. 'You're right, Tibs. As usual.'

Archie had just gone into the empty theatre to begin setting up and testing the lights before the musicians came in to start tuning up, but was first checking that nobody was lurking behind the curtains or in the little back room where the turns waited to go on.

He and Jack had taken what Kitty had told them about Tressing very seriously, which was more than a certain young policeman had done.

When Kitty had talked to Constable Browning at the local station he had promised faithfully to pass on her information – *her allegations*, as he had called them – to his superior, but had actually been more interested in getting her to promise that she'd send him a signed photograph. It wasn't every day of the week that he got to meet an up-and-coming star of the music-hall – even if she was a country girl and a bit barmy.

But honestly, murders in the East End being done by a doctor living over in Belgravia? Old Sergeant Miller would never stop taunting him if he passed on that little nugget.

Miller had been at the station twelve years ago, when every kind of nutcase reckoned they knew who Jack the

Ripper was and drilled into all the new recruits, Browning included, that you never, ever took notice of an hysterical woman. It would only end in tears or, he had hinted, in something far worse.

Archie was standing facing the proscenium arch with his back to the main door into the theatre, fiddling with the row of limelights along the front of the stage, when someone spoke to him in the unmistakably plummy tones of Dr Bartholomew Tressing. 'Miss Wallis. Where is she?'

Archie twisted round and stared.

'Are you stupid as well as crippled?' Tressing asked, striding towards Archie, his snow-dampened opera cloak flapping about him like great satin-lined bat's wings. 'I made myself quite clear, didn't I? I wish to speak to Kitty.'

Archie thought quickly. 'Wait here and I'll get her.'

'I'd rather . . . surprise her.'

'I don't think so . . .'

'Is this any of your business?'

'Look, I'm sorry, but I work for Mr Fisher and if I let you . . .'

'*If you let me*? Get out of my way.' Tressing pushed Archie roughly to one side, wrong-footing him and sending him crashing to the ground.

He fell on his shoulder with a painful whack.

Tressing was almost at the door of the waiting-room at the side of the stage. 'Kitty?' he called. 'Kitty? Are you in there?'

This was Archie's opportunity. If he could just push him inside he could lock the door and trap him while he called the law.

Scrambling to his feet, Archie lunged across the stage at Tressing's legs.

'I'm going through to the theatre to fetch Polly's dolls,' said Tibs, buttoning her thick topcoat up to her neck and slipping her hands into her fur-lined muff. 'She loves them toys. It was so kind of Archie giving them to her.'

'How did they get left in the theatre?' asked Kitty, putting the final touches to her hair with the curling tongs.

Tibs shrugged. 'I had 'em in me bag earlier and must have just forgot.'

'So you didn't leave them there on purpose to have an excuse to go in and talk to Archie on the quiet?

Tibs grinned. 'You're getting worse than me, you are, Kitty Wallis.'

'Well? You two do seem to be getting very close lately.'

'No closer than you and Jack.'

Kitty said nothing, she only smiled happily to herself.

'If Archie's there I might just see if he fancies coming out for a bit of supper with us after the show. Don't exactly feel like celebrating, but we've still gotta eat.'

'What happened with that Harry Fitz-Whatsisname who asked you out tonight? The one with all the money.'

'I can't be bothered with them flashy types.'

'You like Archie a lot, don't you?'

Tibs nodded. 'Yeah, Kit, I do. You know, for a while I was right dubious about him. But I admit, which ain't easy for me, that I was wrong. Very wrong. I misjudged him. He's a good man. Kind and all.'

'And Polly thinks the world of him.'

Tibs dropped her chin and said softly, 'And so do I, Kit. Trouble is, after the life I've had I'm suspicious of people.

343

But it don't always mean I'm right though, does it?'

'Go on, Tibs, go and find him. But don't go slipping over in the snow. I don't fancy having to go on solo.'

Tibs stamped her feet on the coconut mat inside the pub door, knocking the snow off her boots, took her hands out of her muff and shook it dry, then ran up the stairs and into the theatre. She looked around, but had trouble seeing in the dim light that was coming from the single row of lamps fronting the stage. 'Archie?' she called, squinting into the semi-darkness. 'You in here?'

'Tibs, get out! Go and get someone,' she heard Archie yell from the wings. 'Get help.'

Then there was a loud crack, a grunt of pain and the sound of something, or someone, crashing heavily to the ground.

Instead of doing as Archie had told her, Tibs ran to the stage and clambered up over the lights.

There in the wings she saw Tressing, with his sword stick drawn back, ready to thrust it into Archie, who was lying unconscious at his feet. 'Leave him alone!' she screamed.

Tressing spun round, his face distorted with madness. 'You, a trollop, dare tell me what to do? Me, Dr Bartholomew Tressing. The greatest surgeon who has ever lived.' He stepped over Archie and moved towards her, with the sword stick flashing in the limelight above his head as though he were the demon king in the pantomime.

Tibs screamed at the top of her lungs as she stumbled backwards, desperate to get away from the wild-eyed lunatic advancing determinedly towards her.

She was at the edge of the stage with nowhere else to go.

Again she screamed.

Tressing raised the sword and thrust the blade at her.

With a terrified wail, Tibs fell to the ground and rolled over to the edge of the stage. Her coat snagged in one of the lights and caught her there, a dead butterfly pinned to a board.

By the time Jack and Kitty came bursting into the theatre, in answer to Tibs's frantic screams, Tressing was gone, already outside the pub and melting into the crowds who were gathering to celebrate the coming of the new century.

Kitty stood in the doorway, staring at Tibs lying on the stage, with blood soaking through the sleeve of her coat, illuminated by the ghostly glow of the limelight.

'Tibs?' she breathed. 'Tibs?'

Then she started running.

She fell on her knees at her friend's side, whimpering like a wounded animal, 'Jack, please. Do something. Please.'

She climbed on to the stage and cradled Tibs's limp body in her arms, rocking her back and forward like a baby. 'Tibs, wake up. Wake up.'

Jack ripped off his jacket and gently put it round Kitty's shoulders.

'She'll be all right, won't she, Jack?' Kitty looked up at him, her eyes wide with fear and dread.

'I don't know, Kit . . . '

'Jack. Jack.' It was Archie, he was staggering across the stage towards them, holding his head. 'Tressing. He came in here. Looking for Kit.'

'*It was my fault,*' she wailed.

'Where did he go?' Jack demanded.

'Down the stairs,' he gasped, his words coming in short, winded breaths. 'Only a minute or so ago. Go and find him. Go and find the bastard.'

Jack vaulted off the stage and sprinted after him. 'You. Go and get the law,' they heard him holler to someone in the bar.

Archie knelt down and took Tibs's hand in his and touched it to his face, tears flowing unchecked down his cheeks. 'I'll see him hanged for this,' he sobbed. 'He was bragging, *bragging* about all these people he done in. Even that Albert.'

'He said that?'

Archie nodded, the tears pouring down his cheeks. 'I never told her, Kit, but I loved her. I'll always love her.'

Her shock giving way to grief, Kitty too was now crying. 'And she loved you, you know, Archie.'

'No,' Archie wailed. 'No.'

'Yeah, Arch, I do.' Tibs's eyes flickered open.

'You're alive!' Kitty screamed.

'Course I am, you silly daft cow.' Tibs gasped with pain and clutched her wounded side. 'Who'd look out for you if I wasn't about?'

Jack pushed his way through the crowds. There were no toffs in silk top hats around the dock area tonight, they were all too busy celebrating the eve of the new century in their fine houses and posh clubs in the West End.

Jack was shivering, about to give up when, as if it were the most normal thing in the world, he spotted Tressing walking perfectly calmly down towards the river bank in the direction of Tower Bridge.

It took Jack less than a moment to decide what to do. Silently, he followed the doctor until they were well away from the crowds.

Joe, the young barman whom Jack had ordered to get the law, had found Sergeant Miller who was on his way home from Leman Street Police Station and Sergeant

Miller was not best pleased about it. Especially as the only information that he could get from the impossibly soft-spoken Irishman was some rambling story about a murder in a theatre. He wasn't exactly sure whether it was a crime or a play he was being taken to. But the barman was insistent.

The sergeant sighed. Why him? Not only was it bloody parky out, but he was already in Mrs Miller's bad books, having explained that he would be on duty when her sister and brother-in-law arrived to share the celebrations with them. Now he was going to be back late as well. He could just imagine the earful he had to look forward to.

Joe was practically dragging the sergeant into the Dog, when Jack caught up with them. 'I saw the man who attacked the girl,' he panted.

'So there *was* an attack?'

Jack nodded, trying to get his breath back. 'I chased him down to the bridge, but couldn't catch him.'

The sergeant rolled his eyes. The bridge. Bugger. It would be bitter down by the water. 'So where is he now?'

'He threw himself into the river.'

Yes! Sergeant Miller could barely suppress a grin of relief. 'This is a job for the river police.' Let them freeze their arses off.

Jack nodded again. 'I'll send Joe to tell them while you come in for a drop of something to warm you up, officer.'

Joe didn't look too thrilled with Jack's idea, but Sergeant Miller could have kissed him. Legitimate business and he'd be in a pub! Mrs Miller, her sour-faced sister and her big-nosed brother-in-law would just have to get on without him.

*

347

'The rest of the show will go on,' said Jack from the stage, 'but due to unforeseen circumstances, Sweet and Dandy will be unable to perform as billed.' He raised his hands to quell the hisses and boos. 'But despite having injured her side in an accident, Miss Tibs Tyler has agreed to join Miss Kitty Wallis in singing you a song to see in the New Year. And,' he added, 'there will be a free drink for everyone on the chimes of midnight.'

With the cheers ringing out around him Jack checked the clock with Mr Tompkins, then signalled to Archie in the wings that it was time for him and Kitty to help Tibs on to the stage.

'So, although the river police are on the case,' said the sergeant, holding up his empty glass in an inviting sort of way for Jack to see, 'I don't hold out much hope for them finding him. What with the river being so busy with people out celebrating and getting drunk.' He looked meaningfully at the bottle of rum that Jack had fetched to his table at the back of the theatre. 'It's bad enough in the fog, but when it's a night like this with everybody making merry . . . '

Jack took the unsubtle hint and gave him another drink.

'I've seen some horrible things in my time, you know, son. I remember, back in 1888 . . .'

'Listen!' Kitty shouted from the stage. 'The bells are chiming midnight!'

Tibs, leaning on her friend for support, grinned out into the audience. 'It's the New Year and we ain't been struck down. The bible bashers was wrong. We've all made it, thank Gawd!'

'And thank Gawd I ain't over in Trafalgar Square,' said Sergeant Miller, ignoring the fact that Jack, like everyone else in the room except him, was now on his feet; that no one was listening to him any more and that the whole place had erupted into a sea of cheering and kissing, and demands for free drinks.

'It'll be madness over there tonight,' he went on, pouring himself another rum. 'I've seen it. They'll all be singing and dancing to the bands, climbing up lamp-posts and jumping in the fountains, sky-larking about like little kids. It's the lights of London, see, draws 'em in from all over the place, it does. And goes straight to their heads. Specially if they ain't seen the likes before. Still, can't blame 'em, it's a beautiful place all right, this home town of mine. And even better when Mrs Miller ain't here to stop me having another little drink.'

'Look out there!' someone shouted, and pointed out of the window to the fireworks flashing and cracking in the sky, and reflecting back off the dark, secret waters of the Thames.

Jack, who had finally managed to fight his way to the front of the theatre with Archie and Polly, climbed on to the stage and gently cupped Kitty's chin in his hands. He looked deep into her eyes and kissed her softly on the lips.

'About bleed'n' time,' said Tibs and, with a wince of pain, planted kisses of her own, first on Polly's head and then on Archie's startled face.

It was seven o'clock in the morning on the first day of the first year of the new century and Teezer was snoring loudly, curled up in the corner of the gently bobbing skiff. He'd passed out hours ago, a result of all the booze he'd swallowed in the past twenty-four hours. Even Teezer had his limits.

But Buggy was still awake, thoroughly enjoying helping himself to the remainder of the purl. It wasn't a bad

349

life when it was like this. Nice and quiet. It suited him.

He reached into the cauldron to scoop out another cup of the now almost cold alcohol, but was shot forward as the boat hit something with a dull thud.

'What's up?' mumbled Teezer sleepily.

'Nothing,' Buggy assured him hurriedly. That's all he needed, Teezer waking up. He'd have him relighting the fire, mixing up more purl . . . Hang on, what was that?

Buggy stared over the side. Aw, no, it was a sodding body. Teezer would have him dragging it into the boat. It'd be really heavy and soaking wet.

He grabbed one of the oars and poked viciously at the sodden lump, trying to shove it away.

'Buggy. What are you doing?' Teezer grumbled, his eyes still closed. 'Can't you see I'm trying to rest?'

'Sorry, Teeze, I was just pushing something out of the way before we bashed into it again.'

'What is it?' he asked, sounding slightly more awake.

Recognising the interest in his boss's voice, Buggy shoved harder, even though he had thought for a moment that he'd seen the gleam of a silver-topped cane and maybe the hint of a satin-lined opera cloak. That was all he wanted, hauling a river-soaked corpse over to St Thomas's. Especially after the amount of purl he'd swallowed and, worse, it would start Teezer off again about how he'd dragged a real beauty out of the river that time, but the ungrateful cow had never even thanked him. And he'd go on and on and on . . .

'I said . . .'

'It's all right, Teeze.' Buggy gave his final effort every bit of strength he possessed. 'You go back to sleep, it's just a bundle of rubbish.'

With that, the final remains of Dr Bartholomew

Tressing snagged against the splintered side of a passing night soil barge and were dragged downriver, where they provided a tasty New Year treat for the eels and crabs of the Essex salt marshes.

Postscript

Friday, 8 June 1900.

'I'll be two minutes,' Tibs called down the stairs. 'I've just gotta do something.'

Standing there in her smart new silk coat and matching hat, Tibs picked up the scissors and carefully cut two items from the *Daily Messenger*. They read as follows:

Today, the parish church of St John in the district of St George's in the East is the surprise venue for a celebration of marriage. In this poor and overcrowded part of London's East End, the two famous music-hall stars, Miss Tibs Tyler and Miss Kitty Wallis, more widely known as Sweet and Dandy, will be marrying Mr Archibald Hutchinson and Mr Jack Fisher in an unusual double wedding, to which celebrities and local people alike are said to have been invited. There is excited speculation about Miss Polly Tyler, who will be in attendance as bridesmaid. Miss Tibs Tyler has not been married before.

A pawnbroker who, over five months ago, bought a leather case from a mudlark who found it on the banks of the River Thames at low tide, is trying to find a buyer who will be interested in a curiosity that is expected to fetch a considerable sum. The novelty is not the bag itself, but a diary that he has only just found hidden in the lining. It purports to be the confessions of none other than Jack the Ripper, the perpetrator of the notorious Whitechapel murders of 1888.

Coincidentally, the diary links to another more recent scandal, as it is supposedly written in the hand of one Dr Bartholomew Tressing, a colleague of Dr Lucian Mayerton who was only last week publicly disgraced in the abortion outrage, which was brought to light after an anonymous tip-off to the police. According to hospital associates, Dr Tressing disappeared about six months ago after becoming unwell. The hospital has declined to give a public statement about either of its two ex-employees.

Tibs tucked the two cuttings into an envelope, slipped them into her bag and went over to the window.

Kitty, Jack, Archie and Polly, all dressed up in their finest, were standing by two ribbon-bedecked motor cars – the first ever seen in Rosemary Lane.

'I'm ready,' she called to them with a smile and a wave, and hurried downstairs to begin her new life.

Also available from Arrow in paperback, *Dream On* by Gilda O'Neill.

Read on for an exclusive extract:

'Ginny? Gin? It's only me.'

Dilys Chivers was shouting at the top of her voice as she barged, uninvited, through the open street door and along the narrow passageway of number 18 Bailey Street.

'Come on, you lot,' she went on, throwing her coat over the end of the banisters, 'if you don't get a move on, you know what'll happen. That greedy mare from number 20 will have stuffed all the grub. She'll be dancing with all the fellers. And you'll all still be—'

As she stuck her head round the kitchen doorway, Dilys quite uncharacteristically shut her mouth and stood stock still in puzzled silence.

Sitting in the kitchen, hunched over the little scrubbed table, nursing a cup of tea, was a miserable-looking middle-aged woman. 'All right, Dilys?' she muttered.

'Whatever's the matter, Nellie?' Dilys, recovering her composure, pulled out a chair and sat herself down opposite the woman. It looked as though there might be a story to glean here and, young and pretty as she was, Dilys was as partial to a bit of gossip as any of the elderly battleaxes of Bailey Street.

'Honest, Nell,' she went on, pulling off her hat and tossing it on to the table between them, 'you look just like you wanna go for a' – she flashed her eyebrows – '*you know*. But you've gone and lost the key to the lava-tory door.'

'It's this party, ain't it?' Nellie answered, her lips pursing in self-pitying anger. 'I can't go, can I?' She tilted her head to one side and stared sorrowfully into the middle distance over Dilys's shoulder. 'And after surviving all them years of war an' all. Putting up with the Blitz, and what with the doodlebugs ...'

Dilys might have relished a bit of scandal, but putting up with Nellie Martin's tale of woe was a price she wasn't prepared to pay. Dilys had never been a patient sort of person, and while she wanted the full story, she didn't fancy the boring moaning bits that looked like going with it.

'You just forget all about them bad memories, Nell,' Dilys said briskly, slapping her palms on the table. 'You just tell me what this is all about.' She paused, then added firmly: 'Briefly, like.'

Nellie's lips twitched. 'It's her, ain't it?'

It took Dilys a moment. 'D'you mean Ginny?'

'Yeah,' spat Nellie, unable even to speak her daughter-in-law's name.

'What on earth's she done to get you into this state?'

Dilys's forehead pleated into a frown; this was getting really confusing.

While there wasn't exactly any great love lost between Nellie and Ginny, they usually managed to rub along well enough together. With Ginny keeping her mouth shut and doing as she was told by her husband – Nellie's son – and with Nellie not giving a bugger about anyone but herself, in its way, the household functioned. So all this upset, especially on a day like today, well, it just didn't make sense.

'If you must know, she's shut herself in the bloody front bedroom and won't come down, that's what,' Nellie spread her hands in wretched supplication. 'How am I meant to go to the party by myself, Dilys, eh? You tell me that. I'll be a laughing stock. Everyone'll have their families with them – except me. And I can just see that Florrie Robins . . .'

Nellie paused for a moment, visualising the woman who was her oldest friend and, therefore, her oldest rival. 'I know her. She'll be sitting round there at her daughter's street party in St Stephen's Road, with all her grand-children round her, acting like flaming Lady Muck, while they all wait on her, and fuss over her, and make sure the old cow's got everything she wants.'

Nellie's face puckered in on itself until she looked exactly as though she was sucking a lemon. 'And you know what everyone'll be saying, don't you? I can just hear 'em. But I swear on my life, Dilys, he never so much as touched—'

'Hang on, Nell,' Dilys interrupted, 'why're you so worried about Ginny not going with you? You can go with your Ted, can't you?'

'Him!' sneered Nellie, astonishing Dilys by showering her son's name with almost as much venom as she would probably have trowelled on to her daughter-in-law's – had she allowed her name to pass her lips. 'You wanna ask her about him.'

Nellie lifted her chin and stabbed her thumb ceiling-wards. It was a gesture reminiscent of the one that the minister from the local evangelical hall used when he admonished the sinners, telling them they should be list-ening with their hearts to the Lord of Heaven, and not with their throats to the landlord of the Prince Albert. But it would have been obvious, even to the unbeliever, that Nellie's reference was not exactly reverential.

'Go on,' she hissed, 'you go up and see if you can get any sense outta the snivelling little mare, 'cos I'll be buggered if I can.'

'Gin. Gin, it's only me, babe.' Dilys's voice was tender

and wheedling as she tapped gently on the door. 'Come on, girl, let me in, eh?'

A muffled sob came from inside the bedroom.

Dilys stuck her ear to the door. 'What was that?'

There was another low whimper.

'What?' Dilys knelt down and squinted through the keyhole, as though it would help her hear more clearly. 'Speak up, Gin. I mean, I can't help you if I can't hear you, now can I?'

Ginny blew her nose loudly, then croaked in a tear-sodden voice: 'Leave me alone, Dil, please. Just leave me.'

'As if I'd do that, you dopey cow.' Discarding the softly-softly approach, Dilys gave the doorknob a good rattle. 'Now you either open this door, Ginny Martin, or I'm gonna go along to Tommy Fowler's and borrow his ladders. And then I'll stick 'em up against your front wall and I'll climb in through the bloody bedroom window. How'd you fancy that?'

She paused, listening for a response. 'I mean it, Ginny. You know me.'

Ginny did indeed know Dilys – for as long as either of them could remember, in fact – and Ginny also knew that once Dilys Chivers had made up her mind about something, there was no stopping her. And Ginny didn't much relish the idea of having her clambering up the outside of the house and messing up all her VE-Day decorations. Especially not in full view of the neighbours, who had all been out in the drizzle-slicked cobbled street getting the party ready since first light.

With weary resignation, Ginny decided she had no choice. 'Hang on, Dil,' she sniffled, 'I'm coming.'

'I knew you would.' Dilys grinned in self-satisfied triumph as she straightened up from the keyhole. She smoothed the silky fabric of her new dress down over her thighs, tossed her head and patted her dark, shiny, permanently waved hair back into place with a little sigh of contentment.

The bedroom door opened and Ginny stood there, her head bowed and her arms dangling loosely by her sides.

'Blimey, Gin, will you just look at yourself,' chirped Dilys without a trace of compassion in her voice. 'You look worse than Nellie and that's saying something. Whatever's got into the pair of you?'

Without even pausing for a reply Dilys executed a neat little pirouette on the tiny lino-covered landing, flung out her arms in best pin-up style, dropped her chin and peered seductively through her lashes. 'Well?' she demanded. 'Ain't you gonna say nothing about me new frock, then?'

Before Ginny had the chance even to wonder how Dilys had managed to get something as expensive-looking as that – when they both knew she'd used up all her clothing coupons ages ago – Dilys was shoving her back into the bedroom.

'So,' she whispered conspiratorially, rolling her eyes and jerking her head towards the door in the general direction of the stairs, where Dilys presumed Nellie would be standing earwigging – just as she would have been doing in her position – 'what's been going on with her down there, then?'

Ginny slumped on to the double bed she shared with her husband and started picking at a loose quilting stitch on the pink satin eiderdown.

'Come on, Gin, you know you can tell me.'

Ginny shrugged. 'I dunno, Dil, do I.' She shook her head, making her soft blonde curls bounce around her face. 'I really don't.'

'For Gawd's sake, Ginny, pull yourself together girl. You're like looking at a bleed'n' wet weekend. Even

Violet Varney's making more effort than you,' Dilys gestured dramatically towards the window and the street
beyond. 'That woman was out there last night till all
hours doing up her front with a bit o' bunting.'

'So was I.'

Dilys huffed dismissively. 'Yeah, but her old man's in
a bloody prisoner of war camp.'

Ginny looked up at her pitifully. 'At least she knows
her Bert'll be home soon.'

'Whatever you on about now?'

Ginny turned her head so that Dilys couldn't see her
tears. 'Look, Dilys, I know how much Nellie's looking
forward to the party and I really hate letting her down,
'cos I know it ain't her fault, it's mine. And I feel terrible.
But I can't go out there. I just can't.'

'Why not?'

A sob shuddered through her body. 'It's Ted. He's
not been home.'

'He's *what?*' Dilys sprang up from the bed and stuck
her fists into her waist. 'The rotten, stinking, swivel-eyed,
no-good cowson of a . . .' Her fury got the better of her
tongue and Dilys ran out of insults.

Ginny covered her face with her hands. 'Don't say
them things, Dil. Like I said, it's my fault. No one else's.
I must have upset him somehow. But I've been sitting
here racking me brains—'

'I'll kill him,' Dilys fumed. 'I'll bloody well kill him.'

Ginny dropped her hands and looked up at her friend.
'You're a good mate, but it's down to me to sort it out.'
She turned her head away again and said in a voice
so small that Dilys could only just make out the words:
'You and your mum are really important to me, Dilys,
you know that, but since losing my own mum and dad
. . .' Her shoulders shook as she rubbed the tears roughly
from her cheeks with the back of her hand. '. . . Ted and

Nellie are all the family I've got. And I just don't know what I'd do if Ted left me. I do try to make him happy, but sometimes I just seem to get on his nerves. He gets so wild with me. Now he's started staying out all night. What am I gonna do?'

'That's it. I've heard enough.' Dilys took Ginny firmly by the arm and pulled her over to the polished walnut dressing-table, which took up almost the whole wall beneath the window of the cramped front bedroom in the little terraced house.

'Now you listen to me, Ginny Martin. You sit yourself down on that stool. Go on. Do as you're told. And you get your war-paint on. You're going to this sodding party whether you want to or not. We'll show bloody Ted Martin that he can't get away with this; he'd better start watching his step or he's gonna be in for a nasty surprise, a very nasty surprise indeed. 'Cos if he ain't careful, the bastard's gonna have me to deal with.'

ALSO AVAILABLE

Dream On	Gilda O'Neill	£5.99
Rose of Tralee	Katie Flynn	£5.99
Rainbow's End	Katie Flynn	£5.99
Still Waters	Judith Saxton	£5.99
This Royal Breed	Judith Saxton	£5.99
Every Woman Knows a Secret	Rosie Thomas	£5.99
Chloe's Song	Leslie Thomas	£5.99

ALL ARROW BOOKS ARE AVAILABLE THROUGH MAIL ORDER OR FROM YOUR LOCAL BOOKSHOP AND NEWSAGENT.

PLEASE SEND CHEQUE/EUROCHEQUE/POSTAL ORDER (STERLING ONLY) ACCESS, VISA, MASTERCARD, DINERS CARD, SWITCH OR AMEX.

☐☐☐☐☐☐☐☐☐☐☐☐☐☐☐☐

EXPIRY DATE .... SIGNATURE ....

PLEASE ALLOW 75 PENCE PER BOOK FOR POST AND PACKING U.K.

OVERSEAS CUSTOMERS PLEASE ALLOW £1.00 PER COPY FOR POST AND PACKING.

ALL ORDERS TO:
ARROW BOOKS, BOOKS BY POST, TBS LIMITED, THE BOOK SERVICE, COLCHESTER ROAD, FRATING GREEN, COLCHESTER, ESSEX CO7 7DW.

NAME ....

ADDRESS ....

....

Please allow 28 days for delivery. Please tick box if you do not wish to receive any additional information ☐

Prices and availability subject to change without notice.